Pink Ink

ALSO BY AVINA ST. GRAVES

Death's Obsession

Skin of a Sinner

The Saltwater Curse

Fiery Little Thing

Midnight Message

Eldrith Manor

Scorpion

Pink Ink

A Dark Romance

Avina St. Graves

G

GALLERY BOOKS

New York Antwerp/Amsterdam London
Toronto Sydney/Melbourne New Delhi

Gallery Books
An Imprint of Simon & Schuster, LLC
1230 Avenue of the Americas
New York, NY 10020

First Gallery Books trade paperback edition August 2026

Interior design by Julia Jacintho

Manufactured in China

10 9 8 7 6 5 4 3 2 1

Library of Congress Control Number: 2025950889

ISBN 978-1-6682-1898-3 (pbk)
ISBN 978-1-6682-1899-0 (ebook)

For those who dream of being fucked by
their serial-killing professor who murders people
for their university assignments.

Too specific? Fine.

This is for everyone who wanted to fuck their professor.

(I hope you're doing well, Mr. B.)

TRIGGERS

Nut allergy (but make it romantic), unadvised use of a paintbrush, unethical university conduct, trauma art, impact play, breath play, exhibitionism, roleplay, cock warming, sex without a condom, gore, bodily mutilation, serial killers, torture, sacrilege, scarring, arranged marriage, cheating (not between main characters), reference to off-the-page SA and CSA, drugging (in a movie), reference to self-harm, death of parents caused by cancer and a car accident (off the page), reference to off-the-page child abuse, and assault against the main character (not by the love interest).

PLAYLIST

"Forbidden Fruit" by Cray, in collaboration with Avina St. Graves for *Pink Ink*

"Running Up That Hill" by Kate Bush

"Never Felt So Alone" by Labrinth

"Sick Thoughts" by Lou Bliss

"Psycho Killer" by Talking Heads

"Good Looking" by Suki Waterhouse

"my strange addiction" by Billie Eilish

"White Lie" by Lenii

"Money Power Glory" by Lana Del Rey

"Tainted Love" by Soft Cell

"Knee Socks" by Arctic Monkeys

"older" by Isabel LaRosa

"Art Deco" by Lana Del Rey

"Talk" by Hozier

"Teacher's Pet" by Melanie Martinez

"Rhinestone Eyes" by Gorillaz

"Serial Killer" by Moncrieff x JUDGE

"Happiness Is a Butterfly" by Lana Del Rey

"All I Wanted" by Paramore

"Drowning" by Banks

"get him back!" by Olivia Rodrigo

"Flawless" by the Neighbourhood

"Verbatim" by Mother Mother

"One More Hour" by Tame Impala

HIERARCHY

Grand Magistrate

The supreme and undisputed leader of the Order.

High Saint

The second highest rank an acolyte can hold.

Six individuals are elected every five years as the high saints of their respective houses. Each high saint represents and commands the acolytes pledged to their house.

The current houses are House Shaw, House Dornmont, House Hopkins, House Sutherland, House Ellis, and House Ortiz.

Medicus

The prestigious rank granted to high saints' relatives, and acolytes of exceptional influence.

A medicus holds authority over lower ranks and often extends their power beyond the Order, into financial or political spheres.

Paladin

The second lowest rank within the Order, yet one that bears significant responsibility.

Paladins execute crucial assignments with the ambition of one day ascending to medicus.

Neophyte

The lowest rank within the Order, reserved for new recruits and Cresswell students. They represent the vast majority of the Order's population.

Neophytes perform menial, unsavory tasks, learning the Order's ways through service and obedience.

Acolyte

The general term encompassing all who belong to the Order, regardless of rank.

1

REYNA

I've always been fascinated by death.

I thought my life would flash before my eyes as I lie there dying. I'd see my mother taking me to my art lessons. I'd see the day my father gifted me my first camera, right before disappearing for the rest of the year again. I thought I would relive each moment like it was yesterday.

I was wrong.

There's a certain serenity that overcomes me whenever I'm killed; it washes off the burdens of my day, and for one peaceful second, I'm free.

I have a part to play in all this that makes the sweet call of death feel more like acceptance than fear, because to die is to know what it means to have lived.

Warm liquid oozes from a single, vertical slash above my still-beating heart. He trails the back of his latex-covered fingers down my cheek, smearing the wetness with a lover's caress. I blink up at him against the hazy yellow light, meeting his deep-brown eyes. His gaze pierces through me, as if we've found love moments before the grave catches us.

I've lost track of how long I've sat in this chair, focusing on the weapon in his hand and the heat emanating from his touch. I've stopped struggling against the ropes tying my wrists together as I surrender to the inevitable. Death is death, no matter what way it comes.

The tip of the kitchen knife brushes along the column of my throat, like an artist tracing a figure in pencil before permanently marking it with ink. He cups my cheek as he stands behind me to face the darkness together.

In a single swipe, the blade slides along my throat, and I choke on air.

He undoes the rope around one of my wrists, then lowers my bound body onto the cold tile floor. My lungs burn with my shortening breaths, but I don't cry or pray.

This is how it has to be.

"Hold."

The thick pink liquid gurgles from my neck, pooling around my twitching body. It seeps into my hair and sticks to my skin. I lie still, unblinking, as footsteps sound around me. A beady black eye appears before my blurry vision. The shutter of a camera fills the silence to capture the moment I meet the grim reaper.

He kneels beside my head and moves my arm to point a single finger toward the lens as if I were reaching for God like in *The Creation of Adam*.

Then he rises to his feet and leaves me on the floor.

Five.

Four.

Three.

Two.

One.

"And *cut*," Nicole calls.

I slump against the tile and stare at the ceiling. Two seconds is all I give myself before untying my wrists.

I'm exhausted to the bone.

Everyone in the room starts murmuring, and someone in my periphery slaps my dickhead of a co-star's back as if *he* were the one who had to pretend to die. That takes some serious skill, and I'm not the theater major here. I should be the one *behind* the camera.

"Hold up."

I freeze. *Please, for the love of God, no more.*

We've been filming for thirteen hours, and this is the fifth time we've had to redo this scene. My back hurts, I have a rope burn, and I think I'm developing an allergic reaction to one of the products the SFX artist used. To top it off, there wasn't enough pizza for me to have a slice.

If I have to sit through *another* round of hair and makeup to reshoot the scene, I'm going to nose-dive straight into hysterics.

I need food, solitude, and sleep. Immediately.

"Wait, nope. We're good," Nicole says, reviewing the tape even though it's meant to be my job since this is for my assignment. We take turns being on the other side of the camera whenever we have a project due for this class.

Biting back a yawn, I attempt to untie myself, silently cursing Chad and the SFX artist he's chatting up. Was he a Boy Scout or something? We aren't *actually* trying to hold me hostage here. The least this dimwit could do is give me a hand.

Look, I get it. It's been a long day, and my call sheet hasn't exactly been followed to a T. But the sooner I say the holy *W* word, the sooner we can get home, and I can wash the goddamn glitter out of my hair.

I regret letting Kimi sprinkle glitter into the fake pink blood to take pictures for her portfolio. It went everywhere. That's poor planning on my part because I've spent the whole day sparkling in certain lights—which could've ruined my tapes. If any of it shows up in my footage, I'll have to claim it's an Edward Cullen moment.

When I'm less tired, I'll come up with a metaphor that will make Professor Bradford raise a single bushy brow, hum, and then go back to pretending I don't exist.

Or I could spend an unholy number of hours editing it out in post.

Right now, I prefer the sound of the former.

Kimi rushes to my side with a towel in hand and easily undoes the rope. "They're talking about going out after this, but the only shot I'm planning on taking is a diazepam," my roommate whispers, glaring at Chad, who's still flirting with the beautician I'd rather not lose.

I snort, rubbing the towel into my hair to absorb as much of the pink blood as possible. "Lucky for some. I have a hot date with hours' worth of film." *And an essay I've procrastinated on for far too long.*

Plus another online quiz, and a wedding video I still need to deliver.

Nicole yawns, swaying slightly as she rewatches the A-roll. If you had told me thirteen hours ago that she'd stay the whole time, I'd have called you a liar. Yet here she is, spending her entire day assisting on a project she won't receive any credits for.

Fair's fair. She had me waist-deep in a lake three weeks ago when I was helping her with her assignment that Professor Bradford hailed as a masterpiece, proving that he *is* capable of giving out A's. Just not to me.

This entire day has been a collaborative effort that theoretically benefits everyone.

Chad can use the video for auditions, Lindsay can use it for her social media, and the pictures Kimi took will be for her portfolio—even if her art degree is just an excuse to attend university to get out of her mother's hold.

Three short films down. Four more to go.

It hurts that thirteen hours of filming will only amount to a seven-minute film.

I wish I could vent to Mom about all of this.

Kimi helps me to my feet, and I snatch the knife covered in pink goo off the floor so no one injures themselves, then watch the most recent scene with Nicole. I hit pause when the camera pans to my fallen frame on the floor, and pull up the crime-scene images on my phone, careful to angle it away from Nicole, and triple-check the pose is the same.

No one here needs to know they're helping me re-create real-life murder scenes—a side effect of my unhealthy obsession with true-crime podcasts and dream to direct horror movies. This whole thing we're doing is a byproduct of having a "friend" who likes to play show-and-tell with the juicy murders that come through his precinct.

Like this particular one.

I frown, scrutinizing the composition of the corpse. According to my guy on the police force, the subject was a hotshot lobbyist who fell from grace after doing something he shouldn't have.

Lawrence never gives me any details about the investigation or the victims' names, so usually I make them up, except the late Mr. Hogarth has been all over the news for embezzlement.

For the sake of art, I improvised and guessed he was a lonely man with nothing but a job and an empty house. That's what we filmed today—except Chad's dingy flat was my unfortunate substitute for the fancy apartment overlooking the Manhattan Bridge.

Lawrence tells me about any murders he thinks might have been committed by "my guy." He and the rest of his precinct are unconvinced there's a prolific serial killer roaming around, but I'm *certain* there is. All of my projects for this class are based on the murders committed by Böcklin's Shadow, or the Shadow for short—the serial killer I named that the police have been too useless to notice.

There's no obvious MO or trophy collection that I've been able to identify, only the artistic touches to each scene. Sometimes, it isn't so obvious—a strategically placed hand here, oddly symbolic clothing there, things so artfully done that it's too perfect to be an accident—but then came Mr. Hogarth.

The reference to the most well-known painting in the world is so obvious it's mind-boggling, and borderline embarrassing, that not a single detective has spotted it. The killer is making a mockery of New York's finest, with Mr. Hogarth as the star of the show. He was pointing at a cross like in *The Creation of Adam*. The fact that he's half naked and lying on a green towel is a literal dead giveaway that the Shadow was re-creating Michelangelo's painting.

It's dark, depraved, and simplistically genius.

Even with the forensic team's bad angles and flat lighting, I could stare at the crime-scene photos for hours, picking apart every detail, questioning whether the Shadow added certain items into the frame as filler or for symbolic meaning.

I've seen thousands of artworks throughout my life because of my mom and the years I spent working at the museum. None have come close to the artistry of his kills.

He's the inspiration behind every film I've produced this year.

For this project, instead of God, the camera I'm pointing at is Big Brother, all-seeing and omnipresent. But Professor Bradford might be too thick to make the connection.

I hope I've got the shot. Even if I don't, none of us have the time or energy to refilm the scene. Especially since this is due next week.

Screw it.

"Okay, that's a wrap," I call out the glorious *W* word.

The collective exhale makes me feel only semiguilty for making everyone stay longer than planned.

"Thank fucking Christ," Chad huffs.

That's it. I'm never asking him to join again. He wasn't exactly butterflies and roses to work with either. The prick. His ego, bad acting, and shitty attitude were the reason our eight-hour day turned into thirteen. I'll get revenge by picking the footage that makes him look like the tool he is.

Alas, someone needs to act like an adult. "Thank you, everyone, for all your hard work today. You all did amazing"—*Not you, Chad*—"and I couldn't have done it without you." *That last part wasn't for you either, Chad.* "I'll email the final edit next week, but please don't post about it anywhere until the end of the semester."

Everyone—except Chad—smiles and contributes to the clean-up process. Nicole helps me pack up the combo stands and the other film gear while Kimi and Lindsay clean up the rest, peeling gaff tape and wiping pink liquid off the floor and props.

By the time we've all said our goodbyes, it's almost midnight, and I can hear my bed crying out my name.

"I think I threw my back out when I fought off Chad," I grumble to Kimi, hugging my light stands as we trudge down the streets of New York City, looking like a couple of basket cases from the pink corn syrup still on me.

"I wish you had punched him for real."

I chuckle and readjust the strap biting into my shoulder. My back feels like it's going to break from the weight of the equipment.

Maybe I should have agreed to Kimi's offer to call us an Uber. But I've said yes far too many times in the past year I've been here. This city isn't exactly the best place to live with limited funds.

Our moms went to high school together back home in Indonesia, and drifted apart when Mom moved to the States before I was born. They didn't reconnect until Mom got diagnosed with cancer two years ago, shortly after Dad died.

By then, they both had very different lifestyles. My mom was single and worked every day, while Kimi's mom married her boss and didn't have to lift a finger ever again. Kimi got to grow up as a trust-fund baby with an endless bank account, zero responsibility, and living parents.

My inheritance pays rent, the scholarship covers most of my tuition, and I'm hired as a videographer often enough to cover the bare minimum of my expenses. The money from my dad might have been sizable to some, but if I wanted to make it last, I shouldn't have moved to one of the most expensive cities in the world.

"I just had the most depressing realization." Kimi's jet-black braid slaps her cheek as she whips her head toward me. "I have class in nine hours. Maybe I can skip it."

Oh. Good. It's just a *her* problem. Actually . . .

"Shit. I have a quiz tomorrow morning."

She curses. "I have a test tomorrow—which reminds me, I'm gonna need to pass on going to that exhibition. Mom is forcing me to meet with her and her friend who coincidentally has a son our age."

Shrugging, I say, "It's no big deal."

It's a bit of a big deal, but it's my issue to bear. I just need to get over myself, because I shouldn't need someone to hold my hand to do the things I used to do with Mom.

I'd have more friends and a support system or whatever if I hadn't moved across the country and transferred to Cresswell University, an Ivy League school, in the final year of my degree, after Mom died last year. But it was my only choice. I need to know more about my father's life before he died. Why he was never around. How my mom could love a man who only ever kept us at arm's length.

Am I any closer to figuring out why I only saw him once a year? No.

Has moving here felt like a waste of time and money? Partially.

After months of researching, I still have no idea what his life consisted of beyond the usual *My work keeps me very busy, Reyna. Just listen to your mother and do as she says.*

Really sage advice, Dad. Thanks. Appreciate it. So glad we had our annual bonding sessions before you carked it.

My phone buzzes, and I play a game of Twister to fish it out of my inside pocket. Lawrence's name flashes across the screen, and the corners of my lips tip up at the message.

LAWRENCE:

I've got another case for you.

2

REYNA

There's something to be said about human creativity. Give a person a piece of paper, and they might fold it, draw on it, or turn it into ash.

It's one of the reasons I chose to go into the film industry. If three people are given a camera, not one will capture the same exact footage.

Mom loved art because of that too.

My footsteps hum through the otherwise deserted exhibition. It's a hollow, foreboding sound coming from the creak of a decades-old wooden floor, combined with a high ceiling and glass roof that lets in light from the slate-gray sky.

Thunder cracks in the distance, promising a long, dreary day. Paired with the flicker of a single sconce, the weather drags the space back into the ages long before digital cameras were ever a reality. The official gallery of Cresswell University is the picture-perfect definition of melancholy, built for morbidly curious minds.

I've been studying here for a year now, and not once have I made the trek to the south end of the university to see any of the exhibits. I've been telling myself that if I'd befriended a fine-art major, then I would have gone. Unfortunately, I've found the whole *befriending* part rather difficult.

I tap my fingers against my leg, trying and failing to focus on the art. I check my phone for the tenth time in ten minutes. Lawrence still hasn't replied to my question about how far away he is. He's not about to look at the art with me, but having him here will make me feel a little less alone, and like it's not wrong of me to be here without Mom.

She took me to every art event and exhibition that was held in our city—sometimes, she even had her own work up on display. I'm sure she's beside me in spirit, critiquing the ever-living shit out of the pieces hanging on the cobalt walls. She's probably happy as can be right now, finally reunited with her soulmate. But I'm selfish. I wish she could be with me instead.

Taking a deep breath, I slip my phone into the front pocket of my pinafore and move away from the odd light display to return to the paintings. Neither Mom nor I had an eye for conceptual or contemporary art, but it didn't stop us from pretending that we did.

Each work of art I pass has me imagining the ruthless things she'd whisper when she thought no one could hear her.

She used to be a surrealist painter with an Indonesian flair. She still has her art displayed in museums all around the world, even one in the Merdeka Palace. The portion of her royalties that she didn't leave to be donated to charities back in Indo have been accruing in a trust I can't touch until I'm twenty-five.

She may not have known the first thing about operating a camera, but she taught me the art of cinematography and sent me to every class that came up so I could become the very best.

Or at least try to be. I seem to be woefully failing in that department if my grades are any indication. Before Mom died, I had a stellar GPA. Now I have—well, nothing worth bragging about.

I stop at a painting of a shepherd herding a pack of wolves through a maze, and a pit forms in my stomach from the memory of Mom's dying words.

Find shepherd.

I never got the chance to ask whether there was meant to be a *the* before *shepherd.*

Honestly, I'm probably looking into it too much. Mom was never very religious, but as she was nearing the end, she sought comfort from anything she could, even if it didn't make sense to me. Whatever it was that went through her head, it's too late for me to get answers.

I pause in front of a painting of a dead angel hanging upside down. Folding my hands behind my back, I tip my head to the side. The piece in front of me is . . . fascinating, to say the least.

Shaw's pieces usually are. Mom took me to his exhibit in Chicago a couple years back. She had been watching his rise to fame ever since he first hit the news as a teen. The man has talent, but he's nowhere near as good as he used to be. I suppose what comes up must come down.

The angel is holding together his shattered body with broken fingers. Midnight hues and flecks of crimson blot along his porcelain skin. Pools of scarlet and royal-blue velvet, vases, jewels, and golden filigree decorate his surroundings.

The longer I look at it, the clearer it becomes—the subject is a woman, not a man.

I edge closer to get a better look. Her eyes are hollow. Darkness colors between the cracks of her skin, except for the dull light trickling though from her center. Her fragile hands and fraying threads of gold hold her shattered pieces together. Skin flaps at her hairline like she might have been scalped. Once I lean in, I realize she's wearing a wig.

The most jarring realization isn't that she's trying to hold her body together; she's covering the swell of her stomach where the shadows within are five shades lighter.

Sat against the backdrop of the neoclassical building of the fine-art department, and the sullen hues from the indignant sky, Shaw's painting is beautifully grotesque.

The level of detail and thought that has gone into this piece is nothing short of genius. A hundred years from now, critics will look back at this and sing praises about the masterpiece. Any art major could have a field day trying to unpack its meaning. Except something fundamental is missing.

I want to know more about the woman. But I'm not knocked off my feet. I'm not going to go to bed feeling the soul-deep ache the artist is trying to achieve. Simply put, it's lacking.

"Quite the piece."

I whip my head toward the person beside me and nearly jump out of my skin. How long has he been standing here?

My eyes widen before I force my attention back to the painting, imprinting his side profile into memory. Dark hair, chiseled jaw, glasses, tall, *British accent.* There's a relaxed, alluring air about the way he stands, and my God if it doesn't make me feel a little unsteady.

We can add him to the list of artworks in the building.

If I sneak another peek, I might gawk, and I was raised to be better than that. I can see him out of the corner of my eye, observing the painting just as I've been for the past ten minutes. But all I can focus on is the six-foot-something *fine* specimen beside me.

And the fact that I have no idea what I should be doing in this situation.

What would be normal in these circumstances? Nod? Hum my agreement? Say something mundane about the shitty weather?

"You can tell it was painted by a man."

Shit. Too direct.

He snaps his attention to me. "Is that meant to be an offense?"

Retreat. Retreat.

Fuck, I should have mentioned the weather. I shift my weight to look him directly in the eyes—which is a big mistake on my part. They're the most stunning shade of green I've ever seen, with deep rings of emerald and rivers of sage. It's almost unnatural.

My fingers twitch with the urge to draw my camera to capture the details of his face, like the dip beneath his bottom lip and the dark flicks of eyelashes. Even the way the strands of his perfectly styled hair fall atop his head—clean and tidy, but effortless, as if he rolled out of bed, ran his hands through his hair with his fingers, then stepped out the door.

He's got the whole English countryside business attire down pat with the knitted vest, button-up, Chelsea boots, and a tweed jacket hanging from the crook of his elbow. The five o'clock shadow he's sporting is the cherry on top.

Actually a lens wouldn't be able to capture his refined beauty. If Aphrodite saw him walking down the street, she would smite him out of jealousy. Maybe I shouldn't have engaged at all.

My breath stutters as I rack my brain, trying to remember what he said. I clear my throat, then respond, "An astute observation made by someone with an eye for detail."

It's a physical feat not to stare at how the tendons in his forearms ripple as he places his hands in his pockets. I'm not falling for the nonchalant demeanor he's dishing out. If I weren't studying every angle of him, I would have missed the slight flattening of his thick brows.

"And what made you draw this conclusion?"

I could listen to that British accent all damn day. Deep and elegant, it even sounds like he's smoldering.

He straightens, silently challenging me, with every expectation that I would back down, and by *God* does that irk me. He looks like someone who's used to getting his way.

Unfortunately for him, I'm sleep-deprived, stressed, overcaffeinated, and I have many things to say. He can stare me down with those pretty green eyes of his all he wants, nothing will change the fact that I would kill for a distraction right now.

I don't want to think about the corrupted footage waiting for me once I get home. Or the essay I haven't started. Not the ridiculous test I have for an elective class I only chose because of how it worked in my schedule.

Pursing my lips, I twist back to scrutinize the painting. If this man wants to argue over something I'm right about, then I'm game.

"There's profound meaning behind the piece—that much is apparent. There's harmony, the detailing is phenomenal, the colors are complimentary, and the composition is superb." I look over my shoulder at him. "But it lacks intimacy."

Lately, all of Shaw's works do.

He scoffs like I might really be insane. "It's hardly meant to be a piece about love."

I roll my eyes. Typical man brain. This is probably the first time he's stepped into an art gallery.

Honestly, I'm not a hundred percent sure that Shaw's the artist. I haven't looked at the plaque. It simply looks like something he's made.

Mom and I would never read the inscription until we were about to leave. She'd always say that you haven't done a good enough job if you need to read something to understand it. The painter has made it clear that there's *meant* to be some level of relationship to the woman. I have no idea what it is.

Herein lies part of the issue.

The other problem being this guy's attitude.

"To be understood is to know intimacy, as they say. The artist knows the subject; beyond all the symbols, and the pretty background, the people do not. It's a one-sided relationship between a painter and an object."

Now would be a good time for me to shut up. Our stares are clashing. His irritation is rolling off him in waves, and I can feel him burning holes into the side of my head.

Yet I continue, "Take Maria van Oosterwyck's paintings for example. They're just bouquets of flowers, yet you can feel the connection with every stroke of the petal and each angle of the leaves. She worships those flowers, adores them with every fiber of her being, and she wants you to as well. Only a woman could love something inanimate like that. This?"

I narrow my eyes at the name on the plaque. I was, predictably, correct.

"It seems like *Shaw* is more interested in showing off his fine motor skills than making a strong connection. That woman is a subject, not his muse."

It's not always obvious if a piece of art was created by a man or woman, but back in the olden days—especially when artists ran in the same circles—it can be painfully apparent. But sometimes, throw in a bit of critical analysis, and it's as clear as day.

"It's a violent painting." I hazard a glance his way. He's so rigid, he looks carved from stone. "There isn't meant to be *intimacy*," he says through gritted teeth. "'When it comes to art, it's important not to hide the madness.'"

Maybe he deserves more credit than I gave him if he's quoting Atticus. "That's right. But what else? There's blood and gore, and . . . ?"

"Are you a painter?" he says abruptly.

I frown, taken aback. "No."

He raises a brow. "Sculptor?"

"No, but—"

"Illustrator? Designer? Photographer?" he lists. "What about an art degree?"

I shake my head, my annoyance rising. "Not technically, however—"

"What qualifies you to be making any of these comments? You're clearly not any kind of esteemed *critique*."

Ass. *Hole.*

He shouldn't have started a conversation about the damn painting if he couldn't handle a difference in opinion.

I huff. "Maybe I should have been asking your earlier question: Are *you* offended?"

His eyes harden. "No. I don't see any merit in listening to the baseless opinions of someone who has no skill, experience, or expertise in the area."

So he's just insecure. Got it.

"To put your art on display is to bear your heart open."

That's what my mom told me the first time I submitted a short movie for my school's film festival and bawled my eyes out when the judges ripped into my work. She sat me down, held my hand, and said, *You're a Sinaga, Reyna. A* naga. *Dragon. You don't wait for acceptance. You take it, and you burn everything in your way if you have to.*

"Maybe you shouldn't be going to an art gallery if you're going to get hurt on another person's behalf," I say.

"Or maybe you shouldn't comment on things you know nothing about."

My heart lurches when he rounds on me. The proximity of his towering frame feels like I have fingers wrapped around my throat, slowly seeping oxygen from my lungs.

I'll be damned if I let him try to intimidate me. "If I'm not mistaken, Maddox Shaw isn't a woman. So my observations are neither baseless nor incorrect."

"Please," he scoffs. "Your ability to read makes you as qualified as a grade-schooler."

Fine. If he wants to talk shit, then I'll talk shit.

"Look up *Before the Mirror* by Édouard Manet, then *Woman at Her Toilette* by Berthe Morisot. Put them side by side, then ask yourself if you can tell which was painted by a woman. One comes down to the objectification of the subject; the other is the romanticization of it. A painting is a story condensed down to a single frame. The only thing Shaw is glorifying is his ability to use a paintbrush."

The vein in his forehead throbs like he's holding back from detonating. "Remembering the names of famous paintings doesn't make you a valid critic. It makes you a nobody with too much time on your hands and no talent of your own."

Wow. Low blow.

I can't imagine why he'd take such personal offense to a critique on someone else's work.

"Your inability to formulate a valid response to counter my observation is extremely telling of your so-called *qualifications* since the only comments you've offered are weak attacks on my person." This is reminding me of childish bickering. "Come to think of it, the last time I used that tactic was in middle school."

He stares at me like he's trying to rip me apart in his mind.

I hold my breath, counting the seconds, waiting for the next attempt at degradation. Then I stand there dumbstruck, watching him storm out of the exhibition. Did he just . . . run away?

I blink.

What the fuck?

This needs to go in my imaginary book of bizarre encounters.

Whatever. He's got some problems he needs to unpack with someone who isn't me. Shaking my head, I check my phone to see Lawrence is still twenty minutes away. I wish I'd brought my laptop so I could make use of my time. I've already been here way longer than I'd intended.

At least I got to talk art with someone.

By the time he arrives, rain is battering down on the glass ceiling, and I've looked at all the installations and got in a good glower at Shaw's *Fallen Angel* painting.

His face splits into a beaming smile that makes me uncomfortable on a cellular level because I feel nowhere near the same level of glee at seeing him.

Lawrence has a familiar face, one I feel like I've seen a hundred times before—the conventional attractiveness of an average man in his mid-twenties.

He's someone's type. Just not mine.

"I got you something." Rainwater sprays from his bleached-blond hair as he shrugs off his backpack.

Excitement thrums through me as he pulls out a folder, and I resist the urge to snatch it from him. I've been waiting for him to bring me another one of Böcklin's Shadow's kills for weeks. If Dad were still alive, he'd lose his shit if he knew I was in cahoots with a cop so I could be a "copycat" killer who doesn't properly kill anyone. Even Mom would be mortified that I was probably the one and only person in the Shadow's fan club.

It's not like his kills . . . didn't have it coming, as bad as it is to say. Every subject I've managed to identify has had reasons to have enemies, and a past worth dying painfully for—not that anyone deserves to die. But I can see why the killer thought they did.

I grab the folder from Lawrence before his arm has fully extended, and flip open to the first page. Yes. *Finally*, I can get some inspiration for—

"I, uh, got you something else too."

Oh no.

I slowly turn my attention away from the photo of the dead guy up to Lawrence, who's wearing a bashful expression that I might have called cute in another life, down to his outstretched hand. A part of me dies to keep my expression neutral.

Chocolate-coated almonds.

Again.

The one thing in this world that I'm allergic to. How romantic.

Lawrence and I met last year when I called the police after someone broke into Kimi's and my apartment. We left it at that until I ran into him a couple of nights later at a fantasy-themed bar that Kimi dragged me to. He gave me his number, and for some unknown reason, I accepted.

I blame it on the three "lunar mating" cocktails I had, and the first positive interaction with a stranger since Mom died. One year later, I am solidly team platonic while he edges the line of "Why not more?"

It's been a solid no from me since day one.

If I hadn't based my entire project on his help, I would have cut ties the second he started giving me puppy eyes a couple of months ago. But it was nice having someone who could understand what I was going through. He had lost his mom recently too.

And he knew the one thing that would help: a distraction.

He gave me crime-scene photos and tried to look into my dad, and I dropped him so many lunches as a thank-you that he started to believe we're on the path to be more.

I give him the warmest smile I can muster. "Lawrence, you shouldn't have."

"I wanted to." *If you also wanted me to die, you should have said so.* "You were there when I needed someone last week, and it's the least I can do."

Guilt leaves a sour taste in my mouth as I offer him a supportive smile.

He's given me the same thing how many times now? And how many times have I told him that I'm allergic?

I have no intention of taking our relationship beyond the realm of friends, which I've made clear to him numerous times. In fact, I've said it, word for word.

Lawrence, I think we should just be friends.

Lawrence, I'm not looking for a relationship.

Lawrence, thank you for the gift that I am incapable of eating, but we're still not happening.

Maybe I'm a bad person for not doing the right thing and cutting ties to save him the heartbreak, and maybe it's my fault he's getting mixed signals. We hung out a bit after we realized that we were both sad and traumatized and could bond over our shared misery. But that's where our compatibility ends—other than the fact that we have a shared interest in, well, dead people.

"Thank you." I awkwardly hide the packet in my satchel before refocusing on the pictures. "Why do you think this is my guy?"

Lawrence clears his throat and shrugs. "It gives off the vibe."

The vibe. He doesn't believe me at all. This man really is just happy to entertain me.

I flip through the crime-scene photos. It's a gruesome sight, no doubt about it. But it doesn't look staged. Eight stab wounds, bruises, and several broken bones. It's a crime of passion more than anything.

Damn it. "It's not him."

"Are you sure?"

"It's too messy. See here?" I point to the picture of the victim's face, which is black and blue with a boatload of red. "He would never do something like that unless he's trying to make a statement that involves the face. Maybe gouging out the eyes or pulling teeth would be more his style. He'd make it symbolic somehow. This is a simple beating."

Lawrence frowns at me. "There's nothing simple about it. This man was brutally murdered, Reyna."

My lips part. Right. I forgot that I'd desensitized myself to death. I'm *meant* to be mortified by this. "Sorry, yes. It's awful. But . . . usually, people are killed like this for a reason, right?"

"Uh, yeah. Sure," he agrees, though his lips curl in disapproval.

I clear my throat. Time to change the topic. I pull up a photo on my phone. "I've been meaning to ask you something since you've lived here your whole life." *I think.* "Does this building look familiar to you?"

I have a total of five photos of my father, all taken at different times during my life, except this one. He must be in his early twenties here—I'm guessing. It's hard to tell because it's of his profile. I wouldn't have realized it was him if Mom hadn't kept it.

I found it underneath Mom's bed after she'd died. It's the only lead I have.

Lawrence squints at the screen as I zoom in on the high ceiling. All I've been able to figure out is that it's a vaulted room of some sort. The marble ceiling has a honeycomb-like pattern with different symbols painted in each hexagonal shape. The picture's quality isn't clear enough for me to figure out what the designs are. The door behind him also has a filigree design that I can't make out.

My stomach sinks as Lawrence pales. Taking a big step back, he clears his throat and shakes his head. "Nope. Never seen it before."

I frown, moving forward. "Lawrence—"

"But if I *did* know where that was, I'd stay the hell away from it."

Unease ripples down my spine. *He knows where it is.* I've been searching for this place for *months*. I've asked so many people and spent even more time searching the internet. Nothing.

Both of my parents were taken from me before I had the chance to say goodbye. Learning about my dad is my chance to get a part of him back. If I get to know him, maybe I'll be able to love him the same way Mom did, and understand all the times she cried over him.

He might have been my father, but he wasn't present enough to be my dad. He loved his work more than anything else, and I deserve to at least know what he did—not the shitty lie he told me about being a businessman. As a kid, I imagined him working for the CIA, and that's why he never stayed for more than a day or two per year. Who knows, those childlike suspicions could be true.

That there's something more to it. I feel it in my bones. Mom and Dad hid something from me. They begged me never to go to Cresswell, and threw me a *Just trust us* when I'd ask why.

When I lost the only family I had, I started searching for the one I was meant to have.

I move closer. "Lawrence, please, if you know something—*anything*—tell me. You can trust me. You know you can."

"No, Reyna. I mean it," he presses. "Chasing a serial killer is bad enough. You leave that to rest, and don't ever ask me about it again. I'll help you with your guy, but that's it."

I've never seen Lawrence this serious before. He's been bending the law for me for months, and *this* is where he draws the line? A picture? What could possibly be so bad about a damn building?

I'm not about to lie through my teeth and make him promises I won't keep. Still, I nod to keep the peace. This isn't over.

My parents are gone, along with the secrets they kept from me. I'll keep digging until I hit bone. I don't always believe that the dead should stay buried.

3

REYNA

Pink Ink? God, why did I think the premise of this project was a good idea? Re-creating murder scenes with pink blood? That shit is a nightmare to edit to get the tone *just* right. Don't even get me started on what a pain in the ass it is when the vibrancy of the corn-syrup mixture differs from batch to batch. I've stared at my laptop for so long I'm starting to see double.

The idea came to me when I was eight and I just got caught watching *Carrie*. I told Mom it would be less scary if the blood was pink. She shook her head, told me I could do that when I'm older, then instilled the fear of God in me for sneaking out of bed.

Bradford laughed at my concept. If he does it another time, Nicole will need to hold me back from supergluing his desk drawers shut.

My alarm goes off, and I tap my screen a little too aggressively. Grumbling under my breath, I pack up my things and shuffle out of the library. I don't want to say that the assignment I'm submitting tonight is a pile of trash. *But* I'm not saying my mom wouldn't compare it to my classmate's work and passive aggressively point out everything they did better than me.

Some of the framing is definitely off.

Is it worth a C? Absolutely not. Is Professor Bradford going to give me a C? One hundred percent.

I am not sure how many more of those I can afford before I lose my scholarship. I've been getting decent enough grades in my other classes, but he's single-handedly annihilated my GPA. Even the psychology elective I'm suffering through is going substantially better.

Hell, maybe Mom and Dad didn't want me going to Cresswell because they have issues with Professor Bradford and no one cared to enlighten me about it.

I exit the library, going down the grand steps, toward the fountain that has water pouring from the mouths of sea monsters.

Behind the Gothic gate, the traffic noise disappears, as if this university exists on its own plane. The spires of the neo-Gothic library casts the barest shadow across the courtyard pavement, cutting through the fog where skyscrapers should be. The campus looks like a jigsaw puzzle of buildings erected across multiple centuries. On the left, past the russet four-story Victorian-era liberal arts building, is the Cresswell Art Gallery.

I can *just* see it beside the glass cheese-grater-looking monstrosity that stands out like rotten fruit. I call it my personal brand of hell. Everyone else calls it Cresswell Law School. It replaced the neoclassical brownstone that burned down about a decade ago.

People walking to and from buildings, wrapping themselves tighter in their coats, juggling books, and balancing canvases. Some perch on the edge of the fountain to eat their late lunch or hang out.

I lower my head to avoid making eye contact with anyone. It's a big place, with an even bigger student body. Everyone doesn't know everyone. But anyone who knows who I am, knows I don't belong here. I'm considered . . . *odd* because of my circumstances. The girl with dead parents who moved across the country midway through her final year to make "fucked-up" videos, as someone from the film club called them.

It doesn't help that I didn't sign up for any groups or societies. Everyone I know at Cresswell, I know through Kimi. I'm just her tagalong friend. Lawrence didn't see me that way, and I liked that too much.

Music blares through my headphones, just shy of my ears bleeding. It's doing a crap job of keeping me from falling asleep while standing. As if that's not bad enough, I'm panting and peeling my scarf from my sweat-slicked skin after needing to run across campus to the very edge of the east side and into the Victorian brownstone that houses most of the lecture halls.

I need to get to class early so I can ask Bradford to explain why my last assignment was only worthy of a C. He's usually pissy after needing to teach, so hopefully he'll be in a reasonably decent mood if I catch him now.

The music cuts off as I lower the headphones down around my neck. The last time I walked into Bradford's class with them on, he threatened to confiscate them like we were back in high school—but a much prettier high school that takes pride in always having art displayed on the walls and proper mahogany desks that have somehow survived abuse from students.

The muscle in my jaw twitches and prepares to interact with the human embodiment of a viral infection. Except Bradford isn't lounging behind his desk, hand over his beer gut. His stale stench doesn't assault my nostrils the second I step inside. No, there's something . . . masculine lingering in the air instead—like bergamot.

The room is empty except for the man leaning against the cedar desk, with his sleeves rolled up to his elbows and glasses pushed right up his nose. His imposing frame is relaxed, casual yet refined, lost in the book he's reading. I can't help dragging my eyes from his polished shoes to his black slacks, up to his woolen vest and plaid button-up combo with tie. Then to the five o'clock shadow and full lips and, finally, his poison-ivy eyes.

Oh.

Oh no.

"It's you."

His gaze snaps up to mine, and the temperature plummets ten degrees.

"You." He sneers, British accent lacing the single syllable.

Shoot me.

"Where's Professor Bradford?" I whip my head around the room in case I might spot him hiding in the corner. I'll pick the Grinch who stole Christmas over the Lord of Darkness.

"Unavailable."

"Is he dead?" I probably sound a little too hopeful. I've been watching too many horror movies.

"No." He raises an eyebrow like he's only partially amused by my response.

When he doesn't elaborate, I follow his line of sight to the whiteboard behind him, where two words are written in cursive letters: *Maddox Shaw.*

Shaw, like the artist I openly criticized last week. *Shaw*, like the man I looked right in the eye and said that his painting is lacking.

The only thing Shaw is glorifying is his ability to use a paintbrush.

Oh, I definitely fucked up.

I'm going to lose my scholarship.

"Feel free to drop out of this class," Shaw says, stirring me out of my existential crisis.

My jaw drops. "It's midway through the semester."

Getting my liver plucked out by a big bird every day would hurt less than this interaction. I knew Shaw taught at Cresswell; I just didn't expect him to look like . . . like a goddamn dream.

"Not my problem." He shrugs, returning his attention to his book as if I'm an inconsequential speck of dust.

This is the great Maddox Shaw? Color me livid.

I can't move a muscle. I'm stuck, dumbfounded, and seething.

He's the one who wanted me to explain the observation I made about the painting. *He's* the one who started the conversation to begin with. Now he's butt hurt and wants to be a threat to *my* career? Absolutely fucking not. I have come too far to have it all thrown away by an obnoxious, overly sensitive, entitled man.

Moss-colored eyes flick up to me from above the black frames of his glasses. "Didn't your mother teach you not to stare? Although, I'm sure she forgot to teach you a lot of things to do with basic respect."

My blood boils to near-deadly levels at the mention of my mother. If he knows she's a sensitive topic, what's the likelihood he'll use it against me for the rest of the semester?

I'll be damned if I am going to sit by and let some arrogant asshole talk shit about my mom just because he's too egotistical to take criticism. Shaw can dish it out, but he can't take it.

"Yes, just like teaching you how to put emotion on canvas would be a lost cause." I'm not sure whether it's the stress or lack of sleep that's making it so that I don't give two craps about the trouble my mouth will cause. Logic and reason aren't registering right now.

His nostrils flare. It's barely noticeable, but I'm paying attention like my life depends on it.

Shaw slams his book shut, places it on the desk, then casually walks to the storage room near the front of the classroom. Beneath his touch, the old, rickety wooden door releases a squeal that comes from the bounds of hell.

He holds it open, waiting for me to follow. Now *that* makes me pause.

But any hesitation I have evaporates when he makes a show of checking his watch like I'm boring him. I storm ahead.

It's like walking myself into a slaughterhouse.

This was a bad idea. There are far worse things than death. Failing this class and being kicked out of Cresswell is one of them. But turning around would make me seem weak.

Shaw strikes me as the type of person who's never had anyone challenge him. I'm happy to oblige—even though the only thing I *should* be doing is shutting up.

The small, enclosed space surrounds us, closing in on me as if my soul is about to separate from my body. Old cassette tapes, paperwork, and junk are stacked atop more crap on the old shelves. But it's he who takes up the most space. I've never understood claustrophobia until now.

Dust particles float between us, the only barrier between me and him. Beneath the must and scent of old books, is him. It's heady, and suffocating, and it makes my lungs squeeze because if I keep breathing him in, the wires in my brain are going to stop firing.

"Name?" he asks.

I blink hard, reorientating myself. "Why? Will you try to guess whether the assignments were directed by a man or woman? I assure you it can be just as painfully obvious."

There's no point resisting. He's got access to all student records. It'd take him all of two minutes to figure my name out.

Slowly, Shaw closes the distance, stalking forward like a beast cornering its meal. Maintaining eye contact is like I'm threatening a lion, and I am nothing if not a stubborn idiot sometimes.

Shivers ripple down my spine under the full weight of his attention. I raise my chin, willing my fraying nerves to stay put for the next two hours so I can leave this class with what little sanity I have left.

And with my scholarship still intact.

His voice a low rumble only God and I could hear. "Hear me when I say this: You are unqualified. You are inexperienced. You do not matter. Your opinions are inconsequential."

I pause.

This grade-A *asshole.*

I don't give a rat's ass what my résumé looks like, no one deserves to be so demeaned. Shaw represents everything bad about this industry: the ego, the entitlement, stepping on those he deems *lesser* because he's set himself up on the gilded pedestal that he made.

I'm getting under his skin, and he hates it. If he wants someone to kiss his ring, there are people in this class who would volunteer to do his laundry. If he wants someone to push around, he's barked up the wrong tree.

Folding my hands behind my back, I ask, "And what qualifications do you have to teach this class?"

He narrows his eyes. Heat zaps through the air between us, electrifying each of my blood cells. I have to hold my breath to stop taking in his addictive scent. He's close enough to trail my fingers along the curve of his cheek. Three steps and I could press myself to him to feel his strength against me.

Pretty people like Shaw are giant red flags until proven otherwise. Men like him make you stupid. The fact that I'm still thinking he's the most attractive man I've ever seen while he's looking at me like I'm the greatest inconvenience in existence is evidence enough.

"Maddox Shaw. Look up the name."

"Why? Does your Wikipedia bio confirm that you struggle with conveying emotions? Maybe some crayons would help."

Not only is my inability to keep my mouth shut going to get me kicked out of this university, but it's a blatant lie. *Feeling* isn't the issue. There's just a disconnect with what he was trying to achieve and the execution. The look on his face tells me that he thinks I believe my words.

It's on the tip of my tongue to backtrack. Mom would never say anything like that unless she backed it up with suggestions on how to improve. He beats me to it before I can.

"Get out."

I fight the urge to cower. "You first."

With how much I need this class to get my degree, an army of the undead couldn't drag me out of here.

"I'm your professor."

"You're our temporary teacher," I correct. "You have no authority to kick me out of a class I've paid for when you are neither the convener nor named in the syllabus. You're a fill-in. Your demand holds no weight."

Shaw stares at me for one long, tense moment, and it's like a switch goes off in his head. He straightens. Any hint of burning emotion that was flashing through his eyes is gone in an instant. "Very well. I look forward to receiving your assignment tonight."

My stomach drops. I forgot about that.

I should apologize. Maybe make pretty promises not to misbehave. Shit, I should call a truce. Except I spin on my heels, exit the storage room, and take a seat behind Nicole, who has her nose shoved in her laptop. The lecture hall must have quickly begun to fill while Maddox and I had our little spat.

The vast majority of arriving students are drooling over our new teacher. If I didn't have prior interactions with him, I'd be falling victim to his charm.

Maddox Shaw is a Cresswell legacy known worldwide for his morbidly beautiful pieces. Born into wealth, he made a name for himself at sixteen. He was the recipient of the prestigious Henry Locket Award for Artist of the Year at age twenty-two, making him the youngest person who has ever received it. He has two paintings in the Louvre, another in Buckingham Palace, and one in the Pentagon.

And I just insulted him.

Again.

I don't need to look him up, because I know all his accolades. I just didn't know what he looked like.

Shaw didn't just jump into stardom; he plunged into it. I can't remember the exact name of the piece, but I recall seeing photos of it when I was a kid. Even Mom was thoroughly impressed by it. She nudged me and said that I'd be a bigger deal than him one day. It was her way of saying that she was enamored by the piece.

At sixteen, he made a life-size mixed-media painting where he sculpted a woman onto the canvas. She was cloaked in an intricate white cloth, painted with a lace pattern, and she had torn black sinew wings that hung from the canvas, ripping a king's head off. Parts of the man's face were shredded to reveal a real pig skull beneath.

The only reason I remembered it was because it traumatized my nine-year-old brain. I asked Mom if a demon made it.

It enraged the animal-rights activist groups. When Shaw was asked about it, he smiled and said that's part of the art. Saying, people will make assumptions about things they don't understand based on a single glance. Then he provided evidence he used a diseased pig that died long before Shaw got his hands on it.

That kid turned into the legend standing before me today. God, I'm an idiot. I need to get a handle on myself and make it onto his good side. Give him a gift basket or something. Shaw's mentorship would be invaluable and push the bounds of my abilities to turn me into the type of person that people make documentaries about.

Still, I know I won't take all of it back. Buying his forgiveness would be fruitless.

Shaw used to create masterpieces. What I saw in the exhibition wasn't one. It's been years since I've looked up what the critics are saying about him, and I don't imagine it would be very good.

He's been on his high horse for so long that he thinks people will settle for his mediocrity.

It's hard to believe that his fall from grace landed him here to be Bradford's substitute. I mean, it makes sense why he was chosen. Shaw has taught many theory-based classes and written several research papers on the history and modernization of art through various mediums, such as film, photography, and 3D printing. Mom told me he held a photography exhibition three years ago involving corpses and skeletons of all species—a decision that shocked *many* critics. I suppose that makes him qualified to teach this class—even if his mediums of choice are paint and clay.

Shaw clears his throat and introduces himself to the room. I'm sure most students here haven't got a clue who he is beyond the fact that he belongs on the cover of *Vogue*. Every fine-art major knows his name. The film students? God, no.

"Professor Bradford had a fall and is not in a state to teach—rest assured, he is still alive, but less than well." Shaw looks at me when he says it, and I try not to glare back. "I will be teaching this class for the foreseeable future."

The girl beside me does a mini fist pump. I haven't met anyone who likes Bradford, either as a person or as a teacher, so while the situation that resulted in his absence is unfortunate, I would have been over the moon if it were quite literally anyone other than Shaw subbing in.

He doesn't bother explaining his background. He proves he's perfect for the job within the first five minutes.

Shaw slowly paces the small space at the front of the class, clicking through the slides to a screenshot from a film I'm not familiar with. Half of the subject's face is pooled in shadow, softer beneath his eyes.

It's a moody scene. Dramatic. A lower angle to show us we're lesser than the character. It's shorthand for power.

"What does this one image tell you?" When no one immediately answers, he continues. "Pay attention to the contrast, where the light falls, the angle. It's more than a mood. Every frame says something. It's telling a story. What is the subtext?"

Nicole raises her hand in front of me. Shaw nods at her. "That the character is ambiguous."

"Correct." He offers Nicole an approving head tilt that makes my stomach dip unpleasantly. "You can only see half of his face. In a single frame, you know he is half myth, half man. Legendary and unknowable. It's a world where morality is obscure."

Fuck me, I didn't even pick up on half of that. Now that he's said it, I see it, and I hate it because it means he's highly competent and perfect for this class.

"Can anyone tell me what the combination of the soft light and the lower angle represents?"

I glance at the guy on my left. We've never spoken, but Austin is always happy to give his two cents. Like now.

"It's slightly off-center." It is? Shaw is throwing me off my game. "The lighting is basically nostalgic, so it's a memory."

"Yes, it's tilted from where your eye expects it to be because we aren't in the present. The light, the low angle, and the subject being off-center tells us one more thing: It's a melancholic power, and it's fading."

He pauses, dragging his eyes over the class, conveniently missing me.

I've never seen this many people so focused in any of my classes. There must be about seventy students here, and there isn't a phone in sight. Even the guy who usually plays *The Sims* in class is fully engrossed, and I'm pretty sure the pupils of the girl on the other side of me have turned heart-shaped.

"Lighting and angle isn't for visual flair. It *is* the story. This is not just the act of recording. Angle can become a thematic device. Lighting is a language, and you need to learn how to speak it."

The room is silent enough to hear a pin drop.

The longer he talks, the more on edge I am. Oh, he's good all right. Too good.

To Bradford, a camera is just a camera. To Shaw, a camera is an extension of art. Passion oozes from every eloquently worded concept with enough detail to understand without making the waters murky. Even though he's a grade-A prick, he teaches in a way that ensures we absorb everything he says because he truly wants the best for us.

Or at least, the best for everyone but me.

Not once does he look my way during the whole two hours.

I'm screwed if he kicks me out of this class. I'll have to retake it next semester if Bradford is back by then; if not, I won't be able to graduate.

No, I need to get it together, keep my head down, and not look a gift horse in the mouth. Maddox Shaw can be the reason this university adds me to its book of legendary alumni.

Let him rip into my work. In fact, I hope he hates me enough that he won't hold back from telling me all the reasons why my work is terrible, so I can learn and make him scramble for a single bad thing to say.

Mom said I'll make it big one day. She was right. I will. And Shaw is going to help me get there.

Game on, Maddox.

4

MADDOX

A loud crash booms through my studio office, followed by an aggravating, grating "You got any food? I'm hungry."

I shut my eyes and take a deep breath before pointing my paintbrush in the direction of my half-eaten lunch. I have neither the patience nor the neurons to deal with the verbal diarrhea that my brother might choose to let loose today.

"By all means," I grit as I glare at the canvas in front of me. "Please, damage the hundred-year-old door."

"Sorry," Spencer murmurs, humming an annoying, nasally tune that has me approximately two seconds from murdering him with the aforementioned paintbrush. My patience is limited on the best of days. Lately, there isn't a speck of it in existence.

He doesn't come up behind me to look at my painting. He knows I won't allow it. "You know that chick that I met at the bar last week?"

Here we go.

"Which one?" I turn to give him my full attention. Looking at the painting will only piss me off further.

"Not important." He waves me off. Ever since he turned twenty-one, he spends half the week drinking and the other half flirting with every woman in New York. "Anyway, it turns out she's a lecturer here."

Oh, bloody hell.

I swipe my hand down my face. I swear, if this little shit gets me fired—I take a deep breath. Sure, I love him, and he has a great many redeeming qualities that I'm not in the right frame of mind to recall. It doesn't mean I don't want to kill him eighty-seven percent of the time. He's a fucking twat.

"Who, pray tell, might that be?" So I know whether I should expect an email from HR.

My idiot of a brother shrugs. "Don't remember. Blond, yea high, weirdly bony elbows."

"You've just described a quarter of the teaching body." I give him a deadpan stare. "Can you keep it in your pants for a full twenty-four hours? Is that too much to ask?"

"Probably." Spencer snorts. "I can't help that I'm young, fun, and completely undeniable."

"You sound like you're in your forties."

"Yeah, you would know about that, old man."

"Thirty-two is *not* old." I glare at him.

Although my bloody knees feel like they belong to a geriatric.

Don't even get me started on my back. I almost blew it out trying to break someone's spine last week.

"See this?" Spencer motions at his face. "Not a wrinkle in sight. You should try using SPF, man. A girl in freshman year told me about it, and let me tell you: Game. Changer. I'm glowing like a baby. The MILFs love it."

"If only you had that much dedication to quite literally any other aspect of your life. It's wasted passion." Admittedly, he's too invested in the family business for my liking. It may well be the one thing he truly cares about.

He rolls his eyes. "I'm enjoying my youth, *Dad*." He says it jokingly, but we both know it's gone beyond that now.

I'm nothing like our sperm donor, but I sure as shit play more of a fatherly role than he does. It was me who made sure my younger brother ate, showered, did his homework, and paid for the football fees, and I made sure that his nappy was changed.

It wasn't like the woman who gave birth to us was going to do it.

"Don't be a dickhead." I scowl. "All this sleeping around is going to bite you in the ass one day."

Christ, I really do sound like an overbearing father.

"YOLO." *Fucking hell.* "That's a future-me problem. Plus, everyone involved is aware that it's a mutually beneficial arrangement. No hearts are getting hurt." He grins, snags my food off my messy desk, plops onto the leather couch, kicks up his feet, and uses his chest as a plate. "Give me ten. I've gotta do an online quiz."

"They're meant to be an hour long." I frown.

"Yup." He winks.

The second his headphones are on, the spacious room is doused in calm, peaceful, absolutely blissful silence.

Or at least it *would* be all those things if he weren't chewing so bloody loud.

The overgrown child is giving me gray hairs. If he weren't a straight-A student, I'd be concerned about him half-arsing his classes. He comes here whenever he wants to "shoot the shit" or kill time between classes.

Sighing heavily, I stretch my neck to the side before refocusing my attention on my latest piece. It looks even worse under the harsh afternoon light.

Right.

That's it, I'm throwing it away. There's no salvaging it.

I wish there were a cathartic way to destroy a canvas without stabbing or snapping or throwing paint at it like a petulant child. Then I'd probably have a critic drop from the ceiling vents to dissect meaning and intention.

They'll say I'm a creative genius with an eye for detail. They'll claim I'm reviving art by experimenting with artistic styles and media. Then in the same breath, they'll say that I'm out of touch, that all my work comes from the same disturbing vein, and I've passed my prime. That I lack *vision.*

The most offensive claim going around is that I've *lost my muse* and that we've "come to the end of Shaw's era."

What a load of horseshit.

My muse is every man who dies by my hands. They leave the world bent to my will. It's the one and only time they would ever be anything close to beautiful. Art begets art.

Yet it's slipping further from my fingers with every passing day that I move closer to becoming my father's full-time dog. Art used to be a way to untangle the ties holding me together. Now, I don't know what's beneath the binding.

I glare at the painting of a human skeleton morphed with a cow's. The metaphor is in the concept. I even took it a step further, texturizing the canvas with newspaper clippings of my kills.

Lack the vision.

Those fucking cunts.

The *Fallen Angel* piece at the Cresswell Art Gallery was meant to be my chance to prove that Maddox Shaw is still here. It was inspired by a rich Wall Street type who pushed his pregnant wife down the stairs, killing her and their baby in the process. Tatiana died, and the police did nothing. Now he's dead, and his ground-up veneers are in the golden filigree and jewelry of the painting.

I delivered justice, and I'm repaid by some student lecturing *me* about *my* painting?

As if being told I had to teach a class of film students wasn't bad enough, I found out that the Louvre doesn't want to extend the loan on two of my paintings.

The Order made me spend days searching for someone to replace Bradford while he's suffering the consequences of pissing a secret society off. In the end, Shepherd deemed me the only suitable and available person to take the position, given that the paper I recently published was on the symbiotic relationship between film and fine art. And when Shepherd tells you to jump, you jump. He'll break your knees if you don't.

Picking up after Bradford wouldn't be an issue if I didn't have my own classes and an art exhibit coming up, with no finished pieces.

After all that tedious fiasco, I went to the exhibit to check on my latest piece, only to find a girl staring at my painting for easily five minutes or more.

It hit me then: The perfect distraction came in the form of long hair, grabbable hips, and legs that would look impeccable over my shoulders. That's when she opened her mouth and said the same thing as every critic before her—albeit, far more openly and methodically than anyone else I'd encountered.

I returned after storming out, prepared to outline all the ways subjectivity trumped any claim of *intimacy*, but she stopped me short.

She was still there, staring at *Fallen Angel.*

I watched her, lost in thought like she was trying to dissect and absorb the very essence of the piece. She wasn't looking at it like she hated it, nor like it was an offense to art *or* subpar in comparison to my other works.

It felt like a lifetime since anyone had looked at my work with awe. Yet she was doing exactly that.

When she walked into my class, I thought the fates were punishing me for my crimes. It was the most difficult class I'd ever taught—not because the content was hard, I could've done it in my sleep. But I kept wanting to look at the enigma that's rendered me speechless twice now. She was magnetic, and bloody fucking infuriating.

It's truly baffling how disappointed I was when she walked out at the end without uttering a word to me. I was hoping she'd raise her hand to argue with me again—about quite literally anything, so I had a reason to stare at her, hear her husky voice, and attempt to put her in her place.

Is this what has become of me? Getting my kicks from a student who no doubt loathes me?

Huffing, I drop the brush made out of my victim's hair into the water, then fall into my computer chair, lowering my glasses to pinch the bridge of my nose. The printouts of Maria van Oosterwyck's still-life paintings, *Woman at Her Toilette*, and other pieces of art created by women in that era taunt me out of the corner of my eye.

What Reyna said was right. I found her name after class and looked her up. Had I known of her connection to Moraly Sinaga—a woman whose hand I've shook and pieces I've admired—I would have kept my opinion to myself, because her mother would have castrated me alive for talking to her daughter in such a way.

My knuckles bleach as I sneer at the canvas I've been working on since the day Reyna told me to do better.

I've failed. Again.

I see it now, the understanding she was talking about. It's embarrassing I never spotted the subtle nuances in my work. It took a *film* student saying I paint like a man for me to notice the flaws in everything I've ever made.

The hard truth is that anyone who has ever said that I've created a masterpiece was mistaken.

Spencer's groan drags my attention over to him. I raise a brow as he shucks off his headphones with a pained expression. "It's Mom."

Give me strength.

Our parents have a sixth sense for knowing the precise moment we're down, so they can perfectly time when to kick us. I've ignored eight of my birthgiver's calls yesterday, five more this morning. It was only a matter of time before she used different methods.

Spencer looks at me skeptically as he sets the phone on the coffee table and presses the dreaded green button.

"You're with your brother," she states. "Hand the phone over."

No *Hello, Spencer*. No *How are you, my second born*. Nothing.

Annabel Shaw is a woman of few words, just as she believed in minimal parenting. My skin holds the evidence of it.

"Mother," I drawl, pulling my turtleneck away from my throat as pain twinges my back.

"You've been ignoring me."

"Really? I hadn't noticed."

"You've also been ignoring your wife."

Both intentional. "She's not my wife."

In an alternate universe where I get everything I want, there wouldn't be a woman that I'm betrothed to. Abigail Dornmont can barely stand being in the same room as me—a mutual feeling. It's hardly a grievance that my so-called fiancée and I have made no attempt to form a relationship beyond discussing the weather or how she spends every second summer in the Bahamas.

I'm not one to assume someone's intentions, but I believe the whole "killing for fun" thing may be leaving a less-than-pleasant taste in her mouth. I suppose that's why she's scared to be in my general vicinity or worried that I'll accidentally cross paths with her boyfriend and send him to the morgue.

I'm guessing she only knows about what I do because her parents warned her to be careful. My extracurricular activities are a mystery to everyone other than the high saint, the grand magistrate, and most likely Abi. Anyone else who knows is dead.

It's a secret I've kept from my own brother.

I won't, obviously—kill her, that is. I assured her of it four years ago. Twice. I see no point in repeating it a third time.

"You were seen without your ring," Mother says. Engaged men of our secret society are required to wear them—they're big on their symbolism, especially since my engagement is a political move.

"I misplaced it." In other words, I gave it to a homeless woman to pawn.

"For the third time?"

"Fourth." I set one on fire, buried another when I was sculpting, tossed one into the river, and *accidentally* dropped one on the street. "It would be unfortunate to get paint on an object that holds such significant meaning."

I can practically hear her grind her teeth over the phone. Her plastic surgeon isn't going to like that.

The more money the woman who gave birth to me feels compelled to spend to replace such a meaningless item, the better. It won't compensate for her neglect, but inconveniencing her is mildly satisfying—a priceless feeling these days.

If I think hard enough, I can recall a few glimpses from my childhood where she displayed some maternal instincts. At first, Roland was the sole reason for our broken home. Mother was simply trying to survive, while occasionally remembering that a child needs to eat three times a day. I even remember her smiling at me once.

But her lifeless eyes became colder every time my father stripped away another part of her. Once Spencer came, Mother became an active contributor to the poison in the family name. Someone had to stop Spencer from becoming another victim. There's nothing glorious about being a survivor.

"You're meant to be getting to know each other and establishing a common connection to strengthen both our houses." Mother reiterates the spiel I've basically memorized, with how often I hear it. They're not her words; they're my father's. Annabel Shaw hasn't thought for herself since the day she married her husband. "If you don't start making an effort, no one in the Order is going to believe your marriage."

I roll my eyes, and Spencer snickers at my suffering. The shithead doesn't realize I've agreed to marry his friend for *his* benefit. "Again, no one with more than two brain cells believes we're even remotely interested in one another."

Everyone in the Order knows that my father is one of the six high saints of the New York faction. He moved us to the States for the chance to climb up the ranks. Roland wanted power. Relocating was the only way to get a seat at the table. If not, Roland would be like me, a medicus. Not quite at the top, but high enough that there are still two ranks below and above me.

Much to Spencer's chagrin, he's essentially the dirt of the Order. He was automatically accepted by virtue of being the son of a high saint, but he's still a student, and a student can't be anything more than a neophyte at the very bottom of the food chain.

House Shaw was voted in fifteen years ago, and like the five other high saints, Roland is vying for the seat of grand magistrate so he can reign supreme over the Order. It's why Abigail's father and mine both think it's a fantastic idea to marry us off to each other. Forcing two of the high saints' children together is the perfect arrangement.

The high saints and the grand magistrate will do anything to convince the rest of the acolytes in the Order that their house is strong and should be voted in for the next five-year cycle. If the Shaws and Dornmonts provide a united front, it guarantees our two houses seats at the table. Thus, the Shaws and Dornmonts can continue running the world as they see fit.

It's why every man, woman, child, and dog would happily sit as a neophyte at the bottom of the food chain, eating crumbs the higher-ups let trickle down. Being an acolyte means they've touched power, and through it, when they eventually die, for better or worse, they've left a mark on history.

True separation of powers doesn't exist in this universe. There are four branches of government: legislative, executive, judicial, and the Order of the Hallowed Hive. Only one of them carries real weight.

And men like my father, they'll settle for nothing less than the crown. Even if it means wielding both offspring as a bargaining chip for reelection.

It never ceases to astound me that a four-hundred-year-old secret society that meddles in government election fraud practices democracy. It is, however, still incredibly corrupt.

Spencer leans back on the couch, wearing a smug expression as he kicks his legs up on the armrest. I've given up on telling him to show my furniture the respect it deserves.

"Need I remind you of the arrangement, Maddox?" Mother says, far too smug.

My muscles stiffen. "No need."

Everything in this godforsaken world is about some form of contract. The only time I can simply *be* is in front of a canvas. At least that used to be the case. Now, I'm second-guessing every stroke. Everything that's ever given me any semblance of control is slipping through my fingers, and I have no idea how to get it back.

"What arrangement?" Spencer mouths.

By my design, my little brother's knowledge of the inner workings of his reality is abysmal. I would have abandoned everything to do with the Shaw name the second I finished high school if it weren't for the person dirtying my sofa. Hell, I would have moved back to England, or anywhere my father isn't. Maybe even purgatory, since Roland is guaranteed to be in hell.

As it happens, Spencer wants to stay here to study, so he can work at Wilson Shaw and eventually take over from our sperm donor to run the family's global accounting firm. I protected my brother so well that, at the ripe age of twenty-one, he still thinks Roland is a god.

I've fucked up successfully.

"Then I'll have Jessica arrange for the two of you to have dinner at the yacht club on Friday night." Mother's voice holds the same arrogance it always does. Except this time there's a tilt that matches the battle she thinks she won against me.

Everything in this town is a scheme.

Dinner at the Order's breeding ground on the busiest night of the week would send a hum through the grapevine. Abi and I have been playing this charade for years; we have a public outing every once in a while, pretend like we can stand each other's company, then live our separate lives. Spencer finds it amusing.

A couple of years ago, I moved her into one of the properties I own to sate the vultures. And I do visit the property. Not to see her, of course. But every person deserves to have a place where they can clean, bleach, and grind parts of the human body without anyone around to hear. I can't very well be doing that in my studio on campus.

I've been ignoring Abi's calls as well. She isn't going to get me out of my artistic block, so why bother wasting time with her when the only thing we have in common is our desire not to be married to one another?

"Very well," I relent. "I suppose I should look forward to a night of mind-numbing boredom this Friday. How exciting."

"Your father and I have concerns that you are not as enthusiastic about this proposal as you should be. If you're having reservations, Roland will consider alternative options."

My grip tightens around the armrest of my chair. My sperm donor has been lording Spencer's happiness over me since the second he came out of the womb. The threat is simple and effective: Stay in line or your brother's next.

I'm not worried about swapping engagements with him. Abigail and Spencer are already friends—her boyfriend is on Spencer's football team. My concerns are for the more nefarious sides of the Order's dealings that he'd be dragged into. The real reason I sacrificed so he didn't have to.

"Are the bells I'm planning on wearing not loud enough? Or should I hire a mariachi band for dessert as a declaration of my adoration?"

"Find the ring, Maddox," Mother warns.

The line goes dead. Spencer snatches the phone off the table and frantically taps away at the device, grinning to himself.

"What shit are you stirring?"

He shows me the screen where he's turned Mother's contact name from *Birthgiver* to *Sauron*. "She wants the ring."

"Bloody hell." I chuckle, shaking my head. "Please don't show her that."

"She'd probably poison me."

I won't disagree.

My own phone pings. I click the notification to see the pin-drop emoji that was texted to me.

Good. Someone needs killing. It's like my muse is being handed right to me.

5

MADDOX

"Who is it?" I say, voice low, standing to the side of the counter where Shepherd found himself a place to sit. I keep my attention forward so it doesn't appear like we're associated with each other. Still, I don't miss the men and women from the second rank within the Order, standing guard around the coffee shop.

Glancing back, I glare at Shepherd and the light reflecting off his bald head as he takes a sip of his coffee. Fucking Americans and their obsession with the drink. There's a coffee shop on every corner, yet I haven't had a decent cup of tea since moving to this damned country nineteen years ago.

I spy the barista making my order. It'll end up in the trash once I'm a block away. The wanker's insistence to meet at cafés has always been a means to fuck with me. An oh-so-pleasant reminder that I'm not in control.

Shepherd took me under his wing and trained me up to do the Order's bidding not long after my family joined the society based here. Through my kills, they can continue controlling the city and meddling in politics, the economy, and everything in between.

Shepherd takes his sweet time sipping his drink before answering. "Matthew Collins."

I wait a beat. Two. "That narrows it down."

His annoyance is radiating off him, and I couldn't give two shits. After being his bitch—apologies, *protégé*—since I was fourteen, working for him isn't exactly my cup of tea anymore.

I'm Shepherd's star pupil. So if he called for me, whoever this Matthew person is, he's done a good job pissing the Order off.

Any acolyte would kill a man as long as someone as high up as Shepherd says so. But as they say, *Pay peanuts, get monkeys*. Send a neophyte if you want a mess, a paladin if you want the job done, a medicus if you want it done right, or me if you want to send a message.

Very, *very* few know what I do, but I excel at making a point. I advanced through the ranks quickly for that reason.

Only a handful of individuals are aware of who the Order's *boogeyman* is. To everyone else, I'm just Roland's son who fucks around with paint and clay. Some people within the society suspect that I've spent time training under Shepherd, but nothing eventuated from it.

Shepherd has plenty of people to carry out his kills for him. My morbid curiosity for all things macabre made me a natural—a fact Shepherd picked up on before anyone else did.

He introduced me to death. I learned on my own that it could become art, a form of expression, something I could create solely for my sake. Whether I've chosen my victims because their eyes remind me of my father's—cruel men who have never known good—or because Shepherd directed me to them, I see death for what it is: an opportunity. A chance to be free from judgment, and experiment as I wish.

A black USB clatters at my feet. A moment later, Shepherd's chair scrapes against the wooden floors and the bells above the exit chime.

I pocket the USB and leave without waiting for my order. Excitement thrums through my veins. If I'm being given information on their sins, it means I'm allowed to be creative.

Lack the vision? The *understanding*?

If only they knew.

"There are twenty-seven bones in the human hand. Do you realize how long it's taken me to be able to break each and every one of them?"

The tears staining Matthew's cheeks don't dissuade me. Did he stop when his wife screamed and asked for mercy? Begged for God to grant her salvation from the monster before her? No, he didn't stop until her jaw broke beneath his fists.

My father thought punching someone was barbaric. Heaven forbid he splits his own skin. His methods always involved another object when it came to me. For Mother, an open hand sufficed.

Shepherd's file painted a pretty picture of how much Matthew deserves to suffer. His death will make a fine-art installation for the police.

If only it were Roland instead.

"Please." Big, fat clumps of snot trickle down his nose, dampening my creative experience. "I'm sorry."

They always say that. *Sorry.* I don't think I've ever heard that word come out of my father's mouth. I doubt he'd lower himself to say it, even when death is knocking at his door.

Usually, I wouldn't have the slightest clue what they're sorry about. Whatever grievances they have with the Order are always left out of the file, unless Shepherd wants me to be creative with those with grave sins to atone for—the type of subjects I'd pick for myself. Men who prey on their own family.

Any kill authorized by Shepherd means I'm free from repercussions. Unless I've chosen the subject myself, the only question I typically have is whether or not to make it look like an accident.

The Order would never care for the domestic affairs of random citizens. If Matthew here isn't in our ranks, whatever he's done must have been bad enough to warrant *my* attention.

The first time Shepherd nudged me toward a target, slipped their file into my hand, and said "Let it all out" was a monumental point in my adolescence. I finally got a taste of true, unrestrained freedom. It would change any nineteen-year-old.

Normally, my own *passion projects*, as one might call them, take weeks of meticulous planning: storyboards, the perfect song to play in the background, color analysis, lighting, any subsequent paintings or sculptures inspired by their deaths.

All I've had with Matthew is forty-eight hours and a prayer to the art gods, and it's paying off. New York's finest will appreciate the beauty in this one.

They say every masterpiece requires a little suffering. I take that literally.

The blood-soaked mallet crushes the distal phalanx of his left index finger. He screams and thrashes, like he did with every bone prior. Ambience is an important part of the process, but the incessant screaming is more irritating than anything else.

"Have you been counting?" He might have. I wasn't really listening.

I'm still not sure what to name this particular piece, or what to create from it.

"Please. I d-don't know who you are. Take my money! You can have it."

He cries when the proximal phalanx shatters.

"No, thank you. I have enough of my own."

I carefully adjust him to keep the blood within a certain parameter. If it soaks into the rug, I'm going to be *really* upset. I may even need to start again.

"I—I have a wife and kids."

"Ah yes. Linda. I visited her at her work. Lovely lady." Nothing like my mother.

"My kids—"

"Are staying at a friend's house. I'm aware."

"You can't—"

"Do this? I believe the word you're looking for is *shouldn't* do this." I line up my next hit. "Let me make it easier for you to understand by putting it in a sentence. I, Matthew Collins, *should not* beat my wife."

"No! I'm a family man," he pleads. Roland says the same line during his high-saint reelection campaigns. "We go to church every week. I—I would never touch—"

"What number are we up to?" Another bone cracks beneath the mallet. "Thirteen," I answer for him.

He screams, attempting to squirm his way out from under my boot. I press harder into his shattered elbow, worsening his wails.

I inspect my work. The blood from his knees, feet, shoulders, and elbows pool onto the wood. The bones in his hands are broken beyond repair, but there's only a speck of crimson on the wedding band still wrapped around his crooked finger. *That one's for you, Mother.*

Matthew is as naked as the day he was born, ready to be cleansed for a divine reckoning.

"Thirteen," I repeat. "Two syllables, yet the number thirteen holds many meanings. Do you know what they are?"

He shakes his head, sputtering on his tears. "It's—It's the devil's number."

Well, yes. Close enough.

"Some ancient cultures believe that it means femininity for the number of menstrual and lunar cycles in a year," I explain. "In Judaism, it signifies the age that a boy matures and—"

"I'm a good man. I—"

The last finger bone breaks. "*Fourteen.* It's rude to interrupt."

He whimpers and clamps his lips shut, muffling his pathetic cries.

"In Norse mythology, Loki was the thirteenth to arrive at a feast in Valhalla. The number thirteen is both good and bad. In your case, it's the reason why I'm here." It's not like he's in any position to call me out on my lie. "Thirteen. That's how many times you've sent Linda to the hospital in the past four years."

Mother was never given the opportunity to seek professional care for her injuries—not unless it was a "car accident."

I run the instrument over the grooves, feeling for the middle bone before I lower the mallet again with a gut-curdling *thwack.*

"For fuck's sake," I growl. Not only do I lack imagination, but apparently, I don't have hand-eye coordination either. I've hit the bloody fourth bone as well.

"Fuck you!" Matthew howls, trying to hit me with his left arm. It's an amusing sight since the chef's knife in his wrist is effectively nailing his hand to the floor.

"Such vile words, Mr. Collins."

There are eight bones in the human wrist, tightly bunched together to make it nearly impossible to break individually.

I hit it three times for good measure.

Three.

The perfect number.

Three phalanges in each finger.

The triad. The Trinity. Body, soul, and spirit. Past, present, and future. Beginning, middle, and end. Art, science, and religion. Heaven, hell, and purgatory. Birth, life, and death. Hear no evil, see no evil, speak no evil. Hands, head, heart.

Unfortunately, men are made with only two hands. If there were three, this process would be as perfect as the number.

No matter. Sacrifices must be made.

Moving to his left hand, I make my way through the fingers and stop at the one with the golden band. It's hideously bruised and mangled.

It'll do.

I hum beneath my breath as I rummage around my leather pouch for the correct chisel. This is what it feels like to be in my element. Just me, my tools, and a canvas ready for me to unleash whatever I desire.

No cotton canvas has stirred such a feeling from me in years, the way living flesh does. Killing has been the only art that proves I'm not an utter failure. There are no critics here—no rules.

I angle the cutting edge of the chisel in the small space where his finger bone meets the knuckle, directly beneath the webbing. With a single blow, the chisel slices through the skin, tears through ligament, nerves, tendons, and muscle, cleanly severing the finger.

There's something so satisfying about seeing blood sputter. Like watching paint mix. It pools onto the carpet, soaks the woolen threads, and seeps into the floorboards.

"You're a fucking psychopath!"

"I assure you, I feel plenty." Rage, exhaustion, irritation, boredom. The occasional curiosity.

I purse my lips, holding up the severed finger, admiring the thickness of the phalanges. Three little bones. The possibilities are endless. I could grind it up like usual. Or carve it into a small design. Jewelry, perhaps. However will I choose?

The finger gets carefully placed into a cloth and neatly folded for safekeeping. Then I grab another trusted instrument: a knife.

An artist doesn't need tools to create, but one sharpened just right can make a world of difference.

The steel glints under the light, and Matthew's eyes widen. He thrashes, dislodging the knife from the floor, wailing, blubbering, and snotting up a storm. I roll my eyes. He's trapped by the limitations of his own body.

The tip of the blade dips into his skin. "*Confess.* Last chance." Warm spit hits my cheek. Slowly, I wipe it away and lock eyes with him. "Thank you for deciding for me. Your tongue *does* have to go."

I see the moment my words register in his puny brain. But it's too late for him to do anything. I'm prying his mouth open before he can say his goodbyes to the organ.

He screams.

Well, he tries to.

They all try to scream. It's amusing, if you ask me. They always end up choking on blood or their own tongue. It makes for messy work, but it's a necessary evil.

I tear a strip of duct tape, then slap it over his mouth, sealing it shut along with the appendage.

Finally, quiet.

Or at least it would be if Matthew didn't ruin the silence.

Coughing ensues. The thrashing amplifies. He manages to lift his hands and spray crimson over the perfectly white rug. *This motherfucker.* It was meant to be ironic. A bloody massacre beside a pristine, picturesque scene. Juxtaposition. The duality of man, and the unreliability of what meets the eye.

Am I so incapable of creating a masterpiece now? This was meant to be my failproof Holy Grail, and—

I take a deep breath. It isn't too late. I can still salvage this.

There's no such thing as perfection in art. There will always be the one stroke that could have been better, or the dot spotted too late.

The tip of the knife trails down the column of his bobbing throat, down to the jugular, where the knife spears through skin and is dragged down his chest to the spot above his belly button. The second and third incisions follow, diagonal lines across his chest that intersect over his heart.

It isn't straight enough.

He's squirming too much. The cut is too jagged. I've ruined it.

No, I can spin this. It's an imperfect line on an impure soul. It's a metaphor. I have to trust the process.

Fuck.

Fuck.

I rise to my feet and scrutinize my piss-poor art piece. What is this? I don't want the police to see this. It has to be my worst kill to date.

There are galvanized nails waiting for me in my kit. Yet I don't have it in me to nail his eyes open. The concrete mixture I was going to pour into his ear is going to waste as well.

What would be the point of doing more? I've fucked the whole thing up already. My anger swells the longer I stare at the so-called art.

Out of touch.

Out of *fucking* touch.

I grab the lamp beside me and throw it across the room. The space plunges into darkness, so I no longer need to witness the evidence of my failures.

I was going to call this *The Rule of Three*, but this is too embarrassing to be given a name. I'm a pathetic excuse for an artist.

My hands wrap around anything I can get my hands on: beer bottles, tables, chairs, nothing is free from my grasp as Matthew swallows his last breath. Furniture and ornaments go flying around the room in a haphazard mess. I don't stop until the fury boiling in my veins threatens to topple me over. Only then do I step back to survey the destruction.

I know what this night should be called.

End of an Era.

6

REYNA

It's another dreary day that looks like it will only get worse. My coat does nothing to stop the chill from cutting into my bones, and somehow, power walking to the subway makes me exponentially colder.

It's only minutely better once I'm seated inside the car. I still can't feel my fingers, and it makes it hard to grip my pen and scribble down my ideas into my notebook for the next assignment.

It was the Shadow's kill. I'm certain of it.

Every mark on the victim's body appeared intentional. The incisions down the middle of his body are artful, like he measured out the proportions to get them exactly right. And the missing ring finger—Was he an adulterer? Why the blunt knives through the wrist? Was it to demoralize the victim?

Böcklin's Shadow is meticulous in his set design, but the subject is *always* the focal point. Nothing is overlooked, whether it's the cushions' layout, the odd way a throw has been folded, or even the amount of water sitting in a nearby cup.

Sure, this scene screams *crime of passion*, but I think something happened to cause the upheaval of the room. He might have gone wrong somewhere and tried to *scrap the painting*.

I glance up when someone drops their phone on the floor. Our eyes meet for half a second before he leans down to pick it up, and dark locks fall onto his forehead. He's in one of my classes—Andrew or Alex or something? I should probably know it since I see him on campus all the time. Maybe I should befriend him too so I have more than three friends in this city.

I expect him to smile in greeting or maybe start up a conversation and ruin my creative flow, but he turns away, completely ignoring me.

I sag in my seat, scrubbing a hand down my face. Whatever. I need to focus on my next assignment anyway. I've spent the last week losing sleep over the mental ass-whooping I'll get once Shaw releases the grades. He seems like the type of teacher who would fail a student out of sheer spite.

That's a lie. His reputation as a professor is impeccable. Any grade he gives would be justifiable. On the other hand, his reputation as a general member of society is severely lacking. Mom once called him, and I quote, "A prickly, vindictive asshole."

The only thing I have on my side is that I'm substantially less caffeinated than I was at our last interaction and I'm no longer stressed up to my eyeballs. That means that in his class later today, I will *not* be making comments about his artistic abilities, or speaking in general.

The clouds have morphed into a sea of blotted gray by the time I climb up the steps from the subway. Petrichor hangs in the air like a cloying fog with the promise of a coming storm.

Shades of charcoal begin threading through the sky as I pass the wrought-iron gates into campus.

A single drop of rain hits my cheek, and everyone around me seems to feel it too. Students hurry along the pavement, clutching bags, and using their jackets as makeshift umbrellas to protect their books. I rush past the fountains and up the marble steps into the library just as the skies open and water pelts the ground.

The battering rain is white noise against the empty quiet of the grand, Gothic space. I can hear each cough, the glide of pens against paper, the tap of fingers against keyboards, and every soft turn of a page. The sounds travel through the stone hall that rises three stories up to the vaulted ceiling. Daylight filters through the stained glass, scattering colors across the rows of mahogany tables.

My panting bounces off the arched walls as I climb the steps to the second floor. I've already spent an ungodly amount of time scouring the library for information about where the picture of Dad might have been taken or any records about him during his time here.

A year later, and I have nothing to show for it.

Until today.

At least, I hope.

"Hi, Sue." I smile, sidling up to the research counter where the librarian is using a single finger to type.

She squints at me over her glasses, wrinkling the pale skin around her eyes. "Oh! That was quick."

My cheeks heat. An hour ago, I received her email saying she found the alumni book I've been searching for over the past two months.

"I thought you'd be at least a day before you came to look at it. You know, I wasn't even trying to look for this book at the time. Isn't it funny how that works? I was going through the archives, and what do you know, there she was. You wouldn't believe where I found it," she rambles, Southern twang harsh as she starts opening and closing drawers. "It was all hidden away, under a pile of unrelated books. I'm gonna have to have a word with Tim because it wasn't *close* to the correct section. They wouldn't even be considered in the same darn continent—Ah, there it is."

She groans as she bends over. With a huff and a joint click that doesn't sound pleasant, she manages to fish the big book out from the bottom shelf, then all but wheezes when she slides it my way.

"You can't take it out of the library." She drops back onto her chair. "But you can spend as much time as you like with it."

Gripping the book in my clammy palms, I say my thanks and rush to the desk near the back wall, away from prying eyes.

The leatherbound cover thuds against the table when I throw it open. The register alphabetically lists every student who graduated from Cresswell that year, including what they studied, how long they were here, and the job they had lined up. Sue claims it was for recordkeeping and statistics.

Dad studied business, but I don't have the slightest clue where he went after.

The smell of old books drifts from the yellowed paper as I flip page after page, scanning each line in case there's a wayward *T* where there shouldn't be.

The hairs on the back of my neck stand on end. I still, waiting for it to go away. The feeling of being watched sticks to my skin, and I whip my head around. Something flickers out of the corner of my eye, gone before I can see it clearly.

The empty space behind me feels like a taunt. Or maybe a threat.

I'm being paranoid.

The prickling sensation doesn't go away, though, as I slowly turn back to the book. It gets worse when I make it to the very end without coming across anyone by the name of Richard Talbot.

I check every page twice over before flicking to the very start of the book to look a third time. It takes me a moment to register the symbol embossed into the bottom corner of the paper.

At first, it means nothing. Just a honeycomb stamped on the end page of the book. A distant familiarity. But my gut turns the longer I stare at it. I must be overthinking this, right?

I fumble through my bag for my phone, then pull up the image of my dad in the room with the hexagon ceiling. My eyes flick between the screen and the book. Over and over until there isn't a doubt in my mind that this specific book is connected to my dad somehow.

I was wrong about the picture. It's not just a ceiling design; it's a beehive.

I trace the bee sitting in the center of the honeycomb. The university's logo is a boring old crest. Not this. Is the honeycomb stamped in the other alumni books?

I rise to unsteady feet and glance around. The feeling of being watched doesn't go away. Swallowing the lump in my throat, I grab the first alumni book I can get my hands on.

There's no symbol.

One by one, I check fifty years' worth of books.

Nothing. Still.

That can't be right. I couldn't have checked fifty of them already. Frowning, I go back to the shelf to count each and every book.

Some of the years are missing. How didn't I notice that before?

There's no logic or numerical order to any of the gaps. Getting my notebook, I make a tally of all the missing years, dating back to the eighteen hundreds, where the records end—any older ones would likely be kept safe in the restricted archives and artifacts room. They've probably been misplaced somewhere, like the one Sue found was. Would those missing books have a stamp in them?

A thought hits me. I fire up my laptop and open the document containing the handful of names I managed to find of the Shadow's victims through countless hours of online sleuthing.

My finger flies over the mousepad to flag the six men who studied at Cresswell and dig out their corresponding folders filled with information about their lives. Then cross-reference the years they graduated with the books on the shelf.

Five out of six of the years aren't there. Having one or two registries missing is one thing. Five?

If I knew more of the victims' names and worked out where they studied, would I find that their books aren't on the shelves either?

The link to the Shadow has to be a freak coincidence. A lot of his victims never attended Cresswell. But a lot of them did. Maybe the killer himself is connect to this university.

All these questions, and not a single answer about my dad.

I glare at the ceiling. Just once I'd like to see the finish line. Just *once* I'd like to have a decent lead.

It's days like today that I especially resent Dad for not being around more. I feel so utterly hopeless, like if I had asked him the right questions, then I wouldn't have uprooted my life and moved across the country to do what I never did when he was around.

Shaking my head, I pack my things away. Great, this might have been a pointless endeavor. I can't wait to lose sleep over it.

I lumber down the steps to find Sue and show her the embossing.

"Do you know what this is?"

She pushes her glasses up her nose and inches closer to look. She tips her head to the side, and the chains attached to the arms swing and clink against her pearl earrings. "Can't say I do, hon."

"Are you sure?"

Sue stares at it for a moment longer. I've given her the background of my life, and she's been more than accommodating in my search. "Tell you what. How about I have a look around to see if anyone might know?"

"I would be eternally grateful. I've also noticed that quite a few of the alumni books are missing."

She rolls her eyes. "I bet you it's Tim. That boy has been nothing but trouble since the day he started. Things have been goin' missing like it's nobody's business."

I give her a tight grin. I have no idea who Tim is, but I know Sue's hated him since she witnessed him covertly throw out some of her baking.

I wave her goodbye, and because I'm clearly in the fates' good graces today, I have to break into a sprint the second I'm outside. The sky batters the ground with hail and one of the seven plagues of Egypt.

I *love* that I forgot to bring my umbrella.

That's just fan-fucking-tastic.

By the time I stroll into class and claim the seat farthest from the front, I'm the human equivalent of a drowned rat.

Dirt and chips of stone stick to my long boots, and my pantyhose are so soaked that they're glistening against my black dress. Not to mention the water dripping from my scarf and coat is bound to make every cleaner in this university hate me.

Whether or not Shaw noticed me clomp inside bringing the outdoors with me will remain a mystery. I subtly glower at him as I unpack my things, and *Christ* if it isn't infuriating how effortlessly handsome he is. Couldn't he be horrifically disfigured? Or at the very least have bad teeth?

The man encompasses the very essence of suave, and I want to push him into a pool to make him lose his composure. But I bet he'd glide out, soaking wet, looking more godly than Poseidon himself.

Because winning the genetic lottery wasn't enough, he's nailed the hot professor look too. I never thought I'd be attracted to a man in a knitted vest, but it's doing things to me that Maddox Shaw shouldn't be.

Life is so unfair. Why must natural selection be so cruel?

As more students trickle in, I pretend not to notice Shaw while I stare blankly at the graphs for my psych class. Nicole's away sick, so I'll need to face Satan alone.

My face suddenly heats with awareness. Unlike in the library, this feels like a searing burn, the kind that comes from being in the center of a bull's-eye.

The dark, foolish part of my soul is telling me to raise my chin and look Shaw dead-on. The practical part of me—the part that holds the occasionally dormant survival instincts—tells me to ignore him.

It's the mature choice.

But I still want to look at him because he's damn easy on the eyes. Every woman here is swooning; it's in the flutter of their lashes and the overly enthusiastic way they say, "Good afternoon, Professor Shaw," and it mortifies me that I'm one of the ones heating up just thinking about him in his stupid fucking vest.

It makes me hate him more.

Attractive, smart, and arrogant. The traits of a man who isn't worth my time. Regrettably, it's an honor and a privilege to be taught by said man. So shutting up and ignoring him is, unfortunately, the *right* choice.

Class starts, and all of us hang on every word he says. It's enrapturing to watch him teach. What he lacks in practical film skills, he makes up for in theory—and *man* does he know his theory.

My brain is fried from information overload by the time class ends. I've learned more in the past two weeks than I have in the entire year Professor Bradford was teaching us. I take my time packing up, because I only have a couple of assignments to work on for once, and a video I need to upload and deliver to a client. Nothing is burning—except the stats formula for psych I still don't understand. In my books, that's called a moderately relaxing night. I might even spoil myself and rewatch *Midsommar* while researching the insignia I found in the library.

"Miss Sinaga, a moment."

Shaw's voice freezes my insides.

This can't be good.

Taking a deep breath, I shoulder my satchel and try not to seem so begrudging about finishing my day with verbal abuse. I might have the sleep and caffeine levels to tolerate his bullshit, but there's only so much one woman can take.

If he mentions anything to do with my mother, all bets are off. I'm going for his jugular and writing a scathing complaint to the dean. Hell, get a couple of drinks into me, and I might start buddying up with all the critics giving him a hard time—*yes*, I did spend far too long searching him up online the other night.

For a second, I'm self-conscious about how I might look when there isn't a single part of him that's out of place. Then I realize that I don't give a shit. He has luxuries that I can't afford and priorities that aren't in the same tax bracket or realm as mine.

If he's got a problem with my appearance, he can choke on it. I wasn't put on this earth to look pretty for someone else. Especially not him.

I stop beside his desk, not-so-patiently waiting for him to reorganize the books and folders he referred to throughout the class. My stomach swoops when his gaze flickers to my legs for the briefest moment; I'm convinced I might have been imagining it.

Shaw's attention fixes on me, and a small part of me simultaneously dies and comes alive. He's even more attractive up close. More imposing. The natural light filtering through the windows casts dark shadows beneath his jaw to make him seem all the more intimidating, yet alluring, the way a sailor is distantly aware that his ship is about to crash as he drifts closer to the siren.

Holding eye contact is crippling. It's like he wants to dissect me and work out how I tick. It's exhilarating all the same. He opens his mouth.

Let the degradation commence.

"I'm sorry to hear about your mother."

What? Are my ears deceiving me? His shoulders are lowered, the creases around his eyes soft. His voice is more like warm honey than the sting of a wasp.

"She was a lovely woman and well respected within the community."

I suck in a sharp breath. "You've met her?" I think I need to pinch myself.

"Once." Maddox nods. "At an awards dinner. Mora was telling people to keep an eye out because her daughter is an up-and-coming director."

My eyes mist over, and I quickly blink them away. That sounds like Mom. "Oh."

Ever since I was old enough to use a camera, she told everyone I'd be in Hollywood before they knew it.

I swallow and look down at my feet. *I miss her so much.*

I think she'd be disappointed that I chose to come here. She and Dad wanted great things for me that didn't involve Cresswell or New York, even if it has produced some of the most legendary directors.

"Thank you." My voice breaks. I clear my throat. "She was crazy but loved."

Maddox huffs out a breath that could be mistaken for a chuckle. "I remember. She was quite intimidating when she wanted to be."

I smile softly to myself. "You can say that again."

Strangely so, comfortable silence stretches between us. It's been a long time since I've been able to talk to anyone new about Mom. It's nice to be around someone who knew her.

As grateful as I am for the interaction, this isn't the only reason he wants to talk. "Was there something else you wanted to discuss?"

Shaw's eyes stay on me for three heartbeats too long. My pulse ricochets against my skin the longer he stays quiet. It gets worse when he finally puts me out of my misery by nodding at the laptop opened on the desk. "Your assignment."

"You've graded it?" Professor Bradford usually takes a month or two to mark anything.

"Not officially. There are some things I want to go through with you."

I scan the empty room like there might be a line of students he's said the same thing to. Shaw doesn't strike me as the type of man to *offer* his time outside of scheduled hours. He's a good professor, but he's never been known as a generous man.

Apparently, he's changing his whole act just for my benefit.

He pulls out a seat for me, then lowers himself into his own, looking at me expectantly.

I realize what this is. An olive branch. A fresh start.

Mom, you absolute psycho, I owe you for this one.

Reluctantly, I sit beside him. My little heart is going to be shredded to pieces because it's never easy being told that my work isn't good enough. But I *want this*. Any critical feedback is helpful in a highly competitive industry. If I don't find my backbone today, I'll be damn sure I find it by the time our grades are released, because I can tell he won't give me the A that I so desperately want.

I take a deep breath and regret it immediately. Add his scent to the list of his crimes. Maddox smells a hundred percent man, and a thousand percent divine. There's another note that I never noticed before that has me berating myself for finding him more appealing.

Bergamot and *paint*. My new weakness.

Clearing my throat, I narrow my eyes at the screen. If I can't *actually* be focused, pretending is the next best thing.

Shaw motions at the scene where the character—well, *me*—is slowly losing it in an office.

"Why did you choose a static wide angle for this scene?"

"Going wide would emphasize isolation and emptiness," I answer.

"Fair." He nods, considering. "It's a measured angle, but it does not match what you are trying to portray. Emptiness is about dissonance and space. It would have been achieved by going handheld to break the frame so the audience can feel her anxiety. Be there for every hand tremble. Every tear. Feel her paranoia each time she looks out of the window thinking he's out there."

It's maddening that I agree with him.

We go through scene by scene, and he points out each time the movement is too fast, the color is oversaturated, or the lighting falls flat.

"You delivered this part well."

Somewhere in the distance, there's a disc scratching. Did he just . . . Is that a compliment?

The Maddox Shaw—the very Maddox Shaw I insulted—thinks I did something *well.* Hell must be freezing over.

My cheeks burn at his praise, and there's a mini-me doing a happy dance inside my head.

He moves on before I can pepper him with questions or get him to say it again. From the downturn of his lips, I think he might be regretting his decision to voice his opinion, but all I can think about is that not everything I've done is unworthy.

Shaw pauses on a frame where the subject is backlit. "You mirrored this motif at the beginning, even at the risk of appearing repetitive."

That's precisely what I thought. "Was that the wrong choice?" I was on the fence about it.

"No. This was earned repetition with structure and rhythm. You're echoing the thematic element of isolation to perpetuate that they're the killer's sole focus."

I try not to smile to myself, but I do.

"It's different this time. She's more of a silhouette, and there's less clutter in the frame." He noticed that? "The character is losing their identity as they become the killer's single-minded focus."

If Mom were still here, I would run home giddy with excitement to tell her someone *finally* understands my art. After nearly two semesters of Bradford's negativity, I was starting to think that any talent I might have had was imagined. But *he's* seeing it.

Sure, it's not perfect, but it's fixable. He *wants* me to succeed. It's been a long time since anyone was rooting for me.

Maddox continues, then taps the space bar when we get to the scene filmed in Chad's kitchen. The grand finale.

Nerves rack my stomach as I stare at Maddox's profile. Out of everything I've ever filmed, this portion is what I'm most proud of. Even my acting wasn't too shabby.

"The mise-en-scène is too clean and rigid for the characters you're trying to portray."

What?

"The coffee mug is filled to the top when the supposedly exhausted coffee-addict protagonist hasn't been home all day," Shaw explains. "Plus, there's a plate with a half-eaten sandwich. Do you know what the problem with that is?"

My lips part. No one's ever called me out on set design before.

"Your broke, so-called clean-freak protagonist up and left a club sandwich that would have been from the day before. It would have worked if you laid out the set better. There's no other meaningful clutter on the table that provides any insight into her personality. You could have put an ashtray, a two-week-old newspaper, an empty single-use drink bottle, and maybe a gum wrapper. Your set is too clinical."

"Maybe that was intentional because the killer wanted some level of cleanliness." There's no point arguing, because he's right. I'm making excuses.

Maddox snorts, and I damn well almost gape at him. "Throat slicing is a messy kill. Do it fast enough and there'll be far-reaching blood splatter. Slow, and it's a blood bath because they'll be thrashing around. The best way would've been to—" He stops himself, slightly shocked, then schools his features.

No, I want him to finish what he was going to say.

"If your goal was to make him fastidious and clean, then show me the tarpaulin he's set down and the synthetic rope that won't dirty the second blood gets on it."

The Shadow had a kill like that.

I shake my head. "The killer is obviously well researched based on how he's lured her in"—*and how I've written him*—"but he lacks practicality. Look." I point at the clock in the background showing it's eight at night. Obviously, I was taking liberties with the exact details of the Shadow's kill. "Anyone could have heard the commotion and come barreling in. But she stayed completely silent and struggled far less than she could have, indicating an element of trust."

I'm honestly surprised he hasn't raised any issue with my choice of pink blood. For the sake of my ego, I'm going to say that he agrees with my creative vision.

"You've portrayed intimacy between the characters, and then you threw it all away by killing her behind her back," he states.

I open my mouth to say that I doubt the Shadow killed that lawyer front on, but think better of it.

Maybe it isn't a good idea to admit to following a murderer around.

"Up until this moment, it was about watching her through his eyes. Romanticizing everything she does, and how he yearns for her." Shaw pauses the footage at the moment where the blade touches my throat, right before I'm meant to die. "Here, at the most pinnacle moment where they're finally united, you made it about his kill, not her death."

Shit.

He's right about that too.

The romanticism dies the second Chad stands behind me. If we were gazing at each other as it happened, it would be a moment shared.

Shaw stares at me as if expecting me to argue. I swear he short-circuits when I say, "I agree."

He says nothing, eyes lingering on me before watching the scene play out again, until I'm on the floor, pointing at the camera.

"Big Brother is watching you? The take was interesting enough with the stalker aspect, but this concept is on the nose and overdone."

I blink. "Have you read the written portion?"

"Miss Sinaga, you submitted your assignment six days ago. And if you're suggesting that I need to read an essay in order to understand your so-called brilliance, then I suggest you quit while you're ahead."

Professor Douchebag is back.

I'm too stunned to be upset at the dig. *Worse.* I can feel my lips threatening to curve up into a smile because I couldn't agree with his statement more.

"I'm wearing a nude camisole, a blue hairclip, and green nails," I cautiously say.

He looks at me blankly. "That makes little sense from a cinematic point of view, and I don't imagine *Vogue* will be covering your stylistic choice anytime soon."

"Being in the nude, sky blue, green earth, pointing at an omniscient being . . ." I trail off, beginning to doubt every single choice I've made for this project. Maybe I got my hopes up too soon.

My project actually sucked. *He* can't even see it.

Shaw raises his brows, a silent request to get to the point.

"It's *The Creation of Adam.*" The words come out more timidly than I intended.

He says nothing for a beat and glances at the screen for what has to be the longest ten seconds of my life. Then the room seems to plummet twenty degrees, and I'm bristling in alarm. Shaw swings his attention back on me, and I think I might pass away under his stare.

I can't decipher the meaning behind the parting of his lips and the widening of his eyes. It seems more like bewilderment than rage. Within a heartbeat, it's gone, and I'm left reeling, wondering if I imagined it.

A mask falls into place as he gives me his undivided attention. "What inspired you to kill someone in such a way?"

What a messed-up question. A good one nonetheless.

I scramble to find a diplomatic answer that doesn't reveal that I'm re-creating a real murder. "I . . ." *Come on, Reyna.* "I recently saw an installation about reimagining *The Creation of Adam.*"

He leans forward an inch, but he may as well be invading every one of my senses. There's a predatory glint in his eye that has me ensnared to the spot. The greens of his eyes darken with interest like I've caught the attention of a wolf.

"Really? Who's the artist?"

I pale. Now would be a really good time for someone to come in or, better yet, for me to evaporate into thin air. I shift uncomfortably in my seat, and Shaw's gaze drops, watching every minuscule movement I make, scrutinizing every inch of me as if I'm an art installation.

"He . . . uh . . . Böcklin's Shadow." I don't mean to sound uncertain, but it comes out like that anyway.

"Where, pray tell, did you discover this . . . *artist*? I don't believe I've heard of him."

Shit. Shit. Shit.

"You wouldn't have. He's super niche. Up and coming. He, uh . . . he's pretty low-key. I—I stumbled across him. You—You wouldn't like him. It's not your type of thing. You—"

Shut the fuck up, Reyna.

There's no way he knows I'm basically stealing a serial killer's art. I clear my throat and notice his attention flit down to my twisting hands. I quickly tuck them under my thighs and force a smile that I can only hope doesn't make me look insane.

"Interesting," he muses. "Maybe I'll look him up."

"No—" *Not interesting at all. Be a lot less interested.* I swallow. "I mean, yes, of course. Go ahead. But he doesn't have a social-media presence or anything. So it'll be hard. But I'm sure you're good at research. So I'll leave that to you to figure out. There isn't much on him online. If anything. But his stuff is cool. So, I—yeah."

Somebody sedate me. Please. I am *begging*.

There's no way he's not suspicious of me now.

Maddox tips his head to the side. I'm pretty sure I've seen hyenas do the same thing before they eat someone. "Are you all right, Miss Sinaga?"

No. Not at all.

"Great." I clear my throat, reach for my satchel, and scramble out of my seat. "I—I really need to go. But thank you for your time, Mr. Shaw. I appreciate it. Totally agree with what you said. I'll keep that in mind for the next assignment. That was some really great feedback. I can't thank you enough."

I'm so screwed.

A slow smirk spreads across his lips. "I look forward to seeing more of your serial killer."

7

MADDOX

I have a stalker.

My student is stalking me.

In my thirty-two years of life, I never thought those words would go through my head.

I've had plenty of overeager groupies during my time in the limelight. A couple of paparazzi here and there when a few overly sexualized videos of me were making the rounds on social media a couple of years ago. There was also Tracey from eighth grade who followed me around school for about a week.

But this?

My own student?

The moment she explained the ending of her film, I *knew*. It was an indisputable fact I felt deep within my soul. I couldn't convince myself that her assignments were a coincidence when it was clear as day that her inspiration was taken from the very flesh I molded to my vision.

Still, I felt compelled to know for certain. Test the theory so there's no arguing it. I needed to watch her look at my creation once more to prove to her that *intimacy* isn't what I'm missing—what my art is lacking.

The cold air assaults the exposed skin of my face, and I adjust my hood to preserve warmth. The long coat I'm wearing isn't doing enough to combat the evening wind. My clothing is the only layer of invisibility I have, out in the open for anyone walking past this alleyway to see.

The kitchen window of this particular apartment I chose faces the fire escape, giving me sufficient view through the window to watch Reyna investigate my crime scene now that enough days have passed for the police not to return.

Matthew's death was a complete failure, so I decided to play God and kill a man once more to know without a flicker of a doubt that my student is getting inspiration from my kills.

Nathan Barton has been on my personal list for a long time. For this, and for her, I decided it was time for him to go.

The most bemusing aspect of it is that she has no idea it's *me* she's fawning over. Maybe she hasn't crossed the threshold of "fanatic" yet, but I would say this is skirting that line. People often steal and rip off my art. Usually I'd be upset, but when it comes to my kills?

It's rather flattering, actually.

And I have to hand it to her, I'm impressed. From my limited line of sight, it looks like she doesn't leave a single stone unturned, taking pictures of every item I've moved or placed to set the scene—or the mise-en-scène, if you will. Although I can't tell if she's paid any mind to the broken cathedral ornament sitting in a container of water on the windowsill.

Three weeks ago, Reyna called me Böcklin's Shadow. If she knows her paintings, she might register the reference to *The Chapel* by Arnold Böcklin.

Call it curiosity or plain stupidity, I want to see if she'll connect the dots back to me.

Either through the well-known artwork or the hot-pink gel pen I left for her on the dining table.

If she works it out and runs to the police, I have no issue with attending an interrogation. There is nothing she can say or do that will stick. My father's rank as a high saint and mine as the designated rodent exterminator affords me a level of immunity. The Order has the police in its back pocket and politicians in its front. The governor only has her position because the grand magistrate allowed it. Nothing goes on in this city without the Order's involvement.

Reyna stops suddenly, body going rigid. Her attention snaps toward the front door. I reach into my pocket for my knife. Nathan had no ties to the Order, but that means nothing if she's been digging her nose where it doesn't belong.

Shepherd ordered Benjamin Hogarth's death, the man who played subject for my re-creation of Michelangelo's painting that Reyna investigated. She could have gone looking into countless other Shepherd-sanctioned murders.

The Order has never hesitated to take out a civilian they deemed a nuisance. They aren't about to start now. If Reyna has seen too much, they might decide it'll be better for her to be put down.

She becomes a blur of movement, dropping behind the dining table, attention still set on the door. My pulse hammers against my throat as I step out from the shadows, gripping the blade's handle. I lean forward to get a better view of where she's looking, but can't see more than the living room.

Whatever threat she heard must pass because she rises to her full height, blows out a breath, and resumes her investigation.

I slump against the wall with a sigh. This game we're playing is far too dangerous. Not only could her life be on the line, but Spencer's freedom too.

And yet, I stand here and watch. Enraptured by her every move.

The gods are testing me, and I'm failing. Staying still is like fighting the call of a siren. Unable to help myself, I grab my phone and take a photo of her through the window.

For insurance purposes, of course.

Not for me to look at later.

Really, she should be thanking me for this kill. The location was picked specifically for the view into the house, the low likelihood of interruption, and because it's a safer neighborhood. I'd rather not have her death on my conscience.

The corners of my lips twitch upward when she bumps into the table and scrambles to stop things from falling. I'd wager that she'll drop out of my class the second she realizes who and what I am, which would be so unfortunate since I've found myself rather enjoying our interactions. Not to mention that it's profoundly pathetic how many times I've watched the short film she submitted three weeks ago. She has real talent.

I never wanted a fan or recognition for my murders. Even if some of the kills were ordered by Shepherd, the methods of their deaths were solely for me and my art. If the media catches wind of my masterpieces, great. If they don't, I couldn't care less.

But watching someone—her—admire my kills? Taking videos and reimagining it to be watched on-screen?

When I was younger, I enjoyed studying people's expressions of admiration as they viewed my art. I'd try to decipher what they were thinking or simply bask in my inflating ego. It's been years since I've felt anything remotely similar.

No one has looked at my murders before. No one has understood it for the art that it is. But she has. Little Miss Reyna.

I want to know what it means each time a divot forms beneath her brows, and when she tips her head to the side. Is it curiosity or confusion? If she taps her fingers against the camera, does it mean she has a critique? How does the blood splatter on the wall make her feel? Is she repulsed? Intrigued? At which point does the inspiration come?

And could she stay like that? Teeth clamped on her bottom lip with the slightest crease at the corners of her eyes as she surveys the room. Could she remain perfectly still *just like that* so I can transfer it to paper? Immortalize her with graphite to sate the urge to touch.

My fingers itch to wrap around a pencil. I'm hardly sure whether I'd be able to capture her curiosity. Trap it into a single moment where the bronze threads in her irises shine with the flicker of a fire. Or how the golden strands of her hair contrast against the dark ones, framing her perfectly symmetrical face.

How is one meant to make a masterpiece out of a masterpiece?

My heart stalls when she takes a photo of the cathedral ornament on the windowsill. She noticed.

Fate truly has a sick sense of humor, because the person who tore into my craft and disrespected me in my own classroom is the sole reason I don't currently feel like a failed artist.

She looked me dead in the eyes and called me out on my shit. Usually people do one or the other, never both at the same time. Yet she's done it *several* times now, fixing those damn brown eyes on me, and moving her full lips as if she were the succubus history has always warned men about.

It's agonizing that one person can have so much power.

The truth is, I'm fascinated.

It's been a long time since I've been fascinated by anything, and I'd rather that it had not been my student.

Reyna moves with an untrained elegance. Her steps are sure yet hesitant, similar to how she kept her chin up while hiding her trembling hands behind her back when we had our altercation. It's admirable. It would make her more endearing if it weren't for the fact that most of our interactions involved verbal sparring.

It's awfully hypnotic to watch. Knowing she's here for me makes it all a truly heady experience.

By heady, I mean that I'm developing a migraine from the mixed emotions.

I'm not a good man as it is, and that short brown skirt she's wearing is testing me. She's paired it with tights, white socks, a camisole over a turtleneck. Then there's that damn leather harness that serves no practical function but for me to grab on to and fuck her over the spot where I killed a man to get the truth from her.

The outline of a tattoo I can't make out peeks through the thin pantyhose every time she bends over. I hate not knowing what it is. Before today, I'd only noticed the speared sacred heart on her forearm, and it's utterly fucking maddening how desperate I am to see what other pieces of art she's hiding from me.

I have no right to imagine my student naked. Thinking about how her tattooed thighs would look squeezing my head while she screams is far beyond the realm of acceptability.

How ironic that I frequently engage in murder but draw the line at fucking my student.

I can't afford to lose my job if I want to keep Spencer out of trouble and still be able to do art as I please. Staying away from Miss Sinaga is the logical thing to do.

I've tested my theory. Now it's time to move on. Still, I stay and watch.

By the time Reyna steps out of the house and into a cab, my body is numb to the cold. I snap a photo of the departing vehicle, then tuck my phone into my back pocket. If, for some reason, Reyna's whereabouts are unknown tomorrow, I have the driver's license plate and a new murderous idea I'd love to carry out.

Once the car is out of sight, I slink onto the street and into the apartment to catalog what remains of my work. Nathan Barton was an ambitious family man who was just as interested in other people's families. He loved kids a little *too* much.

When I first got here, there were kids' toys all around the house, scattered along the floor, and hidden down the side of the couch. The number of group photos he had of his children during school trips and summer camps made my stomach churn.

I didn't necessarily walk in here with a plan this time around. I figured inspiration would strike when I needed it to. And it did. All it took was to see six photos of his daughter and her friends at ballet, and my decision was made: bound hands, broken feet, and a lasting plié that would make Edgar Degas turn in his grave. I took the liberty of putting all the children's toys away, out of Nathan's reach and thoughts. Then turned the photos around so he couldn't see them.

It's all relatively the same as I left it, although it's hard to tell which part has changed because of the forensics team and which is owed to Reyna. There's one new addition to my scene.

A cobalt-blue metal pen, left on the table my student bumped into.

It wasn't there before, and it wasn't left by any professional.

North View High, it reads.

My stalker's high school.

She's a walking liability.

I haven't decided whether it's a good or bad thing that Miss Sinaga is still alive.

Good because the cab driver lives to see another day. Bad because I'm going to go insane. She's everywhere I look, even when she's not there.

In the three days since I've seen her, my mind hasn't stopped replaying the sight of her staring in awe of my *Fallen Angel* painting, and the way she looked helping herself to my crime scene. I can still picture the slight wrinkle in her forehead and the curve of her brow. Even the way she intently listens to me speak in class—as if I'm not a talentless hack—is all-consuming.

Not to mention her *fucking* legs.

I scrub my face and chuck my scarf and gloves on the couch before dropping into my office chair. My ears are still ringing from all the yelling at Spencer's football game. I hadn't the time, patience, nor the energy for such dramatics, but he asked me to be there, and I couldn't say no.

A faint throb begins at the back of my head as I log in to the university portal. It's another thing I don't want to do, grade the assignments for a class I never wanted to inherit. The cursor hovers over the name at the very top of the alphabetized list. Reyna is near the bottom, and I likely won't get to it for another week. That's seven agonizing days of wondering if she made a video of the kill I laid out for her, or if she did someone else's.

Screw it.

I click her name. A second time. Double-clicking the third time. Fingers tapping the table, glaring at the circle spinning in the center of the screen. Has my computer always been this bloody slow?

Reyna's re-creations aren't replicas of my kills, rather she incorporates overarching themes to bridge the gap until they're entirely hers.

The criteria for this assignment is that there mustn't be any dialogue or music, a project I have no doubt she will excel at. In all of my classes, she's the student who holds the most promise.

The film opens with three loud booms in total darkness. Then the door opens to reveal a young man silently listening to something on the phone. The hero is welcomed into a messy, yellow-hued living room. I watch with skepticism as the camera follows the host into the kitchen and switches focus between his hands and his face as he prepares a cup of coffee for them. An anatomical heart tattoo pokes out from beneath the protagonist's long-sleeve shirt when he drops powder into one of the mugs.

Within a matter of seconds of sipping the offered drink, the hero slowly tips sideways, eyes drooped open.

Maybe it was a coincidence after all. It's entirely possible that she's investigating and re-creating any murder she deems inspiring. I've never drugged anyone like that, let alone been in a position where my subjects trust me enough to drink what I made.

The lack of connection to my kills is all the more evident when the protagonist throws the victim into the trunk of a car and drives through the city, passing loud streets, littered sidewalks, and well-kept brownstones, to a basement cast in a red hue.

All sound dies but the reverberation of footsteps through the concrete room.

The only time I've taken a subject to a second location is upon Shepherd's specific instructions. Nor has a basement been involved.

None of this aligns with my work.

Sipping water does nothing to remove the bitter taste in my mouth that Reyna might have taken inspiration from another killer. She's the first person to recognize a pattern in my murders, but I was wrong to think that she finds my work special or unique.

It doesn't matter. I still have to grade her.

The kidnapper places the semiunconscious man on a chair without bothering to tie him down. The directorial decision seems deliberate. I've yet to understand why.

Reyna opts for another close-up of the kidnapper's hands hovering in indecision between the hammer, chef's knife, and pliers. Again, the heart tattoo peaks out as he reaches for the knife before cutting to a close-up of his face.

An idea that I can't quite grasp forms in the back of my mind. I've seen her previous work. Her choice of focal point is too intentional for it to be a matter of chance.

The scene shifts to an over-the-shoulder shot of the kidnapper, where all that's seen of the victim is his silhouette. Toying with the pen on my table, I watch as the blade glows amber from the flames of a blowtorch. A shock of yellow against the red room.

The protagonist stalks forward, head cut out of the frame. There's not a single sound to be heard when he presses the scorching blade against the lower half of the victim's face. All that can be seen is the killer's arm and the steam rolling into the air as the skin melts away.

My jaw tenses. I've never done that either.

It's not my kill. Reyna isn't following my work.

It's frustrating that I can't see or hear what's happening to the victim. *Finally* the camera pans, following the killer out of the basement that's now cast in blue lighting, and my lips part at the sight.

Three different bodies sit limply on separate chairs. One with the skin of his mouth melted. Another with dried pink blood running down his ears. The last, a woman with a cherry-pink rag tied over her eyes.

The killer shuts the door behind him, plunging the room into darkness. The screen goes black, followed by three knocks.

I stop breathing.

Speak no evil.

Hear no evil.

See no evil.

Head. Hand. Heart.

Yellow. Red. Blue. *Primary colors.*

Littered streets. Pristine brownstones. A murder den. Perfect balance in the midst of carnage.

The cursor darts across the screen to pull up her supporting essay, and time suspends. At the very top of the document is the film title.

The Rule of Three.

Reyna *knew* it was me. My failed kill. The one that was *End of an Era.*

She understands me, and that might be the worst thing of all.

8

MADDOX

I'm hallucinating. It's nearly the witching hour, I'm sleep-deprived, and this is the first time I've left my studio in two days.

My exhibition is in two and a half months. It's meant to be my last attempt at making a comeback into the art world, and I don't have a single piece ready. The last thing I need is a distraction. Yet my hindbrain is conjuring up the woman who's the sole reason for my hellish state.

Because there she is. A ghost gliding across the courtyard bracketed by towers that have stood the test of the ages.

She's haunting me.

I can't stop myself. I slink toward her, sticking close to the wall. Reyna crosses the courtyard, glancing at her surroundings every few seconds—conveniently missing me in the shadows.

Fate, you dirty bastard. I'm meant to be keeping my distance, but the universe is insistent on tormenting me by putting her in my path when my grasp on control is as strong as a fraying thread.

It's well past midnight, and my student has decided it's the right time to be walking alone on a deserted campus. What type of person does that? Right, the type who visits murder scenes when they have the survival skills of a newborn puppy.

Reyna is going to send me into a heart attack. It's a good thing our interactions will drop to zero come the end of the semester. After that, I'll be free from the chains she's put me in, and I'll never have to lose sleep over her. No more plotting murders that are specifically designed for her to see. No more picturing her as I paint. None of that. It'll be like she never existed.

For now, I can sate my curiosity, see how she thinks, and—

No, I need to turn left to go home to my townhouse to drink myself into a stupor. I have to catch up on sleep and pull myself together so I can be ready for my exhibition. Reyna Sinaga isn't my problem and never will be. She's an adult who can make her own decisions regarding her safety. If she chooses to be an admirer of my kills and walk alone at night, that's her prerogative.

She's no one. Nothing.

A rude student with attitude problems who just so happens to be attractive.

An irritant. Inconsequential. A nuisance.

She doesn't matter to me.

She and I have no business talking to each other.

I jog down the stairs and turn right.

Maybe I'll look into getting Reyna removed from my class so I can escape the spell she's cast on me. Witchcraft is the only explanation for it.

I don't want anything to do with her. Any person who speaks the way she does and visits crime scenes for fun is problematic, and the last thing that I need is more problems.

This is a bad idea. I know it. The gods know it. My dead uncle knows it. (May he rest in peace. A literal knife in the back is a bad way to go.) So tell me why I stalk toward her, like the absolute fucking idiot that I am.

A complete tosser who's been picking on her in class just because I want to hear her voice. She never puts her hand up to answer willingly, and she talks too quietly with Nicole for me to catch what she's saying, and I've been utterly deprived of the sound of her voice unless I call her out in the middle of a lecture.

She was flustered the first time. Irritated the second. Now, she just glares.

Not once have I needed to correct her answers.

Reyna is the best student in this class. Bradford was a fool for not seeing it.

That same craving hits me as I creep closer to her. The need to hear her voice.

An odd sensation that holds juvenile familiarity vibrates through my veins. It changes the rhythm of my breaths and the thud of my pulse. I haven't experienced anything like it since primary school, when the girl I had a crush on sat next to me. A fucking *crush*.

This is a *very* fucking bad idea.

This needs to stop. *Right now.*

The sandstone pavement scrapes the bottom of my shoes as I turn to leave. I should never have approached her to begin with—both here and at the art gallery. This ends now. There is to be no further interaction with Reyna from this moment on.

"Mr. Shaw?"

Fuck.

The unwelcome sensation in the pit of my stomach turns molten, heating my body by two degrees.

That's the second time she's called me *that*. I barely have a grip on my sanity as it is. If she calls me *Mr. Shaw* in her husky voice a third time, I'm going to kill the first person I see, no questions asked.

I'm a grown man getting hard from the sound of my star pupil's voice. Someone once suggested that I need therapy. Perhaps it's time to seriously consider that option.

The muscle in my jaw feathers as I turn around, facing the girl who's unknowingly stalking me. All the air rushes from my lungs in one fell swoop.

Reyna Sinaga is breathtaking.

No, *breathtaking* isn't a strong enough word. I could spend a lifetime scouring every dictionary in existence, and I would never find a descriptor that would come close to what she is.

Words are caught in my throat as I take her in. She's a whirlwind of sharp edges and soft curves—harsh jaw, button nose, a cupid's bow pointed enough to cut, and round, almond eyes.

I've always known that she was stunning. It was the first thought that crossed my mind when she looked my way at the art gallery.

I've caught myself staring at her one too many times during class, and walking through campus alone. And when I crept away into my studio, staring at a blank canvas, she came to the forefront of my mind.

Our breaths plume into the night air, filling the space between us, and I have the urge to move closer to feel her against my skin.

Nothing is stopping me from turning around and pretending our eyes never locked, that she never drew me in. But I can't bring myself to move. It's unsettling enough that she's visiting crime scenes by herself. Seeing her walk around in the middle of the night has the black part of my soul rearing its head.

The only reason I'm so concerned is because she's my student who shows the most promise. Yes, that's it. If something happens to her, there'll be a plethora of paperwork and investigations I'd rather not be part of.

People will talk if anyone sees us out here. There's no telling what would happen to us if word were to go back to my parents *or* the faculty about this midnight meeting. I *need* to leave. Despite that, I stay exactly where I am, hands pressed to my sides so I don't do something idiotic like try to touch her.

The silence between us grows, and it sours as I take in the rest of her. Reyna lacks self-preservation of any form if she thinks it's a good idea to wear a jacket that thin when it's this cold.

She's doing a terrible job of hiding the fact that she's shivering. My first thought is to offer her my coat and get her into my office. My second is, *again*, it's none of my bloody business what she does.

I'm both pleased and displeased that she's wearing a skirt that falls past her knees, instead of the minis that drive me insane.

She drives me insane.

"You shouldn't be walking around alone after dark, Miss Sinaga. You never know when a killer might be on the loose."

"I don't fit his MO."

Her eyes widen with her slipped confession. I wipe the grin off my face.

God, she's infuriating.

She clears her throat, yanks her satchel forward, and frantically unclips the front pockets to grab a can of mace and a switchblade. A KitKat, a bag of Cheetos, and an EpiPen hit the ground in the process, and she scrambles to put them back in her bag.

My brows flatten. Why the bloody hell does she have an EpiPen?

Reyna holds out her weapons and tips her chin up. "I have protection."

How cute. She's trying to salvage her mistake.

That doesn't make her any less of a liability to me and to herself.

"Those aren't permitted on campus—or in this state." In fact, she seems to be breaking as many laws as I am. Although at a different scale. But sometimes, it's about quantity and not quality. I can be a numbers guy.

"Neither of those two things in your hand will offer any sort of protection unless someone is willing to give you five seconds' head start to take them out of your bag." I take a step forward, and those plump lips of hers part. The temptation to reach out to see what they'd feel like between my teeth is overwhelming.

She's walking around. At night. Underdressed. Alone. Visiting murder scenes and who knows what else. With no real defense.

It's not my business.

Not. My. Business.

"I do hope you don't intend to use those for anything outside of your nighttime strolls."

I just can't help myself, can I? Talking with her is too enjoyable.

Reyna pales beneath the glow of the lampposts. I can see the six words pinging around in her head: *He knows about the crime scenes.*

Oh, darling, I know.

"No." She shakes her head quickly. "Not at all. Just for safety. At night."

Talented, stunning, occasionally quick-witted, and the newest pain in my ass.

I've never met such a horrific liar. It's rather beguiling.

Another step and her shoulders are curling upward, ready to bolt. "Is that so?" My voice drops several notes, shrinking the space between us until she's a measly five feet away, and I can *just* feel her harsh breaths.

Reyna is even more beautiful up close. Her thick lashes aren't long enough to brush her cheek, but they line her eyes in a way that makes the flecks of bronze in her irises stand out. The shadows play with every part of her face, dipping and curving in certain areas, exaggerating her features.

She nods frantically. "Yes. You know. Walking, in the subway, going out. All very reasonable, normal stuff."

The dim lights of the streetlamps give her the sort of morbid elegance that would suit a woman standing at the end of a balcony, holding a dying tealight. My studio is practically tugging at me as the image takes form in my mind. It's coming to me clearer than anything else has in months—years even.

I want to grab my phone to capture a photo for reference later. Her films and the one image I have of her from the crime scene aren't sating the creative beasts demanding to be fed.

One more step. "Are you lying to me, Miss Sinaga?"

Her lips open and close, and I'm fairly certain she's stopped breathing. So she'll argue with me fine. Disrespect my work without batting an eye. Yet lying is her kryptonite?

Fascinating. Everything about her is so goddamn fascinating.

I should have gone home.

"Are you going to places you shouldn't?"

Her throat bobs. "No?"

"Is that a question?"

"No," she says, a few decibels quieter, twisting the objects in her hands.

I have to bite back a smile. It's refreshing to be around someone so unfiltered—even if she is lying straight to my face. The fact that she does it so badly makes me appreciate it the slightest bit more. "Where are you getting your inspiration from?"

"What?" she practically squeaks. "Nowhere. I mean, I—I told you about—"

"Are you visiting crime scenes?"

Her eyes double in size. "What would make you think that? Of course not. That's illegal. And wrong. I'd never do that. No. God, no. That's too far. And dangerous. And—"

"Miss Sinaga."

Her mouth snaps shut.

I tip my head to the side. "How about we try that again?"

My gaze drops to the swell of her bright-red bottom lip. She gnaws on the pillowy flesh, distracting me for a moment.

"You've based your entire project around gruesome murders that you claimed were inspired by an artist going by Böcklin's Shadow—someone with no presence in the media." I almost feel bad about how stricken she looks. Unfortunately for her, I don't plan on leaving until I hear the truth from her lips.

She clears her throat and shifts her weight, eyes never meeting mine. "Murders? I don't know what you're talking about."

"I am going to ask this one more time, and the next words out of your mouth better be the truth." Watching her squirm would be enjoyable if my patience for her reckless disregard of her safety weren't becoming paper-thin. "Are you visiting murder scenes?"

Reyna hesitates. "Am I going to get in trouble if I am?"

"Are all your films based on the same killer?"

Her throat bobs.

Come on, love. Tell me what I want to hear.

She nods once, and fuck if that doesn't make me wild.

I already knew what she was doing, but her confirmation that she only cares for my murders is like finding the edge of a cliff and throwing myself off it thinking I might grow wings.

Not one person on the police force has linked the murders together. Yet a twenty-one-year-old film major figured it out. I'd laugh if my sanity didn't loosen with every second I'm around this woman.

"Why do you call him Böcklin's Shadow?" I could hazard a guess as to why, but I want to keep hearing her voice.

Reyna fidgets with the weapons in her hands. "He, uh, has a fascination with mortality and how it intertwines with reality. Like the painting *Self-Portrait with Death Playing the Fiddle*. He isn't murdering for recognition or attention. He's doing it because he's an artist, and death is his medium of choice. He's a man working alongside death himself," she says. "Plus." She forces a chuckle. "It was an inside joke with myself that the killer is playing with his victims like a fiddle." Reyna clears her throat and straightens when I say nothing. "That's not funny, sorry."

I stare at her for a beat. Two. Then a third. Taking her in from head to toe and wishing I could delve into her mind and pick at it for hours. Not a single soul has ever understood my motives the way she does.

She's fucking brilliant. Absolutely, completely, utterly astounding, and—

Reyna Sinaga is just my student.

There's nothing interesting about her at all.

This is bad.

This is very, very bad.

Why couldn't she say that she spent two minutes on the internet and chose the first name she saw? How am I meant to dispel her from my mind when she talks about me like I'm a god?

It has to stop. All of it.

"Never look into his murders again, and do not, under any circumstance, visit his crime scenes."

Reyna jolts back. "What?"

It's too dangerous—on so many levels. All it would take is for Reyna to stumble upon the wrong Hive-ordered kill, and she could be right in their crosshairs. As much as I appreciate her admiration of my work, it isn't worth her getting hurt or murdered over.

Not to mention I need to be *less* involved with her. Speaking to her out in the open is risky enough, but if she keeps talking to me with that husky voice and showing me how phenomenal her mind is, I worry whether my fleeting control will be enough to pull me from the brink.

Reyna will need to stay away for both our sakes. If our only crossover is the classroom, then there will be no reason for her to be anywhere near my periphery, so I can focus on rebuilding my career.

"It ends now. It's too dangerous for you."

"No."

"Yes."

She grips her weapons like she may well use them on me. "I made it this far by myself just fine. I'm aware of the risks and everything that could go wrong. But this is my decision to make."

For fuck's sake, I don't have the time to watch her to make sure she's keeping in line. The Order *will* come for her, if they haven't begun watching her already. Unless I find more hours in the day, the only thing I can do is dissuade her from continuing down this path.

The Order has remained in power for so long because they've never hesitated to take someone down. People like my father and the other high saints don't just play god, they *are* gods.

Tech billionaires, real estate moguls, governors—the vice fucking president, they're all in the Order, and are only where they are *because* of the Order.

Any one of them could go to the grand magistrate for permission to kill Reyna, and not a single person would bat an eye.

She has no idea what she's dealing with.

I grab her arm. Her lips part at the contact, and I hate how the sight of it disarms me. Again, my first thought is how badly I wish she weren't wearing all these layers. The second is a proverbial slap because she's my *fucking student.*

"And what if someone kills you?" I snap. Any hope of sounding composed goes out the window.

I drop my hand and take a wide step away. I can't think clearly when I'm touching her.

Everything about her is messing with me. I was trained better than this—to never let my emotions best me, because showing anything other than rage is a weakness. Yet here I am, showing her all my cards.

She glares at me. Shrugs. "We all die eventually."

That's the worst possible thing she could have responded with. It would have been better if she didn't speak at all.

"Death could be a bloody fucking blessing compared to what could happen." I've passed the point of irritation, transcended the realm of anger. Her willingness to die for a film project sends white-hot rage up my spine. *"You aren't going."*

This hobby of hers is stupid beyond belief.

Fire blazes in her as she crosses her arms over her chest. "Like I said, that's not your decision to make. You're not my dad. You're not my husband. You're just my professor."

Hearing the words *you're*, *my*, and *husband* makes my brain short-circuit in a possessive way that I don't like. Not one bit.

"Yes, that's right. I *am* your professor. And as your *professor*, I am telling you to stop going to those crime scenes and sticking your nose in places that it doesn't belong."

"As if you haven't done anything reckless for your art."

Touché.

"There's a difference between us: I haven't gotten caught."

"Yet."

This little shit.

"You have no idea what you're dealing with." My fingers itch to grab her high school's pen from my coat pocket to prove that it's a matter of time before someone else notices her slipups.

"We all have our vices. I'm sticking with mine while I can," she says, tone even and calm. "So let me make this clear: *I'm still going.*"

"Do not fight me on this, Miss Sinaga," I warn.

"You can yell at me, scream at me, berate me, and I'll still be going where my passions lead me." Each word comes out poised, with a faint air of hostility. "Other people might bend to your every whim, but I'm not going to give up something I enjoy just because you told me to. If you want a pet to sit and stay put, then I suggest you get a dog. Now, if you'll excuse me, I have an assignment to write. Good night, Mr. Shaw."

She dips her head, turns on her heel, and storms away, breezing off into the night with regal grace very few could pull off.

"Reyna," I call, and the brat has the audacity to ignore me even when I call for her a second and third time.

I scowl at her back, watching her slink out of view. It's not a difficult decision to follow behind her. It seems someone needs to ensure she gets home safe. I have half a mind to catch up with her to finish our conversation. Except I know better than anyone that a verbal scolding will do nothing to curb a creator's obsession. Common sense and reason go out the window for the sake of art.

Ask for forgiveness, not permission.

In all truthfulness, stopping her from doing what she is clearly talented at feels like a crime worse than murder. She's an artist with a vision, and once that spark is gone, it rarely ever returns.

Still, I will not be the reason she dies.

9

REYNA

Don't bite the hand that teaches you, or whatever the saying is.

My argument with Shaw is just as stupid as my decision to climb the three flights of stairs to his office instead of taking the elevator. I'm only delaying the inevitable.

Just because I'm aware I should own up to my mistakes doesn't mean I like nor want to. Alas, I must re-salvage whatever professional-nonprofessional relationship we have.

He scared me shitless when I heard him coming up behind me last night. Whatever relief I felt from it being *him* and not an attacker was short-lived when I ended up (regrettably) stunned by how well he wears the smart-disheveled look. Then I became immediately ungrateful that I was getting verbally attacked.

Thank you for your concern, Mr. Shaw, but kindly fuck off. Oh, and don't let this impact my grades, pretty please xoxo.

My phone buzzes in my pocket. I stop in the middle of the marble steps to shove my chunky screenplay textbook into my satchel, and my shoulder immediately screams in protest.

LAWRENCE:

What are you doing tomorrow night? My buddies from work got me vouchers to some restaurant.

My sigh threatens to shake the foundations of the old building. I really want to cut ties with Lawrence, but I can't. He has information about my dad and is my only access to the murders. It's not like the kills are appearing on the news. I'm stuck with him.

ME:

I can't, sorry. I promised Kimi I'd accompany her shopping.

Grocery shopping. So it isn't a complete lie.

I tuck the phone into my pocket and ignore the next text that comes through.

I give tight-lipped smiles to students and staff passing by and swallow my envy that they aren't on their way to open Pandora's box. I could technically put this off until after class tomorrow, but I'm bound to lose sleep over it if I do. I'd rather rip out the anxiety in my chest. It's not good for the soul.

I swipe my sweaty hands on my dress as I climb up the final set of steps. Of course, he gets the nicest floor in the building. The hallway is grand, much like the rest of Cresswell, with high ceilings and arches framing each solid-mahogany door.

Paintings from various alumni adorn the corridor, and a Renaissance-style mural sprawls across the ceiling. It seems to come alive beneath the low, golden light coming from the gilded sconces.

There's only one door at the very end of the hall, secluded from everything else.

Fitting for the harbinger of death.

Taking a deep breath, I rap my knuckles on the old wooden door and give the entrance a wide berth in case he decides to rip the thing open and knock me out with it. The seconds stretch on as I wait. And wait.

And wait.

I knock again.

Maybe he's not here.

I don't think he's teaching any classes this afternoon. It's definitely outside of his scheduled office hours. I mean, I did decide to leave it until five to talk to him, so it's entirely possible he's gone home for the day—

The door whips open to reveal Shaw standing there, scowling like Satan himself has come to shit on his parade.

His hair stands at odd angles and brushes the skin of his face; it's beautifully tousled and made to run fingers through. Dots of navy paint cover part of his hand, and there's a blotch of white on his dress pants. The top buttons of his shirt are undone, sleeves rolled up to the top of his forearms; his usual tie and vest combo is nowhere to be found.

He's the most attractive disheveled mess I've ever seen, and *God* I can't get enough of the smell of him. I want to touch his ridiculously gorgeous face, feel his hands on me, and listen to him rip into me in his lethally addictive British accent—the simple things in life.

Wait, is he wearing yesterday's clothes?

Venomous green eyes widen before his brows knit together in a deep frown.

"Did something happen?" Maddox—*Shaw* sounds genuinely concerned.

The question takes my axis for a spin. The same fuzzy feeling I felt last night fizzles in my chest. I expected a comment about how this isn't his office hour, or how I should have booked an appointment if I wanted to speak with him—word on the street is that he's *very* particular about when he can and cannot be disturbed.

"Can we talk?" I clasp my hands together to stop myself from tugging on the sleeve of my cardigan. "About last night."

Something dark crosses Shaw's eyes. He considers for a beat, then steps back to let me inside after sticking his head out the doorway like he's making sure no one saw his dirty little secret. My plan to question his behavior dies.

His studio is *stunning*.

Without permission, I help myself into his space.

The room is situated at the corner of the building and wraps toward the opposite wing in an *L* shape. The afternoon sun illuminates the canvases spread throughout the entire studio, hanging on the forest-green walls, stacked on the floor, or on the easel taking center stage. Clay sculptures are scattered throughout, some that just need finishing touches, others that appear far from complete.

Everything he could possibly need is in here. Against one of the walls is a kitchenette complete with a fridge, portable stove, and microwave. There's a rumpled blanket sprawled over a leather couch, and a pillow dangerously close to falling onto the Persian rug.

I don't know of any other professor who's been awarded this much luxury. I'm fairly certain every art teacher here gets a dingy little office and a studio they can book if they want to paint. Yet here he is, like he's the king of kings. I guess he'd need the big space for his massive ego.

Shaw makes no move to stop me from going farther into the room, and I take it as his silent invitation.

My lips part as I absorb every half-finished piece of art. I have to shove my hands in my pockets to keep myself from going through the stacks of discarded canvases, and unveiling his sculptures. The easel in the center of the room beckons me closer until I'm only a couple of feet away from Shaw's current piece.

One thing crosses my mind: *He's back.*

A faceless woman stands at the edge of a cliff, staring into the distance as a taper candle melts onto her hand. Six feathered seraphim wings are spread high and proud, but she holds herself like she's exhausted, pained, as if she'd be swaying if the painting weren't stilled in a performance that never ends.

We aren't looking at her front on, but from a low angle and to the side, like we're a devotee worshipping at her altar.

I don't know how long I spend staring at the painting. Colors have been set down everywhere except her face, like he hasn't quite decided how she's meant to look. The sight of her already makes my heart ache.

It's almost unrecognizable compared to what I've seen of his work. This woman was painted through the lens of a lover. It's intimate.

"Quite the piece," Maddox says, like the first time we met.

"It's beautiful." It comes out on a breath, and I mean it wholeheartedly.

"Your words mean nothing."

Two steps forward and one step back.

Irritation flashes through me. I turn in time to catch the bitter amusement passing through his expression. "Great. I'll say it again in a year's time while holding my bachelor's. Or would I need a doctorate to be considered qualified by your standards?"

Shaw shakes his head, frowning at his work. "I'd say the same thing if it were Rembrandt himself telling me. It's incomplete and lifeless, far from any masterpiece."

"Sometimes you have to trust the process."

"I don't trust anything."

"That must be exhausting."

He huffs a humorless laugh. "There's no rest for the wicked. I'll take a break when I'm dead."

I roll my eyes. How dramatic. "Or you could rest now. Have a hard reset before you end up in an early grave—which probably sounds more like a holiday for you since you seem to love all things tortured."

The full weight of his attention falls on me, holding me in place. The violent intensity in his eyes tells me that I'm barely scratching the surface of that truth. As fucked-up as that is, it excites me.

"And you?" Maddox raises a brow. "Following a serial killer? Poetizing murder for the screen? You have an affinity for the morose."

"I find peace in the dark and the macabre."

"That's awfully grotesque of you, Miss Sinaga." A slow half smile pulls at his lips, and mine curls to match. My pulse hammers at the same time a swarm of wingless butterflies flitter through my stomach.

My cheeks heat, but I can't bring myself to look away from him. I've never seen a genuine smile on him before. I wish I had my camera on me so I could capture the moment and set it in stone the only way I know how.

In another life, I think we could be friends. There's too much difference in this one.

And he's an arrogant bastard.

My eyes catch the images stuck onto the wallpaper behind him, and a boulder lodges in my throat. At least six annotated printouts of Maria van Oosterwyck's paintings, as well as countless other pieces of art done by women in the same era.

He listened to my opinion. He listened even though he thought I was wrong.

"And?" Maddox asks. At my questioning look, he gestures at his painting. "Penny for your thoughts."

I suck in a sharp breath. My skin feels too heavy for my body. The warmth unfurling in my stomach makes it hard to think clearly. Maddox Shaw is asking for my opinion. He *wants* it. Even after everything he said.

My throat bobs. There are a thousand different things I could say. If I call him remarkable, he won't believe me. If I say it's lackluster, I'd be lying.

"Why is she faceless?"

The muscle in his jaw twitches in frustration. He doesn't answer for a while, and I'm left stewing that I've chosen the wrong thing to say.

"I'm deciding whether I've met her yet."

I frown at the painting. It could be anyone. The image I have in mind will never be precisely the same as his.

"*The King of Kings*," I say, referring to the name of the pig-headed king mixed-media piece that put him on the map when he was sixteen. "You should bring her to life like that."

"Is that a suggestion or a critique?" He cocks a brow at me.

Maybe it's bad that I'm enjoying this banter with him. When he's not degrading me, his companionship is rather enjoyable. It helps that seeing him look like a man at his wit's end makes him more relatable. Human, almost.

I lift a shoulder. "It'll still be priceless either way you portray her. If you want my true thoughts on it, then I'd say that your talent is once in a generation. This?" I stare at the painting again. "Once you get her face right, I think it'll be better than anything else you've ever created. I'd say you'd have outdone yourself, Mr. Shaw."

When I look over at Maddox, his attention is on me, not the masterpiece in the making, looking at me like he isn't sure whether I've lost my mind or, dare I say it, like *I'm* the art. It sets my skin ablaze.

I need to turn away to free myself from the trap he has me in. Nothing good can come from what's happening.

But my body has other plans. I sway closer, wanting a taste of his depravity.

I'd love to spend a single day seeing how he views the world. I want to know what makes him pick up a paintbrush, or if there are colors he's too hesitant to use because they don't match the shades he's given the universe around him. But I can't, and I never will.

He's my professor, and a legend in the art world. I'm just his student.

Maddox breaks the curse before I get the chance to understand the meaning behind the way his eyes darken more the longer they stay on me. The vehemence in his expression dissipates, replaced by the cold exterior he wears like armor.

"What did you want to see me about?"

"Oh, um." I clear my throat.

Right, the whole reason I came here. The uninvited tour of his office has thrown me, and now I don't feel like bringing up last night's conversation.

I take a deep breath. "I'm sorry about how I acted earlier. You were watching out for me, and I took it poorly. It's been a long time since I've had anyone around to look out for me or tell me what to do, so it was a bit of a shock to the system." Kimi is more likely to get me into trouble than out of it. "However, I do appreciate your concern, because you're right, what I am doing is dangerous."

"Were," he corrects. "What you *were* doing."

I narrow my eyes at him. "I believe that's not what I said."

I take it back. I want nothing to do with his beautifully creative mind.

"It isn't," he says matter-of-factly. "That's why I corrected you, since you will not be visiting any more crime scenes from here on out."

Like a petulant teen, I cross my arms over my chest, face him square on, and speak slowly so he hears every word loud and clear. "I'm going to continue doing what I'm doing, and you have no say in the matter, *Professor* Shaw."

"The faculty would be interested in knowing."

My heart stops for a second. I don't understand why he's pushing so hard. I should shut up, agree, then secretly keep doing it. But lying was never my strong suit.

He has nothing but audacity sometimes.

That's fine. I'll bite.

"Good luck convincing them."

Shaw glares at me, though his eyes glint with amusement. "The police would be equally as interested."

"Do I need a lawyer?"

The corners of his lips twitch like he's holding back a grin. "I'll mark you down for plagiarism."

"Where's your proof? That'd be easy to appeal." I raise my chin. I feel more like a kid arguing over toys than something that could seriously harm me and my scholarship. "If you're done with your threats, we can agree to disagree that my dates with the Shadow will continue."

His entire being hardens like I just said something downright offensive, but his face goes expressionless. "If you took your education seriously, you wouldn't be going on dates with anyone."

My jaw drops. Oh my God, I'm going to kill him. "If I took my edu—" I clamp my mouth shut and take a deep breath. "You don't need to worry, I take my education *very* seriously."

I clap my hands together because slapping him isn't an option, then say, "If we're done going around in circles, we can call it a day and both be on our merry way. And if your free will also involves attending crime scenes, then I wish you all the best."

He uncrosses his arms and places his hands in his pockets, shoulders relaxed, resuming the deceptively relaxed facade he dons so well. "Fine. If you want to act recklessly, then so be it."

I blink.

Oh. That was easy. I expected more of a fight.

"Good."

"I'll be accompanying you from now on."

Wait.

Back up.

"Come again."

His gaze turns heated. "That's not something you want to say to me, Miss Sinaga."

What is that supposed to mean—

Oh.

A shudder rolls down my spine. I don't think my heart is beating.

He grimaces, then brushes it off like he didn't just insinuate *that*. "Anytime you intend on visiting a crime scene, you will tell me, and we will go together."

Huh? "No."

"Yes."

"Absolutely not." No fucking way.

"I apologize if you mistook my statement for a suggestion. If you want to go, I'm accompanying you."

I gape at him. "I take my apology back. I am very much *not* sorry. Stop being so overbearing."

"You want me to be more palatable, I want you to stop putting yourself in danger; not everyone can get what they want."

"I don't need you to be my goddamn babysitter."

"Then it's agreed. You're acting like a child."

I take a deep breath, look heavenward, then count to three. I can't believe we're having this conversation. "Right," I say, heading for the exit. "Thank you for your time this afternoon, Mr. Shaw."

He shifts to the side, effectively blocking my exit with his imposing frame, trying and failing to appear relaxed. "I didn't dismiss you."

"Then it's a good thing I wasn't asking for your permission to leave." And here he was calling *me* the child.

Shaw can give me his detached demeanor all he wants. I heard the dark rumble in his voice. The man is two seconds from blowing up. "We aren't done here."

"We never started."

"Why are you being so difficult?"

"Why are you being so insistent?"

He scowls, stepping forward and invading my senses with his intoxicating presence. "Because you are so adamant that your safety is meaningless. Someone needs to make sure you don't get yourself killed."

Gone is the crappy, nonchalant exterior he tried fooling me with. The irritation is rolling off him, and I fucking love it. He's fighting me *for* me. My professor genuinely cares.

"And that someone is you?" My words lack the tenacity I've been wielding for the past five minutes.

"Yes." He takes one more step forward. I take one back. The tremor returns to my hands, and the stupid fuzzy feeling in my stomach goes completely haywire. "That someone is *me*, your fucking *professor*." He says the last few words like he hates them. It turns my blood molten and my pulse skyrocketing. "Do not fight me on this, Miss Sinaga. My patience has scarcely been present, and my tolerance for disobedience is even more rare. You have no idea who you're taunting."

I can't speak. Can't move.

Too much is flaring behind his eyes. Frustration, anger, want, *heat*. Things that he shouldn't be feeling.

Goose bumps rain over my flesh. Maddox's harsh breath fans my face; it trickles through the strands of my hair and kisses my warm skin in the softest caress. Molten desire floods through me and turns my senses into a live wire. Every sensation feels forbidden. This close, I could lean forward on my tiptoes and brush my lips against his. I could run my fingers through his hair and feel the roll of his muscles against my skin.

These are not thoughts that *I* should be having. He's my professor, for God's sake, and I didn't move across the country to screw my damn teacher.

The glint in his eyes frightens me at the same time it lures me closer. The greens in them brighten the way nature's most deadly plants would. It's feral and predatory, the type of deranged that could kill within the span of a heartbeat, and devour in less. I commit the sight to memory, letting our ragged breaths fill the searing space between us.

I break the spell before I'm forever trapped. Swallowing, I keep our eyes locked as I move for the door, saying under my breath, "Have a good evening, Mr. Shaw."

One of us should. That's not in the cards for me anymore.

10

MADDOX

She likes my art.

That's the only thought that has gone through my head for the past three days.

She likes my art.

When I was eighteen, a member of the British royal family commissioned a painting. At twenty-four, I had a four-page spread in *Vogue* for my creations. Not a single one of those things, individually or combined, amounts to the rush I felt when Reyna complimented me.

She thinks I'm *talented*.

My mind is in disarray because of a student and her sinful lips. Which is possibly the worst thing I could think of when amongst Order members. It's made me feel like prey in this pit full of vipers. If there were ever a place that I needed to be ready to kill—both figuratively and literally—it would be here.

My eyes drop to the ornate wooden floors, and I debate counting the grains. The high saint of House Dornmont stands at the center of the room, surrounded by pews full of people in long black cloaks. The six blocks radiate out from the center, a section for each of the houses.

House Shaw—mine, regrettably.

House Dornmont—my fiancée's, unfortunately.

House Hopkins—hate those fuckers. It's basically a glorified frat house right now.

House Sutherland—where my vote is going.

House Ellis—painfully boring, yet incredibly efficient. The traits of acceptable leaders, I suppose.

House Ortiz—highly respectable and unproblematic. Again, boring for my tastes.

The room is fashioned in a way that acolytes sit behind the houses they affiliate with.

They don't need to vote for the high saint of their house. At the end of every election cycle, once the high saints for the following years have been chosen, they can move to a different house, should they choose.

The grand magistrate sits on a platform along the outskirts of the room to symbolize his superiority and *all-seeing* power. Regardless of which house an acolyte pledges themselves to, we all serve him.

Frederick Dornmont waves his arms about as if we're attending Sunday Mass. The flames from hundreds of candles flicker against the walls, at the end of each pew, and around the dais, with a single candelabra in the very middle. The smoke threads up to the hive-shaped ceiling—toward God.

The truth is that the men who began the Order were religious for performative purposes. The only gods they believed in were themselves.

The Order of the Hallowed Hive secretly meets in a hexagon-shaped room with a roof with more hexagons on it. A bit on the nose if you ask me.

Roland stands beside Frederick Dornmont, nodding his head along every once in a while. The two red ropes crossed over their chests that represent their status shift against their black robes as they move. The forced attire is rather pompous. Just another attempt to set us apart from the "peasants" unworthy to join our "force."

Dornmont drones on in Latin about the "importance" of the Order and how society "relies" on us and our decisions, as if we aren't a group of self-interested bastards.

My Latin is piss-poor on a good day, and I'm only catching every other word of what he's saying. Over half these sad saps in the room understand even less than me. Why the Order insists on making the language a requirement of our lifetime membership is beyond me. The only time it's ever spoken is by these old fools when they feel like being especially elitist during our monthly gatherings.

I'm sure I'd see boredom written over everyone's faces if we weren't all wearing pitch-black masks beneath our hooded cloaks.

And Frederick and Roland wonder why they're ranking so poorly in the election polls. Keeping tradition "alive" means fuck all if it means needing to keep up with Duolingo.

Movement from the corner of my eye has my elbow immediately finding Spencer's ribs. His phone nearly flies out of his hand.

We subtly glare at each other. If his general fidgeting wasn't bad enough, this is the second time the fuckwit thought it'd be a good idea to text in the middle of the assembly.

"Chill out," he hisses.

He's lucky there are too many people around for me to slap him upside the head.

Attendance isn't mandatory for all the acolytes, but it would be blasphemous if the members of the high saint's family weren't present. So *texting* during it, while sitting at the very front, feels like tempting divine wrath.

We're not just the children of the high saints. We're a sign of power, another piece on the board to be wielded as the Order deems fit. Soldier or pawn—there is no difference.

This centuries-old society was here the year Cresswell was built. More accurately, the university was built for the Order, because what is an academic institute if not the breeding ground for the future's brightest?

It's how the vast majority of neophytes in this room were recruited. Each house has a dedicated person whose entire job is scouting for potential acolytes to join the organization. Once they've proven themselves and are initiated, they sit in the rows of their respective house.

Mother spears me with a look from my fiancée's side, and little Miss Abigail Dornmont stiffens.

How am I expected to spend my life with a woman who quivers like a leaf whenever we're under the same roof? It's exhausting just looking at her.

I think I've made it abundantly clear that I couldn't give two shits about what she does as long as it keeps my parents off my back. In fact, as long as she's playing her part, she's under my protection. Unless her boyfriend becomes a problem, we're staying out of each other's way.

She's attractive, I guess. Hazel eyes, with long brunette hair. In another life, I could have been into her. But she does nothing for me. No one does.

Except for *her*.

My fucking student.

The fates have an exceptional sense of humor, I'll give them that.

Acolytes suddenly start clapping for Roland and Dornmont as they descend down the steps. I missed their closing remarks. What a shame.

Roland takes his seat beside Mother, casting me a sideways warning glare as we all fix our masks back into place. I guess he noticed Spencer's insolence. I'll sign him up for toilet duty once he finishes his shift as a server. Lord knows he could use humbling.

The respectful applause turns into a roar as Daniel Flores makes his way down the pews of House Sutherland's section.

And if that isn't a bloody beautiful sound.

I can *feel* people's eyes light up behind their masks. The cultish fashion choice keeps the acolytes' anonymity from each other to avoid a lower ranked from naming names, but there's one thing we all seem to agree with: Daniel is one charismatic chap.

Or as my father likes to call him, "a liberal socialist twat."

Roland is absolutely *seething* in his seat. Nothing makes my day quite like it.

Five years ago Daniel was a nobody paladin who'd been loyal to House Sutherland since day one. But he's now risen to be the greatest threat to my father and future father-in-law.

He's the one contender who could replace one of the current houses. Daniel has the acolytes eating out of the palm of his hand—something my father hasn't been able to pull off.

Daniel is everything he's not: He's young (late thirties) and fun, has a full head of hair, and is actually likable.

Someone hoots, and it's truly fantastic not needing to hide my grin behind the mask.

"Thank you, my brothers and sisters. Please, I don't deserve such a warm welcome." Daniel beams, placing a hand over his heart.

"So humble," Spencer quietly snorts from beside me.

It helps that Daniel isn't wearing the two red ropes that high saints wear. All he has is the cloak like the rest of us.

"Many of us are strangers to each other, but every month we come under the same roof for the same reason. For generations we have held the power to make this world better." Try corrupt, dangerous, immoral instead. "We've written the footnotes of history while others got the headlines. We carry the burden of the unseen, day in and day out. We do it for us, and our children, and our children's children."

Kill me now.

Look, the guy knows how to move people, and I agree with what he's saying. I simply want no part in witnessing any of it. I have a running list of things to do that impact my livelihood, and none of those things involve the Order.

"Except we aren't doing it for our children anymore."

Here we go. Time to make Roland's eyes roll.

"For all the influence we hold in this world; the blood, sweat, and tears we've spilled for our houses—What have we gained? Where did the wealth go? To serve the few in the hopes that we may one day be in their position." He looks amongst the crowd.

Daniel caters to the neophytes and the paladins, the lowest ranked that Roland and Dornmont are falling behind on. They forgot who bleeds so they can have their money. Daniel hasn't.

"I stand here before you not to rule you. I am here to be your partner. Someone you can trust to act in *your* interest and your children's interest, and the interest of your children's children."

Okay, let's wrap it up.

"So as you vote this cycle, I ask only one thing: What do you value?" He walks in a slow circle around the dais. "Our power comes at the price of corruption, but what matters is what you intend to do with it. Be puppets or be the ones holding the water while the world above is on fire? Remember, we work together in the shadows to live in the light."

Fuck it. Maybe I'll vote for him instead of House Sutherland.

The room erupts into applause as Daniel returns to his seat, and I do what any good son must to support his father's campaign, I bring my hands together and clap louder than any other person in our row.

Daniel stands up on the platform, smiling like a man who already knows he's won. The question is, whose seat is he going to take: Father's, the Dornmonts', or the Hopkins'?

The grand magistrate's right-hand man drifts up the platform to the center candelabra to extinguish its flame with a candle snuffer.

And that concludes the ceremonial part of tonight's gathering.

People jump to their feet almost instantaneously. Most of the acolytes will be leaving here in their robes and masks, changing right before they make it to the public eye.

I'm not a jealous person, and yet I envy every person who gets to leave. More so when Roland comes right up to me as soon as I stand. Abi and Spencer—those lucky bastards—make themselves scarce.

My sperm donor removes his mask and orders me to do the same. Obviously I keep it on.

I grit my teeth when he wraps an arm around my shoulders and pulls me against him like we have a healthy, functional father-son relationship. It's part of his "family man" show.

He tugs me forward, to join the very back of the masses exiting the building.

He lowers his voice and keeps his expression easy. "I don't know what games you're foolish enough to think you can play, but you are here for a purpose. The moment you stop serving that purpose, I will find someone more useful."

The mask hides my scowl.

His arm drops from around me as we file out of the room, and like a good, leashed dog, I follow him into his study down the hall. The chandelier lights up and illuminates a room that's straight out of a 1960s Hollywood Mafia don's lair. It's an obnoxious mixture of mahogany and red, and the occasional splash of black.

I tug off my mask and cloak to hang in the wardrobe. Looks like Spencer has already rushed here to drop his things. Roland hands me his own, and because I'm still his bitch, I put it away too, making sure it'll get nice and wrinkled in there.

"Listen here," he starts.

It takes far more effort than it should not to walk straight out the door. Slowly, I turn around, attempting to keep my posture relaxed and face expressionless while he looks down his nose at me.

"You are going to prove your worth and do everything in your power to ensure we *keep* our seat and get rid of Daniel."

I snort. I'm not much of a tattletale, but sometimes one must adapt. "Absolutely. I'll put in the request to the grand magistrate." We can't very well go around killing each other unchecked. Murder is fine as long as it's not upon another acolyte—unless our leader grants us permission, that is.

To be an acolyte is to be protected. Killing one without approval? I'd love for Roland to find out the repercussions of such a decision. In fact, I'd volunteer to liberate his soul from his body.

He stiffens—a reaction I appreciate greatly. "He is a threat to the Order."

"I'll put that in the request."

The corner of his lips twitch. The signet ring on his pinky glints against the golden light. I still have its mark permanently indented into the outside of my knee from when he took a swipe at me for stumbling over his shoes.

"I didn't raise you to be disrespectful to your superiors," he snaps.

"You didn't raise me." *You did, however, beat me to the point where I didn't dare speak to or look at you anymore.* Pre-Shepherd days, of course. It wasn't until Spencer came along that I grew a backbone and turned my silence into rage, then made it into art.

"No? Who paid for you to get where you are?" he asks, English accent thick as he pours himself two fingers of scotch.

"As a businessman, I expect you to know the difference between raising and funding."

The only show of Roland's rising anger is the twitch of his hand before he sips the amber liquid. Shepherd and Roland are alike in that sense, but my sperm donor has always been more liberal with his words.

"Enough of the attitude. You like to think you're so tough just because you know how to use a knife. Need I remind you of the commitments you have been woefully neglecting? Perhaps it's time I consider how to fully integrate your brother into the Order."

A kill.

The Order recruits Cresswell students and tests their loyalty in different ways. Most of them trade secrets or favors; but a select few earn their place through blood—so far I've spared Spencer from being one of them.

"You'll have to be more specific of what those are. I'm a man of many talents," I say, attempting to appear casual while I'm grinding my molars.

"Let me spell it out for you. People have noticed your absence at home and by your future wife's side. They are beginning to see the farce behind our alliance with the Dornmonts. Your lack of enthusiasm is costing me my campaign. It's because of *you* that we're losing voters' confidence," he spits out.

It's on the tip of my tongue to wish him all the best with the campaign because I'm calling off the wedding—but I know better.

"Should I lose this election because you failed to play your part, I will ensure that everything you've ever loved withers away until all that's left is for you to fall to your knees and beg me to end the pitiful remnants of your life. Do I make myself clear?"

"Crystal," I say through clenched teeth.

He gives me one final look of disdain before dismissing me with his departing words. "Learn your place or be put in it."

11

MADDOX

I don't like interacting with people on the best of days. On the worst of days, taking a cyanide pill would be more pleasurable.

Which is why, as I usually do, I start a one-hour timer for the *mix and mingle* that follows each monthly Order assembly.

Any less, and I'll be in trouble. Any more, and someone would end up dying.

The room is buzzing with medici, high saints, and any lower-ranked members who are considered the elite in the big world: tech moguls, CEOs, judges, politicians, multibillionaires.

It doesn't matter who I speak to, they don't look all too impressed with talking to me either. They don't know me as the man Shepherd calls if he wants someone moved out of the way. All they see is the washed-up son of a high saint. A talentless hack.

Four years ago these people were begging to get a piece from me to hang up in their office. Now they wouldn't take it even if I were giving it to them for free.

I'm grabbing a drink from the bar when Spencer's distinct voice catches my attention.

A girl is walking away from him, giggling while a friend of mine stares my brother down—my brother, who should be walking around serving food and drinks, not pissing off the heir of one of the most ruthless Mafia families in the country.

I cross the room in case I need to help Spencer pick his organs off the floor.

"Breathe in my sister's direction, and you'll find out what your kneecaps look like on a platter, Spencer," Angelo growls out at Spencer, who's grinning like a bloody fool.

Angelo Zaccardi could break my brother's spine with his pinky while sipping a glass of bourbon. I wouldn't be surprised if he's done it before. His family didn't make it to where they are through their kindness.

He and Theo Sutherland are the only acolytes whose company I've enjoyed since befriending them almost nineteen years ago. They're two of the very few people aware of the part I play in the Order. Turns out we all like bouncing ideas off each other to see how creative we can get with murder.

"Keep it in your pants for two hours, will you?" I tell Spencer off. Everyone is getting on my last nerve tonight.

My brother grins. "Junior has been locked up for seven days already."

"I didn't need to know that," I mutter at the same time Angelo says in disbelief, "You named him *Junior*?"

"Unsurprising," Theo mutters. How Sutherland's been elected a high saint when he's a bitter bastard on the best of days has always been a mystery to me.

Theo's family has held their position within the Order for almost two centuries. House Sutherland's reelection is a sure thing.

"Yup." Spencer shrugs. "I'm still tossing up between that or Lord Hardwick."

I shake my head. It's a wonder how we grew up under the same roof.

"You know they have me cleaning up the candle wax after this," Spencer complains to no one in particular.

"And the toilets."

He frowns. "I've only been put down for after-party and chamber floors."

"Then I suggest you recheck your schedule."

"Dude, you're fucking with me." He glares at me in disbelief. "I have practice tomorrow morning. At this rate I won't be finished until the ass crack of dawn—and I had plans after this."

"You should've thought of that before making hookup arrangements during the assembly."

Spencer looks at me like I just kicked a puppy. But something behind me makes him change his tune.

"Never mind." Spencer slaps my back. "You've got a bigger fish to fry."

The little fuck disappears and drags Angelo with him before I can ask him to explain. My mother's ear-piercing voice is all the answer I need.

The torment continues.

"There he is," she singsongs, so sickly sweet it turns my taste buds sour.

She waltzes through the crowd in her stiletto court heels, blond hair back in a low bun, wearing a satin peplum dress worthy of the Duchess of Cambridge.

Half the room knows her to be the venomous snake she is. The other half thinks she's a goddess made into flesh. Me, on the other hand? The five-inch scar on my back knows Annabel Shaw for who she really is: the woman who helped turn me into a serial killer.

I still remember the look of disdain she gave me the first and only time I went crawling to her, bloody and bruised, with my back torn open after Roland decided to carry out his *teachings*. She didn't wipe my wounds or offer any words of support that a child might expect from their mother. The woman who gave birth to me threw me a towel and told me to wipe the trail of blood that dirtied her floor.

I may not fully blame her for being a horrific mother after what she's endured under Roland, but I do fault her for turning her pain into a weapon to inflict on others.

She glides toward me, my betrothed in tow. I toss my whiskey back without tasting it. I need to see if the bartender has absinthe. If not, bleach will do.

"Mads," Abi greets with faux endearment.

I throw up a little every time she calls me that. She keeps her eyes trained somewhere in my general vicinity and never directly on me, like she's scared I'm going to shiv her when she least expects it.

She stiffly ambles up to my side and loops her arm around mine, just *barely* touching me. I've had broken bones that hurt less than the pain I'm feeling from staying still. She plants a timid kiss on my cheek, and it's even more of an effort not to recoil.

Mother dearest glances around like she's making sure someone saw the most unconvincing show of affection in history. Her eyes snap down to my left hand, and the lack of reaction is enough indication that she approves of my ring.

I got it from the Dollar Tree. I plan on making someone choke on it in the foreseeable future.

"Maddox," Eric Hopkins—heir to House Hopkins and overgrown boarding school twat—booms, clapping me on the shoulder like we're old friends.

I would say that our friendship is akin to how close Icarus was to the sun. In other words, it's on my bucket list to set him on fire.

"Aren't you two a sight for sore eyes," he says loud enough for the whole room to hear. "When's the wedding?"

Mother interjects before I can say *never*. "We're finalizing a date at the moment. But you can expect an invitation soon for the start of next year."

Excuse me?

When the fuck was anyone going to tell me about this? I was led to believe that it would happen between eighty months to never from now.

Fuck.

Fuck.

Being tied to that woman for an eternity sounds like a death sentence. But I wouldn't just be tying myself to Abi; I'd be entrenching my position within the Order. Playing hitman keeps me on the sidelines just enough to stay out of the political limelight. With Abi, I'll be marrying into the Order. There would be no chance of escape.

What's the alternative? What if our sperm donor gets Shepherd to take Spencer under his wing?

My brother would never survive that training. I barely did. Getting beaten because I was too slow to block a kick. Starved for my insolence. Degraded for the barest sign of weakness.

Before making my first kill, I hesitated for half a second. A heartbeat of doubt before slitting a man's throat. I was sixteen. Forty-eight hours in a pitch-black room with no bed, food, or water was my punishment.

Shepherd may not have carried out the torture himself, but he was the one who gave the order.

It was all a mind game. Strip away their armor, then give them just enough to need you again. He brought me unimaginable pain, then held my hand as he took me to an art museum and told me the history behind each piece. He's the one who bought my first slab of clay.

Images flash of my brother losing the light in his eyes as he takes his first life. Killing isn't for everyone, and Spencer is more likely to adopt a fly as a pet and teach it tricks than end its life.

I have to figure out a way out of this ridiculous marriage without ruining his life in the process.

Abi looks woefully unsurprised by our wedding revelation. I narrow my eyes at her, and she freezes.

Oh, spare me the dramatics.

"The grand magistrate has confirmed his attendance," Mother boasts.

I grind my molars, hating the phantom pains that flare up from the scars along my back every time I'm in the general vicinity of either of the two people who sired me.

Eric turns his attention to me. "Where's the venue?"

The man is fishing, and he's not even decent enough to do it discreetly.

Mother blabbers on with her answer as I bite back a yawn. I've had six hours of sleep in the past forty-eight hours. Shepherd, the faculty, and my latest painting have left me running on steam, and I haven't had a chance to sit down to watch Reyna's latest assignment.

The video has been sitting on my laptop, waiting for me to press play. It's all I've been able to think about. As painful as it's been, I've managed to refrain from watching it until I've done enough of the cliffside painting that I've earned it. *Finally*, tonight's the night.

My phone's silent timer goes off.

I clap my hands together, startling my betrothed. "Well, I wish I could say this catch-up has been lovely. But we all know it never is. I'm off."

"Going so soon?" Mother inquires, a silent threat to stay put.

"Not soon enough." If I heed her warning, I'm going to turn Eric into Reyna's next short film.

Just as I'm about to leave, Abi sinks her nails into my arm. Like a damn deer in headlights, she flushes white and releases me.

Right.

Most people bid their would-be spouses farewell. I look at her. Then my mother. Then back at Abi's hopeful face. My gaze drops down to her lips, and it's an effort not to curl mine into a scowl because another pair comes into mind.

Reyna's.

Abi must see my inner turmoil, because she takes one for the team and leans over to brush a kiss on my cheek that I can barely feel.

I pull away and storm out of the room like hell is on my heels—I'm ignoring Roland's calls for me. I don't have the mental capacity or the energy to speak with him.

Reyna's video is sitting on my laptop, waiting for me. No god—or evil—is about to keep me from it.

My shoes click against the marble floor as I make my exit and spill out into the chandelier-lit hallway. To avoid any further interaction, I use the underground passageway. Cold air slams into me. It's a welcome distraction. I shut the entranceway behind me, turn my phone's flash on, and navigate the underground system most acolytes refuse to use because, and I quote, "it's cold as shit" and it gives them "the creeps."

Why they'd feel such a thing surrounded by thousands of human remains is beyond me. They're dead already. Well past the point of decay. It's rather childish to cause such a fuss over it. I personally find the stacked femurs and skulls artful.

The cold seeps through my coat as I pass through the catacombs and to the storage area. Beyond it is a spiraling stone staircase.

Carefully, I inch the hidden door open to check no one is there before sliding the bookshelf back in place. The campus is mostly deserted at this time of night.

As I keep my pace up on my way to the art building, I can't help but take hopeful glances around in case I spot one student in particular slinking through the darkness. Shaking my head, I all but run up the stairs to my studio.

Since the day I watched Reyna root around my crime scene, her videos have been playing on repeat. All the short films she's posted online, her previous assignments, the student movies she's featured in. I'm starved for new material.

I pour myself a glass of scotch, settle behind my desk, and boot up my laptop. It's been too long since I've seen her, and I'm itching for my next hit.

The scene starts with a view of the sunrise from a footpath beside a river—

I swear to God, if I find out that Reyna makes a habit of hanging out underneath *bridges* in the early hours of the morning, I'm chaining her to me.

Her husky voice vibrates through the speakers and down my spine, flushing away the irritation. As the film progresses, I forget all about her questionable safety practices. Her shots are immaculate. She's taken every piece of advice I gave her. Like her other projects, I'm not quite sure yet which of my kills she's reinterpreting.

It isn't until the camera pans to her standing before an architectural landmark that it clicks.

Vincent Horven. An architect I killed over a year ago. I carved out his bones, washed them, then put him back together.

From what Shepherd told me, he was associated with the Order. Based on my own research, I discovered that his penchant for violence made him lose visitation rights to his children.

I've also dug up and read through everything I could possibly find on Reyna's movements, medical background, and university records. I know for a fact she hadn't moved to New York yet when I carried out the hit. Was she piecing my kills together over a matter of years, or once she moved here?

Another realization hits me, and my knuckles go white around the crystal tumbler. It's something so obvious, yet it never clicked before.

Reyna studied every incision, each meticulous placement of limbs, and droplets of blood. She saw the death and destruction I caused, and she wasn't terrified. Even more, she was inspired.

She didn't run for the hills, or call the police about her discoveries. No, that girl knows how monstrous I could be, and she still investigates my crime scenes. She even took photos and made several short films that anyone could stumble across. I'm torn between being exhilarated by the realization and downright pissed off.

What if the serial killer she was following around wasn't me? What if she stumbles across a kill carried out by someone else in the Order?

I'm half tempted to put a tracker on her so she can't go anywhere without me knowing since her safety is nowhere on her list of concerns.

I pause the video when the scene cuts to Reyna, sitting at her desk, staring off into the distance as the golden light from a small lamp licks her bronze skin. It's the only source of light in the frame, and if I hadn't paused it, I would have missed the skull design on the candle beside the lamp.

A smile splits across my lips, and I let out an amused laugh. She's re-creating the painting of *The Repentant Magdalen* by La Tour.

Brava, Miss Sinaga. Well done.

The scene shifts to a bathroom, where a tub brims with steaming water. I stop breathing altogether when Reyna enters the frame in nothing but a thin cream singlet. She's turned away from the camera. All I have to go off is from her waist up, and fuck if the sight of those tiny, breakable straps doesn't drive me feral. My cock twitches to life at the thought of her naked as water trickles between her breasts. She'd lean back and spread her legs to—

I clear my throat and readjust myself to alleviate the pressure.

She's my student.

She's eleven years younger than me.

She's an innocent civilian who's not part of the Order.

I'm getting married soon.

All of these things are *clear* signs that I should have zero interest in her and keep my distance. Yet I would sacrifice anything to have her turn around so I could see what she looks like through the thin material.

Almost her entire back is covered in black and gray ink. I wish I could strip her so I could study the art she deemed worthy to brand onto her body for the rest of eternity.

I want to be the only person she bares herself before. I want to be the only one who sees the tattoos she hides from the world, and I'm turning murderous thinking about anyone else seeing what she looks like in that goddamn singlet.

My breaths grow shallow as the scene progresses, and I'm mildly tempted to ask her who was holding the camera, so I can liberate their soul from their body. The scene focuses on the dips of her rib cage, the delicate curve of her vertebrae, and the roll of her shoulder blades, before she steps into the tub. Slowly, the pieces fall into place.

She's washing her skin and bones, like I did to the subject of that art installation.

Reyna is turning herself into my pretty little muse.

My dick pushes against the zipper of my pants hard enough to cause pain.

I am aware that what she's portraying is a ritualistic act of cleansing and purification. The foretelling of connection between the victim and the killer waiting on the other side of the door. But I've lost the war to my hindbrain. My base instincts drive me to undo my belt, slip my pants and briefs down, and fist my cock.

I curse, dropping my head against the chair, imagining her soft hands gripping me. Pleasure zips down my spine as I draw my hand up, tightening the pressure at the tip. I can already hear it. *See* it. What she'd be like under me.

She'd moan my name and shudder as she flicks her tongue out to taste me. This woman is wearing me down every single day, and she doesn't even know she's doing it. I'm hooked when she hasn't raised a finger.

Precome leaks when her bare back appears on the screen. Soap suds and water trickle down her skin as she cleans herself with a plain white bar of soap. Half of her body is hidden beneath the bubbles, but it doesn't stop my pulse from pounding against my chest.

My fist picks up speed. That's what I'd see if I fucked her against a wall. Reyna's hand braced next to mine, crying out as I drive into her until she can't hold her own weight.

Tension draws from the base of my cock.

Even her bloody bare back drives me insane. Not knowing what her face looks like as she comes is enough to make me go completely mad. Fuck, I need to hear her say my name. I'd be completely and utterly done for if she did.

That husky voice of hers. The curve of her ass. Her fucking legs I need choking me as my nose rubs against her clit while I taste that cunt of hers.

The pleasure takes me over the edge. Ropes of white cover my hand as light flashes behind my eyes. It's nowhere near enough. Nothing compared to what it'd feel like to be inside of her.

When I look back up, electricity flows through me with a different need. I want to draw her. Need to. It's a soul-deep desire as necessary as food and water. I pause the film to trace the dark lines permanently etched into her back.

It's a dragon. A *naga*.

And just like that, lightning strikes, a dam breaks somewhere in the distance.

I know what my main piece is going to be.

12

MADDOX

I have a pile of assignments waiting to be graded.

An exhibit to prepare for.

A research paper to draft.

Someone to kill.

A brother to protect and a woman I'm meant to be marrying to protect said brother.

Yet as I move through the dim-lit library, ostensibly to chip away at the endless list, something intrinsic in my soul, like a compass pointing north, makes me turn my head right and peer around the shelves.

Reyna.

The organ in my chest gives an unfamiliar stutter as I come to a stop. Finishing to the thought of her three nights ago has only worsened my desire for her.

The very last thing I have time for is a student who already occupies far too much of my thoughts. Every part of my brain is screaming at me to leave her well be.

But that compass is still pointing, and my soul and body are at its whim.

"Miss Sinaga."

She doesn't hear me, lightly bobbing her head to the music playing through her headphones as she concentrates on the screen. The cold glow of the library computer brushes her tanned skin, creating a stark contrast against the green light streaming from the desk lamps.

Dark-brown eyes flick my way, and she jolts back, yanking her headphones off. "Mr. Shaw," she gasps, glancing at our deserted surroundings.

She's beautiful. I think that every time I see her.

There's no one around to witness our interaction. This place is usually a ghost town past dinnertime. The idea shouldn't thrill me, but it does—if she tries to run, I'd be the only one here to catch her. I almost wish she would so I would have an excuse to chase her. I'm sure the faculty would love if I did exactly that.

Reyna's too busy being shocked—and just as confused as I am by my stupidity in approaching her—to notice those dark thoughts.

"Another late night?"

And there I go starting up an actual conversation. No wonder Roland thinks I'm a fool.

Reyna glances at her screen. "It's seven."

"As I said, it's late. Not exactly the safest hour." I frown at the bright-yellow object sitting a couple of inches from her bag. "Why is there an EpiPen on the table?"

This is the second time I've seen her with one.

Red kisses her cheeks. "Just in case I need it. I thought there were nuts in my takeout a couple hours ago. I took some antihistamines as a preventative but . . . yeah. Sorry. Coast clear, I guess."

Reyna laughs nervously and shoves it into her brown leather satchel.

She has a nut allergy? Why was this not underlined in red in her student profile? This is pure negligence on the university's part. I'll be having words with the administration manager to ensure this doesn't happen again.

"What specifically are you allergic to?" Ignoring her protests, I take the EpiPen out of her bag.

"You can't just grab things out of my—" She reaches for my arm, and I hold my breath in the hopes she closes the distance. My pulse hammers as she drops her hand back onto her lap, stopping short of touching me.

I turn the pen in my hand until I find the small black inscription. It expires in two months. "Is this the only one you have?"

She nods. "I only need one."

Incorrect. She should have one in her bag and another in her pocket at all times.

There should also be one in every room she enters, and every class she has. Another oversight on the university's part.

"What type of nuts can't you eat?"

"Um, just tree nuts."

I nod.

I'm willing to admit my own shortcomings. Not knowing the classes of nuts is one of them. A fact that will change before the day ends.

Her throat bobs, and the traitorous, torturous, perverted part of my psyche pictures her splayed out on her back, head tipped over the edge as I watch her choke on every inch of my cock I feed her. Not exactly something I should be thinking about when discussing anaphylaxis.

"What are you doing here?"

My eyes snap to hers. Fuck. If I stand for another second with her mouth in line with my groin, she'll see just what she does to me.

Invading her personal space yet again, I lower myself into the chair next to hers and start reading the screenwriting assignment she never offered to show me.

"I-It's not very good. It's still a draft. So don't judge it—or read it for that matter. I'm just getting the skeleton down," she rushes out, but doesn't seem to dare move closer as her eyes flicker between me and the two inches of space between our knees.

Her bloody throat bobs again.

There is quite literally nothing stopping me from fucking off back to my office because Lord knows I have a lot of things to do. None of which include picturing myself throat fucking my student.

Instead, in a move that can only be described as willful self-sabotage, I nod my head at the document on the computer. "Is anyone dying in it?"

She blinks, mouth opening and closing before she realizes what I'm referring to. "No, but someone cuts off their own leg," she says skeptically.

"How?" *Not why.*

She notices that too, if her narrowing eyes are any indication. "An axe."

I hum.

"What?" Reyna crosses her arms, and I curse every god in existence when it makes her breasts swell over the neckline of her chocolate-brown dress and—fuck my life—her skirt rides up her thighs. "You think it's screwed up and disgusting?"

I frown. I, for one, very much dislike the implication that someone might have said that to her. "No, I was going to say it's overdone. Why not a standard wood saw?"

Her lips part on an *O*, and the soft blush that kissed her cheeks earlier blazes pink. It's like a candle flickers to life behind her eyes, because she brightens and the lines around her frame soften.

She shakes her head. "Too time-consuming."

True. Messy too. "A chainsaw is quick."

"But not personal enough."

"A cleaver," I suggest.

A soft divot forms between her brows. It's the same look she gets whenever she's thinking hard in class.

"A bread knife would be kind of comedic—or a cheese knife." A subtle grin twists her lips as she speaks, and it takes everything in me to fight back my own.

"Just as time-consuming as a saw."

Her long hair drifts over her shoulders as she tips her head to the side. "I'm actually curious to know which one would be faster."

Don't offer to find out for her, I tell myself. But I mentally note to discover the answer. For myself, obviously. Professional curiosity.

The irony isn't lost on me. She's learning composition; I'm perfecting decomposition.

I shrug. "Money's on the bread knife. Worse grip, but sturdier blade."

"Huh. That's a good point." She purses her lips, the corners tipping upward. "It might work, actually. I have him making himself toast every morning as part of his monotonous routine."

She's practically hand-feeding me ideas for my own work. I believe I have a chef somewhere on my kill list. "Will the blood be pink in that assignment too?"

Her brows shoot up her forehead. I dislike that I don't know the reason behind her shock at such a simple question. "That's reserved for your class. Bradford hated it." She rolls her eyes.

I scoff, risking leaning back now that I'm not about to stab her in the eye with my cock. "Bradford can't recognize talent."

"And you can?"

"Yes." My own work may have gone to shit, but I still have eyes.

I take it back. My cock may still demand her attention if she keeps innocently biting her lip like that. How have I become so easy?

"Who would you consider to be the most promising student in our class? Bradford thought Nicole was a natural," she says a couple volumes lower.

Reyna's fishing, and I won't be the one to tell her what she wants to hear. That would take this to another level we shouldn't go near. But my answer would be her. In all of my classes, she's the one who shows the most potential for greatness.

"It's unprofessional for me to pick favorites, let alone discuss them with you, Miss Sinaga." I keep my tone scolding, and it's like lighting a fuse beneath her. It's good to know she's as reactive as I am.

"And discussing methods of dismemberment isn't?" she argues.

I almost prefer it when she acts like she hates me, because then I can fool myself into loathing her. For a couple of seconds at least, before the sick thrill of her attention on me drags me closer to the edge of completely losing it.

Every inch of her was carved by a being of the divine, and each sentence past her plump, biteable lips seems to have been strung together to keep me in her web.

"Everything can be turned into an artform. Just as you've made blood pink. I'm curious to know what the thought process behind it was. It was never explained in your prior assignments."

I'm curious about everything to do with her.

"What's your take on it?" She says it like a challenge, as if she thinks I'll never figure it out—and bloody fucking hell does she have me right where she wants me.

I *feel* myself sitting straighter. Feel the cogs turning in my head, the beat of my heart. It's like going into a test where I'm ninety percent certain I know the material better than the back of my hand, but there's still the ten percent.

"It's never simply an aesthetic choice where you're involved."

The barest hint of a smile ghosts over her lips. It's the knowing kind, like I've acknowledged a secret that's been weighing her down. It's distracting.

And it's going straight to my head.

I fear the library isn't big enough for how easily she stokes my ego.

I clear my throat. "One, that there's a significant gender disparity in the film industry. Of the top films, under ten percent of directors were women, and about sixteen percent of all directors, producers, writers, editors, et cetera, were women. Which leads to two, you mentioned being able to tell if the creator was a man or a woman. No male would choose such a color."

Reyna's wide brown eyes have me feeling like some kind of idiot for wanting to puff my chest out like some pubescent attempting to woo a high school crush with basic knowledge.

"Thirdly, one I believe may just be a happy coincidence, the softening of violence through the weaponization of a stigmatized color, and making the murder feel surreal, dreamlike, or even innocent." She's still staring. I clear my throat for the second time, skin warming under her attention. "Just to name a few."

Her mouth is open in astonishment, and all I can still think about is what it would look like to have those lips wrapped around my cock.

I cross my legs, resting my ankle on my knee as I ease back in my chair. "Miss Sinaga, I could draft a dissertation theorizing your intentions, but I'd rather hear it from the source."

"What you said. Plus, there's two more parts to it."

She sits straighter. Her tone is even and confident, tinged with a spark of preemptive anger, and a splash of defensiveness. Bradford's doing, I assume.

"On one hand, there's sentimentality. On the other hand, like you said, society has prescribed notions of femininity and masculinity to specific colors.

Using pink as the blood is the feminization of violence typically caused by men. It's ironic, contradictory, and elicits emotional dissonance. Jarring, and it makes men uncomfortable. The word *girly* sits on the tip of their tongue, but they never say it, because the level of brutality of the crime was fueled by testosterone and male ego. A color is a color. Whether the liquid bleeding from a puncture wound is green or blue or even purple."

There are many firsts in my life that I will never remember. My first steps. The first painting I did. My very first purchase.

Now, I will always remember the time I got completely hard listening to a student discuss the interplay of social constructivism, art, and death.

My cock is throbbing.

Having an intellectual discussion with Reyna is making my cock *throb.*

And unless I move, she's going to see the bulge in my slacks, and I'll have an appointment with the dean first thing.

Reyna must know something is wrong, because she frowns when I lean forward to balance my elbows on my knees and clasp my hands together.

"What's the other part? What's sentimental about it?" Bloody hell, did my voice just break?

Her eyes drop to the floor. "Mom liked to 'make things pretty.' Growing up, she was a big fan of dressing me up in pink, and she found it hilarious when I'd throw a tantrum over it." She smiles sadly to herself, looking back up at me. "But I was a *tomboy.*" She puts it in air quotes. "I was into scary movies and sci-fi and all the other things little girls weren't meant to be interested in."

Reyna leans back in her chair, more relaxed than I've seen her before, as if we're old friends sharing stories.

Another thing I'm enjoying too much.

The boner is here to stay, but I like hearing about her life far more than a professor should of their student. It's a part of her she hasn't put on paper, and she's giving me a piece of her just for me to hold and study, and I want so much more of it.

"Mom was the old-school type with traditional ideas for some things. You know, like how girls should be playing with dolls, and always sit with their legs crossed, and wear cute dresses and always look put together. Get married and start a family, even if she didn't . . ."

She drifts off. I want to pry, but it's not my place to.

"Anyway, one night Mom caught me watching a movie I wasn't supposed to. She said it's not for girls because it's too scary. I asked her what would make it less scary, and she answered, 'If the blood were pink.' I guess I recalled the conversation when I decided on my project."

"This is why it's always best to hear it straight from the source." I clamp my teeth to stop my lips from curling. "And the ink? You titled your project Pink Ink, yet you've never used it in any of your films."

"No one's ever asked me that before." Reyna might as well have sucker punched me, because it would have the same effect as seeing the smile that splits across her face. She glows like the power of the heavens is radiating from her.

I understand now why people speak of being knocked off their feet because of a smile. I never fully saw the beauty in the movement of muscle beyond how the contrast creates dimension and provides the subject with emotion.

But under the harsh light from the screen monitor against the warmth of the surrounding lamps, I see it, and it really is beautiful. I could stare for hours and never stop feeling that glow penetrating the darkness of my soul, and as I watch her lips move, I understand addiction, crawling back to the high that could ruin me.

"Ink leaves a stain, but if you scrub it hard enough, it'll disappear from the naked eye, but traces of it will always linger as long as you know where to look. It's a reference to grief and the everlasting stain of death."

My chest is heavy listening to her speak, because I know I'm well and truly fucked. I'll never come back from Reyna. Never recover. Never move on.

I need to run as bloody far as I can get and put an ocean between us so I can have a fighting chance of purging this sickness from my body.

She lifts a shoulder. "And to your second point, ink is a bitch to work with and doesn't have the same consistency as blood."

My first guess was that she intended to use ink but quickly backtracked.

"Did your mother support your affinity for the dark when you got older?" I can't stop myself from finding out more.

That glow dims, and I regret asking. "As I grew up, she was happy as long as I was happy, but I knew she never understood my interests . . . or how I came to like them."

"How did you come to enjoy looking at and re-creating murders?"

Brown eyes lock on mine, and without a hint of embarrassment or regret, she answers, "I think I was born with something off-kilter about me."

And that may just be my favorite thing about her. "Some people were made to be that way."

"That might be worse because that means there's someone to blame."

I frown at the discomfort building in my chest. This is getting too close and personal for my liking. I've been in her presence for too long, and it was a reckless decision on my part to approach her out in public.

I stand, shucking my coat on to leave like I should've done ten minutes ago.

"Let me walk you to the subway."

Reyna shakes her head, fighting me on every turn as per usual. "I'll still be here for a couple more hours. I want to finish this assignment tonight, if I can."

"Miss Sinaga, you cannot be walking—"

"Thank you for your concern, Mr. Shaw." She cuts me off.

The absolute gall of this woman. "We've discussed this before. It's not safe for you. I can either call you a cab or walk you to the station."

"No, thank you."

I sigh, exasperated. "Miss Sinaga, must we keep going around in circles?"

"It appears we must." She grabs her headphones off the table. "Enjoy the rest of your night, Mr. Shaw." Then she turns around, plays her music, and pretends I'm not standing here staring at her like some lunatic.

Add one more thing on my to-do list: escort Reyna home without her noticing.

13

REYNA

"Guess how much these cost me." Kimi taps her acrylic claws on the table, half an inch away from my bowl.

I could guess, but either way, it didn't come out of her wallet. Whenever her dad limits her bank account, random men step up—hair, nails, eyelashes, Botox, weekly facials, massages, all the things I wish I were in the tax bracket to even *think* about doing.

"You could take an eye out with those things." I spoon the disappointing, Westernized nasi goreng into my mouth.

She holds her hand up, admiring the flowery design. "Exactly. You know who to call if you need them for one of your scenes. As long as it's not too fucked-up, I'm in."

There are those words again. *Fucked-up.*

I brush them off because I know she doesn't mean it as an insult. She supports what I do and what I like, but she doesn't see what I see. "Don't get too ahead of yourself. I need to come up with a new concept for that to happen."

There are plenty of kills by the Shadow that I could choose from for my next project, but none of them have me hooked. The recent ballerina-esque murder was inspiring, except I don't know anyone who does ballet. My two left feet sure won't be playing the victim in it.

Obviously, I could come up with my own murder idea. In fact, I really want to. But it weirdly feels like I'd be betraying the Shadow if I did. So unless he has a new kill, I'm stuck with the ballerina idea. But . . .

"You took dance when you were younger, right?"

Kimi grimaces. "I did hip-hop for, like, six months, then got kicked out for arguing with one of the other girls."

"Arguing?"

"I threw my shoe at her," she clarifies.

"Same thing." It's a wonder how she's never spent a night in jail.

"I love that you support women's wrongs." Kimi grins.

I roll my eyes. "That's not a blanket rule. A lot of women do terrible things."

"And we love it. A woman doing wrong is just a woman acting the way men get away with—wait." Kimi double-taps her phone to check the time. "Shit. I'm so late." She jumps to her feet and contorts her fingers in an unnatural angle to hold her iced coffee, phone, wallet, keys, and books in a single hand.

Frowning, I check my watch. "Our next class doesn't start for another two hours." We both picked psychology as our elective paper. Turns out, we both suck at stats, so we're like dumb and dumber in that class.

Kimi winks at me. "I have a hot date."

"With a new flavor or an old one?"

"A rich one. *Owen.*" She sings his name.

"What happened to Jake?"

"Jack," she corrects. "Jake was the one before him. I saw him run up the stairs, and immediately got the ick. His personality was nice while it lasted—and he didn't last very long."

I chuckle at the innuendo. I'm not sure how that girl manages to go on a date every week. Over eighty percent of the time, it's with a new guy. "You really need to stay away from guys whose name starts with *J*."

"Babe, you haven't lived unless you've been traumatized by at least one dude with the letter *J* at the start of their name. It's usually the Joshes," she says as she saunters away.

"Wear protection," I say a couple of volumes too loud.

And I'm not just talking condoms. Something that could take a man out for long enough to run. There's no way in hell I'd fall asleep at night without knowing she can keep herself safe.

"Okay, Mom!" she throws over her shoulder as she rushes out of the cafeteria—if it can even be called that. This place is pretty much a gourmet food court.

Way back when, this Victorian building doubled as the on-campus dorms—or orphanage. I can't quite remember. They've kept the mess hall operational ever since Cresswell opened, with exposed wooden beams above our heads and antique picture frames displaying the university's original blueprints.

The whole "old timey" open dormitory vibe is an odd contrast to the food stalls with neon signs that clearly didn't exist when this place was built.

The mess hall has every cuisine imaginable, and everything is *well* out of my budget. But every once in a while, I agree to meet Kimi here and order the cheapest thing on the menu.

Does this fried rice taste like it's worth twenty-five dollars? Absolutely not. Is it at least close to how Mom would make it? Fuck no. They're not even on the same planet. I could get the same thing back in Indonesia from a stall on the side of the road and it would cost me two bucks and taste a thousand times better.

I take bite after begrudging bite, until there isn't a single grain left on the plate. I'm not wasting my inheritance on expensive bad-tasting food I don't finish. I don't get hired as a videographer nearly often enough to pay the bills.

I nurse my half-decent coffee in my hand and mindlessly scroll through my phone. I have a hundred other things that I should be doing right now, like planning my next film project, working on my other assignments, or attempting to comprehend a statistical analysis on the behavior of chickens. Instead, I've spent over forty hours searching for a hint of what the honeycomb symbol could be. There's nothing helpful online, and I haven't found anything in the library.

Searching for the symbol and the ceiling in Dad's picture while simultaneously working, studying, and filming has made me hungover from life.

I'm at a dead end with my investigations. My creative well is drying. I got a bad grade—a B—on the screenwriting assignment I thought I did really well on. I woke up at 4 a.m. to help Nicole film her assignment. I'm on the brink of losing my scholarship. I just forked out close to a grand on new film equipment because my camera stopped working.

Honestly, I'm tired.

I want my mom. I want to know the father I never really got to have. And I want to be the star they always thought I could be.

I'm failing on all fronts.

Although, it was nice to have Shaw recognize my art and my macabre interests. It's making me feel minutely less like a total screwup.

Sighing, I pack up my shit. If I'm going to mope, I might as well do it in front of a computer. That way if I find it in me to churn out five minutes' worth of work, that's still five minutes I've shaved off.

The weight of my satchel digs into my tense shoulder, and I mumble profanities under my breath. I think I need a full-body massage on top of a two-week nap.

I turn around, and gasp when I collide with a hard wall of muscle. The half-empty cup of coffee falls from my hand, and I stumble back, reaching for the chair behind me to stop myself from slipping.

Strong hands wrap around my waist to keep me steady. Bergamot and paint assault my senses, and my gaze clashes with poison-ivy eyes and a venomous scowl. *Maddox.*

Dear fucking God, I feel like I'm a real-life Wattpad character.

I follow Shaw's line of sight.

To the man who's still touching me.

Warm hands squeeze my waist, and I tense under the stranger's hold. "You all right there? Sorry about that; I should have watched where I was going."

It takes a beat before the cafeteria stirs back up.

"I, uh . . ."

If looks could kill, he and I would be dead ten times over under Shaw's stare. Darkness pools into his eyes, and there's something in his expression that I can't quite make sense of. It's an emotion I've never seen on him that sends chills down my spine.

Beyond the war behind his eyes, he looks like he's been through hell and back, and got the shirt to prove it. It unsettles me in a way that almost makes me start asking questions about his well-being. Is it his art? Work? Family? Has he lost someone?

I have no right to know any of these things, but I'm no less curious. There's a reason behind his Jekyll and Hyde personality. He seems to wear his arrogance like it's a suit of armor, but everyone knows armor weighs a person down and makes it easier to drown.

Just like the last time I saw him disheveled, I can't help but resonate with him.

He lost his art, and right now, I'm losing mine.

I clear my throat, stepping out of reach of the stranger.

The two men are like night and day standing next to each other. Maddox, with his dark brows drawn together, five o'clock shadow, heavy bags under his eyes, radiating murderous energy. The other man with bright-blue eyes, an easy smile, and the kind of casual Shaw wishes he could convince people he had.

"You have to let me get you another one."

I stare at the man standing beside Shaw. He looks like he could be my age. It's hard to tell with the stubble he's sporting. "Another what?"

He motions toward the coffee splattered across the floor. "It's my bad. Really, I owe you another one. It'd be rude not to." His eyes twinkle to match his dazzling smile.

If Kimi were here, it'd be a hook, line, and sinker.

"Uh, that's okay." I shoot an awkward glance over to Maddox, who's glaring daggers at the space between me and the guy. My gaze shifts to the hand Pretty Boy has moved to my elbow. It's soft enough that I barely notice his grip, but there's no mistaking its insinuation.

"What about dinner, then? I know a really nice steakhouse overlooking the river. Consider it my way of apologizing." He gives me a bashful grin. "The name's Spencer by the way."

Dinner?

For one stupefying second, my deranged little brain wishes it were Maddox asking me out instead.

The last time someone offered to take me on a date within thirty seconds of meeting me would have been at a house party freshman year. He was smashed and slurring his words. Since then, the only male who has shown a modicum of interest in me is Lawrence, and that's clearly going fucking great.

"She's busy."

Our attention snaps to Maddox. From the bottom of my heart, *what the fuck?*

"She has an assignment coming up."

Spencer stares at Shaw in confusion, and my brows hike up my forehead. Who does Professor Audacity think he is? I was going to say no, but now that Shaw said that, I've changed my mind. I'm now very interested in going to dinner with a complete stranger. Why not? I do far worse things.

"Actually, I've got time. I'm almost finished with my next film." A complete lie. There is zero coherent thought swimming through my head right now. I need all the time I can get to frantically pull a fake murder together.

Either way, Shaw's assignment isn't due for a few more weeks. So what the fuck is he trying to imply here? That I need extra help or something?

Here I was thinking we were making headway after our interaction in the library.

I mean, I did visit a crime scene last night without Maddox, and I'm on the fence as to whether it was the Shadow. The artistry was there, but so was a bag of Cheetos and a packet of KitKats—my two favorite snacks—which is odd on so many levels. Both were placed near the body, modernizing the scene in a way that didn't match his usual style.

The autopsy report Lawrence sent me provided that the victim had consumed an abnormal amount of almonds prior to his death. I'm certain it was the killer's doing, I just can't figure out why. My biased brain keeps pointing out my allergies, but that couldn't have anything to do with it since the subject didn't die from anaphylactic shock.

Still, I took photos and looked around in case I end up getting inspired by this kill that may or may not be his. My heart was pounding the whole time because I thought Maddox was going to waltz through the front door to tear me a new one for visiting another crime scene.

"She's your . . . student?" Spencer asks slowly.

Shaw says, "Yes," at the same time I say, "Not really." It seems the only language we know how to speak to each other is combat.

Spencer narrows his eyes at my professor. "Define *not really*."

"It means she's unavailable," Maddox answers for me, wearing a mask of indifference.

I chastise the butterflies that are going for a joyride around my stomach. I'm meant to be livid over his whole controlling act, not ready to twirl my finger in my hair and giggle.

I whip a scathing glare his way, innocently answering, "It means that he's substituting in for my *actual* professor—who should be back at work any day now."

There are a million other things I'd rather do than go on a date with Casanova over here, but I'll go if it means sticking it to Maddox.

First, he was dictating what I can and can't do. Now, he's trying to have a say about who I can and can't see. I think the fuck not. We've been getting along, to a degree. There's no reason for me to rock the boat. But in my defense, he started it.

Spencer glares at him for a split second before a light bulb goes off in his head. A grin spreads across his lips. I'm too annoyed at Shaw to decide whether I like the look of it or not.

"Since it sounds like you're available," Spencer starts, shifting unnecessarily close while sending Maddox a dirty side-eye. "How about tomorrow night? Five o'clock. I'll pick you up."

It takes me a beat to recognize what he's doing, and *boy*, does it make me happy. Someone is pissed off at the good professor too. I give Spencer a smile so sweet it makes me sick. I'm not the flirting kind, but I'll be one if it upsets Maddox. God knows what has his panties in a twist.

He frowns like he'd rather do laps in the River Styx than let that happen. "We have a meeting scheduled for then, Miss Sinaga."

The line of Maddox's shoulder is pulled tight enough to snap. Yet he remains expressionless. If he looked like he had aged ten years when I first saw him today, then he's a new man now. Malice has given the Lord of Darkness back his youthful glow.

"This is the first I'm hearing of it. We'll have to reschedule."

Good. I sound nonchalant. *Not* like I'm developing an embarrassing middle-school crush.

I cross my arms, feeling Spencer's attention flick between us. I'm sure if there were popcorn available, he'd be clapping and enjoying the mini showdown.

"After I've shifted my schedule for it? That's inconsiderate of you." The vein in Maddox's forehead pulses.

"I'm sure you must have forgotten to send me the meeting invitation. It's a simple mistake. Unfortunately, it appears that I am now booked during that time."

He diverts his murderous attention to Spencer. "You don't even know her name."

"It's Reyna." I offer my hand to Spencer.

"That's a pretty name," he all but purrs.

Gross.

"Thanks. I was born with it." I can't help but deadpan.

Spencer places his hand on my back, and Maddox is a foot away from the man before I can blink.

"I suggest that you remove your hand from my student," Maddox states, voice deceptively calm.

The swarm of unholy things swoops low in my stomach and weakens my knees. There's that feeling of being cared for again, and *hell* if that crazed look in his eyes doesn't do sinful things to me. The way he says it is almost like he's . . . jealous.

My core tightens at the prospect.

No. Bad, Reyna.

My skin is on fire with the ridiculous blush I seem to always sport around him. There is no conceivable universe where Maddox Fucking Shaw is jealous of *anyone*, let alone some random frat bro for hitting on me. *Me* of all people. No way. Not possible. I'm imagining things.

Spencer responds with a smirk and holds his hands up in surrender. "Of course."

He turns to walk away, sending Maddox a backward glance, and there, written in white on his football jersey, is the name *SHAW*.

Wait.

They're brothers?

Maddox glares at me. "Five o'clock tomorrow. My office. Don't be late."

Then he stomps after his brother, leaving me reeling from whiplash.

What the fuck just happened?

14

REYNA

"Get on your knees, Miss Sinaga."

Hungry green eyes stare down at me. My breath catches as I lower myself onto the plush carpet, staring up at Maddox's naked body. Heat unfurls low in my core, sending tendrils of desire to every corner of my being.

The smell of sex and sweat sticks to my skin from the hours we've spent in his office, unleashing every whisper of tension that's been brewing between us. My nipples pebble in the cold room, and I arch my back in search of friction.

"He can't touch you the way I can." His thumb skates over my bottom lip. "Tell me you want me to bend you over the—"

An alarm blasts through the room, yanking me out of my lust-addled haze, and I slap my surroundings to put an end to the sound. The blankets twist around my body as I pant, blinking away the vivid dream. The duvet wedges between my thighs and presses against my swollen center. Desire swirls in my stomach, and I clamp my mouth shut to suppress a groan.

My legs curl around the thick maroon fabric to increase the pressure, and my eyes flutter closed to relish in the sensation. The foggy haze of sleep edges my mind as I move my hips against the blanket. It whispers the same tempting words that Dream Maddox said to me.

That's it. You can take it.

My fingers snake down my waist, beneath my sweatpants. My hips buck at the first caress against my clit.

So responsive, Miss Sinaga.

The pads of my fingers press against my aching core. Sparks of pleasure thrum up my spine, and I shudder when I imagine it's Maddox dipping his—

I jolt upright, snatching my hand out from my pants.

No. Nope. *Wrong. Wrong. Wrong.*

Having a sex dream about my professor is bad enough. I am *not* about to have an orgasm because of him. That's crossing way too many lines.

Jesus Christ. No. He's an ass. Not to mention *my teacher*.

Plus, I'm late. And Maddox doesn't deserve my climax. Or my dirty dreams.

I rub the back of my neck, glaring up at the ceiling, cursing the sound of cars on the other side of my bedroom's window and of Kimi chatting away on her phone in the kitchen while something sizzles in the background.

Huffing, I drag myself over to the end of the bed and intentionally don't make eye contact with the pile of laundry I dumped on my computer chair. My room isn't messy per se, but I'm not about to welcome guests with open arms either.

A couple of books I thrifted are lying around, waiting for me to make space for them on my shelf. I dumped my filming equipment in the corner after helping Nicole with her project yesterday. It's also been on my list to get double-sided tape to stick down the corner of one of my movie posters that's lifted from the exposed-brick "feature" wall—my guess is that it was a cost-cutting decision. The landlord special.

So much to do. So little energy.

I force myself to extract my body from the comfort of my bed and all things associated with the deplorable things my professor did to me in my dream last night.

"Morning sunshine!" Kimi twists around from the stove when I whip open the door.

She gives me a once-over like she knows what I was dreaming about, and the thought that she might have caught me makes my stomach flutter in an extra concerning way.

Fucking hell. I need a cold shower.

I walked into the biweekly film workshop early with my chin high and every intention of getting on with my life and pretending like whatever weird shit went on yesterday never happened.

After tossing and turning all evening, I boiled Maddox's reaction down to stress and exhaustion. What I thought was jealousy was probably just irritation that his brother was potentially harming his career.

I'm not sure how far the scope of fraternization goes, but it probably covers family members dating your student, right? Public perception doesn't need a contract for that type of stuff to be considered wrong or taboo.

To make matters substantially worse, the dirty words Dream Maddox said to me in his sultry accent keep playing on repeat in my head, and I can hardly focus.

Frankly, I don't think I can look him in the eye ever again.

I expected Maddox to glare at me when I arrived. Maybe he'd sneer or scowl or make some scathing comment about my abilities, but nothing. Nada.

I respectfully said, "Hi, Mr. Shaw," as I passed, and he didn't acknowledge me.

His pen momentarily faltered, but he didn't look up from his notepad or even nod his head.

Undeterred from trying to be a half-decent person who did not have a sex dream about her professor, I beelined for an empty chair in the middle of the room, turned on my computer, then waited while everyone else trickled in, and *still* he didn't look my way. He just stationed himself in the corner of the classroom, sketching something on a pad.

Only half of the seventy-ish people who've signed up to the class attend this particular workshop time. The others take an early-morning one. And Maddox is all *"Good afternoon"* for every single one of those thirty-odd people who says hi to him.

An hour and a half later, once we've all been given today's assignment, there's nothing more for Shaw to do other than sit back in his brown leather wingback chair and answer questions whenever one is asked. But still *nothing*. He didn't even throw a single question my way.

Well, he did respond when I put my hand up to ask for clarity on a concept—in the same tone he would to any other student. The exchange felt like I was talking to an entirely different person.

I didn't like it.

The Maddox Shaw I've come to expect is a raging dick who forces me to participate in class, has strong opinions on my extracurricular activities, and maybe potentially probably was not jealous of his brother for touching me.

Mr. "That's a good question. We can circle back to that in class next week and cover it in more detail" is *not* my Maddox Shaw. Not that any version of him is mine.

When I feel the heat of someone's gaze on me, I look his way to find his nose in his sketchpad.

Fine. If he doesn't want to look at me, I'll shamelessly look at him.

He's beneath the light of a single desk lamp, backdropped by the green chalkboard covered in his elegant writing.

It's enthralling to watch him be so focused. Even with the bags under his eyes, it's the first time I've fully seen him this relaxed. Occasionally, he tips his head to the side or frowns at whatever it is he's drawing like he's committed some kind of offense.

The tendons and veins in his forearms ripple with each minuscule movement. Flashes of those fingers curled inside me have my core tightening. I regret not *fixing* the issue before I left for class this morning. Now I'm going to spend the whole day with the lady equivalent of blue balls.

Even picturing the way his hands would look pulling my bra down before his lips descend on my—

No. I am *not* lusting after Maddox Fucking Shaw.

I swear I need to be tied up like a damn werewolf on a full moon whenever I'm ovulating. I don't recognize myself.

Actually, I take it back. I don't need to be tied up. I need to be put down.

Watching Maddox is making my deprived libido even more depraved. In that dream, he told me to put my hands on the painted canvas while he fucked me from behind. Since the most creative thing I've done is get on my hands and knees in bed, that dream is permanently ingrained into my brain.

I could sit here for hours watching the way his hands move while he's in his element. I'm half tempted to creep closer to sneak a look at what he's drawing, but he's positioned himself perfectly so no one can see the sketchpad on his lap.

If I'm insistent enough on getting his attention, maybe I'll get a reaction out of him. Which probably isn't a good idea since I apparently have a meeting with him soon.

In all honesty, I'll be screwed if Bradford comes back. Shaw gave me an A– on the last assignment, which isn't great, but it's bumping my GPA just enough to make me feel *slightly* more secure that I won't lose my scholarship by virtue of bad grades.

"What I would give for five minutes alone with him," the girl next to me says dreamily.

I look away from the murder scene I'm editing from a previous assignment. I recognize her as one of the girls in the Cresswell film club. If memory serves, she's best buds with the club president, who told me I lacked the "credentials" and "background" to join.

What she really meant—based on what I overheard her tell the girl beside me—was that she thinks my work is "messed up" and "too inappropriate" to represent such a prestigious institution.

I glance at Nicole to see if she was listening before flicking my attention back to the girl who's staring at Shaw. The lust in her eyes has me questioning if I have what it takes to be a killer.

"He's a busy man," I say through pursed lips.

"A busy man still has needs." She smirks.

Beyond a smile here and there, I've never interacted with this woman before. I don't even know her name. Now she's telling me that she wants to fuck our teacher? Seriously, is Nicole hearing this?

I don't know what has me twitching more: the unprofessionalism or the fact that she could sleep with literally any other teacher and I wouldn't bat an eye.

But *him*?

The girl's gaze flicks to my screen, and I watch her remember, in real time, why she never interacts with me. Her face morphs, lips pull into a scowl, nose turns up in repulsion, and I hear her thoughts without her saying a word: she thinks something is wrong with me.

My chest tightens as I stare blankly at the screen. I almost exit out of the video to work on an essay for another class, but it's a fleeting moment of weakness.

Screw her, and her predictable, unoriginal films. People glance my way as my fingers tap the keyboard a little too loudly.

Nicole takes her earbuds out and leans over. "You good?"

"Perfect."

"You sure?"

I hum my confirmation.

You know what? They can go sleep together. It's none of my business. They're both adults who can do whatever they want. If they end up together afterward, then good for them. I'll be sure to keep an eye out for their stupid wedding pictures, and the annoyingly beautiful babies they'd make together.

"What is that?"

Maddox's voice pulls my attention away from the computer. Half the class gawks at our professor, who's giving the student a couple of seats down from me the death stare.

The guy—I think his name is Corrin—has his hand suspended in the air, about to put something in his mouth. He glances behind him like he's checking if he's the correct recipient of Maddox's wrath. "Uh . . . cashews?"

I mentally confirm with myself that I did bring my EpiPen. It's fine as long as I don't eat them. It'd be painfully embarrassing if I went into anaphylactic shock in the middle of class.

"Get out."

My eyes widen. The entire classroom goes quiet, and everyone stares at Maddox like he's grown two heads.

"What?" Corrin stutters, looking around the room, silently begging someone to come to his rescue.

"This is a nut-free class."

"Since when?"

Yes. Since when, Maddox?

The guy next to me was cracking open pistachios last week, and no one batted an eye. In fact, I don't think there's a single class at this university with a nut-free rule.

Slowly, Shaw sets his pencil down. "Are you questioning me?"

"Uh . . . Yes—I mean no. *No.* I, um—"

"Out." His tone leaves no room for negotiation. Corrin scrambles for his things as everyone collectively shares the same idea of avoiding eye contact with him and Maddox. When the door snicks shut behind Corrin, the tension in the room is palpable in the stoic silence.

Shaw's eyes clash with mine for one long second before he returns his attention to his sketchpad. It's unlike the fury I'm used to, or the jealousy I was confused enough to think I saw yesterday.

No, this time my head spins and my brain goes through a series of mental aerobics to justify the possession flickering in the depths of his poison-ivy irises.

The implication hits me right in the stomach.

He did this for me.

I don't care how wrong my assumption probably is, or how delusional I am to let a thought like that cross my mind—butterflies are soaring through my stomach.

Red tinges my cheeks as I force myself to focus on the computer screen. I'm not special enough for anyone to make a blanket rule in my favor. Nor am I important enough to have someone kicked out of class for it. This isn't me wallowing in self-pity; it's a hard fact. I'm a stone's throw away from decent, and I'm far from perfect.

I'll let myself have this moment; then I'll go back home and scream into my pillow for having my head so far up in the clouds for thinking a person like Maddox Shaw could give a damn.

Just the thought of needing to be in a room alone with him after this has my fingers trembling on the computer mouse. As far as I'm aware, he's never offered to see any other students after class.

Pull yourself together, Reyna.

I need to stop reading into this. It's probably out of respect for my mom—something that has nothing to do with me. That's how it is most of the time.

My shit is in my bag and the computer turned off before Shaw gives the okay for us to pack up and leave. I don't dare look his way as I dart for the nearest bathroom.

Splashing water onto my face and neck, I squeeze my eyes shut. I need to touch grass or reconnect with nature or something after all the thoughts I've been having about Maddox.

I spend the next hour in the library, attempting to make a judgment call on the latest kill Lawrence sent my way. But my traitorous mind keeps straying back to Maddox. The way he looked at me. The heat of his body. The words he whispered against my ear in my dream.

Be a good girl, and spread your legs for me.

Blowing out a breath, I readjust myself in my chair and glance around to make sure no one is looking. There's a single student a couple of desks down from me, and another milling about, perusing the leatherbound books on the shelves. The dark wooden floorboards let out the barest groan as she walks. The sound of her footsteps is nearly as loud as the typing from the person closest to me.

The third floor is the most deserted section of the library, far away from any books relevant to course material. It's also where they put their most uncomfortable seats. But it's my preferred spot. Hidden away from people. Quiet. Zero distractions.

No one can see my screen when my back is to the wall, and I have the perfect view of everyone coming in and out of the area.

I squint at the crime-scene image, trying to ignore the way my stomach tightens as memories of Dream Maddox fucking me against a canvas burn behind my eyelids. The lust slowly eases enough for me to process the marks on the subject, then any thoughts about him evaporate.

My skin prickles as I trace the hexagonal shapes carved into the man's back. It's like the honeycomb insignia in the missing alumni books of the years the Shadow's victims graduated.

They have to be linked. There's no other way. Whatever this honeycomb is, it'll have answers.

I'm not sure how it links with my dad, but I'm certain it does. Did he ever mention bees or anything of the sort? I think when I was a kid, the one time he stayed for a couple of days, he told me a bunch of things about the hierarchy of the insect; otherwise I don't recall.

I think Mom mentioned he was part of a frat, maybe? What were they called? I don't even remember where he worked while he was studying. He told me once, but that was *years* ago.

Could my killer have something to do with Dad? I think that's too far-fetched. They had something in common, though. From what I could tell, a lot of the Shadow's victims attended Cresswell. So did Dad. Maybe he even knew some of the people who died.

Rubbing the back of my neck, I switch between the pictures to get a better look at the markings.

Lawrence said the organized crime unit took over due to the executional style of the kill and the torture that occurred premortem. The symbols etched into his skin are the only reason Lawrence thought it could be "my guy."

I'm certain it wasn't him.

The jagged lines marking the subject's chest are far from clean. I mean, he could have been struggling against his attacker. But the Shadow always has a level of finesse and artful intent with his work. There's no way he would have made such uneven markings, let alone shot someone in the head, and not do it perfectly centered.

I wouldn't say it's a copycat but . . . I might have seen another victim who was chopped up like this. Or maybe it was branded into them? I remember there being something hexagonal in a murder months ago. It was one of the first ones Lawrence showed me, before he started feeding me files regularly.

There could be another serial killer going around, and this is their signature. But how does that link to Cresswell? Am I making something out of nothing?

A bang thunders through the space. I jolt, exiting out of the picture and snapping my attention to the sound. I look up in time to see a girl throw up her hand in silent apology as she picks up a fallen book.

I sag back into my chair. Maybe I am being dramatic.

But . . . I might as well check for similar murders, right?

My laptop fan works overtime as I open up the internet browser and search the local news for recent deaths in the hopes of finding the subject's name.

When half an hour of checking this week's death-notice and news articles for murder comes up blank, I change tactic and search for any murder victims brandished with a similar symbol, but I can't find a single one. Not even in the law school's database of criminal cases. There's not even a hint of anything remotely close to the shape.

I scrub a hand down my face. Nothing is showing up even though I *swear* I saw a victim who had the symbol burned into his chest.

My foot bounces on the floor. There's a connection somewhere. This university is linked to it—I'd bet money on it.

I shut my laptop, jump to my feet, and head toward the shelving, looking for the books dedicated to Cresswell's history. The older copies are kept in the artifact room, but Cresswell loves preserving their history. So there should be a newer edition or an electronic version of them somewhere.

My fingers hover over the spines until I find one that might help. *The History of Cresswell University*. I grab it and a couple of others to bring back to my table.

I scan the index in search of any keywords that might work, going through book after book until I reach the bottom of the pile. *The Birth of Knowledge and Power.* If there weren't a picture of the school's crest on the front, I'd think this is a random philosophy book.

Within seconds of going through the index, I find a word that raises a red flag in my head: *beekeeping*.

I flick to the page and find the segment I'm looking for. My eyes dart over the words, mind racing and making connections worthy of a hardcore conspiracy theorist.

There's an image of a group of men in suits gathered around a single beehive in front of the fountain in the courtyard. According to this, when Cresswell first began three centuries ago, a group of students, academics, and local officials came together to establish a beekeeping group and donated the honey to locals in the area.

They would meet every week, and as the years progressed and more students enrolled, the men who began the club would go out to recruit new students to join. It was considered a great honor to be welcomed into the group. Supposedly, even the mayors, governors, and random business owners joined the beekeeping society—by invite only.

The men who were granted access were given honeycomb-shaped pins. I pull up the image of the victim, flip the page for the embossing in the alumni book, and peer at the pin fastened to the lapel of the man in the photo.

They're a match. It's the same layout, the same four hexagons. The placement of a bee.

I don't think I could ever imagine Dad getting into beekeeping.

I think I'm losing it, because there's no way I am thinking there might be a deadly group of beekeepers out there in *New York* of all places.

I'm more confused than I was an hour ago.

Christ, I think I'm getting a migraine. My eyes drift to the grandfather clock against one of the shelves. It's a quarter to five. Fifteen minutes until my alleged meeting with Maddox.

Heaven help me.

I throw caution to the wind and buy another cup of coffee on the way to his office. My cup is empty by the time I get to his building, and my nerves are going completely haywire.

What could he possibly want to talk about? The incident with his brother? How he wants me to get into beekeeping? He hasn't released the grades for the latest assignment. What if he's going to tell me how horrifically I've done? What if this is the day I find out that I'm losing my scholarship?

I can't afford the tuition, so I'll be kissing my life goodbye, and I'll never figure out what my dad was up to.

Maybe he's decided to fail me after all. I'll do extra assignments, clean his studio, grade papers, do his laundry, literally *anything* he wants, and I'll do it. Just as long as I don't lose my scholarship.

Hell, I'm even willing to get on my hands and knees to beg for a resubmission.

No, bad Reyna.

I check my watch. Five o'clock on the dot.

It's now or never.

15

REYNA

I steel my spine and rattle my knuckles against the imposing door. It opens instantly, like Maddox was waiting on the other side.

Neither of us says anything. Shamelessly staring at each other. It feels wrong, like I'm rewarding him for pretending I didn't exist hours ago. He doesn't bother hiding his perusal of me now, from my knee-high boots to my lacy tights, up to the silky maroon dress, pausing on the thin black ribbon around my throat. When he licks his bottom lip, my skin flushes a deep crimson.

This happened in the dream.

He looks like he did back in class, except his hair is neater, tie straighter, cologne the slightest bit stronger. There's no paint on him or any evidence of the graphite smudged on his hand. It's the cleanest and most put together I've seen him in a while.

Maddox shifts back just enough for me to squeeze past him into the room, brushing against his hard expanse of muscle.

The smell of him is everywhere. On his clothes, in the air.

It's muddling my brain so much that I blurt out, "You're not sleeping."

A single brow raises as he shuts the door behind him—and locks it. "You really are an astute observer."

There's no going back now. I motion to the blanket folded on the couch, stopping myself from pointing out the bags under his eyes instead. "Why? Are you okay?"

He falters, taken aback. "Careful, Miss Sinaga. You're stepping into dangerous territory asking those types of questions."

"I have a habit of doing that."

His nostrils flare. "I'm well aware of your nighttime rendezvous."

Okay, backtrack. Maybe this has nothing to do with my grades and everything to do with rehashing a conversation we've had ad nauseam.

If I recall correctly, *I'm* mad at *him*.

"Did you invite me to your office to discuss what I do in my spare time, Mr. Shaw? If my exercise of free will is the whole reason behind this meeting, then I want you to know that I hear you and I understand your concerns."

I refuse to repeat our prior conversation. It's easier to steer us toward the topic of his brother.

Clasping his hands together, he strolls to his computer chair and sits down. He crosses his leg at his knees, leans his elbows on the armrest, and eyes me, wearing his aggravating mask of indifference. Imposing on my personal space from the other side of the room.

I feel naked standing here, put on display for his viewing. But I don't move. I let him drag his eyes over me again—I relish in it.

"Do you now?" Green eyes dart to the couch beside him. A silent order for me to sit.

I blow out a breath, hesitating before following suit. Lowering onto the leather sofa, I leave my satchel and camera bag on the floor, place the cushion on my lap, and squeeze my legs together.

This is where my dirty dream played out.

His eyes drop down to my thighs like he knows exactly what I'm thinking.

My throat bobs, and I scramble to string together a sentence that will stop me from picturing how his abs contracted when he thrusted inside me.

I wet my lips and say, "It wouldn't be right for your brother to see one of your students because it would put you in a compromising position. It would be disrespectful on both our parts if your brother and I explored any kind of relationship, and I have no intention of making your life more difficult on that front."

He frowns and says nothing for four seconds. I know because I count them. "Right. Thank you."

Because I'm an absolute idiot who can never leave things be, and I want to see whether he was indeed jealous, I keep going. "Until the end of the semester, at least."

My chest constricts when his eyes swirl with a hint of the beast he hides beneath his immaculate veneer.

"You've mistaken me. Consider my concern *permanent.* You're everywhere I look, and the only thing I ever see. Any more of you, and I will go completely mad. So, *no*, Miss Sinaga, I am not okay, and I'm afraid I will never be until I can purge you out of my system."

What?

The air shifts. It grows pointed teeth and barbed wire that wraps around my lungs. Maddox leans forward in his chair until he's resting his weight on his knees. Towering over me without standing. With how close he is, there's barely enough room for me to make a run for it. He acts like he despises me one minute, then looks at me like he's a man possessed the next.

"Let me make this abundantly clear to you, love: I don't wish to hurt my brother, so don't make me."

Love.

He . . . He *was* jealous.

What is happening?

The cogs in my head race a hundred miles per minute as I white-knuckle the cushion. Then they stop turning. His gaze falls to my lips for the briefest moment. Time suspends. Awareness prickles over my body.

"I don't understand what you're saying." My words are barely above a whisper.

"If you want someone with better words, find a poet." He opens the notebook on his desk and rips out one of the pages before writing on it. Pushing the paper toward me, he gives me a pointed look that borders on complete rage. "While we're on the topic of my *concerns*," he says through gritted teeth. "If you so much as *think* about visiting another crime scene, you. Call. Me."

Seriously, this again? Why won't he give it a rest already?

"I don't think so."

"This isn't up for debate, Miss Sinaga. Nor is this an open discussion. I don't care if you call me, text me, email me, or send a letter by fucking carrier pigeon, you are going to tell me." A growl rumbles through his chest as he speaks, puncturing through every word to give it a serrated edge. "Do I make myself clear, *Miss Sinaga*?"

Maybe I should be scared. I probably should be livid beyond measure that he's still trying to dictate my life. But instead a low, keening moan starts at the back of my mind because of how adamant he is to keep me safe.

It's wrong for my blood to heat. Wrong for my stomach to tighten under his deadly gaze. Wrong that I want to grip his shirt and slam my lips against his, let him feel what he was looking at seconds ago.

I nod once even though I know I'm lying to him. I'll never tell him. I'm not sure if it's because I want to push his buttons or because I've burdened enough people in my life and it's selfish of me to drag another person into it.

He grunts his approval, gesturing to his computer and changing the subject fast enough to leave me spinning. "Your assignment."

The mask from earlier is back in place. The rug has been pulled from beneath me, and I'm sitting on my ass like a dumbfounded idiot. My brain hiccups, reeling left and right as I try to make sense of the last few minutes.

I clear my throat and angle myself sideways so I can see the computer screen against the wall. "Yes, of course."

My pulse hammers as I fidget with the cushion, cycling through everything he's said. The more I think about it, the more insane I feel. He can't possibly have feelings for me.

"You've improved." He says it like an afterthought.

What?

"Thank you," I say automatically. I'm too shaken to register what he's talking about.

"The surroundings tell their own story of the character without distracting from the frame's focal points." Maddox gestures toward the abundance of cleaning supplies amongst the mess on the screen.

Right. My assignment.

I heeded his advice, but maybe I took it too far.

"The color scheme is more appropriate for your Pink Ink concept and makes the pop of color less jarring. The contrast of warm and cool tones in the frame shows the emotional polarity between rage and distance."

My nails dig into the fabric. The *but* is going to drop any second now. He's going to pull a one-eighty on me and tell me how bad the lighting is, or how parts of it are poorly framed.

He doesn't.

Just like last time, we watch the short film together, and he instructs me on the ways to turn my work from good to great. Small nuances that I wouldn't have caught, like a different choice of prop, or spending a couple of seconds longer in a certain scene to create more suspense.

Maddox pauses where the killer is carving the victim up with his blade in the pattern of a skeleton. "You're murdering him with far too delicate a touch."

"That's like saying there's no beauty in death."

I'm transfixed when his lips curl into a half smile. It's such a rare sight that I take a mental snapshot of it and tuck it away somewhere safe.

Then he leans forward and catches a lock of my hair. I become paralyzed. His finger never brushes my skin as he slowly tucks the strand behind my ear. Then he jerks his hand away, as if he couldn't help what he did, and goes back to playing the footage.

The blush that blazes across my face reignites the forgotten ache in my core. I can't concentrate on anything else he says after that, or get myself to give a shit about the composition or the framing or the goddamn lighting.

This is how it started in my dream. Maddox invited me into his office, cozied up to me on the couch to watch my assignment, then one thing led to another, and we were kissing. Then the clothes came off, and the lights in my head flickered when he pushed himself inside me.

My attention catches on the orange tip of an EpiPen poking out of his bag. I'm too wound up to think any of this through logically, because why does Maddox have an EpiPen as well?

"Do you have any allergies?" I blurt, derailing his spiel.

His forehead wrinkles. "Not unless you count my allergy to idiots, then no."

I'm not crazy. He kicked that student out for me. He implemented a nut-free rule *for me*.

I frown, remembering the latest crime scene I visited—where the victim had almonds shoved down his throat. It feels so fundamentally *wrong*. But familiar. A little bell goes off in my head. I almost snort at the absurd thought that Maddox Shaw might be my killer.

Over eight million people live in New York. I'm not self-absorbed enough to believe that the snacks at the crime scene and the almonds were a reference to me. The only people who know about my allergy are Maddox and Kimi, and sure, I always have KitKats and a little bag of Cheetos on me, but it's not like Maddox would know that.

It'd be stupid to even entertain the idea.

How would that conversation even go, anyway?

Maddox, I know what you are.

Say it. Out loud. Say it.

Serial killer.

Yeah, I doubt it.

"What about bees? Are you into them? Beekeeping, I mean." I internally cringe. He's probably not quite beekeeping age just yet.

He stares at me like I've grown two heads. "Do I strike you as the type of person who would be into *beekeeping*?"

That was a stupid question. "Just, um, it's a common allergy." I try to play it off.

"Are *you* allergic to bees?"

"Not as far as I'm aware."

He frowns skeptically at me. "Good." Shaking his head, Maddox continues, "As I was saying, it's the same issue as last time. The kill doesn't suit the crime."

I nod along because I don't trust myself not to say something ridiculous. I need to get off this couch if I want to think about anything other than Dream Maddox fucking me on it.

"Much of the film repeatedly provides themes of purity and cleanliness, yet the murder involves a substantial amount of bloodshed without reason." He looks at me, waiting for me to say something.

"He does choke him," I stutter.

I sound so stupid. That's barely a complete sentence.

The killer doesn't really choke him. It's more of a crappy headlock that didn't result in anything more than the victim's physical struggle.

"You call that choking?" Maddox says, voice low.

His eyes are on my lips.

No, my throat.

The temperature rises too quickly to acclimate before it's burning my flesh, and I'm there again, under him in my dreams, watching him thrust into me. Real-life Maddox is right in front of me, and he too is staring at me like every thought that runs through his mind is more depraved than the last, and he's debating whether to reenact every last one of them.

My chest tightens when his eyes darken like the beast within won the battle, and he's spotted his prey.

"Sit back."

The demand takes me off guard.

Rationally, I know I'm an independent woman who should fight back against a man who thinks he can order me around. Irrationally, I want to know why he's unbuttoning the cuffs of his sleeves.

Following instructions was never my strong suit. My ability to listen to authority is worse. And yet I wet my bottom lip and tentatively place the notebook and cushion aside. My gaze is trained on him, tracking his every move. He does the same to me.

Every flicker of a tendon. The glide of my silk dress against my skin. The fall of my hair over my shoulder. He sees it all.

He rises from the chair. Stalks forward. Stopping right above me. "Do you know what it's like to be choked, Miss Sinaga?"

The tension building in my core makes it hard to breathe. I shake my head once.

He hums to himself, considering. Then slowly, *leisurely*, like he's making sure I'm watching, he rolls his sleeves up to his elbows. Each move is precise. Intentional. Fold by fold, he keeps going until I can see the muscles in his forearms flex with his movements.

Desire unfurls low in my stomach, demanding friction. Through the silk dress, I can feel my nipples harden beneath the bralette that won't hide how he's affecting me.

Maddox sees it. I know he does because he stops rolling his sleeve, stare caught on the rise and fall of my chest. His nostrils flare.

Oh, this is bad.

But I don't want to stop him.

With languid movements, he slides his knee between my legs to lean his weight against the edge of the sofa. He wedges himself higher until he's inches away from the apex of my thighs, forcing my legs farther apart.

I grip the armrest to stop myself from closing the distance. He'll feel how soaked I am if he gets any nearer.

Carefully, like he's giving me the chance to run for the hills, Maddox places one hand on the headrest behind me and lowers the other to my throat. One by one, his fingers curl around my neck, tipping my head back so I have no choice but to drown in the sight of him.

I shiver beneath him and grasp on to the arm that's holding me down. My grip only lasts a second before my hand falls to my side. I wholeheartedly believe that if I told him to stop, he would. So when he squeezes, I stay right where I am.

His green eyes smolder and turn into a deeper shade of emerald; then his pupils blow out completely at the part of my lips.

"There's an art to it. Too much pressure on the front of the neck, and I'm just hitting your windpipe." His voice is low. Barely a rasp. He adjusts his hand to evenly distribute the pressure around my throat. "If I press the sides, you'll still be able to breathe." Dipping his head down, his hot breath fans my warm skin. "Every breath you take is because I'm allowing it. If I want you to stop breathing"—he tightens his grip—"you will."

I try to inhale, but his fingers tighten, and the world narrows to the press of his skin against my throat. The darkness I sensed lurking in his soul is coming out to play with mine, and they're getting along far too well.

Maddox's knee between my legs inches dangerously close, and in a moment of absolute weakness, I shift my hips to meet him halfway. What's left of my breath stutters out in a violent shudder the moment we make contact.

I can't think about anything else when it feels this good to press my aching sex against him. Like how he's my professor, and I'm his student. Or that he's choking me on his couch on campus.

There are a thousand reasons why this can't happen. A million more on why this will tip me well over the edge so that I'll never emotionally recover.

Every cell in my body is singing. My senses heightened, turning my gray world into various shades of colors I've never seen before. I've never felt so alive. No one has ever made me feel this way, and it's maddening because he's barely touched me.

I want to grasp on to the addictive feeling and never let go. After what I've gone through these past few years, I'm craving a slice of this: freedom. Liberation. The chance to let go because I'll fall into a better place.

It's more than a distraction or a means to an end. Just for today, I want to shed the weight of my past and future. Live in the now, and . . . I'm curious about how far this will go.

If he's worried about his job, he can let go, and we can pretend none of this happened.

Until then, the world ending wouldn't stop the cant of my hips against his knee. The friction has me biting my lip to stop from making a sound.

My eyelids grow heavy when a low growl builds at the back of his throat.

"The things I want to do to you, love." His voice comes out hoarse. Strained. Possessed.

Maddox shifts his knee, applying more pressure against my core. A bolt of pleasure goes up my spine. I whimper from the ache thrumming low in my stomach that pulses to a frantic rhythm.

His scent is like my very own aphrodisiac. I'm drunk on his proximity.

I claw at his arms in a soundless request for him to do it again. He curses under his breath and lets go of my throat, placing both hands on either side of my head like he's forbidding himself from touching me.

"Stop me from making a mistake."

Those six words are sobering.

I don't want to be anyone's mistake, least of all *his*. I clamor away from his leg to escape his orbit, stilling when he traps me in place by lowering his face to mine. His stubble whispers against my skin, lips just soft enough to leave the faintest mark. When he speaks, I don't recognize the sound of his voice. It's darker, like another side of him has taken control.

"I didn't say you could get up."

Mixed signals. *Again.*

Maddox's gaze drops to my lips, and he wets his own like he's hungry for a taste.

"You're dismissed when I say you're dismissed, Miss Sinaga."

I shiver at his deep tenor, core tightening with need. If I don't get out of here, I'll be the mistake he thinks I am.

"This is a bad idea." It's barely loud enough for him to hear.

"That's the thing about us. We both like bad ideas."

He stays there for a beat. Watching me. Studying me. Pushing his leg against my core one last time so he can see me squirm. Then he edges back, rolls his chair to him, and sits in front of me, close enough that I can't close my legs with his in the way.

"If you want to leave, then I trust you're familiar with where the door is."

I should.

In the next five seconds, I need to get my ass off this couch and out of this room, because nothing good can come from this. Maddox is my *professor*.

If I screw up, my scholarship is gone. My future takes a hit. My hope of knowing my family will be decimated.

But I still don't run. God knows why I stay exactly where I am, staring at the man who's been setting off fireworks in my stomach. Maddox could cause everything to come crashing down, yet I chew my bottom lip, imagining what type of kisser he'd be. Whether he'd be a generous lover. If he'd keep looking at me like he's obsessed. Sealing whatever *this* is would destroy my psyche.

I've never been the type for one-night stands. I've already lost my parents, and I have no interest in losing anyone else I care about. Sleeping with him will make me more attached when I already shouldn't be.

But I want to feel wanted. Cared for. Like I'm the only person in the room and the only one who matters, and right now, he's looking at me like he can give me those things. Even if it's only for a few minutes. Even if none of it is real. I still want it.

He takes my silence for an answer.

"Give me your foot," he orders, leaning back in his chair.

How is he so calm right now? I feel like I'm about to explode.

Inhaling sharply, I squeeze my legs together, knocking his knee in the process.

"You can't touch me anymore." If he does, I'll fall too far, too fast.

"I won't," he promises.

We both need a line between us.

I swallow, focusing on him to check that he's not about to shift gears on me again. There's a heavy pause before I do as he asks, cautiously raising my knee-high boot up into his waiting hand. He rests my heel against his knee, and his hand slides up my calf to the top of the boot.

Right about now, I'm wishing we never made the rule. I'd kill to feel his skin against mine.

Green eyes stay fixed on me as he leisurely glides the zipper down, one hand kept firmly beneath the back of my knee. Achingly close to touching me. Painfully near the invisible line in the sand that's supposed to stop me from losing it.

We haven't done anything, and I'm already panting. He hasn't touched me, and I already know I'll never be the same.

He sets the boot beside the couch. The muscles in my stomach coil tighter with each inch he unzips, and my body melts as he carefully places my foot on the armrest. The same ritual is repeated with my other boot, and when he moves my leg to the side, the hem of my dress falls to my hips to give him a clear view of my black cotton panties.

It peeks through the tights. Blending into the lace to paint a pretty picture just for him—and a pretty picture it must be, because his eyes turn ravenous when he sees it. Time seems to pause. He does nothing but stare at me. Gaze darting from my core, to my chest, to my face, then back like he can't decide which part of me he's going to consume first.

This is nothing like all the other times I've had sex. They've never held even a modicum of the heat burning between us and in my veins. I didn't even know it was possible to feel like this.

"Take your tights off."

My throat constricts. It feels second nature to comply even though our relationship has been built on resistance. I lift my hips to shimmy the thin material down, but he stops me before I make it past my thighs.

"Slowly."

Blood roars in my ears. I take a deep breath. Hesitantly, I hook my thumbs into the band and ease the material down my legs so he catches every inch of skin that I'm feeding him.

Maddox swipes a hand over his mouth, runs it through his hair, down his face, then curls his fingers into a fist before pressing it back against his lips.

He's regretting the rule too.

I'm not a prude; I'm just a little inexperienced. Sure, I've had boyfriends I've done all sorts of stuff with. The classic lights off, no sound, lackluster sexscapades. The type where I'd go home to finish the job because I was making a grocery list while they got off.

Something tells me that there won't be anything like it with Maddox.

Our harsh breaths mingle in the air between us. The chill from the buttery leather couch kisses my skin. It's another sensation that sets sparks flying through me. He takes the pair of tights from me, leaving me in my dress and saturated panties. Then the seconds tick by.

He's just staring. Concentrating on every detail of my body.

My chest tightens while Maddox inspects my ink. He traces the lines of my tattoos with his eyes. There's a snake wrapped around a scythe and a crescent moon on one thigh, a giant chrysanthemum on the other, as well as a dagger going through a skull. On my shin, creeping up around the side of my knee, are pink peonies with thick black lines. More are hidden beneath my dress.

My stomach hollows when I follow his line of sight to the scars on my thighs. The mortification tastes like acid in my throat. How could I forget about those?

In my teenage years, I had issues accepting why Dad didn't want me. Mom assured me it was because of his work, but I didn't believe it. The only logical conclusion I could reach was that I wasn't good enough.

Maybe if I got better grades, he'd stay. Maybe if I made better films, he'd visit more than once a year. Maybe if I could have been the perfect daughter, my family wouldn't have been broken. Mom would have been happier with the love of her life.

It was my fault. That's what I told myself.

Then I told myself that if it was bad enough—if *I* was bad enough—he'd come home. He'd heal me. None of that happened. So I became angry instead.

I did it for attention, yes. But I also did it because I wanted control over circumstances I couldn't have control over.

For a second—one painful second, I worry Maddox will think I'm not enough either.

Anger flares in his eyes as he continues staring. I've never been ashamed of the scars or felt the need to explain. Yet Maddox is looking at me like he has a string of colorful words ready to lash out at me. I'm just about to put my legs down and cover myself with my dress so I can yell at him when he tears me apart.

"Those bloody legs," he murmurs to himself, so quiet I almost don't hear. "Perfect."

It's on the tip of my tongue to ask him to repeat himself. There's no way I heard him correctly. I'm wearing my baggage on my skin, and he's looking at me like I'm nothing short of beautiful.

"Panties. Off. Now."

I watch him, second-guessing if he meant it. The doubt evaporates when my eyes fall to the sizable tent in his pants, and the pained expression on his face. *I'm* the cause of his suffering. However bereft I feel, this is the gravest torture for him. It's empowering.

My core flutters with need. This time, I'm slow without being told. My attention is fixed on him as I languidly glide the black material down my thighs. There's a little black bow on it and lace trim that flares from my hips. Innocent yet sultry. The perfect juxtaposition to how I feel at this moment.

I loop it out from one leg to let the garment dangle from the other that's balancing on the armrest of his chair, and I swear he stops breathing. With more confidence than I should have, I tuck my heel up closer to my hip, baring every vulnerable inch of me for him to see.

My heart stops beating as I wait for a reaction.

He stares.

And stares.

And stares.

Then finally, something.

Maddox's lips part. Lost. Mesmerized. Frozen.

"Art," I hear him whisper.

I'm sitting on my professor's couch, naked from the waist down, with my legs balancing on his armchair, and he's looking at me like he's found religion.

He shakes his head in disbelief, going to the edge of the seat like he's fighting a battle to stop himself from touching me. "So fucking beautiful," he rasps, gripping the chair.

Power thrums through my veins. I'm practically vibrating from it. I'm bringing him to his knees without saying a word.

"Look how wet you are for me, love," he says in awe.

Love.

It's the third time he's called me that. I could get used to it.

Apprehension skitters through my bones as I trail my fingers down the inner seam of my thighs. The pattern of his breathing changes, turning short and sharp, worsening when I reach the juncture of my thighs.

Electricity zaps through my body when I brush my fingers against the oversensitive bundle of nerves. Streaks of white make my eyes flutter closed as I stifle a whimper.

"No. Eyes on me." His voice is gruff like he just woke up.

My gaze collides with his. Unable to help myself, I do another pass against my clit, and my hips buck at the contact.

It's enrapturing watching his blown-out pupils focus on every touch.

I've never considered myself a sadist. Nor much of a masochist, for that matter. But seeing him pained by having to keep his hands to himself is awakening a sinister part of me. It spurs me on, fueling me with the courage I need to add more pressure and strum my clit the way I like to in the dead of night.

My head drops back against the couch as the pleasure amplifies. I've never had an audience before, and I'm finding I rather like the dirtiness of it. So long as it's Maddox watching me.

His eyes track the beads of wetness trickling down my thigh.

"You've made a pretty mess of my couch."

I hiccup on a groan at the next pass over my clit.

The frills of my bra peek above the curve of my neckline, and he scowls at it like it's a personal offense. Reaching forward, he undoes the tie holding the top half of my dress together. The silky material slips away to give him an unobstructed view of my black bralette.

A lock of brown hair falls onto his forehead from the tousled mess his hand caused. The tendons in his forearms strain with the force of his hold on the armrest, and I let out my first strangled moan.

The sound breaks him. That's the only way to describe how he collapses forward, elbows on his knees as if he only just caught himself from breaking the barrier we've placed.

"You drive me fucking insane, Reyna."

Reyna.

The jade in his irises twists into black with his guttural snarl. It's like he can't decide whether he wants to kill me or fuck me into the sofa. That unhinged look has my muscles contract and stretch, and I can't help sliding two fingers into my pussy. A shudder works through me.

More. I need more.

I forgo any thread of self-restraint I have and add another finger, imagining they belong to him.

"Mr. Shaw," I whimper.

"That's it, love." His voice is hoarse. "Say it again."

I curve my fingers, and my hips jerk. "Maddox."

"Fuck."

Moans fall past my lips unbidden as I continue thrusting my fingers. It feels better than any other time I've ever touched myself. Someone could hear me, and I couldn't care less. I'm addicted to his tortured gaze. Feeding off his wordless desperation.

"If you knew all the ways I've been imagining you, there wouldn't be a second that you aren't drenched at the thought of me." The words come through gritted teeth.

"Like what?" I pant, moisture dripping onto the couch.

All the sounds coming from me are lewd, ratcheting my need higher. I chew my bottom lip and spread my legs wider to take my fingers deeper. My eyes roll to the back of my head at the amplified sensation, and I'm vaguely aware of the string of curses leaving his mouth.

He watches me like a man who's been forced into a prison of his own making, and he's done nothing but try to shake the bars for the last century. The muscle in his jaw ticks, chest expanding with every heaved breath.

"I imagined stripping you until you're in nothing but those tiny bloody skirts of yours. Then I'd fuck you against the window so anyone could see." My breath hitches as he continues. "I'd put you in a hundred different positions so they'll know everything I could do to you."

I'm not sure what's more shocking: the fact that he's saying these things, or that he thinks about me. A voice at the back of my head tries to tell me that he's only saying it because of the circumstances we've gotten ourselves into, but I tamp it down.

"I thought about blindfolding you and letting you roam around my studio, and fucking you against whichever art piece you have your hands on." He shakes his head. "The reality of you is better than any dream I could conjure. Your pussy is a goddamn fucking masterpiece."

My core spasms, and I increase my speed. My hips buck, and my pulse runs rampant. If he touches me—even so much as a caress—I'm done for.

He groans. "You shouldn't have let yourself be alone with me. I'll destroy you. I'll fuck you until you can't walk. I'll make you lose the ability to speak with how loud you'll scream. And you know what?"

I can barely keep my eyes open, much less string together a sentence.

"I asked you a question, Miss Sinaga." It comes out close to a growl.

"What?" I snap. I'm on the precipice.

"You're going to be a good girl and look at me while you come on your professor's couch, and you're going to fucking love it."

That does it.

Lightning explodes through every cell in my body. White heat bursts across my vision. I'm falling. Crying out with no lifeboat to catch me. It keeps going and going until I can't take anymore. Green eyes morph to black and brown and gold as the world spins.

It's not the words I wanted to finish to, but the switch flipped. Maddox took back the reins and got under my skin. I'm in his grasp as much as he's in mine. Whatever tumble we're taking, we're doing it together. Falling on the same sword. Though camaraderie isn't what I'm feeling. It's a mutual connection that is far more dangerous. Potent enough to get sick off of.

A shudder rips through me when I withdraw my fingers and ease my shaking legs to the ground. Before I can move to get myself cleaned up and fix the mess we got ourselves into, he grabs my hand, and his mouth closes around the same fingers I came on.

Maddox's tongue flicks out, lapping at the remnants of my desire. He keeps his attention trained on me. A low sound rumbles at the back of his throat and makes me gasp.

"You were sent to destroy me," he whispers when he finally releases me.

A knock at the door startles me up onto my feet, and I don't think twice about darting away from him with my boots and tights in hand. A blush blazes across my cheeks. Oh God. What if someone heard me?

The only thing worse than a man sleeping with his student is a woman sleeping with her professor.

Maddox mutters profanities I don't catch; I'm too busy frantically shoving my clothes back on to make myself look like I didn't just finger fuck myself in front of my professor. I don't get the chance to go back to grab the panties I left on the couch before Maddox rips the door open and growls, "*What?*"

I don't care to listen to the exchange. I don't dare look at Maddox either. I shoulder my satchel, grab my coat, and spare a quick glance at the student at the door. I recognize him from one of my classes. Alex or Andrew or something.

Somehow, I muster the willpower to act like everything is okay, saying "Thanks" and "See ya" to Maddox before hightailing it out of there.

My thighs are sticky, I'm panting, and I can still feel the warmth of his lips around my fingers.

Dear fucking God. I just fingered myself in front of my professor.

16

MADDOX

I shouldn't be here.

I've done a lot of stupid shit in my life, but this is by far the dumbest of them all. And I've done it three times now. This has the potential to be a giant cock-up.

My eyes dart away from her sleeping form long enough to put pencil to paper and crosshatch the shadows beneath her jaw.

Reyna has a cute little room. An exposed-brick feature wall decorated with old movie posters and art prints, filming equipment everywhere, photos of her mother and friends, a couple of packets of Hello Panda and Kusuka, a bookshelf with four different editions of Mary Shelley's *Frankenstein*, and six special editions of H. P. Lovecraft's works. It's the type of room I pictured her having.

The part that pleases me to no end is the switchblade on her bedside table. It seems she has survival instincts after all. Terrible ones if she hasn't sensed my presence.

Like the other two times, I wait until she falls asleep before letting myself into her apartment. I'm half tempted to throw her over my shoulder and bring her home since I can't seem to find a moment of peace unless she's around.

I can't find it when she's there either.

However, sitting here in the dark, or back in class, with my sketchpad in hand, I find myself enjoying the process of creating again. The pressure is there to do her beauty justice, but the perfectly imperfect drawings have become the rare thing that brings me solace. I'd forgotten what it means to draw for myself, without worry of judgment.

Admittedly, I'm a tad disappointed that she sleeps in pants, fluffy socks, and a T-shirt. I would've preferred she slept nude, though I doubt my Reyna-related sensibilities would have been able to withstand such a sight.

I was less like a man and more like a feral beast when her tights were on earlier today. Once they were off, I was sure the chains around my self-control were going to snap.

She was in my office hours ago, and I still can't get the image of her on my couch out of my head. The sounds she made. The way her legs shook. The outline of her nipples through her bra. The taste of her. The sound of my fucking name on her lips. It sounded like a melody. A torturously tempting one.

She's lucky she kept one foot on my chair to keep me back. If not, I would have fallen to my knees and shoved my face between her divine thighs. My mouth would have been on every inch of her: her scars, tattoos, her luscious, tanned skin.

If it weren't going to be a titanic rip-off, I would have asked her to stay exactly where she was so I could draw her.

But *of course* that acolyte twat had to fucking ruin it. Bloody Shepherd couldn't have sent me a text like a normal person, could he? No, he had to come and ruin my day. The graying twat sent his latest bloodhound in training to deliver my next assignment, and the curious expression Alex gave Reyna rubbed me the wrong way.

Another member of the Order is on the chopping block. An issue I can deal with tomorrow. For now, I can sit here and just *be* next to her.

It was for the best that she left earlier. Something like that *cannot* happen again. There are simply too many risks that I can't afford.

Murder isn't only an art form, it's a method of control.

Because of her, I have none. It's both liberating and vexing.

Worse. It's addictive.

The same way getting lost in a painting is magnetizing and taking a life is thrilling.

I know what the definition of *obsession* is. I understand its implication. Feeling it is something completely different.

She should never have crossed paths with someone like me. This is the last night I will allow myself to watch her sleep. The next time I'm alone with her, I might try to fuck her. If that happens, she'll never escape me, because I'll never let her go.

I'd make Reyna Sinaga mine. But it would cost me everything.

She's avoiding me.

I keep expecting to see Reyna around campus, except I never do. Not once have I spotted her golden highlights running away from me. Which means one thing, and I hate it.

I was worried when she missed class yesterday. In fact, I assumed the very worst. I thought the Order had gotten to her and my father had put a bullet in her head to ensure I solidify the alliance with House Dornmont. I thought she went searching for my kills and ended up in a ditch.

Joke's on me, though, because I found her having bubble tea with her friend Kimi instead.

Thinking that she regrets what we did leaves a nasty pit in my stomach. I sure as shit don't regret it. In fact, the whole interaction is constantly playing in my head. I've been sporting a semi for the past week.

I should be happy she's putting distance between us since it's apparent that I'm incapable of doing so. Instead, I'm livid beyond measure. I'm not remotely pleased unless she's somewhere I can see her, and when I do see her, I'm somehow even more pissed off.

This morning, I hid outside of her film-editing class like some bloody stalker to confirm she was alive. I also paid a visit to her screenwriting professor to bump up her grade from a B to an A–. But several hours have passed. I've killed people for the Order in substantially less time. I'm not sure what her schedule is like this afternoon, but I've been taught how to hunt. I'll find her.

It'll all be much easier once I put a tracker on her.

My phone buzzes in my pocket. I pull it out to read the text.

SHEPHERD:

Confirmed.

Fantastic. More work. Just what I wanted. I don't exactly find it fun playing assassin for a tyrannical system when it doesn't benefit me.

Jogging up the steps to my room, I give a curt nod to the students passing by. It's lunchtime when the university is busiest, so the polite expression slips right from my face after my shoulder brushes one too many people.

At least there's something good waiting for me in my office. I can check Nicole's and Kimi's social media to see if they've posted anything with Reyna in it to confirm she's still fine. Otherwise, I'll stop by the library to see her.

Once that concern is out of the way, I can focus on painting. I've finished the cliffside angel painting and started two new pieces that I've been working on while Reyna ignores me. One of them has pushed me in ways I never thought it would, but all the nights I've spent—

"Mads."

I pause with my foot on the step.

"Mads," she repeats. Quieter this time.

If I turn around, I better not find who I think is standing there. Running my tongue over my teeth, I take a deep breath, and slowly pivot to look at the woman waiting for me at the bottom of the stairs.

Abigail Bloody Dornmont.

Good.

Now I'm in an extra-bad mood.

Her lips curl into a nervous smile as she grips a brown paper bag so hard that it's shaking. Holding back a sigh, I meet her at the bottom of the stairs, where she glances around at the students milling about before leaning in for a kiss that I sidestep.

"What do you want?" I sigh.

"I brought you lunch," she squeaks, and holds the bag out.

I stare at it. Controlling my personal life wasn't enough, now my parents are ruining my workplace too?

"I'm sure I have Mother to thank for this visit." I scowl, then wipe the emotion from my face when she flinches.

If this were Reyna and I looked at her this way, she'd double down and give me a run for my money. I'm pretty sure she gets off on pissing me off. Other than my brother, there hasn't been a single person who's been able to tolerate my candidness. Until her.

Abi lowers her eyes so her gaze is somewhere around my chest. "She said we need to try to sell it more."

Sighing, I squeeze my eyes shut before cautiously extracting the bag from her hands like it might be a bomb, then say my thanks. I can't be mad at her when she's here under orders. Still, "Don't come to my work again."

She hesitates. "But I was told that we need to make more appearances. Outside of our dinners. Mom says that people are saying that the whole marriage is for the election."

"Not all acolytes are stupid, then." I scoff. "It doesn't matter what you're told. My work is off-limits. If you want to organize something, text me. I don't appreciate being blindsided like this."

My voice is moderately soft, but she swallows and stares at her feet like I just yelled at her in front of the entire student body. "Okay."

"Good." I try to give her a friendly smile. The key word there is *try*. "Great chat. Thanks for lunch."

I turn to leave her to do whatever it is she does during the day—shopping, probably. My socialite fiancée's hobby is spending Daddy's money.

And soon mine, unless I can find a way out of it.

Storming back up the steps, I head toward my office and throw the food into the nearest rubbish bin. I wouldn't put it past Mother to poison it or hide razor blades in there to keep me on my toes.

My mood takes more of a nosedive when I pass Alex, the kid who showed up at my door seconds after my religious experience with Reyna last week. He just gives me a sideways glance before continuing down the stairs.

What is this? Am I meant to be seeing every member of the bloody Order today?

Either I need to drink enough to become comatose or I need to turn someone into a creative piece to release some steam. Picking up a paintbrush when I'm in this state won't go down well for me. My exhibition is quickly approaching, and I can't afford to screw it up.

I've barely slept since I last visited Reyna's bedroom. If I keep running on fumes the way I am, I might decide it's a good idea to confront the little *naga* and demand to know why she's avoiding me.

When I get to my floor, my eyes lock with a pair of coffee-brown eyes that look like hers.

Fucking hell. Now I'm hallucinating.

No.

Not hallucinating.

That's her. Waiting in front of my door. Fidgeting with her fingers right before she shoves them into her pockets.

I quickly straighten my tie, fix my hair, and stroll toward her. I'm not sure whether I want to fuck her against the wall as punishment for the doe-eyed, lust-filled, obsessed teenager she's turned me into, finger her until she tells me every single sordid detail of what's gone through her head this past week, or sit her on my face until we both can't breathe.

It's like she's trying to torture me with her short burgundy tartan skirt that would look so much better gathered around her waist.

Or on the floor.

I'm not picky.

My attention lands on her lace-clad thighs, and my semi goes to full mast. Just great. I'm going to have a meeting with HR come morning.

My only saving grace is that her turtleneck is covering her entire chest. Although it still does very little to minimize the temptation to rip her bra off with my teeth and take her nipples into my mouth.

"Mr. Shaw." The three syllables come out in a single breath. I can't tell whether it's nerves, fear, or exasperation.

I don't like any of the three options. So I go with a surprising fourth and final answer: lust.

Dilated pupils. Flushed skin. Subtle panting.

My lips pull into a grin. Well, well, well. It appears we're mirroring the same thoughts. Maybe a repeat of last week is on the table after all.

She clears her throat. "I forgot my camera in your office."

My grin falls.

Swell.

Now I'm pissed off again.

I deliberately forgot to bring it to class yesterday so there was an excuse for her to visit my office. But of course, she conveniently didn't even show. After spotting her camera bag in my office last week, I foolishly thought she'd be on the first train back to campus and knocking on my door. Yet again, she proved me wrong.

Wordlessly, I unlock the door and shove it open, then deactivate the alarm. And because I can't help myself, I say, "You weren't in class yesterday."

"No, I wasn't."

From the corner of my eye, I watch her enter the room. Clearly, I don't give her enough credit. I expected her to lie and say she was sick, or bluster with one excuse or another. No, just a flat, obvious response.

I stride to my desk and grab her camera from the top drawer. I pause for a moment to toy with her black panties that I've kept in there for safekeeping.

There's so much I could say. The first and main one being, why the fuck does she have an image relating to the Order in her camera roll?

Of course, I can't ask her that since I'm sure she'd rip me another one if I confessed to going through her photos. Also, because she isn't an acolyte, and if she became aware of the Order and started shaking trees she shouldn't, the Order would sign her death certificate.

How would that conversation go? *Reyna, you took a picture of the Order of the Hallowed Hive's symbol—Yes, hives as in beehives, not the rash. Anyway, where did you find it? Do you know what it means? Are you prepared to die with the knowledge? Can you spread your legs again, please? I think I'm going through withdrawal.*

I think not.

Other than that, I was disappointed to find zero photos of her in her camera roll. I hoped to find at least one or two self-portraits, clothing optional. Nothing.

I turn to pass Reyna her bag, but she's nowhere to be seen. Like every other time she's come in here, she can't seem to help making herself at home, looking around without asking. I didn't know she'd be here, so I didn't have time to cover the two pieces I'm currently working on—the very two things she's standing before.

My nerves develop a pulse, beating harder with every step I take toward her.

She's become my only glimmer of sunlight, and I'm sick of living in the dark.

For my brother's sake, I need to stay away and wash my hands clean of everything to do with this girl. But one look at her, and I'm questioning whether it's worth losing her or my sanity. The line between right and wrong blurs where she's involved.

When was the last time I made a life decision just for me? Since I was a child, everything I did was because I had to. My brother's happiness has always come before mine.

The arrangement was fine at the start. Beyond escaping the Order's grasp, there wasn't much more I desired in life. Everything I wanted to claim, I did. I made a name for myself within the art community and established myself as a highly respectable academic within my field. I had my art and my kills in between being a pawn for someone else's goals.

But I think I've found something I want for myself. A slice of paradise that I want to keep at the risk of making all my suffering meaningless.

I want to tell her that I'm the one she's been following, because then I'll know whether I'm going to war only to lose in the end. More than that, I want her to see the real me. The side that no one else knows—not even my own brother—so I can know what human connection really feels like.

I don't want walls. I don't want threats. I want to have my bloody cake and eat it too.

With Reyna standing here, in my most sacred space, staring at my uncompleted artwork like I've painted the Sistine Chapel, something volatile settles within me. Her lips are parted, and there's a glassy sheen over her eyes.

Every time I'm around her, I'm helpless. Helpless to her whims. Helpless to the onslaught of inspiration her existence strikes within me. Taking my phone out of my blazer, I take a photo to save into my encrypted album later. If I can't stand here and draw her, taking a picture will need to be the next best thing. My collection of her is growing, and I don't want to share it with anyone. I don't want to share *her* with anyone.

Watching Reyna stare at my art is both euphoric and frightening. I don't care for anyone else's opinion. I only want hers. She's the reason I've stopped worrying about what the critics will think about my exhibition. All I care about is doing the pieces the justice they deserve—it's a perspective I haven't held in a long time.

Every cell in my body is telling me to close the distance and come up behind her, drag my nose along her neck and feel her soft skin against mine. I want to get her back on my couch and see what she'd look like when she comes with my tongue in her cunt.

She makes me want so much I can't have.

Reyna's attention moves from the painting of a woman holding a sword to the sculpture on the workbench. It's far from finished, but there's no mistaking that it's of a woman. The wings still need doing, as do the water ripples, her tail, and her face.

I watch Reyna's eyes slide over the sleeping frame of the five-foot-seven plaster sculpture. At the moment, a cloth covers her backside, and her arms are crossed in front of her to hide her breasts. Part of her body is cut off to look like she's beneath the water. I intend to make it my centerpiece.

When Reyna tips her head to the side, the golden highlights of her dark-brown hair fall from her shoulder and down her back, revealing the red peonies on the neckline of her top. The afternoon sun pours through the window, casting shadows across her face as her skin warms into liquid gold. The glossy sheen of her lips glistens, and I'm overcome with the urge to kiss her like I might be able to absorb everything that's going on in her head, create a connection that will allow me to sleep pretending she's safe next to me.

"Little dragon." I suck in a sharp breath when her eyes collide with mine.

Calling her irises brown would be an insult. Under the afternoon sun, they're rich cinnamon with threads of caramel and marigold. I could spend a lifetime staring at them and I wouldn't get bored.

"What?"

"Naga," I rasp, trying to get myself together. I straighten and manage to get the next words out in an even tone. "It means dragon in Indonesian."

The lines around her eyes soften, and the most subtle shudder goes through her that I wouldn't have caught if I weren't wanting to consume her mind, body, and soul.

She nods even though it wasn't a question.

"Like the dragon tattoo on your back."

Her lips part, and it takes everything in me not to press mine against hers. Just once. But once wouldn't be enough for me. I'll want it over and over again until it's the only thing I'll ever know.

"Yes," she whispers, eyes dropping down to my mouth for a notable second.

She's killing me here.

"Penny for your thoughts, Miss Sinaga." I nod at the art piece.

Inhaling deeply, she focuses on the incomplete painting. "I think it's too soon to tell."

If there's one thing I can rely on Reyna for, it's that she'll always tell me what she thinks when it comes to my art. Not just that, she provides actual constructive criticism. It's refreshing.

Her eyes widen with shock when she notes my smile. I have the urge to move closer when her gaze stays on my lips for long enough that the rise of her chest becomes more pronounced.

Red paints her cheeks, and she whips her attention back to the painting like she didn't mean to be caught staring.

She clears her throat. "Although, I think it could be appropriate to add pomegranates into the empty space over here—since the snake is holding her hostage to the chair." She motions to the empty space behind the woman, where I've already set the values of a pedestal and skull.

"Anything else?" I don't add it was already in my plans to do just that.

She narrows her eyes at my painting while I stare at her. "A candle." She chews the inside of her cheek. "It could be a single candle about to run out, to symbolize her limited time."

A gasp escapes her when I step forward just as she's turning so our chests brush against each other. Even through the layers of clothes, she feels like a dream. Soft. Supple. Like silk.

I want to give it all up to touch her. Push every boundary, break every rule. As long as I get to hold her. *Taste* her. I wouldn't need anything else in the world if I could lean forward and kiss her right now. I don't deserve her, but fuck, I'd kill anyone who tried to keep me from her.

"I'd like to bring you somewhere."

Her brows hike up her forehead. "Where?"

"Do you trust me?"

I hold my breath, waiting for her to answer. She should say no. It's the line in the sand that will keep me at bay from sinking my teeth into her. I'd never do anything to hurt her, but saying yes might result in the end of her. And me.

"I trust you." She hesitates.

My lips twist into a devilish smirk.

Well, she's done it now.

I told her she shouldn't let herself be left alone with me. This was my attempt at saving her from my clutches.

And it'll be the last time I do it.

17

REYNA

Neither of us has uttered a word to each other since we entered the taxi.

I keep thinking someone is going to jump out of nowhere and start screaming that we're up to no good. It's not uncommon for students to spend time with their professors. I've had coffee and lunch with my teachers and tutors. They were always related to my classes, however.

This time feels different. What's going on between us isn't innocent. I should've refused.

Do I trust him not to put me in harm's way? Yes.

Do I trust him with my life? Eh, I'm leaning toward yes as well.

Do I trust him not to get me into trouble? He's an artist and a bad boy in a suit. Whoever made up the rule that you should never color outside the lines is full of shit, and he knows it.

I'm more nervous about getting caught with him than about wherever it is he's taking me. But it's kind of . . . *thrilling*.

It's the same giddy feeling I get before going to a crime scene. It feels like I'm leaping through clouds with electricity in my veins. It's exciting and frightening all at once.

I keep stealing glances at him as we inch through traffic. Maddox has grown out his stubble, somehow elevating his bad-boy edge.

The driver is humming along to the song on the radio, blissfully unaware of my inner turmoil, and the rising tension—*sexual* tension. Every so often I catch Maddox staring at my thighs, and I get the distinct feeling all he wants to do is grab them to bury himself in me—I'm probably making the last part up.

Here I was thinking I couldn't get any more wound up from the memory of last week, but with a single look—or many *looks* in this case—my underwear is ruined, and I'm left squirming. Thank God I'm wearing an actual bra today, or else my nipples would be saying hi to him and every other person in this city.

What would sex with Maddox Shaw feel like? He doesn't strike me as a selfless lover. I bet he wouldn't leave me wanting for more. He'd do whatever makes him feel good, and that'd just so happen to be what makes me feel good too.

Glancing out the window, I break the silence, sounding far calmer than I feel. "Are you going to tell me where we're going?"

"That depends. Are you going to learn to listen to instructions?"

"I seem to remember following them to a T last week, Mr. Shaw." It takes me a second to realize I've shamelessly said it out loud.

I'm flirting with him.

His eyes widen. Maddox clearly can't believe it either.

"Looks to me like you might be the one taking me to places you shouldn't," I add, referencing his comment from last week when I can't take the silence any longer.

He chuckles. Whatever bolstering confidence I felt evaporates when he rests his arm behind my seat, effectively touching me without laying a hand on me. He'd be breaking our rule with the slightest jolt. There's nothing sexual about it, but the level of intimacy involved with the mindless act is making the butterflies in my stomach go crazy.

"I'm curious to know where you think I'm taking you."

I can't respond. Not when he's toying with my hair. I doubt he's aware that he's doing it. He's too casual for it to be anything other than a subconscious action. He's making it seem like showing me any level of affection is second nature to him.

"Reyna?"

Reyna.

I'm in trouble.

I like the sound of that a little too much.

"I do hope you aren't bringing me to your house, Mr. Shaw," I whisper so the driver doesn't hear.

"I'm a respectable man, Miss Sinaga. I would never dare do something so . . ." The fingers playing with my hair crawl closer to my roots, rendering me frozen when he tugs on it. *"Depraved."*

This cab isn't big enough for the both of us. Without breaking our no-touching rule, his fingers ghost over the back of my neck. Desire ripples through my bones. If he doesn't move his hand soon, I'm going to say fuck the rules.

"I expect you to do far worse than that," I respond, voice breathy.

A grin splits across his lips, and he leans closer, inches away from my ear. "You don't know the half of it, love."

I couldn't be more grateful when the taxi comes to a stop. I'm out of the car and on the footpath before I dare take another breath. I probably shouldn't have left Maddox to cover the bill, but I'll be damned if I spend another second in there breathing in his scent.

Maddox strides out of the taxi, buttoning his cashmere coat. Without missing a beat, my satchel is off my shoulder and on his. He plays deaf to my protest, offering me an amused, grumpy side-eye that sets me in a daze.

It only gets worse when he places his hand on my lower back to steer me away from the road and around the corner. If it weren't for the trench coat, I might be able to feel the heat radiating from him, and honestly, I've never loathed fabric more.

I hate how disappointed I become when the hand falls away as we start walking down a street I don't recognize. Potentially to my certain death. We're still in the city, although an neighborhood that's a little quieter.

My pepper spray is now with him, so it's not like I have much in the way of protection. Coincidentally, I forgot my camera in his office. Somehow, I think the ass intentionally made me forget.

He keeps a healthy distance between us—the amount I'd expect any normal professor and student to walk. A pang hits my chest at that thought.

"If your intention is to murder me, do you mind doing that next week? I have a pizza voucher I really want to use before then," I say to distract myself.

"No one needs to turn you into art." He chuckles, referring to the Shadow's victims.

I roll my eyes, annoyance rising. "Why? Because I'm unworthy?"

"Because you already are."

New rule. No flirting. Whatsoever. My ovaries can't take it. Maybe he should go back to being horrible toward me. That way he's just an asshole with a pretty face.

"Even a child's scribble is still art." I grimace at how my killer might convey that type of messaging. It'd take dismemberment to a new level, I'm sure.

"That was truly moving, Miss Sinaga. Really inspiring." He mock-claps.

My glower falls when I make out the sign of the building in front of us. "You're taking me to an art museum?" *Holy shit?*

"What gave it away? The sign or the art?" He points to the sculptures behind the windows.

I don't have a comeback for that. This is an actual date.

Well, he probably doesn't think it is. It probably wasn't his intention either. Nor is it in any realm of likelihood that he'd be doing that kind of thing with his student. But this feels pretty textbook date material.

My throat tightens. He doesn't know how much this means to me.

"Why?" I step inside when he holds the door open for me.

The walls are emerald green set against cherry wooden floor. There's a feature wall showcasing a large contemporary piece, and on the opposite end of the foyer, there's a set of glass doors bracketed between sculptures of Athena and Hephaestus.

At only two stories, Halenbeek Museum isn't large. Frankly, I didn't know it existed until three seconds ago.

"Do you have art here?" I ask before he answers my first question.

Maddox nods at the woman behind the counter and continues through the automatic doors without waiting for me to follow. My boots squeak against the wooden floors as I race to catch up with him.

"Don't you need to pay first?" I stumble, throwing glances back at the receptionist. Capitalism will fall before a millionaire makes their privately owned museum free.

"My painting that was here was recently relocated back to Montana, so not anymore. And to your third question, no, I know the owner," he answers before I make it beside him. Soft murmuring filters down the hallway, getting louder the closer we get to the juncture at the very end. "And the why? You can call it a university field trip."

I roll my eyes. "I swear, you better not be pulling the *everything is a learning opportunity* card on me. I've done enough learning to last a lifetime. My brain is at full capacity."

"Is that any different from usual?"

I whip my head his way, ready to feed the man his own scrotum. But the wild grin he flashes my way makes me playfully hit his arm instead. "I'll have you know that I won my third-grade spelling bee."

"I'm not sure if it counts if only two people were participating," he teases even though he doesn't know that. "But I'm proud of you, love."

I'm about to fire off a retort when he wraps his arm around my waist and leads me left when we hit the end of the hallway. Sparks fly across my skin. The sensation seems to last a lifetime, when he couldn't have held me for longer than three beats.

"You can't touch me," I breathe out.

Maddox halts us both, rounding on me to invade my space. "It appears we have a different opinion on the definition of *touching*." His hand drops to my hip, grabbing my flesh through layers of clothing. He brushes the back of his fingers along my jaw. "This is nothing compared to what I want to do to you."

"You can't." The words come out barely above a whisper.

"Tell me, is it that I can't touch you, or you don't want me to?"

"You *can't*," I repeat like a broken record.

His cologne washes over me and makes it hard to breathe. Maddox steps away, taking his warmth with him. If I don't get it together, I'm going to embarrass myself and make everything worse than it is. I move through the open space, observing the art alongside him, shaking off the desire spiking through my veins.

"I could paint a better portrait than that when I was four," he whispers, breaking our silence. "I could do it in the dark now, and it would still look better."

"I've seen preschoolers with more talent," I agree.

Maddox nods at the next painting. "Miss Sinaga, take a picture and print it out."

"Why?"

"To ensure you never forget what inconsistent tones look like. It's a novice mistake."

I bark out a laugh and slap a hand over my mouth when people look my way. "You're so mean."

He shrugs, and we move to the next painting of an old man with a golden chalice. "I've been called worse."

This is too easy. Being here.

With him.

How long has it been since I've been able to do this with someone? I love Kimi, of course, but Maddox gets it, and it's the most at ease I've felt all year. Actually, it's probably the most fun I've had as well.

Dad died in a freak car crash a year before cancer took Mom, and she wasn't sick for long before she died. It was still the hardest six months of my life. I did nothing but beg a god I didn't believe in and wish for a hundred different things that never came true. Art and creation was lost to me.

If I think about it, I owe Lawrence. If it weren't for the crime scenes he showed me, I would never have fallen back in love with creating.

And this time, there's someone who believes in me. It feels too good to be true.

I'm not sure what hurts more: the warmth unfurling in my heart or the knowledge that there's an expiration date on it.

Motion beside me stops me in my tracks. I flick my attention Maddox's way as he pockets his phone. "Did you just take a photo of me?" I gasp.

"Perhaps."

The smug look he's wearing tells me he most definitely did. He refused to look my way in class a week ago, and now he's not-so-discreetly taking pictures of me. I like what we have going. If it were up to me, I'd see it through to the end.

Crossing my arms, I jut my chin. "I didn't say that you could."

"I never asked."

"Delete it," I demand.

"The student doesn't tell her professor what to do."

My jaw drops. "Are you seriously playing that card right now?"

"Absolutely." He nods. "Whenever it suits me."

I roll my eyes and keep staring at the painting. Or rather I try to. The heat burning a hole in the side of my face makes it impossible to notice anything other than the man beside me. I give it five seconds. Then ten. The sensation doesn't go away. All it does is ratchet up the level of *weird*.

"What are you doing?"

"Looking at you." Maddox says it like it's the most obvious thing in the world.

I blink. That does funny things to my insides I most definitely should not be feeling about my professor. Especially in public where anyone could see us and call us out on all the lines being crossed. "We're at an art museum, Mr. Shaw. I believe you're looking at the wrong thing."

"I'm perfectly content looking at you, Miss Sinaga. You're the only thing here that holds my interest."

All I can do is stare at him. How does he say things like that and still be so composed? Meanwhile I'm seconds away from melting into the floor. Unless we change the subject soon, I'm going to say something I wish I hadn't.

"Tell me what you're thinking."

Nope. That's the last thing I'm going to do.

We need to talk about literally anything that will make the flirting stop.

"I don't know what my next film project will be about, and I hate it."

"Has the serial killer not killed enough people for you?" Maddox muses.

"There's no shortage of people that need to go," I mumble under my breath, then pause. I probably shouldn't be openly condoning murder to one of the people who knows I'm essentially a copycat killer. Minus the killing. Clearing my throat, I explain, "Nothing is speaking to me."

He turns his body, giving me his full, undivided attention. "What is it that you're looking for? Go through his prior kills that you're aware of and look through a different lens—pun intended."

"That was terrible." I snort. "There's this one concept I have—that ideas can be deadly. I've always wanted to come up with a short film based on it, but everything I've thought of has been lackluster and unoriginal—"

"I disagree."

Nope. Not acknowledging that comment. "I'm waiting for that light bulb moment that'll take the words out of my mouth."

He eyes me with interest. "Explain."

I sigh, shaking my head. "I guess I really want to make a film centered around an idiom that can be taken both figuratively and literally. That's the only idea I've got for the next project, and I'm coming up empty on all accounts—especially since I want to keep basing them off the Shadow's kills."

The pregnant pause fills me with hope, then extinguishes it in an instant. I've still got nothing, and I don't have long until the project is due.

"Do you want solutions or to vent?"

I laugh humorlessly. "Unless you can tell the Shadow to go on a creative murder spree, there's nothing you can do."

"That can be arranged." He says it like a promise.

The intensity of his gaze skyrockets to the point that it's uncomfortable.

"Right." I shift my weight and force a chuckle, focusing my attention back on the painting to avoid meeting his stare. Clearing my throat, I add,

"While you're at it, tell him to leave me a bag of Cheetos and a pair of chopsticks so I can snack dust-free while looking around."

"Noted."

No humor, no eye roll. "A drink as well?" he asks.

The tension lifts off my shoulders. It doesn't sound like a joke, but it clearly is. "Some lemon iced tea, please. That way I can get caffeine with a side of sugar."

He's still looking at me like he's preparing a life-changing grocery list.

Time to wrap this up. I can't deal with this tension.

I make a show of checking my phone. "It's getting late." Not completely a lie. It's almost four o'clock. By the time I get back to his office to get my camera for the wedding I'm getting paid to film tomorrow, then take the subway home, it'll be close to six, and I'm already feeling quite snackish.

"Do you have plans that I'm not aware of?" His eyes narrow.

"Yeah, your brother—"

"I suggest you don't finish that sentence."

My grin widens, and I shrug. "I'll leave it to Spencer to tell you, then."

I haven't spoken to the guy since our first interaction. Seeing Maddox drop the weirdness and get all smoldery and angry is a nice ego boost.

I'm not sure what's going on with him. Us. This. It seems too dangerous. I should be running in the opposite direction, not entertaining it. But I like it too much to keep hiding like I've been doing over the past week. All I could think about was how what I wanted—all I've dreamed of—was a repeat of that day, and to see how far we can take it.

He follows behind me, brooding and radiating enough vicious energy to kill the surrounding plants. I can practically hear his murderous thoughts, and I'll admit, it makes a girl feel special.

And confused.

Very, very confused.

18

REYNA

Maddox speeds up in front of me to hold the door open and grips my satchel when I try to take it off him. He follows the whole gentlemanly act with a glare when I don't give him a chance to help me into the cab.

Stuck in rush hour, our conversation drifts from art and film to stories about my mom—his full of the wacky stuff she'd say at shows, mine of everything else.

"You haven't mentioned your father," Maddox observes.

"There's not much to say."

He raises an inquisitive brow.

Leaning my head back, I gaze out the front window. "I used to get a single day out of the year to see him—and he'd spend half of that day playing catch-up with Mom. He usually didn't even stay the night. There was the odd occasion that he stayed, like, two or three days, but I could count on one hand how many times that happened. I mean, he called randomly a couple of times, but that guy was *not* a talker."

That catches his attention. "Used to?"

I nod once. "Car accident. The engine exploded."

"Why only once a year?"

Sighing, I turn to look at him. "His job was more important to him than his family."

I laugh when his lips twist like he's personally victimized by this revelation. "Why? What the bloody hell did he do that he only had one day off every three hundred sixty-four days?"

"CIA."

His eyes bulge a fraction. "Really?"

"Fuck no." I snort as the cab driver yells at a pedestrian. "As a kid, it was a toss-up between that, assassin, Batman, or one of the FBI's most wanted. Five-year-old me thought the CIA was the safest bet. Every time I'd ask, he'd give me some bullshit answer like 'businessman' or 'sales.' Then I got in trouble with *both* my parents during 'bring your dad to school' day when I stood up and said that my dad couldn't come because he was running away from the police—but it's okay because he came and saw me once a year. I finished the speech by making everyone promise they wouldn't tell the cops. Surprise, surprise, the school did. That was my first experience with betrayal."

"Christ."

"He sent me money, though. Dad of the year for that."

Maddox scoffs. "That makes up for everything."

"Oh, for sure. It literally made all the mental illness go away since it just so happened to be the exact amount required to pay for a therapist."

The smile wipes off his face as his eyes drop to my thighs. The attention usually makes me uncomfortable because it's like waiting for a judgment bomb to go off, but instead, he looks pissed.

"Say the word, and I'll kill him again for you."

I choke on a laugh. "I'm pretty sure you're not meant to say that to people who lose a parent."

He lifts a shoulder and drops his hand on the seat, dangerously close to my thighs. "The offer still stands."

And they say chivalry is dead.

"What about your dad? Any trauma there, or is it mainly mommy issues?" It's a rude assumption, but one I'd bet good money on. No one makes the type of art he does and holds such a hateful outlook on the world without having family issues.

He levels a dirty look my way.

"Both, then," I conclude, smirking. His deadpan stare is confirmation enough. "Let me guess, one or both of your parents aren't fans of your art. They think you should have been a lawyer, doctor, an accountant, or something that involves a soul-crushing nine-to-nine corporate job. How close am I?"

He just looks at me, and I grin as I give him an obvious once-over of his overly refined clothes. No one dresses like that without money, and no teenager could have pulled off the art he had made unless his parents had deep wallets.

"I think your mom's on the PTA and is Hermès's favorite client, while your dad's a businessman of some kind who—"

"He's the president of Wilson Shaw."

I stare blankly at him, waiting for him to elaborate, but his irritation slowly morphs to cold amusement.

"The accounting company," Maddox explains.

"Wow. That's . . . cool."

"You have no idea who they are, do you?"

"Not at all."

"Good."

Uh. "Should I . . . ?"

"It's a Fortune 500 company."

Oh. "That explains why you're a pompous asshole."

Maddox bursts out laughing. The sound bubbles out of his chest and rumbles through the car, so jarring that a smile splits across my face—because the only time I've ever heard him laugh is with me. He never does more than a practiced smile in all the interviews I've seen of him. In class, he only ever cocks an amused brow when someone cracks a joke.

"Miss Sinaga, I suggest you develop a filter."

"This is me with a filter."

"In that case, you should lose it. Say whatever crosses your mind."

"One wrong move and you could give me an F. Hard pass, Mr. Shaw. I'll keep my more colorful insults to myself for now."

His lips flatten, and he lowers his voice just enough for me to hear him over the radio and the cacophony of honking and yelling. "I told you that you're aware of where the door is. I'll say it once more, then I have no intention of repeating it. I won't stop you from walking out now. Should you choose to stay, once we cross that line, there is no going back. And don't for a second think that any of this concerns your grades or your continued attendance in my class."

My eyes widen. All I can manage is a single nod.

When the cab eventually reaches the university, Maddox is out of the car and opening my door before it can come to a complete stop. This time, when I reach for my satchel, he doesn't keep it hostage, remaining a safe, healthy distance from me at all times, three steps ahead, and acting like he barely knows who I am.

When you aren't enough, you're forgettable, and the distance is making me feel forgettable.

It hurts when I know it shouldn't. I have no right to feel this way when our entire relationship only exists behind closed doors. The seconds of contact we shared are stolen moments I should have savored because this thing between us was never meant to last.

The harsh late-afternoon light casts the campus in a foreboding glow. Students mill about, some probably going to or from their last class of the day, or starting their travel back home. A few greet Maddox as we pass.

The buildings around us seem grander, the spires of the library behemoths, and us, two little dots on a map. Yet it feels like we're trapped in glass, and everyone can see us, but we can't see them. Their eyes seem to know too much, like they suspect exactly what we've done, and any minute now someone will chastise us. It feels like I'm sinning even though technically, I'm only going to his office to grab my camera.

Once we're in the building and on his floor, the air between us turns charged. It's silent enough that I could hear a pin drop. My breathing grows heavier the closer we get to his office, and the anticipation has my pulse pounding an erratic beat.

I'm getting my bag. Nothing more, I remind myself as he unlocks his room, turns off the alarm, and lets me in first.

I'm not sure why I'm surprised that his studio looks the same as when we left. Somehow, I thought our time together would change everything, and the world as I knew it would morph alongside the rapidly multiplying butterflies in my stomach.

The door snicks shut behind him. The sound sends a bolt of energy down my spine. It vibrates through the room and clings to the fabric of my clothes. I internally wince when the wooden floor creaks under my boots.

Maddox doesn't move far from the entrance, silently watching me as I grab my camera bag from his desk. The severity of his stare makes me feel like cornered prey, except I have neither the fight nor flight instincts to decide how I want this night to end.

Shouldering my bag, I move back toward the exit, lifting my chin to meet his gaze. He takes his glasses off and sets them on a nearby bench. I'm trapped in his orbit. It's odd being unsure whether he's going to say something that pisses me off or turn me on.

"Well." I clear my throat and pause in front of him. "Thank you for this afternoon."

He hums, shifting closer, forcing me to shuffle back until I'm against the door and his front is touching mine. His eyes darken, and I'm assaulted with memories of the couch. He looks as tortured as he was the afternoon I came undone because of him.

A pulse starts between my legs. Every inch of me is acutely aware of where he is; the hand on the wall above my head, his fingers dipping beneath my coat to inch up the curve of my body, his excruciatingly slow ascent from the jut of my hip to the curve of my waist.

Heat blossoms through the fabric and across my skin beneath his touch, and the scent of bergamot and paint makes me shiver.

He can't be touching me, I chant. But the words don't come out. It feels too good. *Right.*

"You have no idea how much I needed it." I keep speaking despite being given no prompt to continue.

Poison-ivy eyes drop to my lips, watching my mouth curve around each word. Still, he says nothing, letting me squirm as his hand descends back down my body and skates over my ass in the gentlest tease.

The motion is so small, but I'm seeing double from it. I have to ball my hands into fists to stop myself from touching him as freely as I've been dreaming of.

His head dips down, nose near mine, lips a breath away from sealing this with something deadly. *Still not touching.*

"I've been wanting to see more of the city but haven't wanted to do it alone. I also didn't know that place existed, so I'm glad I can cross it off my bucket list anyway. I had a lot of fun," I quietly ramble, hoping that the torture of his forbidden touch will end. I'm not sure whether I want him to close the distance or back away.

The muscles in his thick thigh are firm between mine, and it would be so easy for me to roll my hips against him to get the friction I so desperately need.

When he opens his mouth, his voice is hoarse, like speaking is the last thing on his mind. "Keep talking, Miss Sinaga."

"Mr. Shaw?"

His features shudder. "Say my name."

I hesitate before whispering, "Maddox."

"Fuck it."

His fingers thread through my hair, and he captures my lips in a kiss that shatters my axis. The world skitters to a halt while my soul expands with feather-soft light as if I were the one who put the sun in the sky and he's finally getting to see it.

Maddox's grip on me tightens, and he angles my head to take me deeper, like he might lose his grasp on reality if he doesn't. My lips move with the same tender demand as his, but I waver. The kiss lingers, silently communicating what he isn't saying with words. He's giving me the chance to find the door or remind him that we can't touch. I pull away to stare up at him.

This was—*is*—a bad idea. I'm falling, and he's going to walk away the second I land, and he won't be there to help me back up. I'm a blip on his radar. Something that will come along and disappear by the end of the year, when I'll be left picking up my broken pieces, while he'll continue as before.

I'm his *student* for Christ's sake. Nothing about that kind of arrangement is permanent. Once he gets a taste, he'll leave.

And then? I'll be hurt, but so what? I'll live. I can bounce back. At least then I'll remember what it's like to be kissed by Maddox Shaw.

Despite my turmoil, he's looking at me like I'm the only person he's ever wanted and will ever want. Each glance is a risk. Every touch is another nail in the coffin. I want this. Even for a little while.

I don't think it through or give myself another chance to hesitate. Like he put it so eloquently: *Fuck it.*

I slam my lips against his, and this time it isn't loving or tender—it's desperate. Maddox kisses me back like I'm the first drop of water and he's parched.

Our mouths move together with the familiarity of people who've done this a thousand times before, in sync and frantic. The softness of his lips is a shocking contrast to the harsh stubble along his jaw.

When he deepens the kiss this time, our tongues dance together. I let my inhibitions fall away, grinding against his leg, clawing at his shirt, and letting breathy moans fall past my lips. My entire being lights up under his touch, and whatever indiscretions from the past disintegrate with it. Maybe I'll pay for this crime later. For now, I only care about making the most of this moment while I can.

He wrenches his coat and jacket off and throws them somewhere behind him. I fist his hair as he hoists my legs up around his waist, and the air rushes out of me when my back hits the door, rattling it on its hinges.

Desire pools low in my stomach. I arch my back to push my center against the hard buckle of his pants and a whimper escapes me. *I need more.*

Strong hands grope my ass and grind me against his length. My eyes roll to the back of my head as he pulls my bottom lip between his teeth before trailing ravenous kisses along the column of my throat.

Maddox yanks down my neckline, popping the stitches of my top to suck the sensitive skin into his mouth. The silky, dark strands of his hair fall onto his face and against my chin. His belt rubs against my clit, sending jolts of lightning through my bones, and God help me, I think I could come from this alone.

His lips work their magic along my throat as I shamelessly buck my hips to bring myself closer to the edge. I curse from the magnetizing sensations, cradling the back of his head to get him to keep going.

If he'd move his fingers a couple of inches closer to my middle, he'd know how soaked he's made me. He keeps kissing my neck and running his teeth over my skin like a damn vampire, but I don't have it in me to care about the marks he's leaving behind. I keep rolling my hips, getting needier every second I'm left empty.

"Please," I beg. I need more than just this. The single syllable comes out on a whimper, and I'm not sure what I'm asking for. I can hardly string together a complete sentence. I'm so close to bursting, and so far from it at the same time.

Maddox doesn't give himself a moment to catch his breath before his lips are back on mine, and he's gripping my legs, walking us toward—I don't know toward what. I don't think I care at this point. He could be taking us down the hall, and that wouldn't make me break this kiss.

I need this.

I need *him*.

Something cold presses against my back. It shocks me out of my trance long enough for me to scowl as he sets me down on the edge of the windowsill and pulls away so my fingers are no longer threaded through his hair. It's an uncomfortable height where only the tips of my toes reach the wooden floor, and if the sexual frustration wasn't enough to piss me off, the lack of physical touch is.

The thin fabric of my pantyhose tears beneath his hands before I can protest my new position, and a rush of air assaults the apex of my inner thighs.

The Neanderthal just *ripped* my tights.

I gawk at him. "You couldn't have taken them off like a normal person? Those were expensive."

"Send me the link. I'll buy you another." He yanks his tie loose and pops open the button of his collar. He falters, eyes glazing when they drop to the lacy pair I donned today. I felt so audacious this morning when I picked them out. I wistfully thought that something might happen, and I wanted to impress him.

"Three more." The last ones were ruined in my haste to leave. The extra pair is for next time.

Just in case there is a next time.

"Done."

He stops me before I can hop off, and I freeze. I'm sitting on the goddamn *windowsill.*

Overlooking campus.

In the afternoon.

On a weekday.

While there are people below.

"Are you afraid of heights?" Maddox asks.

I shake my head, panting. I need to get down before someone spots us. It's only a five-story building. It isn't like people can see more than just my back against the glass pane, but still, it would certainly raise questions.

His lips pull into a smirk as he rolls his sleeves up like men do before they eat. "Don't look down anyway."

"Are you crazy?" I hiss.

He drops down to his knees before me and spreads my thighs apart with both hands. "Yes."

"Anyone could see us." I try squeezing my legs together, but it's no use against him. My attempt at pushing him back is just as futile.

"That's the point, love." He grins up at me, pulling my shoes and tights off before pushing my panties to the side. A low groan of appreciation sounds from the base of his throat when his eyes drop to the wet mess he's helped make.

"We could get in trouble!" I whisper-shout in case anyone beyond the door can hear. Not like they wouldn't have heard me moaning up a storm when Maddox was letting loose on my neck.

"Then you better stay still so no one knows."

His mouth falls to my pussy. I've never been silenced so effectively before. It's all I can do to bite back a cry. One hand flies to his hair while the other stays on the windowsill for balance.

Fireworks explode behind my eyes when his soft lips wrap around my clit to suck on the bundle of nerves. I choke on a garbled moan and release a string of unintelligible hissed words. I didn't know it was possible to have my mind scrambled by a man's tongue.

"You're doing so well," Maddox praises.

When he flattens his tongue to lick a hungry path from my center to my clit, I'm a goner. I slap the window behind me. I pull him closer and clamp a hand over my mouth to stop myself from alerting the whole building of my impending orgasm.

Anyone would just need to look up to see that I am very much in the middle of something I shouldn't be doing with *my teacher*, and right now they could sue me for all I care. There's not a thing in this world that will make me stop my professor from eating me out like it's his sole purpose in life.

My attempt at composure lasts about ten seconds before I'm thoroughly lost again. I don't stop my crusade of trying to close my legs—mainly because it's too much and not enough. If I were any stronger, I'd be crushing his skull with my thighs. If anything, my unconvincing attempts at freeing myself only motivate him further, because he's lapping at my pussy like I'm better than any Michelin-star restaurant he's been to.

His name comes out on a breathy moan—first name, last name, both at the same time, title—my brain isn't operating anymore. *Stop, keep going, right there*—I don't know what I want.

Maddox curses and sucks harder like *he's* the one getting mind-blowing pleasure out of this. And holy shit if that doesn't push my blood to a boiling point.

My breathing bottoms out, coming out short and shallow with my rising pleasure. The heat from the sun against my back is almost unbearable, but I can't move without risking everyone seeing me in my bra.

"Do you see any of your friends down there?" The deep rumble of his voice sends vibrations through my bones, and my legs curl around his shoulders on instinct.

I shake my head, pushing my hips up to get him to do less talking and more sucking.

"I'm not turning." He doesn't resume his task, and I make a sound somewhere between a whimper and a growl. *"Maddox."*

"Look." Instead of his tongue, he uses the tip of his middle finger to rub achingly slow circles around where I need it most. I've become nothing more than a baseless creature, whimpering and pleading, scowling in frustration, that bastard. "Can anyone see you?"

I have every intention of fighting his command. I really do.

Looking means people could see my face. Looking means everyone could know I'm *that girl* who's fucking her teacher.

Still, I look.

I turn because I'm too wild with need to think about doing anything else but what he's told me to do. There has to be at least ten students walking through the courtyard below. Most are preoccupied with their phones or talking to their friends, but all it would take is one person to look up, and our secret would be out.

"Yes." I choke on a single syllable, and as a reward, he pushes two fingers into me.

"Good," he croons. "It's rude of you not to say hi to your friends."

Before I can tell him that a guy down there is in one of my classes, Maddox curves his fingers and captures my sensitive skin in his mouth with a greedy tug. I'm a puppet on his strings, crying out and buckling over, using his head for support just from a single ministration.

"Inside voice, Miss Sinaga," Maddox chastises right before biting down on the inside of my thigh. I squeal and attempt to squirm away, but of course the sadistic asshole doesn't let me free. He starts pumping his fingers while leaving blue and purple love bites along my flesh that feel like the embodiment of carnal sin.

Curse after curse quietly flies past my lips. All he does is give me an amused chuckle, curling his fingers inside of me. The tension in my lower stomach tightens, pushing me closer to the precipice of my release, so close, yet just out of reach.

Condensation trickles onto the windowsill from his teasing pace. I claw at every inch of him that I can reach, to urge him to go faster and put me out of my misery.

Maddox tenderly kneads and caresses the scarred tissue along my thighs. Our gazes clash, stealing the air from my lungs. Disarmed by the absolute adoration in how he looks at me, I forget to swallow a moan.

"Love, I suggest you quiet down. I'd hate to lose my job for eating the best meal I've ever had."

Heat unfurls to every corner of my heart—the kind that feels like warmth on the harshest days. A makeshift crutch to lean on when everything is too much. I'm so far from perfect that there's no universe where I deserve whatever he's feeling toward me.

It's fake. *Temporary.* He'll move on soon enough. Even if he doesn't, it's for the best that he realizes how wrong it is for him to look at me the same way he looked at the Artemisia Gentileschi back at the museum.

I'm flawed. Beyond repair. Cracked and chipped, held together by weathering glue, and he's treating me like I'm the foundation he'd crumble without.

I never want him to stop, but I need him to. I'm falling deeper. This will end with my hopes and spirit crushed. But I promised myself one day because I know this isn't supposed to last.

Winding his soft, dark strands between my fingers, I let my eyes drift shut to bask in the last remnants of warmth, and the way my pleasure soars each time he moves a muscle.

"I want you to make a docufilm about me."

It takes me a second to realize he said something. Then a solid two more to work out *what* he said.

"Do we have to talk about this right now?" I'm going cross-eyed. This is hardly the right time.

"Make a documentary about me." Maddox curls his fingers and presses his thumb against the bundle of nerves. "Does that feel good?"

I moan out my approval, shifting position to feel more of him.

"Good. I'll make a list of topics I suggest covering."

My eyelids snap open. "Wait. That's not what—"

"It's silent time now, Miss Sinaga."

I scramble to grasp the last vestiges of my sanity. "I didn't agree—"

He does something with his fingers that officially makes me lose my grip on reality. It's like he found a switch that shuts me right up, and my orgasm comes barreling forward.

All of my muscles contract and seize. A bright light flashes before me as if the gates of heaven have opened up. Euphoria bathes my skin and douses my veins in the most intoxicating ecstasy.

My legs tremble on his shoulders as my climax stretches. The death grip I have on his hair is the last thing on my mind because the sadist keeps going. He continues moving his fingers in a way that makes all the lights in my head go out.

I think I'm chanting his name. Or maybe I'm quietly moaning, saying please and thank you a thousand times. I'm not sure. One second my eyes are rolling to the back of my head, the next, I'm cradled in his arms and being carried across the room.

One hand is supporting the back of my neck, the other under my ass to hold my weight. So at odds with the brutal way he was fingering me, he gently lowers me onto the couch and whispers, "Bloody beautiful."

I'm panting and shaking, but when he kisses me, exhilaration floods my veins, and the fall from my high goes back on the rise. The heartbeat-long pause is the only indication I have that he didn't expect it.

But he doesn't stop. Maddox keeps kissing me like he's taking out his pleasure through it.

"You shouldn't have let me taste you," he rasps against my lips.

I shouldn't have done a lot of things when it comes to him.

19

MADDOX

I have a new rule. Under no circumstances will I be involved in any "ice-breaker" activities from here on out. If I need to stand up and introduce myself with my name, occupation, and what I enjoy doing, I will say that my number-one hobby is eating Reyna's sweet pussy.

It's my new favorite pastime. To my utmost sadness, I have only been graced with the opportunity once, and I fear I will never know peace unless I experience it again.

My cock has not fully come down in the six painfully long days since I was blessed with her sublime cunt. Watching her from afar—or from the chair in her bedroom while she's asleep—isn't enough for me to continue functioning.

Four nights ago, I realized I'd never be content with only interacting with her in class. The most rational solution I could come up with was downloading a tracker on her phone while she was asleep. I thought being able to watch the little dot move along on the screen would sate my need to have her in my sights constantly, but if my restlessness is any indication, I was clearly fucking incorrect.

I pull my coat on and wrap the scarf around my neck as I jog down the steps to the courtyard, double-checking Reyna's location on my phone. She's still on campus, moving in the direction of the subway station that doesn't take her to her apartment. If my activities from three nights ago are any indication, I know precisely where she's heading to on this cold, sunny morning.

We both have several hours to kill until I teach her class, and what better way to spend it than in each other's company? She'll likely disagree, but fortunately, I don't intend on asking for her opinion on the matter.

I catch up to her as she passes the campus gates. Because I'm feeling generous, I give her time to change her mind about doing something she shouldn't.

Reyna doesn't, continuing for the subway that'll take her to the crime scene I created for her. Her knee-high boots poke out from beneath her long brown tweed coat as she strides down the pavement, blissfully unaware that I'm eating up the space between us.

"Miss Sinaga," I say when I'm no more than a couple of feet away from her.

She whips around, lips parting on a gasp. "Maddox."

Fuck. She can't just go around saying my name like that in public unless she wants the entire student body to know what she looks like when she comes. It'd be most unfortunate because they'd all have to lose their eyes for it.

She looks utterly beautiful in this weather. Her tanned skin is a couple of shades paler, while the tip of her nose, her lips, and the apples of her cheeks are kissed cherry pink. Reyna stiffens with the look of someone doing something they know they'll be in trouble for.

"Where are you going?"

"Uh, home," she answers a little too forcefully.

My jaw tenses to stop from grinning. "You are many things, a good liar is not one of them. I am going to throw out some guesses, how does that sound?"

"Like a terrible plan." She checks her invisible watch. "Oh, would you look at the time. Seems I have to go."

"I'll join you."

It's cute watching her freeze like a deer in headlights. "Pass."

"Wasn't asking."

"Wasn't offering. Don't you have better things to do?"

I curl my fists at my side and use every speck of willpower I have not to touch her. Or worse: kiss her out in the open. "Nothing that's more important. Now. Where are we headed? And don't bother trying to lie. We both know you're not getting out of this."

"Why are you so difficult?" Lessers would wither under her glare. I, for one, find it endearing.

"It's part of my charm."

I watch her stubbornness melt away in time with her reluctant sigh. "A crime scene."

If I were a betting man, I'd be giving myself a hundred dollars for being right, yet again.

"So kind of you to extend an invitation to me. Please, lead the way." I motion toward the station at the end of the block, in front of the hideous modern monstrosity of a law school building.

Naturally, because Reyna insists on gripping on to the last vestiges of her stubbornness, she doesn't move.

"I'm barely holding myself back from bending you over the nearest bench so I can taste your sweet cunt again. So I suggest we start heading off before I decide I need to paint your pretty skin with my come."

She flushes bright pink, eyes darting around as she leans in to whisper, "You can't say that."

"Which part? That I want to see your pussy dripping for me again, or that I want you bent over and coming on my cock."

"Both," she hisses as her chest rises and falls faster.

I narrow my eyes at her when she puts an extra three feet of space between us. "I told you how to prevent either from happening. What's the address?"

Her glare burns into me like she can make me disappear if she thinks hard enough. After a quick stare-off, she gives up on attempting to perform miracles and tells me the address I already know before spinning on her heel to storm down the street.

I chuckle and follow along. My amusement quickly dies when we both put a respectable amount of space between us and I'm left glaring at the sidewalk and every person in our general vicinity. I need to touch her. It's not a want, or a mere desire. It's a physical necessity that every cell in my body screams for. The distance isn't good enough for me. I'm not sure how long I can withstand it, or what happens next. She doesn't know who I am or about the engagement ring sitting at the bottom of my office drawer. Until then the truth will always stand between us.

That's what today is about. I have to know whether her eyes crinkle with mortification at the truth. I need to know that she *sees me*.

The need to touch her doesn't disappear when we climb down the steps or when I guide her to an empty section of the subway at the back of the car where the seats are empty at our back and front, with no one on the opposite row. A single person sits at the other end, too far to hear us and too invested with their phone to pay us any attention. We're free in our corner to share every forbidden breath before the sky falls.

Reyna's coat parts when she sits, revealing the harness strapped around her waist, just above her lacy maroon miniskirt, and my mind takes the image of her in nothing but the leather, and it *runs* with it. The second the door slides shut, my hand slides beneath her coat and up her thighs.

Bloody hell, I've missed her legs.

Reyna clamps her knees together on pure reflex, squeezing my hand. The blush from earlier crawls up her neck and reddens her cheeks like it did the afternoon she fucked her fingers on my couch, and, *Christ*, if it doesn't make my cock thicken.

"Maddox?" My name comes out rasped as she grips my forearm and nods pointedly at the stranger at the other end of the car.

I lean down until my lips are inches away from her ear. "There's no one around, Miss Sinaga," I whisper slowly, skating my hand up her inner thigh beneath her skirt.

She squirms on her coat that protects her from the seat, and her breaths turn shuddering when she sees the bulge in my pants . . . "Maddox," she whispers. I can taste her aching desire in the two syllables.

"Do you see what you do to me, love?" I grunt. Precome leaks from my cock under her attention.

The edge of my finger presses against her pussy, and she gasps, swinging her wide brown eyes back up at me. I can picture her trapped beneath my weight, staring up at me with her lips parted on a silent gasp as her skin pinks with her arousal.

I rub her clit in slow circles. Reyna's warmth seeps through the material of her tights and underwear, and I learn it's possible to be jealous of fabric just because it's touching her skin.

"Someone could come in and see us." She glances at the door behind us that leads into the other car. Turns more frantic when the subway slows to a stop at the next station, but no one walks in or out.

"Mr. Shaw." It's one part whine, and another part worry. But her hips don't share the same concern, tilting ever so slightly so I'd meet her partway, pressing my knuckles against her sex.

"I like it when you call me that," I murmur, increasing the pressure. Her breath catches, eyelashes fluttering. The doors slide closed, and the wheels squeal against the tracks before it picks up speed again. "Tell me that your cunt is wet and needy for me."

"You're being insufferable." It's hard to make out any hint of worry when her words are moaned out.

"If I recall correctly, you were begging me not to stop what my tongue was doing. You rather enjoy it when I'm insufferable." I grin, gliding my fingers over her slit to make her shudder.

The lights flicker as we travel between tunnels.

She huffs in frustration—the pent-up kind—when I stop to slide my hand back down her thigh. "People would find this inappropriate, Mr. Shaw." Her irritation swiftly morphs into barely restrained lust when I go back to rubbing her clit. She melts against my side.

"Yeah?" I muse, moving my hand out from beneath her skirt to curl my fingers beneath her harness and yank her closer to me. "What's inappropriate is you wearing that to class without considering that I'd be hard the entire time, imagining what it'd be like to grip on to the leather as I fuck you against a wall."

I spread her thighs apart and press the heel of my palm against her pussy. Her body jolts, and I swear I can smell her arousal as I grab one of her knees to keep her legs parted for me.

The barest little broken moan escapes her, and my eyes damn well nearly roll to the back of my head when her thighs crush my hand.

The flimsy fabric of her tights gives way beneath my fingers, and a hole tears right above the entrance to her sex.

"Maddox!" She gawks at me, squirming and flicking her gaze between me and the man at the other end of the car. He's quickly forgotten the second my knuckle is back against her clit, adding *just* the right amount of pressure to bring her close to the edge without taking her to the end.

Her glare is vicious when I stop.

I don't bother hiding my smirk. "Are you going to tell me what I want to hear, or will I need to find out for myself?" I can feel her wetness through the fabric, but I want her to say it. When she doesn't answer, I pull my hand away. If looks could kill, she'd be making art out of me. "So?"

Through gritted teeth, Reyna grinds out a demanding "Yes."

In a single motion, her panties are pushed to the side and my fingers find home. Her warm cunt clamps down around me, and I almost finish like a fucking teenager. Moisture soaks my hand. It feels illegal that I can't sit her on my cock this very second. I curl my fingers and grin triumphantly when she slaps her hand over her mouth to cover her squeak.

Her addictive scent fills my lungs as I nuzzle my nose into her hair and whisper against the shell of her ear. "I'm just making sure you aren't telling me another lie."

Shudders work through her frame, staring up at me through glazed brown eyes. I feel like a fucking king. I draw out of her to slide another digit in, pumping them until she's struggling to stay upright in her seat.

Reyna lets out a sound of betrayal when I pull out of her to slide her saturated underwear back in place, rubbing her over the fabric. I bite back my grin and pretend not to notice her glaring at me in disbelief as I right her clothes, making sure her skirt is lowered and her coat covers her legs for warmth.

Reyna is too focused on murdering me in her mind to notice we've come to another stop and one more person has come to join us in the car.

"Put your headphones on, look out of the window, and pretend I'm not here," I tell her once the doors close and we're trudging along the tracks.

She does none of those things, shooting daggers at my profile the entire time I respond to emails on my phone, sliding my hand up and down her inner thigh, dangerously close to her core only to deny her what she wants.

If my cock is throbbing, then it's only fair that she's suffering too.

The mutual torture lasts several long, painful minutes before we get to our stop and she all but shoves me out of the seat and storms out of the subway, leaving me in the wind. The brat makes me jog to catch up to her and grab her elbow just to get her to stop.

"What?" she barks, whirling to face me.

Something tells me she won't receive my shit-eating grin well, so I only just manage to keep it at bay. Without a word, I grab the scarf from around my neck and wrap it around hers, then forge ahead without her so that it's her turn to huff and walk faster to catch up to me.

It's only a twenty-minute walk to the house, but due to Reyna's most unfortunate wardrobe malfunction, I hail us a cab and use the willpower not even God possesses to stop myself from warming her pussy for her.

The silence must do us some good because by the time we're dropped off a block away from our destination and moving around to the back of the house, Reyna no longer looks like she wants to stage my murder.

Yes, she's vibrating, but it's with the gleam of an artist about to start a new project. I had the exact same look three nights ago as I was climbing up the steps of the back porch.

Jeremy Warren lived in a slice of suburbia fit for a recently divorced Michelin chef who threatened to kill his ex-wife and child and left them with nothing while he got to keep the backyard and the white picket fence.

Like we've done this dance before, we search through the windows of Jeremy's house and our surroundings for signs of life before facing each other.

"Remember, you asked for this. If I go down, you're going down with me" is all the warning I get before Reyna rummages through her satchel, slides her hands into latex gloves, pulls out a black plastic container, glances around, then walks right up to the back door.

I arch a brow as she lowers herself to her haunches, right at eye level with my cock, which is twitching with the wrong idea. I fully harden when she opens the container and starts picking the lock.

Committing a felony with my student is not quite the field trip I expected. One may even call it a date.

Color me shocked and feral when the door clicks open in under three minutes. I don't think I've been this turned on by something so mundane in my life.

Reyna stands, brows pinched, shooting me a hesitant look. Her apprehension sets me on edge. Perhaps I've read her wrong, and she sees the person behind the art as a villain, abhorring the sin while appreciating the nuances only from a lens.

"You're really okay with this?" she asks carefully. "It's . . . this is illegal."

Christ, isn't she just adorable. I nod. "Of course."

"Someone—" She cuts herself off like she wants to choose her words carefully. "Somebody died in there. It won't be a pretty sight. You can wait outside if that's what you're more comfortable with."

I assure you, I was inside when he was killed, and I was extremely comfortable with it.

I don't miss that she didn't say it was disgusting or vile. "I appreciate your concern but open the bloody door before you catch a cold. Let's see what we're working with."

She studies me. I'm not sure what she finds, but whatever it is, it lightens her, and, dare I say it, she almost looks ecstatic about it. I suppose carrying out imprisonable offenses is more fun when someone is there to commit them with.

Reyna offers me a pair of gloves and shoe coverings from her satchel. We both look ridiculous with the white rustling clouds on our feet, but I can't help but fight the smile on my face. This woman is a dream.

Romance isn't part of the syllabus, but neither is homicide. It seems I'm expanding my curriculum today.

I open the door for her while she fishes out her camera, and trail after her, staying close to watch her reactions. She sucks in a shuddering breath when her arm brushes against mine, and I try not to smirk when she tries to hide her reaction from me.

I might hazard a guess and say that little Miss Sinaga is frustrated.

She stays back to let me walk into the lounge first, wringing her hands as she waits for me to take in the room and either back out or faint or do whatever it is the average person does when they see blood coating the once-white walls and dreary gray furniture.

Before I gave this house my artistic touch, it looked more like a bachelor pad, with all white and glass everything, than a home. Now? Reyna doesn't bat an eye or look remotely fazed by the gruesome sight. The most I manage to offer her is raised brows while I survey the area as if I weren't the one who staged it.

The plan was to make the scene as horrific as possible. Seeing as there are bloodstains all over the ceiling and crystal chandelier, I'd say I achieved that goal.

"Do you think your killer did it?" I wonder out loud once she's had enough time to look around.

"Yes," Reyna answers without hesitation. Her cheeks pinken. Is my student embarrassed about being so bloody intelligent? That won't do.

The corners of my lips twitch, and I finally take it as my turn to study her reactions. She watches me just as skeptically. Does my student think I doubt her? If this were a test, she'd be getting an A+.

"What makes you so certain?"

"Look at the place." She motions at the walls and tables like it's obvious. I wait for her to continue. She sighs. "You may school me on mise-en-scène, but here, I can learn from the master."

How receptive would she be to getting eaten out on the couch two feet from where I dismembered a man? Because if she says that again, I'm going to insist we contaminate a crime scene.

"You're impressed by this?" I'm not above fishing.

"Always."

My chest expands. My head probably does too. I doubt I'll fit through the door anymore.

"Do explain how you're certain your killer did this. It's a gruesome, chaotic sight." I sound far too upbeat for someone who is meant to be a level-headed person witnessing the remnants of a bloodbath. But neither of us is normal. There's no point pretending we're something we're not.

Reyna lets her camera hang from its strap around her neck to show me a picture on her phone. Jeremy does *not* look good there. Seems rigor mortis well and truly set in before his cleaner found him.

She points at the corner of the screen. "There's a coin three feet away from the body. Payment for the ferryman, and Cerberus has three heads."

Actually, I had put the penny on his forehead. Someone must have knocked it off. As for the coin, she's right in that it was for the ferryman, only it'd be an insult to pay that amount.

I'll give her seven out of ten.

"You got all that from a penny?"

Penny for your thoughts, Miss Sinaga.

"Yes." She shrugs, walking around with the camera back in hand to document the scene. "Charon won't be granting him passage with that amount."

I amend my answer. She gets full marks.

"You don't believe me." I dislike her defensive tone.

"On the contrary. I believe you wholeheartedly. I want to see this piece through your eyes."

Reyna is full of blushes today. Only this time, she turns her face away in an attempt to hide that she's biting her lip.

She pauses next to the corner table at the end of the couch and motions at the sleek black object beneath the lamp. "An hourglass symbolizes the afterlife, but there's no sand. It's not that the subject's time is up; there's nothing else for him beyond death."

Her shoe coverings rustle against the bloodstained carpet as she ducks down and peers up beneath the lampshade.

"No light bulb." She nods to herself like she's confirming what she already knew. "The banks of the River Styx where the souls who can't pay are left to wander are often described as being dark. Hence no light bulb."

Eight out of ten. She'll get the next two points if she can guess the other reference.

There's a stone from the garden beside the shoe rack in the entranceway. The bulb beneath the fake tree in the dining room is also missing. In his bedroom, I've left out a white hoodie for him on his bed, and a black one in his car.

It's my personal take on *Isle of the Dead* by Arnold Böcklin.

My personal favorite is the fifth version; however, I believe that's too specific to expect Reyna to figure out.

She hasn't noticed that not all of what's on the wall is blood either. Exhilaration floods through me as I glance at the drops of pink ink I've splattered around the room. It's washed out against the red, but I know it's there. The evidence of our kinship, and the risk of losing it all if she were to see me in the art I made for us.

"What's this?" I say, pointing at discoloration in the carpet, because I'm an utter fool when it comes to her. I want her to see me.

Reyna crouches to peer closer. She squints, and I really do try not to grin as she says, "I don't know, but it looks slightly . . . pink?" She makes a sound of contemplation. "There could have been chemicals here that made the blood oxidize or whatever they call it. I'm not a scientist."

Three out of ten. But because she never touched it, showed her working, and is so enjoyable to be around, I'll give her an eight.

I scroll to the next picture on her phone to find a wide view of the scene with Jeremy missing his hands and ears. The cuts are far from clean, more like he was torn apart by an animal.

Jeremy was perfectly silent and pliant as I carried out my experiment. I took a page out of Reyna's book and found a drug that paralyzed him. "What type of weapon do you think he used?" She steps away from a nearby shelf to come up to my side in front of where the body was found. The bloodstains are the worst here. "The coroner's report states the killer used three different weapons."

"I don't care about the doctor's opinion. I want to know what you think."

"I'm not qualified to answer that."

Cop-out. She has opinions.

"Humor me." I'll give out extra marks.

The browns in her eyes brighten. "Well, the report said a serrated blade was used. I mean, here—" She comes closer to scroll through the photos until she finds pictures of his head. "It looks like his ear was ripped off. It's messy."

"Not impressed?" I'll have her know it was difficult to cut off body parts with a bread knife.

But she was right. It was rather comedic.

"It's not that. I'm struggling to think of the messaging behind it. That he's heard something he shouldn't? Fallen for rumors, maybe? Grégoire Guérard has a painting based on a passage where Peter cuts off a man's ear, but if memory serves, the story behind it came down to mistakenly acting in defense of another."

Close, but not quite.

Depending on who you speak to, in the ancient story, Peter cut the servant's ear off to insult a high priest. In this instance, I'm only insulting Jeremy because he's a fucking cunt. He's Roland, but if Roland knew how to cook.

Plus, she may as well call me a fan of her work, because this part was inspired by her take on hearing no evil and the rule of three. Frankly, Reyna is a more creative killer than I am.

"And the hands?" I scroll back to the previous photo.

In the interest of fairness and symmetry, I felt it wise to cut off the same limb at the same angle, from the same spot right below the wrist, using a different tool.

"I think he's trying to say that the subject carried out wrong with his hands while he was alive—maybe because of what he heard—and continuing with the theme of the afterlife, it could be so that he can't commit those harms there too."

I don't think I'll ever have the heart to tell her that I just wanted to cut one side of him with a coping saw and the other with a bread knife because of our discussion in the library. The latter was far more efficient at carrying out dismemberments. But both were equally terrible for the task. It was purely experimental for our mutual benefit.

I appreciate her blowing smoke up my arse either way.

I'll still scale to eight out of ten.

And for the finale, I ask, "When did you decide that the Shadow killed him?"

"Yesterday."

Yesterday? As in, before she arrived at the scene? Just from *photos*?

She casually lifts her shoulders, not remotely smug.

"The victim's name is Jeremy. He owns fifty percent of the shares in a restaurant called *Afterworld*. The photos of him online always have him wearing a signet ring, and from what I could find, he had a phoenix engraved on it. The creature often symbolizes life or rebirth. The penny, the missing hands, and the references to the afterlife—or lack thereof—aren't just to insult him, the killer was sending a message. The future is in someone else's hands."

I stare at her, awestruck, hanging on to every word she says. No one—and I mean *no one*—would ever make that connection but her.

I am completely and utterly enraptured by Reyna Sinaga. She sees me, she knows who I am, recognizes how I think, sees the same picture as I do, even if she hasn't connected all the dots.

She was made perfect for me. That is not an opinion or a feeling or some misguided notion from rose-tinted sunglasses. That is a fact.

Reyna Sinaga is perfect for me.

20

REYNA

Ninety-three minutes.

That's how long I've spent questioning whether it would be fine to let my professor fuck me in front of the entire class.

I haven't absorbed any information, nor have I been able to understand a single word Maddox has said—let alone a full sentence.

I was wound up after Maddox teased the ever-loving shit out of me on the subway. Because I'm apparently broken and entirely desensitized to murder, my libido decided that a crime scene was the right place to go into fucking heat all because my goddamn professor validated my fascination with a serial killer no one else believes exists.

Without thinking, I pull Maddox's scarf higher to bring it closer to my nose. My core tightens as his scent fills my lungs. Even my bra feels too harsh against my nipples. Every time I move, I'm reminded of the tear he's made in my tights and how soaked my underwear still is.

My attention falls to my empty Word document before going back to Maddox. He's just so—infuriating. He's going to make me go crazy, and I think I *am* crazy for thinking that we may genuinely be compatible.

He may be eleven years older and my professor, but once I graduate, neither will matter. We'll still share the same broken edges that somehow fit together.

And as for the rest of him? *Attractive* doesn't begin to cut it.

The black sweater he's thrown over his white button-up is clinging to his chest and shoulders, tapering at his waist, down to the belt I know costs enough to make me cry. His dark-gray pants stretch and hug his thighs whenever he paces the classroom. And is it just me, or is the fabric straining over his bulge more than usual?

Maddox looks like an academic god when he has a blazer on. Without it, he's pure danger. The Clark Kent type that causes the crime. To think the same hand he's gesturing with was between my thighs a couple of hours ago.

I shift in my seat, eyelids growing heavy as my focus drifts back to the bulge in his pants. He feels it, doesn't he? The pull between us.

"Miss Sinaga?"

I blink. The blood rushes to my face. Half the class is staring at me. I clear my throat and sit straighter. "What was that?"

Nicole gives me a look of pity as I try to stop imagining my professor doing indecent things to me.

A slow, knowing smile spreads across his lips, and I glare at him. Jerk. "I was asking what the intention was behind the tonal contrast."

"Um." It takes far too long for my brain to process work.

Someone snorts a laugh behind me, and I fumble, dropping my pen on the floor. My skin burns hotter as I scramble to pick it up. I suck in a sharp breath to regulate my breathing only for it to be thrown out when I look up to find Maddox glaring at whoever it was who was amused by my struggling. Even I'd wither under that stare.

I exhale and try to focus on the projector. The screenshot is from *Hereditary*, a horror film that's hailed by critics and hated by the public—it's by the same man who directed *Midsommar*, one of my favorite movies—a fact I happened to have shared with Maddox in the cab, right before he went down on me.

On the screen is a woman, played by Toni Collette, sitting alone in a warmly lit workshop filled with golden hues, while the rest of the house recedes into shadows behind her.

The class know-it-all beside me stirs in his seat. "Psychological—"

"It shows psychological fragmentation," I say a little too loud before Austin can answer for me. "Aster uses the warmth to deceive the viewer into thinking she's in control, while the rest of the house slips into colder, fractured tones. It's a visual way to mirror emotional dissonance." It doesn't come out any friendlier.

"That's correct, Miss Sinaga," Maddox praises.

I narrow my eyes at him. That rat bastard *knew* I was distracted because of him.

Pissed off, sexually frustrated, and completely and utterly wound up, the moment class ends, I jump to my feet and shove everything in my bag.

"Someone's in a rush." Nicole laughs as she leisurely packs up.

"I have an appointment." With my vibrator. "I'll see you tomorrow." I throw the strap over my shoulder and beeline for the exit.

This is our last class of the day, and we usually walk to the subway together, but I'm not waiting. The sooner I get home, the better it'd be for society. Maddox's voice stops me.

"Miss Sinaga, a moment."

I'm going to kill him.

Maddox is the reason I'm acting this way, and goddamn him for looking so good, sitting on the edge of the desk, legs crossed at the ankle as he flicks through a textbook.

"Good luck," Nicole whispers, patting me on the back as she passes me.

I glower and clutch the strap of my satchel, striding up to him as students pour out of the class. Two students reach him before I can, and I'm left to fester and curse him and his bloodline while they ask their million questions. A solid five minutes pass, and they're still talking. Everyone else has left.

What could they possibly want to know that they can't just look up online? A child could understand the criteria of our next assignment.

I tap my fingers on my arm as I wait. *Finally,* they say their thanks and fuck off. But apparently Maddox has zero consideration for me, my time, or my libido, because the moment they walk away, he turns around and starts packing up as if I don't exist.

The wooden door slams shut, and I take it as my cue to leave as well, but once again, he stops me before I can.

"Lock the door, Miss Sinaga."

My irritation vanishes, and my internal temperature skyrockets when he looks up at me out of the corner of his eye, arching a brow in challenge.

He straightens to his full height and adjusts his belt, pulling my attention down to the bulge in his pants that's doubled in size.

I swallow the lump in my throat. It doesn't go away. "After what you did in the subway, and embarrassed me in front of the entire class, you must be delusional if you think you can order me around." I'm proud of myself for keeping my voice measured when my core is clenching with my internal battle not to stare at his erection.

Maddox prowls forward, eating the distance between us. He reaches out to hold my chin between his thumb and forefinger, and tips my head to the side so he can lean down and say against my ear, "Unless you'd like for someone to walk in and see your pretty lips around my cock, I suggest you lock the door for your private lesson."

Molten desire floods through me. Maddox straightens, eyes falling to my mouth when it parts on a soundless gasp. In *here*? This is a *classroom*.

Every single alarm bell is going off in my head, and each one of them is telling me how stupid I'd be for doing what he says. Yet delicious tension coils through my flesh at the danger that comes from doing something I shouldn't.

Oxygen stutters in my chest as I glance back at the door. Doing as he says will plunge us deeper toward the point of no return, where it'll be so much harder to claw my way back out and try to move on after knowing what life is like with Maddox Shaw.

I'll have to go back to being invisible and living with a brain that no one understands.

This . . . It can't be permanent, can it? Could we actually make this work? Keep what we have going on in secret until it's safe? Does he see us moving in that direction too?

Looking into his eyes, I think I know the answer. It's more than lust or pure want, it's a desperate, visceral need that surpasses mere physical touch. I've written about it before, and have only dreamed of being able to encapsulate it on the screen.

My heart hammers in my chest, and the warmth that follows stings my eyes, because I know without a doubt that I want this to work out between us.

I let the strap of my bag fall and set my satchel and outer layers down. Then, before I can change my mind, I turn around.

"Reyna, if you lock that door, there's no going back."

I pause to look at him over my shoulder. One word crosses my mind: *good*.

The doubts are still there. No one has ever stayed or picked me first—not in the way that really counts. This could always be a game to him. Just a bit of fun with his student to pass the time. But I can't let fear control me.

I keep walking until my fingers hover over the lock, and with a resounding echo that cracks through the room like thunder, it clicks into place.

"Knees."

Three seconds is how long I give myself to accept fate. Slowly, I turn around, afraid that it'll all vanish if I move too quickly. He watches me with the steady surety of a man who decided this moment was happening long before I did.

The air is heavy with tension and words unspoken. The room is charged with something volatile that could strike either of us with the slightest misstep. If I concentrate hard enough, I can hear his pulse beat as rapidly as mine.

I keep walking until there's a foot of weighted space separating us. We stare at each other. Study each minute movement. Maddox reaches for me, skating his fingers along my jaw before tucking a lock of hair behind my ears. The touch feels like forbidden magic, and I'm at the whim of his spell.

"*Knees*, Reyna," he repeats, voice a soft demand.

Another three seconds. I spend each one of them filling my lungs; then I do what fate intended.

My legs shake as I stare up at him, slowly lowering until the wooden floor digs into skin. Black devours all traces of green in his irises, and I can track every rise and fall of his chest.

Backlit by the afternoon sunlight streaming through the windows, he looks like he could be a deity of death and art with his dark clothing, blackened eyes, oozing dominance. Yet from down here, kneeling before him, I feel powerful.

There's power in safety, being seen and untouchable, the centerpiece and every focal point.

My heart stalls as he circles me and pauses at my back. I sense him lowering to his haunches. Goose bumps pepper my skin as he reaches around me to loosen the buckles of my harness to leave my top bare for him.

The electrified air crackles along my exposed, tender breasts. Nerves and desire tighten my stomach. His hand brushes over my nipples as he draws the harness over my shoulders and fastens it in place. The leather feels like silk and sandpaper against my aching flesh.

My breaths stagger as his fingers skate over the back of my arm, sweeping my hair to the side to drag his lips over my shoulder and up the side of my neck, inhaling my scent and leaving a trail of delicate kisses in his wake. His hot breath caresses my skin as his fingers whisper along the underside of my breasts before splaying over my sternum.

"I apologize for putting you on the spot," Maddox mutters against the place where my jaw meets my ear. A shiver rolls through me. "I wanted to hear your voice, love."

"I dislike public speaking." The words come out broken from his touch.

"Let me help you get used to it before you have a bigger audience."

I nod. It's the only thing I can get myself to do as I turn to watch him move back in front of me, putting his bulge in my eyeline. He removes his sweater and sets it down in front of my knees. Heat radiates through my core, part excitement and part . . . trepidation.

"Spread your legs apart."

I blink hard to push aside my thoughts. An innate part of me wants to please him—*impress him*. He opens his mouth to repeat himself, and I scramble to do as he said. The floor catches on my tights before my knees find reprieve against the cashmere fabric that still harbors traces of his warmth.

His head tips as he drags an amused, scrutinizing gaze over my form. "Wider."

I swallow down a retort, hesitating before complying. He chuckles, cradling the back of my skull, and lowers to reach beneath my skirt, dragging his fingers over my sex, touching and teasing, rubbing around where I want him until I'm panting and angling my hips to get what I need from him. Only then does he push my underwear to the side and slide a finger into my entrance.

Stars explode in my vision. I buckle forward, held upright by his grip threaded through my hair. He draws his finger out to add a second. My muscles spasm around him, and a violent shudder works through me when he rubs my clit with his thumb.

His next chuckle is almost mocking. "You might hate getting ordered around, but it makes your cunt fucking wet, doesn't it?"

I curse him with my glare because damn him for being right. When I don't answer, he leaves me empty to pinch the oversensitive flesh. I yelp, digging my nails into his covered forearms.

"*Doesn't it*, Miss Sinaga?" Maddox's stern voice makes me see red.

"Yes, sir," I bite out, and the sadistic asshole tightens his grip in my hair and hovers his hand over my core. It's like he's *trying* to make me bratty.

He raises his brows. "Sir?"

I shrug. "It's generic. Easy to remember."

Apparently the wrong thing to say, because he turns venomous, and I witness firsthand why people call him vindictive.

"If you're going to have a bratty mouth, you better know how to use it." He rises to his full height; any hint of tenderness is gone from him as he winds my hair around his fist and holds my head back. "Stick your tongue out."

Whether my self-preservation has kicked in or my need to get off is strong enough to get me into line, I part my lips, show him the back of my throat, and reach for his belt.

My eyes widen when his wet fingers push into my mouth, coating my tongue in the evidence of my arousal. My gag reflexes kick in, and I sputter, but he doesn't relent, fingering my throat like he's training me to take him. Tears gather along my waterline, threatening to fall each time he slides back into me.

Moisture trickles down my thighs, saturating my panties. I grip on to his belt with one hand, feeling his length drag against the palm of my hand every time I move.

"Can you taste yourself on my fingers?"

He pulls out, and I swallow down greedy gulps of air. My legs quiver, stomach convulsing and spasming at the complete and utter emptiness. I have half a mind to bring my hand between my legs if he's so intent on dragging my suffering out.

"No answer?"

My eyes sharpen on him for a moment before I melt into a puddle because he thrusts the same fingers back into my sex, driving them mercilessly until I'm a panting, quivering mess, clawing at his shoulders and feeling the light around the corner.

Then it ends. I don't have the time to murder him for edging me before I'm gagging around him, feeling a tear leak from the corner of my eye. He holds my head in place so I can't escape—not that I want to.

"Let's try that again. Can you taste yourself on my fingers, Miss Sinaga?"

Maddox doesn't remove his fingers for me to answer. I make a sound that loosely resembles the words "Yes, you sadistic asshole," because if he brings me right to the precipice just to pull away, I might start a fistfight.

He eases up, smearing the wetness over my lips and down my chin. "Good girl. Now was that so hard?" He brightens at my answering glower and looks pointedly at my hand still on his belt. "Are you going to do something about it, Miss Sinaga, or do you intend to just sit there looking pretty?"

I must have developed the strength of God in my frustration, because I manage to yank him closer and unbuckle him with nothing but pure lust-addled fury pumping through me.

He chuckles. *Motherfucker.* I grit my teeth, frantically undoing his pants so maybe the devil would be so kind as to, oh boy, I don't know—how about let me fucking come?

When he pushes my hands away, I release a feral growl. Maddox lowers his pants just enough to pull out his cock. My jaw drops. There's so much to take in that I can't decide where to focus; the precome beading on the head of his cock, the throbbing vein, or the sheer size of him. I wet my bottom lip, fixated on the pearl snaking beneath his crown, down his shaft.

"It's rude to stare, Miss Sinaga." His voice is no more than a fraying rasp.

My eyelids grow heavy the longer I admire him, and another bead of come gathers on the head of his cock, and a light bulb goes off in my head. This is an opportunity.

I inch forward, breathing hard through my mouth so the hot air skates over his length. He twitches, and a strained sound comes from the back of his throat.

If I don't get to finish, then neither does he.

I blink languidly, meeting his stare when I reopen my eyes. Then, ever so slowly, I drag the tip of my tongue over his crown, capturing his arousal into my mouth. My moan makes him curse, abs clenching beneath his buttoned top. And I do it again, reveling in the grip tightening around my hair. I explore him with only the tip of my tongue, and reverent kisses bleach his knuckles white.

Every one of his labored breaths takes me higher as I continue to refuse him. Desire pools between my legs, and my muscles spasm at the emptiness.

A callous smirk spreads across my lips when his thighs start to shake. I finally close my lips around him with a moan and take him as deep as I can. His strangled groan fills the room, and he pays me back for the torture by keeping my head in place so my throat closes around him.

He releases me, and we simultaneously gasp for breath. Except I don't waste time repeating the process of edging him with tentative touches.

He snarls, and I do it again, and again, and preen when he smiles down at me, reading me like an open book.

My jaw aches as I widen to take him, and I choke when he hits the back of my throat. He steals the control back from me, holding my head steady so I gag around him. He pulls back an inch just to get reacquainted with my throat, over and over until tears stream down my cheeks and I'm a wet mess.

"I fucking knew your lips would be the death of me," he rasps.

My body locks up when someone tries to open the door, rattling the handle. Maddox keeps having his way with me like nothing happened. I'm too far gone to warn him that someone might have a key.

He releases me just enough to drag oxygen into my lungs before thrusting as far as I can take him—which isn't very far. I can only manage half of him before I choke.

"Relax your jaw." Voice as rough as stone.

I blink through my teary vision to make him out through the blur. Wrinkles paint his forehead, as another hand threads through my hair. I take a deep breath before forcing myself to loosen my body.

"Go on. Take me—*fuck*," he grunts. "Yes. Fuck. That's my girl."

I moan, and that only makes him buck. My nails dig into his toned thighs, and I give in to the temptation. My eyes roll to the back of my head as soon as pressure hits my sex. The muscles in my neck vibrate with my groan.

Maddox loses it. There's no control to his movements, curled over, jerking, bucking his hips without restraint. Eyes are glazed over, drifting between half-lidded and shut. Brows furrow, cursing and murmuring my name and grunting quietly.

Saliva, tears, and the residue of his come paint my cheeks and swollen lips. We're both too helpless to stop as I chase my pleasure with him in my mouth. The same sick thrill of power courses through me seeing him so gone, fucking my throat like he's operating with his hindbrain because *I* brought him to that state.

Maddox pulls all the way out suddenly, drags me to my feet, and slams his lips to mine, devouring me with as much ruined control. One of his hands strays to the base of my skull. The other wraps around the column of my throat, molding me to his will. He deepens the kiss, backing me up or moving me to the side or—I don't know anymore.

The only thing clicking is him and his lips and that this is the only thing that matters. It's the only thing that's ever felt right.

I can barely breathe from his hold on my throat and his tongue pushing into my mouth, kissing me like a drowning man gulping down air. His hard length is plastered against my stomach, and my core screams with the need to feel him inside me.

The desk hits the back of my thighs, and he lifts me onto the table without care for the ensuing chorus of clattering. There's no care about the nearby window, or the people who might be on the other side of the door. Neither of us breaks the starved kiss until I tug at his top.

Maddox draws back. We breathe hard, staring at each other, only he's looking at me with animalistic glee, dragging his eyes from my parted legs and bunched skirt to my bare chest, then my abused lips that he traces with his thumb, smiling like he's won the lottery.

"Look at you, all nice and pink for me." Time seems to slow as Maddox's hand drops to my chest to twist my tender nipples between his fingers, and he watches mesmerized. "So beautiful."

The air between us grows weight. I can't have him go slow and gentle with me. It'll hurt too much once this is over if I know what him treating me tenderly feels like. I pull him closer by his shirt, plant my lips back onto his, and he's back to pawing at my flesh.

We undress each other at the same time: I'm unbuttoning his top; he's throwing my boots to the side, ripping off my stockings and panties, leaving my skirt and harness. As soon as he's content with his work, my nipple is in his mouth and he's groping my other breast with the same frantic need I have thrumming through me.

This wasn't on my bingo card for this year. Or lifetime. I never thought I'd be sitting half naked on my professor's desk with the taste of his come in my mouth.

I most definitely didn't think I'd be doing it on a weekday while there's still daylight outside and people who are no doubt on the other side of the wall—a fact that hasn't crossed my mind in far too long.

The thought pumps the brakes in my head.

This is the real crossing. Not the locking of the door or the meeting of our lips. This is the next step, the threshold that cannot be uncrossed. I can't think clearly or formulate what I really want to ask, but I need to know that we are really taking that step together.

The question comes out as a blurted "Are we going to have sex?"

He pauses, arching a brow. "I'm not going to have sex with you, Miss Sinaga. I'm going to fuck you. The effect would be the same. Your ability to walk won't be."

My eyes fall to his cock that's twitching and leaking with more precome. My core throbs around nothing, and right now that's answer enough for me.

When I meet his eyes, he's already watching me—not with judgment or the arrogant tilt I might have expected. More like I'm a project he's trying to work out.

I frown when he stops me from removing his unbuttoned top. He rolls on a condom he got from who knows where and lines himself up at my entrance before I can overthink it.

He presses something long and thin against my lips. "Bite."

My lips part on instinct. I glance down at the paintbrush. He can't be serious, can he?

I hesitate before complying with his order, clamping down on the paintbrush. The wood dents under my teeth, and he lowers his lips to my ear.

"Remember, love, not a sound. I'd hate for anyone to hear."

It's the only warning I get. He grips a hand on my harness and fills me with a single thrust. Pleasure explodes through me. I throw my head back, biting down on the paintbrush to muffle the sound. The stretch stings, but it's barely noticeable against the pure bliss of having him inside of me.

My hand flies behind me. Papers and books go soaring through the air, hitting the floor with a hard thud. I gasp, but he doesn't stop driving his hips forward, lost to the motion of fucking me. It takes several tries to contort around to look at the items that have fallen from his bag.

I still. That's . . .

Ice chills my veins at his serious expression. I can't say a word without taking the brush out of my mouth, and he offers no explanation for why there are sketches of me strewn across the floor.

Each one is drawn from different angles and positions: side profile, chewing on a pen, looking over my shoulder, sitting on a chair, lying down. There's one of the dragon tattoo on my back. Some of the sketches were done with pink ink and chalk in various shades of that same color. Others were created with graphite.

This really isn't *just* fun.

This isn't a game for him or an extracurricular habit he has where he fraternizes with students.

My pulse roars in my ears as we stare at each other. I don't dare blink. Neither does Maddox. He rubs my pussy as if I'm already his, thrusting into me like he's telling me something with each drive. And I accept whatever it is he's offering. Skin slaps against skin. I jolt back with every unrelenting drive of his hips.

If the paintbrush weren't in between my teeth, what could I say?

Maddox pinches my clit, and just like that my thoughts vanish with a needy buck of my hips. My body takes on a mind of its own as my hands start to roam over him. I need more of him. All of him. The pressure in my core is cresting, and I'm struggling to keep from making a sound.

I bite the paintbrush until it splinters. He takes it out of my mouth, fucking me with desperate strokes, watching me like the universe moves around me. He gets me to take over rubbing my clit. A big mistake. I forget to stop myself from swallowing my groan.

"Do you need my cock back in your mouth to keep you quiet, Miss Sinaga?"

I nod, then shake my head, then nod again, repeating the same cycle as my climax rushes closer.

He sucks the soft flesh of my neck, and I know this time I won't have any hope of hiding the damage he leaves behind.

My fingers inch beneath his shirt, moving over his collarbones and the expanse of muscles still hidden by fabric. He grasps my wrists before I can stray to his back, roughly kissing each knuckle before grabbing my shoulder and harness as leverage to bring me down onto his length hard.

I hiss his name, and lips come down on mine to swallow my next moan. His pummeling grows jerkier.

Then I'm hit with more force than anything else I've been hit with before. Every cell in my body lights in an explosion, propelling me to the top of the world. It's the fall that blinds me with worry, because I reach my climax hoping and praying and dreading that I better not have read this wrong. Maddox has become one of the few recurring presences in my life, and the only one who sees what I see. I've already lost too many people. I can't lose more.

I force my eyes to stay open when he slams into me, snarling my name between curses as he keeps fucking me until he drops his forehead against mine.

His ragged breaths chafe my burning skin. The weight of what we did blankets us. After this, I'm walking out the door, back to being strangers until the next time we're alone together. And I hate it. I don't like being his dirty secret.

His cock twitches inside of me, and something dangerous settles behind his eyes that scares me. A secretive smirk curves across his face, and it feels like I've just agreed to something.

Maddox's lips suddenly crash against mine in a ravenous kiss. "You should have walked away when you still could, Reyna." He nods to the wall between the windows, farther into the classroom. "Now be a good girl and put your hands on the wall, why don't you?"

My eyes bug. Is he not tired?

"Don't make me tell you twice again, Miss Sinaga. Or would you prefer that I count to three, and you can face the repercussions for not following instructions?"

I glare at him. "Don't you dare."

His lips twist into a devilish smirk. In a single motion, he has his belt unthreaded from his pants and folded in his hands. "Try me."

I make a sound that I don't recognize. Maddox was wrong. He's the one who's going to be the death of me.

21

MADDOX

Romance isn't dead.

Although, its definition becomes debatable when a serial killer is involved.

After fucking Reyna senseless to the point where she couldn't walk, I've been overflowing with ideas. I've come up with several concepts to add to my exhibition and thought of something rather brilliant that will solve both of our creative blocks.

I carefully place the light bulb amongst the bottle of ink and tacky fake peonies before closing my bag. I had hoped to stop by the local florist and pick up real ones. To say I was disappointed to find out they're not in bloom is the understatement of the century.

This is why I'm not a flower person. There's no consistency.

At least the fake pink ones I managed to find are a similar shade to the peonies on one of Reyna's tattoos. So the sentiment remains.

Locking my car, I shoulder my duffle bag and pull my cap lower to keep the rain out of my eyes. It's the ideal weather to create the ultimate crime. Barely anyone is looking out their window this late at night. If they did, they wouldn't bat an eye over a man running through the rain. I'll be completely forgettable. And the drops of water battering the roof will drown out the sound of screams. All in all, it's a fantastic night to make a romantic gesture.

The risks associated with carrying out this plan are endless. Honestly, from an average, sane person's point of view, I'm about to take an uncalculated and potentially premature leap of faith.

So I sat on it.

I went to bed disregarding the idea and had every intention of taking our newfound relationship day by day—where I slowly go mad because she doesn't know the truth.

Except the next day, I saw her tugging up her woolen jersey to hide the marks I left on her body. Later that night, when she thought she was safe in the confines of her bed, I crept in because I can't stop myself, and saw the smattering of blue-and-pink splotches along her neck.

I was already holding on by a thread at that point.

Then, a couple of days later, I invited her back to my office, and she arrived wearing that same bloody leather harness of hers. It was absolutely fucking magnificent to grab on to while I fucked her over my desk and covered her body in more marks.

After that, all my good intentions flew right out the window.

I decided our fates were sealed.

We haven't interacted since then, but my student doesn't know I've seen her every single night since.

She fucked up.

Reyna Sinaga fucked. Up.

She should never have let me in, never let me touch her. She fucked up, and it's too late for her to run from me now. Soon, everything is going to change.

This is a means to prove what destiny has always intended.

She knows me. Sees me. *Gets* me. No one else has understood me quite like her. She calls me out on my bullshit, looks past my messes, and still deems me worthy. If she pieces tonight together, there will be no mistaking that, whether it was by God's will or pure fate, Reyna and I were meant to be together.

I slow to a stop when I reach Paddy Hutton's house. Just as I suspected, lights are flashing from the gaps in the living room curtain.

He's been on my list for the better part of a year. His life is like clockwork: wake up, go to work, hit the casinos during his lunch break, go back to his soul-crushing insurance job, come home, hit his wife before dinner, then waste away on the couch while placing bets from his phone.

Obviously, he changes it up on the weekend. For example, he might go to a gambling ring with Nolan instead of Barry, or stay at a casino from dawn until dusk and give his wife some reprieve. It keeps me on my toes.

Most importantly, he has zero ties with the Order. I triple-checked. It's my new rule: only make art out of men Shepherd doesn't know about. Since Reyna follows my work, it's now quite literally in my job description to give her a safe learning environment.

Water sloshes up my legs as I jump the fence into their minuscule backyard. There's only a faint glow spilling out from nearby houses. Combined with the stormy night, it's difficult to see more than an outline of my surroundings.

With my gloves in place, I slink up the porch and kneel in front of the door. Picking locks is an art form—a boring one, yet art nonetheless. Steady hands and a dash of patience are required. It seems I only enjoy it when I'm watching Reyna do it.

But without Mrs. Hutton home, ol' Paddy over here is probably too boozed up to remember to add the dead bolt. Like usual. Which means that once the lock slides out of its spot, thanks to the WD-40 I added to the hinges a few months ago, the door opens without a squeak.

My pulse thrums—it's the excitement of starting a new project. The type of tingles from being overcome with creative vision. It's my favorite feeling in the world. Second to feeling Reyna's pussy on my face.

I grab a cloth out of my bag and splash my home remedy onto the fabric, then help myself inside. Like every other time I've done it, the moment I cross the threshold, I become a different person. I'm no longer a man, simply an artist.

My senses sharpen, and my everything becomes more vibrant. I can see the depth of color in every grain of the cedar furniture as if the lights were on high beam. The floral-patterned wallpaper pops in the darkness, a cloudy mauve against ivory, and the single dot of vermilion.

The flashes of blue and white from the TV glinting against the glass of the China cabinets.

A neat stack of shoes lines the wall next to the front door, and I pick up notes of a fresh bouquet of flowers from the vase in the center of the hallway. They'll wither away and die soon enough. It's a pathetic man's way of apologizing—throwing gifts and money with no intention of changing.

After all the pitiful kills I've carried out lately, this will be my redemption arc. My mind whirls with possibilities for staging the scene. It may be my greatest work yet, and it's all Reyna's idea. How the tables have turned.

Hopefully, the idiot cop drooling over Reyna can put his two brain cells to use and feed her tonight's kill. The delusional fuckwit seriously thinks he has a chance with her. It's rather sad. He's not her type.

I am, though.

It wasn't hard to figure out who was leaking the information to Reyna since I only had to watch her walk right into the police station, then come out looking uncomfortable as a man guided her outside to have lunch.

Lawrence McCabe. Twenty-five. Six feet tall. Looks like he reads with his finger. A paladin, and a man who still has his uses and can remain alive—for the time being, that is.

I've never been the type to get petty over competition. I've always known my place in the food chain, the Order leaves no room for doubt. The second he steps out of line, his death will look like an accident.

For now, he needs to give Patrick "Paddy" Hutton's file to Reyna.

After that? Who knows. It's been a few months since I've made someone's death look like an accident. What type of man would I be if I didn't brush up on my skills?

I stalk into the house, carefully closing the door behind me before a draft can alert Paddy to my presence. The place gives off olden-day suburbia vibes. You'd think a family with two and a half kids lives there, a barbecue firing up on the back deck every Sunday.

Only part of that is true. Paddy does have a barbecue. It's decommissioned.

The only sounds are the blaring TV and the squeal of the couch every time Paddy shifts. My lips twist when the wooden floor creaks beneath my boot. I pause and wait for a reaction that doesn't come.

Slowly, I slip into the kitchen, past the open, empty pizza box and beer bottles, then through the dining room and into the lounge, where Paddy's too busy frowning at his phone to notice me.

The rest proceeds like clockwork. I get up behind him, place the cloth over his nose and mouth, and hold. He struggles for a bit; I struggle for a bit; then he passes out. It's always the same song and dance.

I sigh, stretching my back out. I'm really not that into fighting. It's cleaner this way. The raging migraine he'll get from my concoction is an added bonus.

Twenty minutes later, the little fella is looking strapping in his Sunday best, tied to a chair in the middle of the hallway between the front and back doors—a poetic tragedy, one Reyna would appreciate if she's familiar with feng shui. With both doors perfectly aligned, the money comes in, and it flies right out. And right in the center of it all is Paddy.

I lay out my supplies on the floor, and by the time I've set up the kitchen and lounge, plucked the petals from the fake peonies, and scattered them around the future corpse, my subject rises from his slumber, frowning and grumbling words impossible to make out.

I don't blame him. It's hard to speak when you have a light bulb in your mouth.

His eyes widen when awareness hits him, and the wheels in that smooth brain of his start ticking like maybe—just *maybe*—he might be in a bit of a bind. A garbled, jumbled mess of sounds comes out of him as he thrashes against the synthetic ropes. He tries dislodging the light bulb from his mouth, but his jaw is firmly clamped around it.

As I watch him squawk, I mentally take notes for future kills. I don't know why I didn't start gagging my subjects earlier. There's no incessant begging or whining. No high-pitched screams, nor any lies about how innocent they are.

I'm not looking for Paddy's confession. I only need him to sit there and look pretty so I can do my work.

It's odd, actually. Usually I can see Roland in the men, and I imagine how he'd react in the situation. I find myself caring very little about what that bastard would do right now. I'm a man with his muse, with no bone to pick and a lady to court.

Lacks intimacy.

We'll see if Reyna still says that once I've finished with this piece.

"Paddy, let's cut to the chase, shall we?" I start. "You're a terrible human being, but I'm worse—for different reasons, obviously. For example, I wasn't accused of raping my wife."

He can try thrashing around as much as he wants; I've stabilized the chair by tying it to the railing of the stairwell and the antique shelf. It's never going to topple over.

Crossing my arms, I lean against the wall and stare him down. I suppose this is a bit of a "villain spiel," but I try to involve my subjects in the process where I can. It gives the project a more profound impact.

"Anyway, I digress." I hold up the extension cord. "This leads to this light bulb." Much to my surprise, he goes completely still. "I'm going to turn it on now, and it would be highly preferable that you bite down sooner rather than later—I want to go home and catch up on sleep." His eyes bulge, wide and panicked as they flick between me and the cord. "I feel it's necessary to remind you that it will get rather hot."

Tears stream down his face, mixing in with the sweat trickling down his temple. He frantically shakes his head and says something that sounds a lot like *please*. I flip the switch on, and his face lights up like . . . well, like a light bulb.

He pulls at the ropes around his arms and legs, and whips his head from side to side, screaming at the top of his lungs.

I tsk. "Don't you start getting any bright ideas about escaping—no pun intended."

Paddy ignores me.

Sighing, I lean against the wall and check my watch. When he hasn't clamped down by the three-minute mark, I begin arranging the petals and the bouquet of peonies so that the flow and placement is perfect.

A ragged cry follows the sound of shattering glass.

Oh good, we're speeding things along.

Stepping away from the lamp I just turned on, I carefully navigate my way back in front of him to avoid stepping on any petals.

I wince once I catch sight of him. "As painful as it looks, I want you to know that you're doing a wonderful job. I think my student will really appreciate this piece."

Crimson falls down his chin onto his pristine white shirt in a steady stream, dripping onto the shards littering the floor. *Bloody hell.* For the sake of art, I would have left the fallen glass alone. I'll have to clean it now because I'll be pissed if Reyna cuts herself on it.

Paddy cries out a truly pathetic sound when he attempts to talk. *Go figure.* I grab the duct tape off the floor, grip his head, then apply strips over his nose and mouth to block his airways. The moisture on his skin makes it peel off immediately. Huffing, I slap his face to keep the edges down despite the blood, sweat, and tears on his skin, but the useless thing keeps lifting around his nose. I pinch his nose together with one hand while his thrashing becomes more extreme. It's not exactly what I wanted to do, but improvise, adapt, overcome.

Right about now—if his choking is any indication—some glass is lodging in his throat.

It's a relatively simple death. Sometimes less is more.

His attempt at fighting me off grows more desperate the redder his skin gets. It quickly dissipates as the purple tinge to his face grows more prominent.

I check my watch before glancing around at my stage, waiting for him to die. I've always found it rather irritating how long it takes to kill someone by suffocation. Sure, his esophagus is all cut up, and there's probably a bit of brain damage going on, but I'm going to need his heart to stop beating before I can wrap this up.

Reyna was looking for that light bulb moment that takes the words right out of her mouth. I can't say for certain that she'll be rendered speechless by what I've done, but ol' Paddy over here definitely is.

Soon, she's going to see what I did for her, and she will know how perfect we are for each other.

Until then, I have to wait approximately four more minutes until Paddy is dead for good.

The things I do to impress my girl.

22

REYNA

I'm sure I'd be put on a watchlist for feeling glad that a serial killer murdered someone. Except the usual excitement isn't there this time around. I haven't felt dread this strong since Mom was in the hospital and every day was a waiting game to see when the lights would go out.

The pit in my stomach has tripled in size, and I feel sick every time I think about the kill.

Sleeping has been impossible since Lawrence handed me the latest file two nights ago. I would have visited the crime scene immediately if it weren't for the wedding I had to film yesterday.

My feet are rooted on the other side of the door, mind conjuring a million different reasons why I'm so nervous.

Sneaking into murder scenes is dangerous.

The killer could be watching me right now.

If I get arrested, I lose my scholarship.

I home in on each because I can't shake the thought that *he* could be behind this.

A coincidence. That's all it is.

Taking a shuddering breath, I steel my spine, and head into the spotless kitchen, camera in my trembling hand. There isn't so much as a speck of dust around, every inch has been wiped clean. I can only assume it wasn't the victim's doing.

My heart stops when I spot the bag of Cheetos and a cup of tea sitting on the counter. I swallow. *No.* It has to be a fluke. *Has to.* Something like that wouldn't happen to me.

It's one of the most popular snacks in the country, and tea is a well-loved drink. It's . . . I clear my throat. That's not enough of a sign.

The KitKats and almonds at one of the other scenes isn't enough either.

Once is by chance. Twice is a coincidence. Three times is a pattern.

It's not *him*.

I glance up at the light bulb, and that dreaded sensation flushes through me again. *It's not a pattern yet.*

The Shadow left every light in the house on. Lamps, chandeliers, candles. For that reason alone, I knew it was my killer before I ever saw pictures of the body.

It only gets worse when I make my way into the living room that's been staged to perfection—the cushions are fluffed, coffee table cleared, and a blanket is neatly folded over the back of the couch. The knickknacks on the shelf are the only sign that anyone lives here.

My attention catches on the three picture frames on the side table. One is a surrealist-style violin. The other, a skull in a different artistic style, and the last is an image of a pomegranate. None match the decor of the house and they are haphazardly placed next to each other—at odds with the rest of the picture-perfect home.

Was it out of place because of the police, or because the Shadow intended it to be? Another puzzle piece.

I creep into the top floor, and my sights stall on the glass bottle sitting on the windowsill of one of the bedrooms. It's small, as tall and wide as my thumb. I inch closer, keeping one ear out for any sound—the last thing I need is to be arrested for breaking and entering a crime scene.

I fish out my phone from my pocket to shine my screen light on the label, and my stomach drops. There, in cursive lettering, are two words that have that sinking feeling in my stomach worsening: *Black Ink*.

No. *No.* It's a coincidence.

I mean, it's not like the ink is pink.

Right, exactly. It's fine.

Bar that one thing, all the other bedrooms are immaculate.

I can't figure out the logic behind it. Is he trying to say that the victim was clean on the outside, but rotten on the inside?

Was the victim grabbing a drink while the Shadow crept in through the window, then dragged him kicking and screaming before drugging him? Or maybe he was in the shower, or the comfort of his bed. He could have been partially conscious as the bulb was jammed into his mouth.

The victim probably begged to be spared as the glass, presumably, tore through his throat. Did the subject witness the killer setting up the scene, laying out the petals, and cleaning the place?

Grabbing the coroner's photos from my bag, I station myself in front of the spot in the hallway where the magic—*brutal murder*—happened.

I try to picture the victim tied up to the chair, and what the killer's thought process was when he was setting every piece of the scene. Theories flood in, but I can't shake that nudging at the back of my head. It's a feeling that I can't put into words. A familiarity that I can't quite pinpoint—refuse to.

Lowering my belongings to the ground, I try to get back in the zone and focus on the mise-en-scène. I place the stun gun on the stairs and my camera on top of my satchel and train it on the middle of the corridor.

Careful not to disturb the blush-colored petals on the floor, I tiptoe to the chair and pause at the very edge of it. With a deep breath, I close my eyes to realign myself, hoping that something will inspire me for my next project.

Right now, I'm not Reyna, or a film student; I'm the guy in the chair with a light bulb in my mouth.

Reopening my eyes, I take stock of the situation from a different lens.

I'm sitting between the front and back entrances, surrounded by pink petals of some sort. The positioning of the chair seems intentional. I don't know why yet.

My hands are tied with synthetic ropes, and the only things in my line of sight are a painting of peonies next to the front door and an antique shelf I can't see inside.

All the lights are on, the house is clean, fairy lights are wrapped around my head, and strange pictures are in my living room.

Why am I here? Do I know the killer? What did I do to make him torture me like this? If he's a stranger, why did he choose me? What kind of a symbolism could these objects hold that's related to me?

The crushed bulb in the subject's mouth. The cords wrapped around his head. House lights. Clean rooms. Snacks on the counter. Tea. Pink petals. Black ink.

I repeat the facts in my mind, flipping it over, and turning it around to get a different perspective until I figure out his message.

All it takes is one bright idea, and everything else goes away.

Air slams into my lungs in a startled gasp.

In the darkest pits of my soul, the most wretched part of me rears its ugly head with a smile from the onslaught of emotions. Betrayal, shock, mortification, and worst of all: exhilaration, and stone-cold satisfaction. I was right.

It's him.

He's Böcklin's Shadow.

It's a fucking pattern.

In the middle of the museum with him by my side, I gazed up at his green eyes with my heart racing, and my body tingling with need. And I told him, *I'm waiting for that light bulb moment that'll take the words out of my mouth.*

The twisted feelings intensify when my wide-eyed stare lands on the peony painting by the front entrance. A *welcoming* door. Maddox did this for me. He knew I'd see all this, and he wants me to know that he sees me too.

He saw the peony tattoos on my shoulder and shin.

Pink flowers paired with black ink. Pink ink.

My favorite snacks appearing on murder scenes. The almonds. Synthetic rope. The penny.

Maddox knows I've been idolizing a serial killer for my film project—knows that I've been idolizing *him*. I've beautified his art, put it on a screen for his critique, and consumption. I've turned murder into our dirty little secret. We visited his crime scene together.

Oh *God.*

I fucked a serial killer.

I bark out a deranged laugh. I fucked a serial killer several times, and I *loved it.*

It's been a little over a week since I first slept with Maddox, and we've both kept our distance as if we've already been caught, and we're pretending to be strangers to lessen the damage. But he's spent that week planning to kill someone for me. Maddox being my professor is the very least of my problems.

Laughter tumbles out of my chest. I can't believe it. Maddox Shaw is a serial killer. Paranoia has me hearing sounds in the house that aren't there, but I can't stop laughing.

All the signs were there; the way he spoke about the murders, the method of execution, and how he promised to pass on a message to the killer. Maddox *warned* me to stop going to the crime scenes. He promised to go to them with me, and he did. I thought it was because he cared about my safety, but maybe it was fear of getting caught and a dash of curiosity.

How could I be so blind? This whole project is about uncovering hidden messages, and I didn't see the big fucking neon sign.

I don't know what to do with any of this information. I upended my entire life in pursuit of my father's memory and ended up falling for a serial killer who left breadcrumbs for me to follow. What's his plan? To make me play his games? See how I'd react? We could have spent the rest of our lives with me being none the wiser, and yet he left *hints* for me to find.

A startled scream rips from my throat when I'm yanked to the side. Pain ruptures along my jaw and cheek when my face hits the banister, turning everything upside down, muting the voice in my head that's yelling at me to escape.

White orbs float into my swimming vision as I scramble to my feet, attempting to orient myself. My equilibrium tilts from the grip on my hair. My stomach lurches with the threat of emptying its contents onto the floor.

The fuzzy outline of a man appears in my vision, and another ragged cry tears out of me when my back collides with a wall.

Maddox knows that I know, and he's come back to . . . kill me? That makes no sense.

My vision clears to find a man I don't recognize. Fingers wrap around my throat, cutting off the oxygen and my scream with it.

Panic shoots through me, wild and hot, ready to explode. My legs dangle in the air as I kick and thrash, desperate to find my footing. My nails catch on the seams of his denim jacket and scrape the stubble along his jaw as I claw at his head. The harder I fight, the tighter his hold gets, until I can barely hear him above the ringing in my ears.

"Where's our money?" He spits out the words, shaking me by his rough hold. "Did you think Paddy's death would wipe what he owes us?"

Paddy?

Darkness blankets my vision as I gasp for breath. The fight in me dwindles with every heartbeat. The knife and stun gun I brought are too far away.

"Where'd he put our fucking money?" he yells, loosening his hold enough for me to sputter.

"Wrong person."

I manage to pry two of his fingers off my neck. It slackens his grip *just* enough for my toes to touch the floor, and before he can utter another word, my knee is smashing into his groin.

My body hits the hardwood next. Coughs rampage through my chest from the rush of oxygen while the man howls in pain beside me. Another figure comes into view, and every cell in me kicks into hyperdrive. It was sheer luck that I managed to get out of that guy's grip. I'm screwed if there are two.

In a reckless split second, I dive for the stun gun in the stairwell before stumbling to my feet and bolting for the front door. The room spins, my head pounds, and then it hits.

More so, it *sounds* like someone being hit.

I twist around with the stun gun raised, one hand on the handle, and my weight against the door to keep upright. For the second time, I can't move. Can't breathe. All I can do is stare as Maddox brings his fists down on my attacker.

Over.

And over.

And over.

The world sways as I try to make out the scene in front of me, my vision going in and out of focus. Fresh blood splatters along the wall with every attack my professor delivers. The man tries to fight him off, but Maddox is behind him, holding him in a headlock.

The pressure in my skull is making it hard to stay put. Hot liquid trickles from the throbbing wound on my cheek, but I don't dare touch it. I'm too busy watching the man claw at a serial killer's arm for mercy. They have to be around the same age. Similar build.

My aim on the stun gun shifts from him to Maddox, then back to the man whose eyelids are drooping closed.

This is my one and only chance to leave while Maddox is distracted. I need to run. Get the hell out of here and move as far as I can. Start over. Forget about my father. Live the rest of my life regretting everything I've done since moving here.

This entire *thing* between Maddox and me could be some sick ploy. A game to pass the time before I become his next victim.

I should be disgusted with him, mortified by his work, frightened to my very core that I could be his next target. Yet all I feel is enraptured.

I should pull the trigger. Turn him in. Scream for help.

I should. I should. I should. I should do a lot of things, but I stay where I am and watch Maddox knock a man unconscious at a murder scene he made for me.

My harsh breaths come out shuddered as I hope and pray to whatever god listening that they'd give me the wisdom to make the right decision. Because the longer I stand here, the more my curiosity blooms alongside the panic.

A bead of cold sweat runs down my spine as I slowly lower the stun gun. Watching Maddox move is hypnotic. How his eyes glint with unrestrained madness, and how the cords in his neck feather with each attack. Sometimes he pairs it with a little grunt that's just like the sounds he makes when he thrusts into me.

My attacker's reddened skin morphs into blue with each strike. Every time someone called me messed up in the head makes sense now because I can't help but feel a sick sense of justice that he's suffering the same fate he attempted to deliver to me a minute ago.

Maddox doesn't step back until my attacker stops twitching and his face is unrecognizable. Watching crimson bleed out of him is cathartic, but I'd die before admitting it out loud. As soon as Maddox's eyes meet mine, a psychotic grin twists across his lips that spikes my anxiety. I raise the stun gun higher and grip it tighter to hide the tremble in my hand.

Fuck, he might actually kill me.

He tips his head to the side in mock amusement. "A gun? Are you flirting with me?"

"No." I gulp.

"Well, it's working either way."

He can't seriously be trying to engage in banter *right now*. A man is bleeding out between us, and he's acting like this is a normal occurrence.

I sink back against the wall when he steps forward. I should have run when I could.

His eyes narrow on my cheek. "I'm going to ask you this once, and only once. Did he leave that mark on you?"

What is he talking about? I frown, following his line of sight, and a flicker of the ache returns with the reminder of the damage my attacker caused. My broken skin is the very least of my problems. For example, oh, I don't know, how about the fact that *I'm standing in front of a fucking serial killer who just . . .*

My attention flickers between him and the body on the ground. He just . . . Maddox just . . .

His jaw ticks. "Reyna."

I unintentionally flinch. It makes him angrier. My mouth opens and shuts, unable to form the words.

"Reyna," he repeats, making a show of relaxing his shoulders. "Was it him or someone else?"

I warily nod, bracing for the backlash.

Without a word, Maddox reaches for his back pocket and pulls out a knife that he offers to me. My lips part as my gaze darts between the blade and the unconscious man bleeding out on the murder scene. He can't seriously be—

"I don't kill people." I'm flustered, and the room sways when I shake my head. Is he crazy? Is he trying to make me complicit as an insurance policy?

He shrugs. "It's a good thing that I do, then." Maddox slaps the man's cheek until he wakes up with a throaty groan. "No one leaves a mark on her but me."

In one swift move, my attacker's hair is in Maddox's hands, and the skin along his neck is splitting apart. Scarlet splatters onto the wall, but the lunatic doesn't stop there. Each slice and jab is unpracticed. There's no art or finesse to the way Maddox mutilates the body. Just short, sharp explosions of movements, with death gleaming in his moss-colored eyes. I stop counting after the tenth puncture wound.

It's a crime of passion.

And it's . . . it's fascinating.

Reenacting murders and watching people get tortured on TV is child's play compared to seeing it play out in front of me.

Better him than me, a small voice says in my head.

Rationally, I'm aware Maddox could do the same thing to me. Irrationally, I trust him not to. He's never hurt me. Believes in me in a way I haven't experienced in a long time. Looks out for me when no one else does. For God's sake, he's brutally murdering a man instead of sending him home with brain damage just because he cut my cheek.

The metallic taste of iron thickens in the air the more wounds he inflicts. Maddox straightens, cleaning the blade on the sleeve of his sweater before tucking the weapon back into his pocket.

"As I said, throat slitting can be a very messy ordeal. I hope you're taking notes, Miss Sinaga," Maddox states, wearing his faux-casual demeanor.

My vision narrows on the blood pooling out of the corpse's gaping holes, crimson soaks into the fake flower petals. It's beautifully grotesque. A painting in its own right.

"You're *him*," I whisper the obvious. "You're Böcklin's Shadow."

A smile splits across his face that chills my internal temperature. "What gave it away?"

"Is that rhetorical?" My voice is just above a rasp.

"I warned you to stop visiting crime scenes."

You didn't say they were your *fucking crime scenes.* "Are you going to kill me?" I croak, becoming more lightheaded with each heartbeat.

"Don't insult me, Miss Sinaga. If you have to question it, then I'm clearly not doing a very good job at showing you my intentions."

Swallowing, I nod. I believe him. He's had every opportunity to harm me when he's known for a while that I've discovered a serial killer. But it doesn't explain why he let me get away with it.

"I'm going to pass out," I rasp, knees wobbling from the piercing pain in my head.

"Please don't. That would be rather embarrassing for you. Out of character too, might I add."

White dots my vision. "My head," I slur as I feel my body go sideways.

"Hey, hey, look at me." Maddox closes the distance in the blink of an eye, holding me against him with a bloody hand cupping my cheek.

The warm liquid smears along my skin, and the coppery scent slams into my nose. I tentatively bring my trembling hands to my face, and pull them away to stare at the fine coat of red on the tips of my fingers.

"You got his blood on me." My voice is hoarse, ragged like I've been sobbing for hours on end.

"Say the word and I could get more—the thickness of the liquid makes it good to paint with. Although, it doesn't age well." His eyes show no amusement as he speaks, only stone-cold worry.

The morbid humor melts away some of my shock to make room for the panic to settle back in. Alarm bells grow louder in my head. He's a serial killer, and I'm the star witness.

I yank myself out of his hold and stumble toward the stairs to put distance between me, Maddox, and his latest victim.

"You're a murderer," I hiss, pointing the stun gun at him in case it turns out *I'm* the endgame. I don't believe it, but self-preservation demands it.

He raises a brow, seemingly pleased that I'm no longer a fainting risk. "Says my stalker."

"I wasn't stalking you," I stammer, forgetting about the dead man on the floor. My head pounds like someone is taking a sledgehammer to it. Everything hurts. "I *wasn't.* I—I was following your work and studying it. That's different."

"Are you or are you not at my crime scene?" He raises a brow. "Might I add that you've displayed clear signs of obsession toward me. I admit, I'm rather flattered."

"Well, I didn't know you were the killer," I try to reason. *Not for certain.*

"Which makes you a *terrible* stalker. Investigative work is not your forte, Miss Sinaga. There's another bag of Cheetos in the cupboard and iced tea in the fridge, in case you missed it."

He's unbelievable. Un-*fucking*-believable. This isn't how any normal person should be reacting—admittedly, he isn't exactly normal. Neither am I.

Which begs the question, what would a normal person do in this situation? Beg? Run? Scream? Go straight to the cops? All of which I'm not doing, and as many times as I tell myself that I should, deep down I know I won't. And that's what makes this worse. There's something off-kilter about me. He knows it. I know it. I'm just looking for excuses to fight it.

"Were you waiting for me to show up?"

"No, I've been following you around." He gives me a blank look like it's obvious.

I gawk at him. "How is that better?"

"I told you that you're not visiting crime scenes alone anymore." At least he has the grace not to remind me of the evidence proving how dangerous my extracurricular activity is.

"You've been leaving me hints. Why would you do that?"

"To lead you to me," he says simply. "I also knew you wouldn't be able to resist seeing this one. You thought of it, after all."

That opens the floodgates.

"No. *No.*" I wave the stun gun at the chair and corpse. "You don't get to put this on me. I didn't tell you to murder someone, let alone like *this*!"

"Love, it was such a bright idea. How could I not?"

A pun now? "I'm done." I shake my head, voice rising in volume. Fatigue rushes through me from my movements. "I'm *done*. This is pointless." I push past him to get my things.

Of *course* the unhinged critters in my stomach flutter their wings. This is a sickly romantic gesture. I . . . I don't entirely hate it.

A hand lands on my shoulder, and I turn around without really meaning to. I regret it immediately because everything spins. The creases around his eyes disarm me and hold me hostage. He's always been the most beautiful man I've ever seen. With red droplets decorating his skin, he's downright striking.

"No." Maddox looks like power—the deranged, dark kind I've been trying to encapsulate on camera. Eyes flashing with energy he has yet to expel. "Don't."

My throat bobs. I won't be told what to do. I've fallen for those green eyes before; I'd be a fool for it to happen again when only one of our cards is on the table. "I won't stand around and talk to you if you won't take me seriously."

"We'll talk somewhere else, then." He shifts closer. "Do you trust me?"

Yes. I suck in a sharp breath. "You're a serial killer." *One who should kill me to protect his identity but hasn't.*

"Let me rephrase. Do you trust me not to harm you?"

His gaze meets mine, forehead wrinkled with worry for *me*—not the knowledge that I hold.

My lungs feel like they might collapse under the weighted silence as I recall every interaction we've ever had and the events of the past few minutes. I know, without a shadow of a doubt, until the day I inevitably die, he'll never lay a hand on me.

"I do."

I trust him, and it might be the biggest mistake I'll ever make.

23

REYNA

The spot on my thigh Maddox was rubbing the entire drive feels hollow and cold now that we've arrived.

Everything is so cold.

The chill has seeped into my bones and rendered me frozen. I don't want to move. I'm not sure I could if I tried. My head hurts too much.

Maddox had the heater on full blast, but nothing he said during the drive made it beyond my ears. I'm too numb to feel the pain throughout my body. I doubt I'd notice if the world stopped turning. Everything is a blur. My brain is spinning with thoughts I can't make sense of, and I can't escape the pressure in my head.

Maddox opens my door. I stay limp as he unbuckles me from my seat and cradles my body against his chest, up the garage stairs and into the building. I have half a mind to fight him and insist I walk, but I don't have the energy. The truth is that the warmth of his arms is the only thing tethering my sanity together.

I felt fine until we got to the car. As soon as I was hit by the silence, my adrenaline crashed and sleep was screaming my name.

"Where are you taking me?" I croak as we walk through the darkness. *Please, don't be a basement.*

"We're getting you cleaned up." His arms tighten around me to keep me still. "I'll take care of you."

The light switches on and hits me right in the retina. A faint ringing sounds in my ear. I fist Maddox's hoodie and bury my face in his shoulder, silently groaning from the ache that spreads through my head.

By some miracle, I swallow a needy whimper when he carefully sets me on the edge of the kitchen counter and pulls away, saying something I miss and taking his heat with him.

I blink my bleary eyes at the low light to survey my surroundings. Maddox's kitchen looks exactly like the aesthetic he maintains. Clean, elegant, the type of man who'd own an English country estate on a hill, with an equestrian ranch beside it. There's a rustic feel to the white marble countertops, polished sage cupboards, and brass handles.

From what I can see of the kitchen and dining room, the house appears like an unlived-in home. There is artwork on the walls and shelves, the odd decorative piece on the table. But no photos or personal effects beyond a stack of books. It's a facade. I expect nothing less from him.

Porcelain clinks against the marble counter as he slides a cup of tea my way. "Drink."

How very British of him.

I sip without tasting it. The hot liquid trickles down the back of my throat and does very little to thaw the chill in my bones. It doesn't dispel the fog clouding my mind or bring me any closer to the present either. It isn't until a warm cloth touches my face that I jolt, becoming aware that my surroundings have changed since I was first placed on the counter. There's now a bowl of water beside me and a first aid kit laid out on the opposite side of the kitchen island.

I rear back when the cloth touches the raw skin of my cheek.

"Sorry." Maddox adjusts his grip to dab at the bruised area with the delicate touch only an artist could master. His brows are stitched together in pained concentration like this is hurting him more than it's hurting me.

"You don't have to do this," I whisper.

It's my fault after all. I should have been more careful. On the other hand, he shouldn't have led me there. I guess we're both to blame.

The tension in my muscles bleeds away as he slowly cleans my wound. His touch is gentle—intimate in a way that seems impossible. For a few seconds, I let myself pretend we're just two ordinary people.

I'm not his student. He's not a serial murderer. Our relationship isn't doomed from the get-go.

When I reopen my eyes, I focus on him, imprinting this exchange to memory. His eyes crinkle at the corners the way they do when he puts graphite to paper, focused like a painter working on his craft.

If I were a portrait painter, his face would be my very first study. Chiseled jaw, full lips, and the faintest wrinkle between his brows from years of frowning.

He must have wiped away the blood splatter from his cheek at some point during the drive, because he looks as put together as the day I met him.

It's hard to reconcile that these are the same hands that have killed, maimed, and mutilated. They've been soaked in blood, and covered in paint. Broken bones, and flayed skin. What's even harder to reconcile is that I don't fear them.

I don't fear *him*.

My vision goes blurry at the sudden pounding in my head and the wave of nausea that follows. My hand flies forward to grab on to Maddox before I can fall. He tucks my head beneath his chin as if we've done this a thousand times before—as if it's as natural as coming home.

And as if that weren't cruel enough, he starts caressing the back of my head.

I want to fucking sob because everything he's doing feels too good. He's making this harder than it already is.

"You probably have a concussion," he says softly.

I push at his chest, though I'm not fooling myself into thinking I'm strong enough to move this mountain of a man. "I'm fine."

Maddox works his jaw, but says nothing. He finishes cleaning my face before sticking a Band-Aid on my cheek. "Either I take you to the hospital now, or I'll take you upstairs so you can rest. Regardless, I'm taking care of you." He drops the cloth in the sink. "We can discuss everything tomorrow."

Tomorrow?

No, I can't wait until then. I deserve answers—I need them more than I need to breathe.

I hold my hand up to stop him. "I don't want to sleep under your roof until we talk."

He places the tea into my hands before moving back.

"Ask away. I'm an open book." He looks like he most definitely does *not* want me to ask away. I get the feeling that none of this is going according to his plan.

I blow out a breath. My brain goes hazy, and I say the first thing that comes to mind. "Why must you be a stereotypical, attractive serial killer? Couldn't Böcklin's Shadow be ugly?"

My comment takes the both of us by such surprise that a laugh rumbles right out of him. It bulldozes through the tense atmosphere, and the smile that spreads across his face catches me so off guard that I find my lips tipping upward too, stopped by the ache in my cheek.

"Forgive me for disappointing." He grins softly. "I had a monobrow when I was ten if that helps. However, I'm open to feedback on how to improve to fit your vision."

"Grow back the monobrow," I croak, fighting the need to lie down.

"I fear my sex appeal would skyrocket if I did. You'd be hopeless to deny me then."

I huff a chuckle, bringing the cup back to my lips. Trust a Brit to brew a good cup of tea. A bloodstained Brit no less.

I should be denying him, or at the very least interrogating him, but when our messed-up conversation flows so easily, it's hard not to just give in. Still, this is too important. My life could depend on it.

Chewing on the inside of my cheek, I sift through the mush in my brain, searching for what could be most important to ask.

How many people have you killed?

How have you evaded authorities for so long?

Do you have a favorite crime scene?

When was your first kill?

Do you keep souvenirs?

Why are you the way you are?

"Did you know he'd be there?" I blurt instead.

Maddox shakes his head, hardening in anger. "Paddy had a gambling problem. I wasn't aware he owed criminals money. He must have been waiting inside the house, because I didn't see him come in."

Oh. It really is my fault in every sense of the word.

"Thank you." When he shoots me a questioning look, I explain. "For coming in—saving me. If you had gotten there a minute later, he could've . . ."

"That's not fucking good enough. I should have known better. He hurt you, and if he were still alive, I would turn his spleen into an art display."

A warm, fuzzy feeling settles over me. I blame it on the possible concussion.

To an extent, I get it. It makes sense that someone so put together could cause so much carnage. He needs a release. An escape. From what I know, those men deserved it.

"Why?"

"You'll have to be more specific, love."

"Why do you do what you do?" I wince when I try to massage the back of my head.

Maybe, if I can know why, then . . . what? I can relate? Sympathize? Understand him better? Deep down, I know why that's the question I chose to ask. I want him to let me in and trust me.

Maddox doesn't say anything for a while. The passing seconds have my hope dwindling. He stares at me with the empty, withdrawn mask he wears in front of everyone else.

The last thing I want is to be treated like I'm just *anyone* to him. Another person he keeps at arm's length so no one can see the real him—not the artist, nor the killer—*him*. I don't get why he let me find out if he never intended to give me an explanation.

"It wasn't a conscious choice I made. I was cursed to be this way." Tormented, his eyes drop to an empty spot on the counter. I want to reach out to take away his pain. Pull him apart so I can see every broken part of him. His stare snaps back up to mine. "Do you realize how broken I had to be to become this violent?" He asks it like a question but it hangs in the air like a confession.

"Your father." It's a guess—one I'd bet good money on given what little he's shared about his parents.

"That's part of it."

"Mother?"

"They say that it takes a village to raise a child. Each person leaves a mark on their lives, bypassing their innate nature to shape them into who they are. It determines how they express themselves, engage with others, and the types of passions they might have. Some people were born with violence in their blood. I was made to become it."

I purse my lips, thinking about the true question that's been burning in my mind since he revealed himself. "Then why aren't you killing me?" His brow hikes. "I just want to understand. It would have been easier for you to let the guy finish the job. I mean, killing me would be outside of your MO, but I know your secret. I know which kills are yours. I could tell the authorities."

Stop giving him reasons to murder you.

"I could ruin your career, and get you sent to prison."

Shut up, Reyna.

"You'd probably get life too."

Idiot.

He closes in, trapping me in place with a hand on my hip before I can escape. The frozen mask melts away to reveal the determination in his eyes. Hunger blazes behind them. It's in the heated way his eyes dip with possession.

No, that can't be right. *Obsession.*

Longing fills me. He looked at me like that the last time we were alone, as though I was his muse. Just as it turned out he's mine.

He traces the edge of my jaw down to my chin, tilting my face up to his. "I've found a kindred soul in you, and the world will burn before I let you go."

My breath lodges in my throat when his lips brush mine. I want so badly to believe it. But part of me needs proof. And time. And a clear head to think everything through.

Maddox has proven he can be an asshole, but violent is the last thing he's been when it comes to me. It's what I've always wanted: to be the one someone chooses. The exception to the rule. Not because it's convenient. Not because they have no other option. I wanted them to pick me *because* I'm me.

As heartwarming as the realization is, he's answering around my questions. He's only showing me pieces of his world—glimpses through the cracks in the wall he's built around himself. Fragments of a person aren't enough for me.

"Maybe I haven't made it clear, love. You are a risk I'm willing to take." He kisses the spot beneath my ear. "I've tasted your depravity, and I want to get drunk on it." He sucks the soft skin of my neck into his mouth, and I swallow a moan from the pleasure that ripples down my spine. "You're intoxicating, Reyna. I haven't been able to think of anything else but you."

My nails sink into his arms even though it hurts to move. His words and the feel of his lips are turning my brain into a jumbled mess. I press a hand to his chest to get him to stop. He doesn't move far, keeping our noses a breath away from touching.

"What happens if I try to walk away?" I whisper.

His eyes darken. "I'll find you. I told you that I wouldn't be going anywhere once we crossed that line. Try to run, and see how little of a liar I am."

"You can't make me stay."

"I'll give you time. I'll even give you space. But this ends one way, and it's not us apart. I'll do whatever it takes."

Just a week ago, I was losing sleep over our *temporary* relationship. Now he's talking about forever, and *doing whatever it takes* to keep us together.

"What will you do to me?"

"What I've already been doing: immortalizing you."

I shake my head. That's hardly a straight answer, and sounds frighteningly like I'm going to land in the obituary notice. "You can't make me do anything, Maddox." His name sounds dangerous on my lips. "I'm not yours to twist and shape into what you want."

"I know. You've done that all on your own." He brushes his thumb over my lips. "Don't be fooled. I'm not good for you. I may even be the worst thing to ever happen to you. But I promise that you'll never be left wanting."

He can't promise me that. I don't know if I *want* him to promise me that. Maddox Shaw is still a mystery to me.

"I—"

Fuck. I think I'm going to throw up.

"Woah, hey." Maddox holds my weight. "I've got you, love."

Everything is throbbing. I groan, latching onto the soft material of his clothes. My head hurts like a bitch, and the tea is making waves up my esophagus. He has me back in his arms and carries me through the house before I have a chance to argue.

"We weren't done talking," I grumble, squeezing my eyes shut. The harsh light is making it feel like my eyeballs are being scooped right out of my head.

"Tomorrow," he grunts.

My eyes drift open just enough to catch the worry across his face. The mattress dips beneath my weight, and creaks when he wrestles the clothes off my frame. "What are you doing?" I ask when he unbuttons my skirt.

"Would you rather sleep in these clothes, or mine?"

My lips part, catching sight of his coat on the nearby chair. This is *his* room. "Sleep? *Here?* You . . ."

"Any murderer worth half his salt wouldn't kill you while you're wearing their clothes. That would be a forensics nightmare."

What the fuck. "That doesn't reassure me in the slightest."

He shrugs. "Do with that what you will, Miss Sinaga."

I shove him with the little energy I have. "I'll kill you if you kill me."

"That would be my preferred way to go." I see his amusement through the darkness.

He tugs my skirt down my legs, and my tights follow suit. My head and stomach swim as I wait for Maddox to return. Without a word, he slides a pair of sweats up my legs, and eases his T-shirt over my head.

"I lied," I pant as he lowers me onto the bed, placing a stack of pillows behind me—probably to keep me from choking on my own vomit.

He falters. "What is it?"

"I'm not fine, I think I'm concussed."

Chuckling, he pulls the blanket up to my chin. "It's a curse, always being right."

24

REYNA

Not to be dramatic or anything, but I really need to see a doctor.

Today, ideally.

Actually, I change my mind. I might push it out for another week. See if it improves on its own before I fork over copious funds to receive basic medical care.

I don't think it's normal for anyone's head to hurt this bad. Maddox owes me Advil, Tylenol, Xanax, and antihistamines (just in case) for the shit I've experienced in the past twenty-four hours.

Groaning, I inch onto my side. I think my ribs are broken, bruised, or I possibly slept wrong. Either way, I'm going to be out of action for the foreseeable future.

Peeling my eyes open, I squint against the sliver of light seeping in from beneath the door. It penetrates to the very back of my eyeballs like a damn ice pick. Pain zaps through my body as I attempt to stand. It takes three tries to make it up onto my very unsteady feet.

My lids fall closed to protect me from the light. I have to head toward the door using nothing but my memory and the will of the gods that I don't knock into something. My heavy legs and weak knees almost send me tumbling twice in my mission to get to the room directly across from me, thinking Maddox—or the bathroom—will be there. I stumble to a stop when the door opens, both because it's blinding and because I don't think I should be in here.

It's an art studio. It feels like an invasion of privacy to step inside, but the sculpture in the center of the room beckons me closer. I can't bring myself to leave, and just like that, the light is almost bearable, the pounding in my head a distant memory.

That's one thing I've always admired about Maddox—and what critics have been discussing since he entered the art scene. He's never stuck to one medium. Going from clay, to oil paint, to marble, to photography, to watercolor. He's a natural at anything related to the arts. Killing included, I guess.

I narrow my eyes on a marble sculpture sitting on a table in the middle of the room. It's half cloaked in a white sheet that my fingers are itching to pull away.

From what I can see, a two-headed serpent climbs up the staff strapped to a woman's back. Poison ivy coils around her hand, pointing up to the heavens. A cross between armor and some kind of silken fabric covers her body, only leaving the hole in her chest exposed.

When I step forward to take a closer look at the half-painted canvas on the easel behind the sculpture, another wave of nausea rolls through me. My arms shoot out toward the floating shelves for balance as my joints nearly buckle instead of supporting my weight.

A whole minute passes before my equilibrium falls back in line. I push away from the shelf, and even though I'm certain I'm a fall risk, I grip the banister and ease myself down the stairs. Concentrating on putting one foot in front of the other.

At the bottom, the only thing I'm more certain about is that my brain is going to detonate. I need to lie down. Pronto. Sleep. Cry. Sleep again. Water would be great too.

Getting to the very last step takes all my focus. So much so that I don't hear the voices until I stumble into the kitchen to find three people staring at me.

Swallowing, I lean against the doorframe because if I don't, I'll be acquainting myself with the floor. I'm sure I look horrific. Based on how the woman is gawking at me, I can only assume that however bad I think I look, the truth is eight times worse.

Spencer turns to a very pissed-off Maddox. He sticks his bottom lip out in a pout. "You had a slumber party and didn't invite me?" He ignores his older brother's death glare to face me. "Well, it appears introductions are in order—"

"Fuck off." Steam is practically coming out of Maddox's ears as he crosses the room to him.

Spencer chuckles, swerving around the counter to put the kitchen island between them. He gestures toward the woman. "I don't believe you've met Abi—"

"I mean it," Maddox growls out, panicked. "Fuck off right—"

"Maddox's fiancée," Spencer finishes.

"You fucking cunt."

His . . . She can't be.

I turn my head slowly and pale when my eyes clash with the woman's—*Abi's*. Her cheeks redden as she offers me a tight-lipped smile. "That's me."

No.

No, no, no, no, no, no.

My knuckles bleach around the doorframe. This can't be happening. Any second now they're going to say sike. They're going to confess that this is one big joke and that my serial-killing, fuck-buddy professor is *not* also a cheating bastard.

But no one denies it.

No one even tries to suggest it's something it's not. Tears sting my eyes. I'm still paying for the events of last night. This bombshell is tipping me over the edge. It hurt less to be thrown against the wall.

"Have a seat." Maddox approaches me cautiously. "It's not—"

The *crack* of a slap rings through the air, and his head whips to the side. "You motherfucking piece of shit."

"Oh, fuck," Spencer mutters.

I can take grievous bodily harm. Hell, I can even take serial killing. *Cheating?* That's where I draw the line.

Tears burn down my cheeks, and I want to throttle Maddox for it. After everything he did—everything he *said*—it turns out that he's getting *married*? How is his relationship status not public knowledge? How didn't *I* know? What the hell was the point of last night's demand if he's *engaged*?

He declared his feelings for me a hundred different ways less than twenty-four hours ago. I was considering being with him knowing he killed people as a hobby. Now *this*? It doesn't matter if I believed a word he said anymore, because the fact of the matter is that he used me. I would've never agreed to do the things we did if I had known he was in love with another woman.

I thought we could never be because of our positions, but it turns out it was the difference in relationship status.

He didn't choose me. He doesn't *care* about me.

I'm the other woman. The second choice.

The one who gets left behind.

"Rey—"

This time, he wraps me in his arms before I can knee him in the balls.

"*Fiancée?* Are you fucking kidding me? I trusted you," I hiss, wrestling an arm free from his hold. Why is he trying to touch me when she's *right there*? "You lying, two-timing piece of shit. You—"

"Let me explain—"

He doesn't get the chance to before I throat-punch him. He rears back, sputtering a cough. I've bought myself thirty seconds at most since my limbs lacked the power.

I don't wait for him to recover to bolt for my satchel on the counter. I'm a fucking coward for being too mortified to look her in the eye, thinking a whispered "I'm so sorry" is enough to say to her after the damage I caused.

I'm back in Maddox's arms before I get the chance to make it to the door.

"Out. *Now,*" Maddox snarls at his brother and his *fiancée* while he easily clamps both my arms to my sides. They scramble out, leaving me alone with Maddox. Bile lurches up my throat. My head is screaming from trying so hard to fight him off. "Reyna, calm down."

Calm down? This motherfucker.

"Let *go of me,*" I hiss. Dots form in my vision.

"Jesus Christ, woman. Stay still for two minutes so I can exp—"

"No," I growl, elbowing him weakly in the stomach. "You don't get to call the shots, asshole. There is nothing you can say because I'm not going to listen to a word that comes out of your lying fucking mouth. I hate—"

"Don't you dare finish that sentence, or—"

"Or what?" I suck in a sharp breath, and flinch back. "Never mind, don't answer that one."

"Bloody hell." He spins me around, and I just about pass out from the sloshing of my brain. Steady hands gripping the back of my neck to force me to look at him. "I'm going to say this once, and only once: I am willing to hurt everyone around you, but I will never hurt you."

"And *her*." I sound so disgustingly bitter, I don't recognize myself. Does *she* know about what he does? Shit, shouldn't she be here yelling her head off at me—or him—for the things we've done?

"It's an arranged marriage," he blurts.

That stops me. Only for a second.

"Bullshit," I seethe.

"It's the truth. She means nothing to me."

I scowl, relishing in the pain along my cheek. Maddox doesn't strike me as the type of man who would sneak around with other women. He especially doesn't strike me as the type who'd say things without meaning it.

Maybe he's telling the truth. She didn't seem to care much that I walked down the steps wearing nothing but his shirt. And she left without saying a word to me.

It still doesn't change that he lied.

I start struggling in his grip again. "I don't care if she's your pretend fiancée. I'm not going to be anyone's mistress. Least of all *yours*."

"I've never cared about her—never have and never will."

"I don't give a shit! You lied to me. You made me believe that I was the only one and you—"

He slams his lips against mine. It halts my traitorous body from its attack. Warmth curls all the way down to my toes because the kiss is filled with more intimacy than any other time our lips have met.

Maddox pulls away before I can come to my senses. His hoarse breath heats my lips as he presses our foreheads together. "I've never had the chance to choose before, and I'm sick of being complacent with the cards I've been dealt. It's you. I'm picking *you*."

Lie. Lie. Lie.

"Stop lying," I croak.

"Only you."

I wish that were true.

"Always," he whispers against my lips.

Tears sting my eyes. "I don't believe you." How can any of it be real if he kept this from me? I understand hiding that he's a serial killer, but keeping a *fiancée* from me?

He grips the back of my neck, making sure he has my full attention. "I see you in every room, even if you're not there. Everything I've told you is true. I've killed for you, Reyna. I've done things for you that no good man would do. There's *only you* for me."

The butterfly wings flutter and send tendrils of warmth over me. Last night's events and years of insecurities make it hard to trust in what he's saying. I wouldn't pick me, so why would he?

"Please. Stop." I choke on my tears. "Don't lie to me."

"I give you my word, Reyna. I'm going to end the engagement."

He should have told me he was engaged before revealing his identity. What if I decided that his engagement alone is unforgivable? That this betrayal trumps all of the violence he causes?

I'm tired of all the secrets. They're the only thing I seem to get.

Maddox holds me tighter when I try to leave. "Why didn't you tell me earlier?" I demand.

"I was going to last night, but you looked like you were going to faint and I didn't want to put more on your plate if it was going to make your injuries worse."

My hands tremble. "Is that why she was here this morning? You were going to come clean?"

"Yes, but my shit-stirring brother tagged along to meddle in my business as payback for looking out for him." He scowls. "This is the first time she's stepped foot in my house."

I shake my head, wiping away my tears. None of this makes any sense. "So what? You're leaving her? Your fiancée—whatever her name is."

"Abigail," he provides, frowning as he massages the back of my neck. I wish he wouldn't, though. I wish he'd stand on the other side of the room. "I was never technically *with* her. We can barely stand being in the same room as each other. We haven't been able to since our parents arranged this engagement four years ago to profit their businesses. I never wanted the bloody thing."

"What is this? The fourteenth century?" Who arranges a marriage for a business deal?

"Of course not. There wasn't any dowry," he deadpans.

I usually like this side of him—the angry humor. It's a part of him that had seemed reserved just for me. But right now I just feel flayed open.

"I mean it, Reyna. I'm ending it," Maddox promises.

This time when he says it, part of me believes him. The most broken part that wants to trust him. But it makes sense, right? He wouldn't risk prison or ruining his career if his intention was to make me the other woman. I mean . . . he wouldn't, would he?

"Then why did you agree to the engagement?" *Convince me that this isn't an elaborate ruse.*

He hardens, and for a second I think he's going to evade the answer. "It was a question of whether the burden would fall on me or my brother. Back then, the answer was always me."

That's chivalrous. I guess.

If it's a question of choosing me or his brother . . . I swallow. "And now?"

"I'm putting myself first."

Tugging at the hem of my shirt, I purse my lips. "Since it was arranged, won't there be . . . consequences for breaking the engagement? Won't your parents be mad? Won't . . . What about the business?"

Maddox scoffs. The facade he wears so well glimmers on the surface, threatening to solidify.

"Fuck them. I've been their loyal errand boy for as long as I've existed. They'll have to deal with whatever decision I make. I am not asking for permission, nor do I care for their forgiveness. You're mine, and I will sooner make my bed in the earth than tie myself to anyone who isn't you."

I work my jaw, debating whether to demand an explanation of everything he's mentioned. Like what type of business deal could involve a marriage? What else have his parents forced him to do? What could they have possibly done to make him who he is?

"Does she know about . . . you know." I wave my hand in a general direction I'm sure a kill has taken place in. "The whole murder thing."

"Murder thing? Reyna, love, repeat after me: I'm a *serial killer*." His lips twist into a half-hearted smirk. "However, I'll settle for a *bloody artist*, as well."

How he's making jokes out of the situation is beyond me. Deep down I know he's trying to stop me from spiraling, but I can't fucking take it. Everything is crashing around me, and he's the cause of the destruction. "You know what I'm talking about."

He tucks my hair behind my ear. "No, she doesn't know exactly what I've done."

"Do your parents?"

Frowning, I see the exact moment that I lose him. Something switches behind his eyes. A thought or a memory. I'm back to questioning how many secrets he's hiding from me. I don't want to keep living in the dark.

"Just give me time to figure out how to end things without causing an explosion in the process. I can't risk you." He cups my cheek, changing the subject. "Let me be your monster, love. It's always been dark around my soul, and you've made me hungry for more."

I swallow, trying to hide my disappointment. "I need time to think."

"As much time as you need. I'll be here waiting for you. For as long as it takes."

25

REYNA

Maybe I should have relented to Maddox's insistence I stay at his place last night, after we went to the hospital. I needed room to think, but Nurse Kimi apparently doesn't have that in her treatment plan.

"Here's your soup, Grandma." She marches in carrying a breakfast tray that I didn't know we owned and props it up on the empty space on the bed.

"I have a concussion, not the flu."

"Same thing." The hot liquid almost spills everywhere when she flops down onto the bed, then rolls onto her stomach to go on her phone.

Shaking my head, I carefully spoon the food into my mouth. I feel exponentially better than I did yesterday, but my brain and body still aren't on speaking terms. "Did you make this?"

She gives me the universal *are you kidding me* look. "Reyna, please. Think before you ask stupid questions."

"Apologies, let me rephrase: Where did you buy this from?"

"That's better." She grins. "I DoorDashed it from Golden Dragon. I had a craving for their mapo tahu."

"Thank you for thinking about me during your cravings."

Typing away on her phone, she gives me a brief nod. I manage about eight spoonfuls before I think I'm going to throw up. Any person would struggle to eat after finding out the guy they're sleeping with is an engaged serial killer who also happens to be their professor and potentially has information about their dead father. The concussion doesn't help.

Life has been empty since my parents died. All I had was work, class, and a wild goose chase. Maddox changed that. Maybe that makes me a fool, or maybe that makes me desperate, but I don't want to go back to not knowing what being alive feels like.

"Are you sure you're good?" Kimi's voice jars me from my thoughts.

"Hmm?" *Oh, you know, I've been sleeping with the serial killer I've been stalking, and guess what!? He's my professor, and it turns out he is—or maybe was—planning on getting married next year. Also, did I mention that the only lead I have on my father's life also happens to involve said serial killer?* "Yeah, I'm good."

"You had a nasty-ass fall, but, like"—she waves a finger at my bruised face—"you have this dead thing going on in your eyes that's weirding me out."

"Jesus Christ." I huff a laugh that hurts my ribs. "What you're seeing is something I call stress, and what the doctors call a concussion." The non-lie slips easily from my tongue.

I'm an awful friend.

"Maybe you should get Professor Psycho to eat you out real good to take some of the edge off."

My cheeks burn bright red, and I throw the nearest cushion at her. "We've done it *once*." Well, multiple times in one session.

"Yes, and you should do it again because you were a better person after you got dicked down. Your skin was glowing in a way that no K-beauty routine could achieve."

I wasn't planning on telling her about my little crush on my professor, and I most definitely planned on keeping our tryst a secret. But apparently, I had a bounce in my step even though I was struggling to walk. Kimi is like a dog with a bone when she smells gossip, especially if it involves my typically nonexistent sex life—or as Kimi calls it, my *regenerated hymen*.

So for better or worse, I relented. Now, every day she'll remind me about the times my professor gave me a religious experience. As if I don't already replay it every night before bed, trying to relive that moment with a vibrating wand.

"If not Mr. Tall, Dark, and Traumatized, then I'm pretty sure Lawrence would come running with bells if you gave him a booty call."

I blanch. "In that case, my hymen will be a permanent fixture."

Kimi nods solemnly. "He doesn't look like a man who knows where the clit is."

My recent attack comes back as a very rude reminder when my entire body screams as I choke back a laugh. "Stop it. Please. It hurts to breathe. He's a nice person."

"Personality doesn't make you come. It's why we all knew Shaw's hands could work magic."

I cover my face with a pillow and groan. *"Stooop."* I can't be imagining his fingers when I'm trying to figure out whether we actually have a future together.

I want to talk to someone—*anyone*—about the full extent of my problems. There are far too many legal issues with telling Kimi about Maddox's extracurricular activities, and I doubt she'd even begin to understand my lack of mortification toward his hobbies. If she knew about the engagement, she'd be researching what type of chemicals we'd need to make his body disappear.

"Fine, fine." She holds up her hands in surrender, flashing the ruby ring Owen bought her the other day. "Just know that any man who gives me *that* can get it." She points at the painting I found in my room this morning, along with the confirmation letter that I've been granted extensions on my assignments for all my classes.

Sucking in a sharp breath, I stare at the portrait of me in a deep-maroon gown under the moonlight, surrounded by foliage. The painting was wrapped up and leaning against my closet door when I woke up this morning. Two realizations had hit me in that instant.

One, he snuck into my room without me knowing.

Two, I'm in too deep, because the first thing I felt was giddy, then embarrassed that I haven't cleaned my room. At no point did it occur to me to be concerned for my safety or even remotely troubled that Maddox is breaking into *my bedroom.*

I guess that's why we're compatible. Deep down, I'm a hopeless romantic, and so is he. Concerningly so.

But I'm worried that none of it will work out, or we'll get in trouble, or I'm made a complete idiot for sticking around when he has a ring on his finger. I'm just . . . scared. Nothing is worse than the feeling of knowing you're alone again.

Kimi's phone lights up, and a deep divot forms between her brows as she reads the message. She buries her head into the blanket with a full-chested groan.

"I would die a happy woman if I never have to do another group assignment."

I snort. "What happened?"

"Men happened," she growls, muttering and cursing as she rolls back onto her feet. "They're fucking useless. He had one job. *One.* Write the conclusion. But guess what?"

"He's MIA or sick."

"*Both.* I'm going to rip this man another one," she yells over her shoulder as she storms out and practically slams her bedroom door behind her.

I chuckle and set the tray on the floor, then curl onto my side. The silence stretches until it grows claws and blocks out the sun. I stare at the other painting on the wall, beneath the *Silence of the Lambs* poster I thrifted. It's hard to tell, but it's meant to be of my father holding me as a baby.

Mom made it for my birthday the year before Dad died. She was upset that she didn't get the warm, enthusiastic reception she was expecting for it. I was bitter and angry that my own father was never around, and hadn't wished me a happy birthday. And I was resentful that she kept pushing me to love him because of "everything he's done for me," as if he were the one who put the stars in the sky.

She claimed he loved me. I believed it when I was a kid. As I got older, it became harder to.

Mom said he was the love of her life. Then her eyes would glaze over as she said that work was the love of his, even if he loved her too. That, I believed.

I didn't shed a tear for him at his funeral. But in the dark of night, when no one was watching, and there was nothing to distract me, I'd cry for the man I never got to know, and the hole that a lifetime of his absence left.

Taking a deep breath, I glance at Maddox's portrait again.

I pushed my dad away before I got to know him, and I regret it every day. I'm afraid I'll regret never knowing Maddox or seeing where our relationship could go.

What if I'm destined to be like my mother: falling for a man who wouldn't put me first? I don't want a life where I'm constantly waiting for my soulmate to come home, sitting on the sidelines as I watch him live life without me.

If he wants to make this work, he needs to prove he's as committed as he claims. That the strength of our relationship won't be dictated by who's watching.

My eyes fall to the laptop on the edge of my bedside table. I have videos from a stationery ad to edit, and no shortage of readings and assignments to work on—all things Nurse Kimi has banned me from doing.

She can't get mad at me if she doesn't know.

I fluff the pillows behind my back and set my laptop on the blankets, squeezing my eyes shut when the loading screen stares back at me. I really don't want to have to pay for a new one. It finally turns on, and I click back into the legal case database I've been slowly reading through these past few weeks. Researching the connection between the insignia, Maddox, and Cresswell is the last thing I should be doing, especially when I'm meant to be resting or at the very least studying.

But I don't open my editing software; I pull up my recent search in Westlaw with all of my filters and click onto the eleventh page of the results. I figured since Cresswell seems to be the common denominator in all my investigations, it was a good place to start. That was until thousands upon thousands of cases showed up.

My bright idea was to narrow down the search to only criminal cases in the past ten years. There are still several hundred, but it's substantially more manageable than the initial figure.

I click the case I was attempting to read before bed last night to pick up where I left off. I skim over the legal crap to see if any details are dropped that might lead me somewhere.

Like the previous ten pages, it is a waste of time.

The next one only mentions Cresswell because the expert witness studied there.

The one after had a fight break out on campus.

In the next, the defendant went to the Cresswell gym—I didn't even know we had one—straight after murdering someone.

One right after another, the wild goose chase continues. I take a snack break before clicking into the next one. I don't know how lawyers can do this for a living. This is killing me. I'm bored out of my mind.

I get comfortable, cozying up beneath the blankets until I'm practically lying on my back. My brows hike when I realize I'm reading a case about a serial killer from nine years ago. That has me sitting back up.

Seven victims. All sliced and diced and found around the city.

Korbin Mitchell Lewis's DNA was found on a piece of fabric that was on one of the victims, and he was seen around the same place as another victim the day they went missing. But according to the police, none of the people who died seemed to have much in common beyond the way their bodies were mutilated.

He claimed not guilty, and pleaded insanity as his defense.

When the police first took Lewis into custody, he insisted he was being framed by bee people.

My forehead wrinkles as I read the line again. It says in quotes, "The defendant alleged the murders were carried out by who he described at the time as the 'bee people.' He later claimed he was set up by 'the people who keep bees.' Lewis became aggressive with the police when they rejected his claim."

Beekeepers.

I scroll through the case until I find mention of Cresswell.

"When giving evidence at trial, Lewis echoed the sentiments given to the police during the investigation. He refused to answer the questions asked, and stated that the 'bee people' earlier mentioned had framed him so the mayor could be elected. When I asked who they were, he claimed they're a secret group of people living beneath Cresswell."

I reread the paragraph several times until there are stabbing pains behind my eye. The decision never elaborates on who or what Cresswell supposedly is, and maybe I'm concussed or dramatic, but he must be referring to the university.

All of the body parts were found in New York. This case was heard in New York.

New York's most prestigious university used to have a beekeeping society that even politicians joined.

The serial killer, Maddox Shaw, professor and alumnus of Cresswell University, has a string of murders where the victims all have ties to the same university.

Every puzzle piece is creating the same picture.

Am I seriously about to believe that the honeycomb emblem is connected to a secret society because of the claims from someone who doctors strongly suggested should be institutionalized? Is this the concussion speaking? Then again, it's too big to be a giant coincidence.

My dad is linked to it somehow; I just don't know how it fits yet. Maybe . . . Maybe he was a member of this bee society? Or maybe he got caught up in it somehow.

But how would Maddox fit? Is he targeting people from the society? Does he work for them? Does he have some kind of vendetta against them?

I debate calling him to ask, but if this society is the type to murder someone like it's just another Tuesday, I'm not sure that's something I want to talk about over the phone. I need to know more about this case first.

I go through the decision front to back, then do it one more time in case I missed anything. There's nothing else about Lewis's claims beyond the judge's deep dive into the many mental health reports and expert opinions.

Anxiety works my stomach as I do an internet search of the people he allegedly killed. It was so long ago that most of them didn't have much of an online presence, and if they did, it's gone now. There are far too many search results for his name. I have to wade through the pages before finding him on the sixth one, and I only find a single article by a random indie print I've never heard of.

Korbin Mitchell Lewis Died Six Days Following a Unanimous Guilty Verdict by the Jury

Prickles skate over my skin. Lewis is dead?

Cold sweat trickles down my spine. I check the date of the decision against the article. They line up. The court document was published at a later date, but it doesn't mention anywhere that Lewis died or that there was no more need for a sentencing date.

The prosecution's case was weak at best, and it was clear he was mentally unwell. He probably wasn't even fit for trial. There . . . couldn't have been foul play.

Except Lewis claimed he was being framed for murders he didn't commit. He was found to be fit for trial, and the jury convicted him despite testimony from the forensic specialists and evidence of his slew of health issues. A week later, he died . . . And for there to be no news coverage of this beyond this one article?

If a serial killer who allegedly chopped up seven people and scattered their remains around the city was found guilty for it, then died in what was likely police custody, I'd expect the local newspaper to have covered it.

My hunch says he was killed. It'd make sense.

Blame it on the person who can't properly defend themselves, then get rid of them once they've gone down for it because they've been opening their mouth and spilling secrets they shouldn't.

And Lawrence, he . . . he *knew* what the hexagon ceiling meant. He must have known that a society or an organization of some sort was involved. Hence why he told me to stay the hell away from it.

Everything points to two things: Cresswell and fucking *bees*.

I'm going to sound like a conspiracy theorist, but I believe Lewis. I think I'm looking into a secret society, and if my theory is correct and I'm not careful, I'm going to be in a world of danger.

And maybe that danger found my father.

26

MADDOX

ME:

Please send evidence that you finished your meal, Miss Sinaga.

I tap my pen against the desk impatiently and watch the three dots appear on the screen.

Perhaps I am somewhat type A. In my defense, the more she eats, the faster she'll recover, and the sooner we can get over this nonsense so she can be back in my bed.

REYNA:

You have no right to be controlling, Mr. Shaw.

Controlling? No.

Obsessive? Maybe.

In dire need of her attention? Possibly.

Scratch that.

Yes. A solid, one hundred percent yes.

Who would have guessed it only took her getting attacked for us to move to the next tedious stage of our relationship: texting.

I'd much prefer face-to-face interaction, but I suppose it makes sense that she needs space. However, in my opinion, there's nothing for her to consider.

I want her. She wants me. Case closed.

Admittedly, the whole *Surprise, I'm engaged to another woman* would have thrown a spanner in the works. So I'll let the distance slide. If the roles were reversed, Reyna's fiancé would be a permanent fixture on the missing persons list.

ME:

Proof of life is also required.

The next message is a photo of her legs perched up on the couch with a movie and a table full of snacks in the background. Before I can demand more, a knock booms through my studio. It's too loud and authoritative to be Spencer's. Scowling, I set my phone on the table and rise from the stool.

Why do people keep bothering me? What is it about me that makes it seem like I am warm and inviting?

I yank the door open, frowning at whoever decided to interrupt me outside of office hours.

"Maddox."

Unease churns in my stomach from the apparition standing at my door. Nothing good comes from being visited by the devil.

I fight the chill creeping up my neck, trying to appear completely unfazed by my visitor. If Shepherd sees any ounce of discomfort, he'll latch onto it and make me bleed for the weakness. Without returning any greeting, I step back to let him into my studio.

In all my years working under him, I've never known Shepherd to make a house call. I come to him. Not the other way around. The only time he plays guest without warning is when the night will end with the host's blood seeping out from under the door.

He wants me unnerved. Off balance. He's intruding as a reminder that I can prance around and live my life, but he's just around the corner.

With a single, calculated sidestep and one controlled glance, I see him catalog every inch of my room. He pauses on my current painting a beat longer than anything else, and my skin crawls at the intrusion.

I don't let anyone look at my unfinished work. This feels like a violation of every degree—especially *that* piece.

When his eyes fix on me, something in the air twitches. A violent undertone masks his face beneath a veneer of diplomacy. I've trained under him. Fought for him. Killed because he said so. Been beaten and whipped under his command, as he tried to tear apart my psyche to make me a better soldier. But not once has he looked at me like this.

Usually, there's the slightest, virtually unnoticeable tell in his facade. Like the barest tilt of his lips, a minute flare of the nostrils, the smallest shift in one of the wrinkles on his forehead.

This time it's completely blank.

Empty.

"To what do I owe the pleasure?" I ask, lounging back on the couch.

He stays standing. The difference in height bothers me to no end.

My lack of hospitality won't be going unnoticed by him. Yet I can't bring myself to fix it. I'm over being used and catering to the Order's every whim.

"I believe you spoke to your father recently."

"Unfortunately." It was the same discussion we always have.

"Then you understand the importance of your union with the Dornmonts."

Oh, for fuck's sake. Not this shit again.

"I've been well informed." From the bottom of my heart, Roland and his campaign can go fuck themselves. Daniel can take my family's station in the Order for all I care.

"And yet"—Shepherd unbuttons his suit jacket and settles into my office chair—"you aren't acting like you understand."

Why is he suddenly interested in my marriage? Over the past four years, he couldn't have cared less. In fact, his only concern was whether it would hinder my ability to carry out the work he required.

"If I recall correctly, I attended a breakfast with my fiancée four days ago." Spencer brought the aforesaid fiancée to my apartment, shouldering right past me despite my continuous refusal to let them in. Abi looked like she was two seconds away from fainting when I kept telling Spencer to piss right off.

Then Reyna came down, and shit hit the fan.

Shepherd studies me for three unsettling seconds. "Remind me, was this before or after you were seen caring for a young woman?"

My stomach sinks below the floor. I'm being tailed, and I didn't even know it. Anyone could have ordered that I be watched. Roland, the Dornmonts, Shepherd, even Daniel could have to get a leg up in the election.

I resist swiping a hand over my mouth. "Before."

"A student."

He better not fucking threaten her.

My breathing grows uneven. Not a question, but I respond regardless. "One I inherited after you asked me to teach Bradford's class."

"One you've been seen with many times."

I don't answer. Can't. There's no lie I can tell. No explanation to sway his assumptions since I have no gauge of how long he's been watching me. He's well aware of the fact that I've kept to myself. I'm sure he knows that I've never been one to bring women to bed. Let alone students.

There's no way he could have seen any video footage of Reyna and me at Halenbeek Museum. Mathijs Halenbeek holds one of the highest positions within his secret organization, and if the Order were to hack into or tamper with his footage, it would be seen as a hostile act. As for the offices on this floor, the only cameras here are owned and operated by me. The only possibility for Shepherd to have gathered information is if someone's got eyes on me.

My fury develops its own heartbeat. It has a deafening roar in my ears that makes me want to tear the entire Order to the fucking ground.

"Following Bradford's departure, she approached me and requested further assistance to improve her grades and filming techniques, as she found Bradford lacking as an instructor. I believe teaching is part of my job description." I stop myself from saying more.

Shepherd stares at me. To make me squirm, no doubt. I know his tactics because he taught me them.

"I am beginning to question your dedication to the Order."

I try to match his callous demeanor. I've been commanded to say that very line to men right before I killed them.

"It would be much more appropriate for one of your colleagues to teach the class," Shepherd states.

The thought of anyone else teaching Reyna—seeing her videos—fills me with blind anger. I'm half a second away from telling him to shove it up his bloody ass, except my desperation would only prove his point.

Because that's what I am.

Desperate.

"Very well. I'll advise the class that Bradford will be returning. What would be his start date?" It would be an absolute disservice to the class for Bradford to start "teaching" again, let alone to do so by video call, seeing as the Order has him under house arrest. Or so I've been told.

"He remains unavailable. Another person from your faculty will have to take over."

"The initial issue we had remains. Very few people are qualified, and those who are aren't available." I faffed around for days trying to find a replacement for the useless wanker, and it was Shepherd who decided that I was the only person who could do it. "I believe there is one somewhat competent student who tutors on the side. However, I will need to speak to the dean to get permission for her to run a class by herself."

Hook. Line. Sinker. I'm the only option.

Shepherd knows I'm not lying either. He had one of his own men looking into suitable options. It was odd to see him so involved, but I stopped looking deeper into things Shepherd takes interest in a long time ago.

The first glimmer of a reaction crosses his features. It's the barest pinch of his brows. "Until we can find a suitable substitute, your attention will only be directed toward one woman. That woman is *not* your student."

Rage slices a path down my spine. I'm vibrating with it. He's *forbidding* me from seeing her? Like fuck am I going to let them get in the way of the one thing I bloody want. I've given them everything, but they always take more.

"Also, I do believe congratulations are in order."

Shepherd's comment makes me frown without intending to. The first crack in my composure. My muscles tighten as he draws his phone from the front pocket of his jacket, unlocks it, then holds it out to show me a live feed of my brother's sleeping form.

They've hidden a camera in Spencer's room.

The blood drains from my face.

"He requires a lot of work but will make an adequate addition," Shepherd states.

I jump to my feet and close the distance until I'm towering over him. "Don't you dare lay a fucking hand on my brother." My fists shake with the need to pummel his face. If only I wouldn't be six feet under the second I lay a hand on him.

When did this start? If Shepherd's watching him and saying *congratulations*, it can only mean that he's recruited Spencer already—and my own brother didn't even fucking tell me. What have they got him doing? Fighting? Killing? Torturing people for information?

It's one thing for Roland or the grand magistrate to require that he takes a life to prove his worthiness to the Order. It's another story altogether if he's being taken under Shepherd's wing to play hitman for the rest of his life, because that means he'll go through what I went through. He'll have the same scars—the same wrecked skin and broken mind.

Unamused, Shepherd stares up at me and slides his phone back into his pocket. The video of Spencer tossing and turning in bed is replaying in my head.

All bets will be off if I discover they've gone anywhere near Reyna.

I will drag my brother and Reyna to the other side of the world if I have to. We're all getting the fuck out of here.

At least that sounds great in theory, but I know Spencer won't go. He's only aware of a *fraction* of what really goes on in the Order. Every acolyte knows that the only way to end their tenure is death, whether by natural causes or at the hands of one of Shepherd's soldiers.

Most members think that people like me are the only ones who do the killing. They don't realize it can be part of someone's initiation into the Order. If people know what the grim reaper looks like, they'll know who to hide from.

So my brother lives blissfully naive thinking that the only people who pull the trigger for the Order are those who want to. He'll learn the truth once he reaches my rank as medicus. Until then, he can sleep his way through the student body, drink, party, play football, do everything that makes him feel like a normal human before it all goes away.

Taking Shepherd out won't change anything. His replacement could very well have a more brutal touch. Either way, he's too well protected by the Order to be brought down, especially by someone like me. I now have not one but two weaknesses, and apparently, everyone knows it.

Shepherd looks at me blandly. "Take my suggestion, and your brother will do nothing more than the basics. Every man should know how to throw a decent punch."

Fuck.

Fuck.

I was willing to drop Abigail and risk Spencer for the sake of having Reyna, but now that reality is in front of me, I don't know if I can guarantee her survival, because Reyna *will* be the next hit that's called out if I don't keep my distance. If anything happens to her . . .

Begging will only feed into Shepherd's agenda, and he'll hang it over my head daily as a reminder that he doesn't *suggest* things. Every order is a threat. Do it or else.

"Am I to turn away every student seeking assistance?"

"Yes. If it's discovered that you are speaking with Reyna Sinaga, further, more drastic measures will be put in place."

My breaths come out hard as I stare him down. Hearing her name come out of his mouth sends streaks of red across my vision.

"Such as?" I grit out.

"You require your hands to paint, do you not?" His head tilts to the side, staring down at me even though I'm standing above him. "Although, you won't be painting if you're dead."

The Order is untouchable. But anything that happens to me or Spencer would impact my father greatly.

"A fortunate possibility for someone who doesn't wish to see Roland as a high saint," I say.

The grand magistrate has somewhat of a soft spot for Roland for reasons beyond me. He's much too virtuous to pull strings to ensure my father's election, and I find it difficult to believe Shepherd will take any steps to jeopardize Roland's campaign.

I step back when he slowly rises to his feet, buttoning his jacket. "Perhaps," Shepherd says simply, heading for the exit.

The object he tosses my way clatters onto the floor.

"I suggest you start wearing your ring."

27

REYNA

Four days of recovery is ample time to spiral into despair.

I hate being left alone with my thoughts.

I hate being ignored more.

I haven't heard from Maddox since I went grocery shopping yesterday morning. While I was there, I had the misfortune of running into a guy from one of my classes—Alex—and had to pretend I was fine when he started asking why I look like I've been run over by a bus three times. It ruined my mood.

Then to be ghosted by Maddox after that? After he asked me to send pictures of my "proof of life." It's nearly unforgivable if you ask me. If anyone gets to ignore the other person, it's me. I'm considering having a chiropractor on retainer because of how much whiplash that man gives me.

I've been left stewing and running through every possible theory on whether a secret society could actually exist. I mean, the idea wouldn't be so far-fetched. The world is already corrupt as it is—or maybe I've just watched one too many movies involving cults.

"Seriously, though, if you need someone to carry you because you think you're dying, let me know so Lawrence can have his knight-in-shining-armor moment." Kimi winks as she climbs the campus steps beside me.

I send her a death glare. I'd provide a proper response if I weren't trying to preserve my energy. Physically, I'm fine, I think. But my anxiety has manifested itself into flu-like symptoms. Which means needing to talk to the Lord of Darkness to see if there's a real future for us.

She checks her phone before dropping it into her purse. "Right, well, I'm going to love you and leave you. Owen said he's taking me to Chicago for dinner."

I come to a screeching halt. "Wait, what? Since when are you on a traveling basis?"

Kimi shrugs innocently while still looking smug as hell. "Since I like him, and he likes me."

"Him or his wallet?"

Her expression sours like the thought of him being *just another guy* hurts. "Him and his personality. His wallet is an added bonus. Besides, we're taking his jet there, so I can carry pepper spray in my bag."

I snort. "Don't do anything stupid, all right? And use protection."

Her eyes light up. "Funny you say that; I was going to email Shaw and tell him the same thing."

I lightly hit her arm, looking around to make sure no one heard. "Don't say that so loud."

Cackling, she sashays backward. "It'll be kinda cute if we have babies at the same time."

Hard pass.

"Neither of us are getting pregnant, Kimi."

"You're not, but with the right financial incentive, I might. As they say, you've gotta get that bread, and I simply wasn't built for the nine-to-five."

For God's sake. This woman is going to give me a brain aneurysm.

Her dedication to the sugar-baby lifestyle is admirable, if not exhausting. I'd be an entirely different person if I had even an ounce of her extroverted energy.

"For sure." If my afternoon goes perfectly, Maddox will dispel my anxieties about us, and I will miraculously have everything I need to uncover my dad's other life.

And whether this society has anything to do with it.

"Good luck. If Jennifer gives you a hard time, I'll light her car on fire." Kimi leaves with these departing words.

I feel bad for lying about who I'm going to see. Admitting that I'm going to corner Maddox won't go down well with her, especially since she thinks we were a one-and-done deal and I'm just a girl fawning over her professor because I slept with him.

I'll tell her eventually. She doesn't need more of my drama when she babysat me after Mom died.

The walk to Maddox's office seems to go on forever. I'm half tempted to leave this conversation for another day, but there's no point delaying the inevitable. He's made his intentions clear; he'll have to show he's dedicated to making this work by being completely honest with me.

Maybe it's too early in our relationship to promise no more secrets, but I won't compromise on it. No more cryptic answers. No more making excuses or putting off conversations. He needs to tell it to me straight. I need to see the full scope of what I'm getting into if I'm going to agree.

I pause with my foot midair at the sound of someone calling my name. I whip around toward it, and it takes me a moment to place the woman approaching me.

Abi.

My mouth goes dry, and I glance around for Kimi. A thousand questions fly through my mind. Why is *she* here? What does she want? Is she coming to see Maddox?

I force a strained smile onto my face. "Hey."

"Hi." Her steps falter for a moment before she decides to close the distance. "We, um . . ." Abi's throat bobs, and I shift my weight, unsure where to look. "We never got to talk the other day because . . . you know."

My skin burns red, and I fidget with my hands. Never in my life did I imagine an interaction like this. "Yeah. Sorry about that."

This time, she offers me a genuine smile as a silent truce, and shrugs. "I get it. When you don't know our world, it's a lot to take in."

As in the world of the upper class? The . . . society?

"Yeah." Awkward silence hangs around us, neither of us daring to look at the other. I clear my throat. "Are you on the way to see Maddox?"

Abi's eyes bug like I just accused her of murder. "No, no. God, no. I've come to see him once, and it was the most painful experience in my life. I try to avoid him at all costs."

"Oh." I can't say that sounds like the workings of a happy marriage. Maddox mentioned something along the same vein. Their dislike toward each other is a balm on my aching wound.

Shaking her head, she continues and gestures to the building behind her. "My boyfriend studies here." Her face lightens up at the mention of him. "Brodie and Spencer are on the same football team, and we were hanging out before they went to class."

"Oh."

Come on, Reyna. Form a proper sentence.

Hearing that she has a boyfriend has the knot in my stomach unwinding. I'm admittedly less repulsed by the circumstances I've landed myself in with Maddox.

"And you don't want to be with Maddox?" I ask carefully. The answer is obvious, but I need to hear her say it.

"I wouldn't want to marry him even if we were the last people on earth."

I tap my finger against my thigh, taking a deep breath of cold air. "You both intend on ending it, then?"

She nods enthusiastically. "He invited me over the other day to assure you that he and I wanted the same thing. When he said he wanted to end our engagement, I almost passed out from relief." Her perfectly styled hair falls from her shoulder when she shrugs. "He must be taken by you. It's literally the first time he's ever approached me for something—actually, I think it's the first time he's willingly spoken to me."

My resolve solidifies with giddy delight. Maddox was telling the truth. He's picking me. *Us.*

My shoulders relax as I let out a breath. "Thank you for telling me. I really appreciate it. You have no idea how much I needed to hear it from you."

"Of course." She nods. "The sooner you can get him and the Order off my back, the better. I feel guilty pulling Brodie along."

Huh? "The Order?"

Abi's bright hazel eyes turn into saucers, widening when they dart to something behind me. I spin around to catch what it was she saw, but there's nothing but students who I don't recognize walking around.

"Uh, you don't—He never told—" She cuts herself off. "Yeah. Yes. Sorry. I was confused for a sec. It's the name of my father's, um . . . what's it called? Subsidiary companies, or whatever? Like an Order of them? You get what I mean." She chuckles nervously.

My forehead wrinkles.

She shakes her head and retreats back a step. "Anyway, just . . . be careful with him."

My breath catches in my throat. "Why?"

"He . . . Um, I don't really know how to put this, and you didn't hear this from me or anything . . . but I've heard that he can be . . ." Her throat bobs. "Dangerous. *Really* dangerous."

My heart hammers as I watch her back away slowly. Is she referring to the whole serial-killing thing? Because turns out, I'm pretty accepting of that. Or does she mean the secret society I'm digging into?

"Yeah, thanks for the heads-up."

She gives me a tight-lipped smile as she turns around and says over her shoulder, "See you round."

All right. What just happened? Her reactions at the end were off.

What did she call it? The Order?

So now the woman who Maddox is—*was*—supposed to marry for "business reasons" mentions "our world" and an "order"?

Shaking my head, I put a pin in what she said and continue on my trek to his office. The conversation threw me, but at the same time it makes me feel more confident—about Maddox and my theories. He's made his intentions clear with someone other than me. It's exactly the kind of proof I wanted to see. A good first step.

I wipe my sweaty palms on my coat before knocking on his door, attempting not to sound timid.

The ball is in my court, I remind myself. I'm the one making decisions here. If I need more time or decide to walk away, that's entirely up to me. The worst that could happen is—

The door swings open. Green eyes slam with mine, hard and forceful. Maddox's nostrils flare when he realizes it's me.

"Miss Sinaga." He scowls.

My pulse ratchets up a notch. This isn't the warm reception I thought I'd receive.

Nodding toward the hand he's keeping firmly on the door, I ask, "Can I come in?"

"Did you make an appointment?" he says flatly.

My hackles rise. "What?" I blink several times. "No?"

"Then I'm afraid I'm busy." There's no humor in his tone.

My brow spears up to my hairline.

Right. *No.* Whatever game he's playing ends now. It's not cute. Nor is it funny. I barge right in, shoving his hand aside when he tries to stop me.

"What are you doing here?"

Is he serious right now? "I wanted to talk with you."

He strides past me to his desk without sparing me a glance. "We have nothing to talk about."

I pale. "Excuse me?" No, I must have heard wrong.

"Like you, I've had a couple of days to think about it, and I've decided you're just a student. We couldn't possibly have anything to talk about." His voice is distracted. Detached. Bored.

My heart cracks in two. There must be something I'm missing. I probably misunderstood him. There's a perfectly reasonable explanation for his reaction.

This must be a joke. It *has* to be. I can't—I choke. I am *not* being put last again.

Clearing my throat, I raise my chin. "I don't under—"

Maddox sighs like this is a complete waste of his time, and he's at the very end of his patience. "Perhaps I need to say it more plainly; nothing will ever happen between us because you're *you*, and I'm *me*."

My stomach sinks. It's like I'm being skinned alive. He . . . No, he doesn't mean that. He *can't* mean that.

I quickly blink away the tears pricking my eyes. "What the hell does that mean?"

Maddox doesn't look at me when he says, "That it was fun while it lasted."

Oh.

It's happening again.

I was right. This was all a game to him. Some fun to pass the time. I was never going to be the one he chose.

For a minute there, I believed that I was worthy of being put first. He really had me fooled. He—I rake my fingers through my hair. I don't . . . Just the other day he was saying—

This *can't* be happening. The pain is visceral.

He . . . He was playing me. He *played* me. And I believed all the stupid words he said. I fell for it. I fell for *him*. I can't believe I was so blind. So *stupid*.

"You're a fucking piece of shit," I hiss. My body is vibrating. Why does this keep happening to me? Was Abi in on this too? Is that why she approached me?

He's the worst person I've ever met. As bad as every other monster out there. I was wrong before. He *would* hurt me. Only he doesn't need to lay a hand on me to do it.

He stares blankly at me as if this is the most inconsequential conversation he's ever had. As if he hasn't ripped my fucking heart out. "You've never been very creative with your insults. I suppose that's why you've always had to work off of someone else's idea."

I rear back like I've been slapped. "No. *No.* You don't get to lead me on like that then throw me aside like I'm nothing." *Not after you got inside my head. Made me think that you cared about me, and that I was special, and the only girl in the world that you wanted.*

What was the point of gifting me the painting? Or revealing his identity? None of this makes sense.

He shrugs, sorting through the paperwork on his desk like I'm not there.

"Look at me, you *asshole.*" I seethe, slamming my trembling hand on the desk when he doesn't. *Just look at me. Why can't you fucking look at me?* "Fuck you and your Jekyll-and-Hyde bullshit."

He just told Abi that he wants to be with me, for fuck's sake.

Finally, *finally*, he looks at me. But it hurts more because he doesn't spare me more than a sideways glance. "Careful, Miss Sinaga. I do not tolerate abuse from my students."

He throws the words out like he couldn't care less if he spoke or not. Like I'm not worth his time or energy. Like I'm forgettable.

Mom would forget that I was there, too busy thinking about Dad. My own father didn't even remember that he had a daughter.

"After everything we've been through. Everything you've told me. The secrets you've shared . . . you want to . . . You're walking away?" I sputter.

Why does everyone keep leaving me? I can't do this again. I can't keep caring for people only for them to be ripped away from me.

Every aspect of me is flawed. *Lacking.* Pathetic. I'll never be a director like I wanted. My father was never going to love me. Mom was never going to pick me over her soulmate. I'll never amount to anything more than a passing phase—a backup—to *anyone*. I'm wasted space. The blank wall between paintings at a museum.

Maddox's jaw feathers as he flicks through the pages of a book. "I do believe I've made that obvious."

There's no inflection in his tone. Nothing that would suggest how he's feeling. His walls are up, and the mask he wears like a second skin is on tight. Our progress was a lie. *Everything* was a lie.

Red tints my vision. I can't stand looking at him. He's so put together while I'm crumbling apart. I want to throw things, scream, ask him how he can be such a vile human being.

"I risked my reputation for you. My career. My safety. My *dignity*. I was going to move past your relationship status. I was going to talk to you and figure out how to move forward. How *we* can move forward. I don't understand. Why are you doing this? I thought . . . I thought we—"

I cut myself off. I won't keep pouring my heart out when he doesn't care. He doesn't deserve any part of me. I said my piece as he leafed through his book.

"*God*, I believed you. I *trusted* you. How could I be so stupid? How many other people have you screwed over like this? Huh? Is this how you get your kicks when killing doesn't cut it?" I growl, fighting the hot, angry tears. *I just want to know why?*

He shrugs as if to say, *Get over it.* "Are you done?"

I swallow down a shuddering breath.

Pull yourself together.

Taking a deep breath, I straighten my spine and look him dead in the eyes. "Yes. Yes, we are."

Fine.

So be it.

Fuck him. Fuck his art. And fuck everything to do with Maddox Fucking Shaw.

I turn as calmly as I can and walk away. My vision blurs the more distance I put between us. It feels like the building rattles when I slam the door behind me. The final nail in the coffin.

The sound of furniture crashing echoes through the hall, coming from his room. Followed by a loud, guttural *"Fuck."*

Yes.

I agree.

Fuck Maddox Shaw.

28

MADDOX

"Miss Sinaga, please ensure you have your essay emailed to me by midnight tomorrow."

She doesn't need the reminder. I say it anyway because it's the only form of interaction I can have with her. The only thing she offers me in return is a curt nod. It's killing me that she refuses to meet my eyes because she's too busy staring at the band around my finger.

I want to melt the bloody thing into a bullet and put it between Roland's eyes for ruining my relationship with her.

I've been tortured several times in my life. I've been waterboarded, electrocuted, beaten, starved, beaten again, whipped, burned, and other rather gruesome acts that I would rather not relive.

Out of everything I've endured, this is the worst torture. Watching Reyna live out her life without me. Looking at me with seething hatred. Acting like I don't exist whenever I'm in her general vicinity. She even changed the premise of her final film project.

It hurt more than I'm willing to admit.

I got reckless, excited about something for once in my life, and became blind to my surroundings. It's been two weeks since I saw her heart break in front of me, and I see it every time I close my eyes. I wish I could take back what I said.

My office fell victim to my rage. I ripped canvases, shattered sculptures, broke furniture, anything I could get my hands on to release the fury that burned through my veins.

I wanted to run out the door and apologize a hundred times over. Explain that this is for her safety. That I'm giving my happiness up so she can *live*. Hold her and tell her that I meant every word I said before that day; none of it was a lie, because she's become everything to me.

I follow her out of class without waiting for the rest of the students to leave, turning onto the path that leads to my office. Reyna will be staying at the library late into the night anyway.

Once I'm in the confines of my studio, I slump into my chair, chuck my glasses onto the table and rub my eyes.

What a mess.

I can't sleep. Can't eat. Can't think. My art has turned into glorified rubbish.

I feel like I need her more than I need air to breathe. My exhibition is in two and a half weeks, and I haven't been able to pick up a paintbrush, because I've lost my muse. In the few months that I've known her, she's become the sole source of my inspiration.

I need her to come back to me. I need her to look at me. To laugh. To call me out on my shit. Make me feel something other than the cloying air that's suffocating me.

Threatening every professor in this university to give her good grades doesn't make up for the things I said. Nor does offering her an "anonymous" scholarship grant.

I slip my hand beneath the collar of my shirt to rub the tension from my shoulders. My fingers skim across the ruined skin, and I grimace, yanking my hand away at the memory of Roland's heated belt buckle tearing the soft tissue apart.

It doesn't matter how far I run, the marks the Order left on me will never disappear.

Right on cue, my phone chimes with a text.

SHEPHERD:

Tomorrow night. Clean.

I clench my jaw, grateful the next kill will be made to look like an accident, because I'm not in the frame of mind to be creative.

My irritation spikes when another message comes through.

MOTHER:

I've arranged for you and Abi to have dinner at the yacht club tomorrow. She'll be ready by 6:30 for you to pick her up.

A minute later, another from one of the few people in the Order I like—usually. Right now, he's getting on my last nerve about the painting I promised to donate for his charity event.

THEO:

ETA on the donation piece.

I shut my phone off. I have neither the patience nor the willpower to deal with any of them tonight. If I get one more text, I might feel so inclined to tell all of them to disrespectfully fuck off.

Sighing, I put my glasses back on. I can't remember the last time I slept more than a handful of hours, because I'm too busy worrying that something might happen to Reyna. At least she's safe in the library, so I can grade some papers on my laptop. I pull up the tracker app I had installed into Reyna's phone to have in the background.

"What the fuck?" I whisper, watching the little dot move through the city, heading in a direction that *isn't* toward her apartment.

I'm on my feet and out the door in three seconds flat. She doesn't have any work scheduled for tonight, so where the fuck is she going?

By the time the tracker stops moving, I'm on the sidewalk hailing a cab. I zoom in on the surrounding area, recognizing one street in particular that's two blocks away from where she is.

The same street Lawrence happens to live on.

Jealousy, wild and hot, surges up my chest. I have no right to it when I can't have her. She deserves to be free and happy, away from the Order and away from the danger I've put her in.

Reyna is too good for me.

I never felt the need to lay claim on anyone or be so utterly consumed by someone that the thought of another man touching them has the most lethal ideas flashing through my mind.

Reyna Sinaga is *too good* for me, and I want her all to myself.

Lawrence had been hanging around Reyna long before the Order set its sights on her. If there's one acolyte she'd be safe with, it's him. He might be a paladin, but from what I've gathered, he sticks to himself and isn't that engaged.

What I should be doing instead of risking both of our lives is grading assignments and prepping for the hit Shepherd commissioned. What I *should* be doing is keeping my brother safe and keeping Reyna as far from me as I can. But I want what I want, and I want her. I need to feel like I'm worth more than what I create with my hands, and only she can make me feel human.

No one has to know.

I'll kill Lawrence if I have to.

Out of an abundance of caution, I change cabs twice on the way there, ordering the drivers to take unnecessary turns before I head into the subway just to go right back out.

It takes far longer than I'd like to get to the restaurant her tracker stopped at, giving me more time to seethe and think of a thousand and one ways to turn Lawrence into a centerpiece. I'm going to gift her his head on a fucking spike.

Two weeks.

Two weeks.

That's how long it took her to move on from me. *Two.* Reyna has been acting like nothing happened between us, and it pisses me the fuck off. It's like she doesn't give a shit about me. As if I'm some guy she hooked up with. Like it—I—meant nothing to her. Meanwhile, I'm losing my fucking mind.

The cab pulls up in front of the restaurant, and I drop a hundred-dollar bill on the seat before powering down the sidewalk.

Images flash in my mind of every possible thing I might find. If she's on a date, they're fucking dead. Reyna can scream at me and hit me for all I care; I'm going to steal her away.

She doesn't get to forget about me. No one else gets to have her attention. *I'm* her fucking man, even if we'll never be together. I'm the one she talks to. I'm the one who's meant to be taking her out to dinner. I'm the only one who can wine and dine her, and see what she looks like without her dress. Not fucking *Lawrence.* Not any random men or women who don't deserve her. Who can't cherish her the way that I can.

Desperate.

That's what I am. I'm desperate for Reyna.

And she doesn't get to move on from me in *two weeks.*

I walk straight into the restaurant. The panicked hostess scrambles to attention, spouting off her welcoming speech as I storm straight past her.

It's a religious experience having my sights instantly land on the back of Reyna's head when the entire restaurant is filled to the brim. She deserves better than this dingy place. I'll take her to every single bloody Michelin-star restaurant in this city to prove I'm the only one who can treat her right.

Fuck the Order and their rules.

My heart beats erratically as I close the distance. I almost stumble when her *date* comes into view.

Are you fucking kidding me? She's moved on from me with some scrawny kid in a Batman T-shirt?

Lawrence looks worse in person. There's no way she could be into that. I refuse to believe it.

Steam practically blows out of my ears as I grab a chair from a nearby table—I don't give a damn if someone was using it—and slam it down in front of the two *lovebirds*, dropping myself into the seat, hoping Batman has a brain aneurysm from the glare I'm shooting his way.

I want to grab her and drag her to my lap, either to put her over it or on it—I'm not sure. What the fuck does she see in this fuckwit?

Dear Lord, does this cop have braces? His stupid mouth is parted, gulping like a damn fish as he flicks his gaze from me to Reyna—I can't explain how unnecessarily upset it makes me when he looks at her.

What pisses me off more is that I'm comparing myself to someone wearing cargo pants. Is this what her type is? Someone who's the opposite of me in every way?

Fuck it. Even if he's her type, there's no way she could date him. He's not good enough for her. He can't be what she needs. He can't take care of her or keep her safe or stoke her creativity. He won't be able to satisfy her like I can.

Really, I'm doing this for her, not me.

"What are you doing here?" Reyna hisses, glancing around like someone might come over and yell at her for my intrusion.

Then her eyes land on me, and one look is all it takes for some of the tension to ease from my chest.

She's finally looking at me.

"I was walking past and decided to stop by." A slight growl makes its way into my voice, making her flinch before hardening into steel.

Reyna gives the wanker a reassuring smile before going back to glaring at me. She should be smiling at *me*, not that fuckwit.

"How kind," she grits out. "Unfortunately—"

"Is there a problem here?" Lawrence must have a death wish if he thinks he can cut Reyna off.

It took the idiot fifteen seconds to read the room. Maybe I'll get his badge taken from him, then cut off his tongue before I kill him.

"No," Reyna says at the same time I say, "Yes."

He blinks, puffing out his chest as if I might be intimidated by someone who wears a smartwatch. What's more amusing is that he hasn't registered who I am—if he had, the lowly paladin wouldn't be speaking to me like he is.

Good. Everything is going my way. He's not about to go running to Roland or Shepherd about my behavior.

"You're the problem. Leave," I demand.

Lawrence gapes at me like I'm out of my mind. I guess I am. "I don't know who the hell you think—"

"Mr. Shaw, it's been lovely to see you this evening," Reyna interrupts, plastering on the fakest, most disgustingly sweet voice she's ever used on me. "If you don't mind, I can email you any questions I have about the assignment." *I mind. I very much mind.* "There's no need to discuss the classwork outside office hours."

"Assignment?" Lawrence unhelpfully speaks.

I ignore him. "No need. I'm here now. Let's walk and talk."

If looks could kill, I'd be dead at her feet from the holes she's burning into me. "I'm in the middle of something, as you can see." She nods at the dry, brick-level cheesecake they're sharing.

Sharing.

My fingers curl into a fist. "I wasn't asking for your opinion on the matter."

There's no universe where I would *let* her go out to dinner with someone who isn't me. Let alone with Lawrence.

He stands to his full height. "Look, if she doesn't—"

"No one gave you permission to speak," I snap. His jaw goes slack, and I return my full attention to Reyna. "I think it's past your bedtime."

Oh, that does it. If she was angry before, she's downright *livid* now. "How dare you? What's your prob—"

Lawrence holds his hand up. "It's time for you to leave, pal."

The chair screeches and skitters back as I take a step toward him, leaving only a foot of space between us. "Cut her off again, *pal*. I dare you. Now, how about you do all of us a favor and take your bad breath to go."

Reyna is turning me into a person I don't recognize. I'd never do something so callous in public. Most definitely not to a police officer. One who happens to be an acolyte devoted to my betrothed's house.

"Careful, Mr. Shaw," Reyna whispers behind me, loud enough for only me to hear. "I do not tolerate abuse from my teachers."

I can hear the chess piece click against the board as she finishes her sentence. *Checkmate.*

She leans closer, fire blazing behind her eyes as a pang of regret hits me in the chest. Her next words come out low and like barbed wire. "Fuck off, you piece of shit. It's over."

Forgetting about Batman, I turn to face her, letting her scent flood over me as I do something I may regret. It's surreal to have her close enough to touch again. Satisfaction unfurls from her shiver when I brush my lips against the shell of her ear.

"You and I, love? We'll never be over." I pull away, resisting the urge to run my fingers over her parted lips. "I look forward to receiving your email tomorrow."

Until then, I'll be seeing a lot of you. Someone has to make sure you get home safe.

29

REYNA

Maddox might be a serial killer, but I'm two seconds away from killing the motherfucker. As they say, the lion, the witch, and the absolute *audacity* of this fucking bitch.

We'll never be over.

Kiss. My. Ass.

He broke up with *me*. Then all of a sudden, he shows up at my dinner with Lawrence wanting to talk and have some alone time with me—and now this?

Please. He's about two weeks too late.

I slam my books on the desk as soon as the last student leaves the room. "What the fuck is your problem?" I growl, glaring down Maddox Fucking Shaw who's standing all prim and proper on the other side of the desk.

Fuck him and his stupid tie. And fuck his knitted sweater, his perfectly polished boots, and the annoyingly cute scarf he walked into class wearing too.

Once again, he showed up to a workshop a tutor is meant to run. I thought I'd be free of him so I'd have more than a couple of days to process what happened and come up with a reason why he showed up at dinner. Him being jealous is not a valid option.

His eyes brighten when they land on me. Maddox can't seriously be happy to see me. "Whatever do you mean?"

Oh. He really wants to play this card?

"Don't play dumb with me," I hiss, pointing a finger at his stupid face. "Why the hell did you have to ruin my"—*gag*—"date?"

I wasn't sure if I agreed to go to dinner with Lawrence out of pity, as a distraction to forget about Maddox, or to see if I could fish information about the society. But when he made clear that any information linked to the society wouldn't be forthcoming—and since it's not like I'm going to keep poking around Maddox's crime scenes—I decided I was done entertaining him for good and cut our evening short. A fact he didn't take particularly well.

Maddox raises a flawless brow in amusement and scoffs. "Bad breath and dry cake ruined it long before I came along."

"I don't understand you," I say, exasperated. "You told me how you really feel, and I listened. I stayed the hell away, and you've been so goddamn persistent with ensuring that *you're* the one who can't leave it to rest."

Ever since we broke up, I haven't stopped feeling like I'm being watched, and I'm so sick and tired of it. Worse, I can't stop thinking that it's *him* who's tailing me. Like, how did he just so happen to "be in the area" of my date? He lives on the opposite side of the city.

Doesn't he realize that I'm hurting? I can't get over something we apparently never had if he keeps showing up to remind me of all my misplaced feelings.

I'm grateful for the desk between us. I feel like killing him, and kissing him, and ruining his irritatingly perfect face, then climbing all over him so he can take me against the wall.

I hate him. I hate him. I hate him.

"What do you want, Maddox?" I whisper-yell, throwing my arms out because energy is vibrating through my veins, and I can't take it anymore: the lies, the secrets, the whiplash. "If you're wanting to have someone on call to fuck you, I suggest trying at a local bar. Or maybe your fiancée." I feel sick saying the words. The thought of Maddox being with anyone but me makes me seethe.

We could have been *great* together. Our lives could've been filled with messed-up acts of romance and bloodstained art. I was ready for the risk. I would have been okay with the knowledge that we'll forever be outcasts, if it meant we would've had each other. All he had to do was show me that he wanted to commit. But the joke's on me, and he knows it.

Maddox works his jaw, staring at me like he has a thousand things he wants to say. Yet "He's not right for you" is all he responds with.

Why is he making everything so confusing? *What does he want?*

I laugh bitterly. "You don't get to say shit about what is or isn't good or *right* for me. You lost your chance of holding any valid opinion on my personal life. You're my *temporary* professor. Nothing more."

I swear he flinches. I keep going before he can say more, because *I'm* the one in control here. There's nothing he could say that would change anything. I'm setting the line in stone, and there's to be no more crossing it. He needs to stop leading me on and filling me with false hope.

"I have strong feelings for Lawrence." *Negative feelings.* "And I would appreciate it if you didn't interfere with my relationship with him, or anyone else, for that matter."

Maddox's eyes darken, and the room temperature plummets as his mask fractures to let the beast through. "I have a list," he starts, words slow to ensure I don't miss a single thing. "It's a list of names of all the men in this city who I'd like to turn into decorative pieces." He tips his head innocently to the side. "It would be most unfortunate if Lawrence were to end up on this list. Or any other men I deem . . . unworthy."

My throat bobs. The idea makes me sick with glee, and mortification that he can twist me around his fingers so easily. "You wouldn't dare."

His gaze drops to my lips for one jarring second. "You have no idea what I would and wouldn't do when you're involved."

I stagger back from the heated change in his tone. I feel like I can't get enough oxygen in my lungs. "Lawrence is a police officer."

"All men bleed equally."

"You're insane." I shake my head, scowling at him.

"I thought we've been over this before, Miss Sinaga." Maddox's voice drops in volume, and the skin of his knuckles turns white. "*You* make me insane."

Tears spring in the back of my eyes. "Stop," I rasp through clenched teeth. "Don't."

Once someone else is interested in his *toy* he threw away, he doesn't like it.

He didn't want me. *He* ruined me like he said he could. He turned me into a fool, and he keeps coming back to do it again.

Maddox starts to move around the table. "Reyna, I meant what I said. There hasn't been a moment that you haven't occupied every single one of my thoughts, and—"

"No. Stop talking. I don't want to hear it. I—" I choke back tears.

I'm so fucking *tired.* I just wanted to make films and get to know my dad.

I can't do this. With him. With Lawrence. With anyone.

"If you ever gave a shit about me, you're going to answer my question." I pull up a photo of the honeycomb insignia on my phone. "Your kills. What is the connection between your victims, Cresswell, and this honeycomb? I know a lot of them studied here, and this symbol—this society has something to do with it."

The blood drains from his face. "There is no connection, and you should stop looking for one."

He's lying—he's fucking *lying*.

"We're done here. Don't ever speak to me again."

I snatch my books off the desk and storm toward the door, using every ounce of willpower to keep my sob at bay.

"Reyna," Maddox calls.

My footsteps quicken and I ignore his calls as I whip the door open and stagger out, narrowly colliding with another student.

"Hey, you okay?"

"Fine!"

My eyes snap up to Alex's, and I almost trip in my haste to get away from him. I spin around and bound down the steps to get away from both men because I'm being reminded of the day Maddox made me think he was interested in me for anything beyond sex. He pointed me to the door and gave me the opportunity to stop before we started.

I regret not taking it.

30

REYNA

I round the corner to the library and leap back, narrowly avoiding another collision. Hands grip on to my shoulder to catch my fall, and my breath leaves me in a rush.

"Oh, Jesus—" I snap my mouth shut. My lips twitch into an involuntary scowl. "Lawrence."

I haven't seen this prick since our pitiful date a week ago. I would've been happy if I never saw him again. Since we don't run in the same circles, I figured it would've been doable.

I glance around at the deserted campus buildings that are cloaked in darkness. "What are you doing here?"

"Reyna," Lawrence grunts, frowning down at me.

My eyes narrow on his hands when they stiffen on me right before he lets me go. My mouth dries when I catch a glimpse of his golden cuff links peeking out beneath his suit.

Bees. Tiny, unmistakable bees.

My breath rushes out, and I take a cautious step back, eyeing him up and down. He's out of his uniform and in a cheap suit and polyester coat instead. There's no reason for him to be on campus at this time of night. The university wouldn't host an event well past dinnertime.

I will my face to relax and pass off as empathetic. "Hey, look. I've been meaning to reach out about the other night." *No, I haven't been.* "I'm . . ." *Come on, just spit it out.* "Sorry about the way things went." The words taste like acid.

Lawrence's smug little mouth tightens. I force a smile anyway and hold out my hand. "Let's let bygones be bygones?"

He considers for a moment. "Sure." He takes my offered hand, and my sights lock on his wrists again. Definitely bees.

I drop my arm, putting more distance between us.

"It was good to see you." *No, it wasn't.* "Sorry, but I really have to go."

His annoying face scrunches up in displeasure and confusion. "Uh, sure."

I smile sweetly at him and continue in the direction I was going, keeping my ears peeled for his footsteps. I spin back around once he sounds far enough away, and rush to the very edge of the building to peer around the corner at his receding frame.

He's hiding something. Maddox is hiding something. My parents were hiding something. I'm going to find out what that is.

Digging my nails into my palm, I creep out of the shadows and keep close to the buildings, following Lawrence across campus—away from the library. My heart pounds as brick and plaster walls watch me stalk through the night.

The frigid air burns my lungs with every inhale but makes me feel like I'm coming alive. The chill penetrates my bones when he turns around. For a second, I *swear* he spots me shadowing him. But he turns around and continues walking, pulling out his phone, completely unaware of my presence. I breathe a sigh of relief and put more space between us.

We're heading into a part of campus I've never been to. Unease prickles the back of my neck when he slips into a side door at the very edge of the university. If memory serves, it's the administration building that holds all the higher-ups' offices. It's one of the older buildings that isn't as well kept, so it sees a lot less traffic.

The anxiety multiplies when I rush up to the door to find it unlocked. I mean, Lawrence doesn't exactly strike me as a competent person, so I'm not surprised if he forgot.

Unless it's to allow more people inside.

No, there could be an entirely reasonable explanation for this. Lawrence is a cop. He could be investigating something.

This late at night.

In a shitty suit.

Without backup.

I mean, I should follow him in, just to be sure.

Plus, it's not like I haven't been in substantially worse situations. It's dangerous, and I'm beyond giving a shit. I've hit more dead ends than I can count, the two men who have any information about my father are conveniently withholding it from me, and I am *so sick* of being kept in the dark by everyone.

If this ends up with me in cuffs, or dead in a ditch, then it can be my father's last act of disappointment. His life will forever be a secret, because if nothing comes from this, I'm done. I came here to find the truth about him, not pine after my serial-killing professor.

With a deep breath, I turn on my phone's flashlight and slip into the building to attempt to retrace Lawrence's steps . . . which is surprisingly easy since every door is closed except the ones I can only assume he's gone into.

I keep turning down various hallways, padding along on the balls of my feet in case anyone is close enough to hear. Being somewhere I shouldn't be is thrilling. It's like taking a dip into the dark side without knowing if something will reach out and drag me under.

My feet stall at the threshold of an office room. Is that . . . What type of Scooby-Doo shit is this? Why is there a hidden entrance behind a bookcase?

As I ease closer, the musty air fills my lungs. I hold up my phone to shine light on the entryway that leads to a winding, uneven staircase descending into the earth. The walls are made of stone and mortar. It must have been made hundreds of years ago.

I feel like I'm in a knock-off Nancy Drew novel.

There's no way Lawrence isn't messing with me right now. He has to know that I'm following him, right? And why would a secret deadly organization have someone like *Lawrence* as a member? Lawrence, the guy who *fed me* the crime-scene pictures of murders that may or may not be connected to that very same dangerous society?

If it's a question of whether I'm dumb enough to risk my safety by going inside, the answer is yes. I am, in fact, stupid enough to follow a crooked cop into a mysterious, secret, ancient tunnel that may or may not lead to a sex dungeon.

I can hear my mom turning in her grave as I take a deep breath and move my feet closer to the potential kink club. The sandstone steps crunch beneath my boots and the echo through the tunnel makes me die inside.

Taking a deep breath, I descend the staircase, shivering at the sudden drop in temperature. It only gets worse the lower I get. I guess the silver lining is that I might die of hypothermia before I get murdered.

When I reach the bottom level, it's like entering into my very own horror movie. Cobwebs and broken sconces decorate the arched stone walls.

Curiosity gets the better of me as I eye the crates lining the tunnel. I lift the lid of one high enough to peer inside. There are a bunch of books, and other stuff like plaques, vases, medallions, and whatnot. I can't look at them properly without causing a ruckus and letting everyone in the vicinity know I'm here.

My knees click as I lower myself to open a big wooden chest. I grab the padlock, mentally crossing my fingers that it just needs a little wiggle to unlatch. No such luck.

I'm about to move on when the insignia on the lock catches my eye.

A honeycomb.

My heart pounds in double time. The distant sound of heavy footsteps travels down the tunnel from the direction I came. Panic seizes my chest in a vise. I kill my phone light, drop to the dirty floor, and wedge myself up against a chaise with a broken leg, tucking my limbs against my body to make myself as small as possible.

"No," a deep voice says.

The single syllable has every cell in my body going haywire. I will my eyesight to adjust to the darkness as I frantically search for somewhere better to hide and notice the white cloth lying on the chaise beside me.

Footsteps grow louder as the man continues speaking in a hushed tone. I yank the cloth toward me, covering part of the furniture and my entire body. I curl as tight as I can, melting against the dusty fabric. I've never felt more exposed.

My pulse roars in my ears. What if I was right, and the secret society really does exist? I'm sure Maddox's victims were killed because of it. What if I'm killed next because I found out? Or would they torture me? What if they killed my dad?

Adrenaline sends violent tremors through my hands as I fish through my satchel for my taser. It tumbles onto the stone, and the sound ripples through the tunnel.

I stop breathing.

The footsteps falter. Silence.

I hold perfectly still. Arm trembling in midair. They're just around the corner. I can hear them. They caught me, and now they're going to kill me.

It isn't until the voice starts again that I dare snatch the taser off the ground and hold it against my chest.

"Maybe I haven't made myself clear. The merger is going through—I said it's going through, and you are going to do whatever needs to be done to ensure it proceeds as planned—"

I hold my breath, clamping a hand over my mouth and nose to stay completely silent. Light streams through the cloth concealing me. It grows brighter with every step. He's right there—right in front of me.

He's not talking. Why isn't he talking? Blood roars in my ears, screaming my impending doom.

Tears burn my eyes, and a single razor-edged droplet runs down my cheek. I'm in way over my head. This is why Lawrence warned me to steer clear. Why Maddox told me to stop looking into his victims.

A sudden realization makes me nauseous. What if they know I'm onto them, and it wasn't Maddox who I felt watching me these past few weeks?

The steps carry through the tunnel, losing volume as he walks right past me. "Congressman Wallace will vote yes, and if he doesn't, you'll make sure he changes his mind, won't you?"

I take in my first breath, not daring to move in case he turns around. The taser continues to shake in my hand.

"Good. I don't want to hear from you until it's—"

He's too far away for me to make out the rest. It gets quieter and quieter until the only sound comes from my raging pulse. But I stay exactly where I am long after the last echo flows through the cold space.

It isn't until every one of my muscles cramps that I muster the confidence to creep out from beneath the fabric. My phone struggles to recognize the touch from my frozen fingers, and it takes too many precious seconds to turn the flashlight back on. Slowly, silently, like I'm a mouse and there's a beast hunting me, I leave my nest.

I start rushing in the direction I came from only to stop when the light shines on another chest with the honeycomb insignia. A war starts in my head.

If following a serial killer didn't end up with me dead, then this will—and there are fates far worse than death. The Cresswell book said the elites were in this beekeeping club, and evidence is pointing to that tradition living on. Mergers? Blackmailing congressmen? Corruption? I'm less than an ant in this game.

But I came here for a reason. I've spent all of my free time researching, investigating, and mulling over dead ends. This might be my only chance to find out more. I have to do this.

Using one arm to hug myself to preserve warmth, I hold my other out, shining the light left and right as I turn back around and continue down the tunnel in the same direction the man went.

My mind plays tricks on me, convinced each long shadow cast by the furniture is a person. Every few steps, I spot another item with the beehive emblem on it. Crates, banners, books, vases; it grows more frequent the deeper I go, until it stops completely.

I follow the sudden turn and stop dead in my tracks. My mouth goes dry as I move in a slow circle. This isn't just a tunnel. It's a catacomb.

Rows upon rows of skulls and femurs are piled against the wall to create an arched pattern. My fingers tremble around my phone as I edge closer.

They look real, and very, very old.

I stagger back, whipping around to face the direction I came from. It's not too late to run and forget everything I saw.

Still, I forge forward for answers that will never bring either of my parents back.

Despite the constant fear hammering at the back of my head, my lips part as I take in the wall. Nightmare-inducing circumstances aside, it's truly astounding.

All too soon, the catacomb comes to an end where a single door awaits. I've come too far to back out now—at least, that's what I tell myself. I turn my flashlight off, set my phone to record, grip the taser, and count to ten before inching the door open.

This is where those "beekeepers" meet up. I know it like I know my first name.

Carefully, I widen the opening enough to see inside—and my heart stalls. It's like sneaking into a portal to an alternate universe and stepping out into Versailles. High, painted ceilings, great big marble pillars and crystal chandeliers, ornate golden crown molding and paneling. It's a stark contrast to the tunnel I just walked through.

How is this beneath Cresswell?

Inhaling, I pull the door wider, waiting for any sound that might indicate someone has been alerted to my intrusion. Nothing.

Emboldened, I stick my head into what looks like a study—an *empty* study. I slip inside and close the door behind me. A chorus of applause in the distance makes my heart jump into my throat.

The sound cuts short. Casting my eyes around the room, I catalog every inch of it, pausing on the painting on the corner wall. Squinting against the dim light, I can make out a man wearing refined clothing from the Regency era with a crown atop his head and a shepherd's staff in hand, standing in a field surrounded by sheep. Three wolves conceal themselves beneath sheep hides, prowling toward the center, where the shepherd king stands.

My mom's dying words whisper in the back of my head about finding the shepherd, drowned out by the thought that the painting looks like Maddox's style. It confirms what I already knew: Maddox is involved.

He probably kills for the society. A deranged commissioned piece of art. Maybe Spencer does something similar, like a murderous family business.

I rush to the door opposite the one I came in through and inch it open too.

"—Mayor Tomin expressed his profound gratitude for House Dornmont's efforts to block the Zone Twenty-Three Bill."

House Dornmont?

Like *Abigail* Dornmont. What did she slip up and say? The Order? Is that what they're called?

The woman's voice is muffled like it's coming from the other side of the wall.

"After a grueling seven months, through your help, we can now begin Project Red, which will be led by House Shaw in conjunction with our Zaccardi—"

My lips part. *House Shaw?*

Ignoring the alarm bells going off in my head, I keep my ears open, sneaking into the hallway and creeping toward the voice. I don't know what I'm hoping to find. Potentially an office that coincidentally holds a registry of every person this society has interacted with? Maybe a list of everyone they've killed . . . because maybe Dad's death wasn't an accident.

The same opulent interior as the study is reflected everywhere I turn. At the end of the hallway is another corridor going in both directions. I hesitate before heading toward the voice.

The place is barren of people, but the applause that explodes down the hall tells me there's a whole crowd in there. The sound of glass and cutlery clinking together comes from farther away, making my anxiety reach new heights. Anyone could pop out and catch me snooping.

Alcoves have been dug into the wall to house statues, giant vases, and armor. A thick velvet curtain hangs above each archway, tied on each side to create the illusion of windows.

I dart from alcove to alcove, pausing each time in case anyone decides to step into the corridor. Some of the curtains are closed to hide various artifacts for reasons I can't explain. I use the hiding spot to catch my breath, then dash to the next one just as I hear a door opening. Footsteps carry down the hall toward me. Panic coils my muscles tighter and makes it harder to hear above the pulsing in my ears.

I don't let myself overthink. I drop down onto my hands and knees to make myself as small as possible, clutching the taser and hoping I'm unnoticeable behind the marble slab.

Their steps are sure and unhurried—slow even. It's torture.

Cold sweat sticks my clothes to my clammy skin. I hold my breath as the person passes, praying to whatever deity exists that I get out of here unscathed. I survived the catacombs and every murder scene I've ever visited. My luck is bound to run out eventually.

But not right now, apparently. The person waltzes right past without a hitch. A door opens, then closes, and the footsteps stop.

My shoulders sag, but the stroke of luck does nothing to calm my electrified nerves. I scramble onto my feet and peek into the hallway to double-check that there's no one there.

With the coast clear, I bolt to the last alcove opposite the room where the sounds are coming from, slipping behind its curtain. The heavy drapes barely ripple when I inch them aside to peer through the glass doors. The blood rushes from my face as I lean down to get a clearer view into the room.

Rows upon rows of people—hundreds of them—sit inside, dressed in a black mask and cloak that covers them head to toe. The pews are set in blocks that narrow into the center, where a woman stands on a platform in the same robe, except she has two red ropes crossed over her body, and nothing concealing her face.

It looks like some kind of ritual with all the lit candles along the wall, scattered at the edges of the pews, and surrounding the dais.

My gaze flicks up to the roof, and my blood turns cold.

It's here.

The honeycomb ceiling.

My hands shake as I scramble to retrieve my phone and locate the picture of my dad that I've spent hours looking at. My eyes dart from the screen to the molding and the ceiling on the other side of the doors, then back.

The one photo I have of my dad was taken here. Right beneath the golden filigree.

The room spins. I can barely breathe. What is this place? Why was my dad here? Why are Maddox and my dad connected to this?

This was a terrible idea. I need to get out of here.

A hand clamps over my mouth. "Well, well, well. What do we have here?"

31

REYNA

My heart lurches into my throat. I swallow down a scream. My elbow soars back into his ribs. He hisses and tightens his grip on me, pressing me flat against his chest directly behind the curtain.

"Remember how good you can be at following instructions?" Maddox whispers against my ear. "How about you do that again, huh, love?"

Betrayal crashes through me, hot and painful.

First, I found out he was engaged. Now, I have irrefutable confirmation that he's connected to my dead father, and I was too busy being a lovesick puppy to see it clearly.

He's lucky I'm not tasing him. I thrash against him, careful to keep as quiet as possible. My nails sink into his arms, and raw satisfaction flows through me at the sound of his strained grunt.

Maddox's arm is covered in the same black cloak as the people inside, and that fact feels like another slap.

He pulls me harder against him, and my traitorous body forces me to suppress a shiver. He still smells heavenly, and it fucking hurts. I can't give him a piece of my mind with his hand clamped over my mouth. So without second-guessing, I clamp my teeth down on his finger. I need him to hurt too.

This time, his grunt is less than lusty, but the way his other hand grasps at my clothes is making my heart send mixed signals to my frightened, rage-filled mind.

At this angle, I can peek between the gap of the curtain and see the congregation of people in the beehive room. The sounds of soft murmurings and the clink of utensils are growing louder.

"Reyna, calm down. I'm going to let go of you. It's in your best interest *not* to scream for help, because no one here will rescue you," Maddox says, voice low.

I pale. What would his people do to me if they caught me here?

"Nod once if you understand."

A tremor goes down my spine from the way the low cadence of his voice caresses the side of my face. I want to turn around to look at him, but I'm scared of meeting his eyes. It'll remind me of everything he said.

I nod, my knuckles bleaching around the taser, letting its solid shape ground me.

Maddox slowly lifts his hand from my mouth, keeping his other firmly wrapped around me. I hate how nice his arms feel, and how I want to close my eyes and bury my face into his chest to breathe him in.

"You need to leave. It isn't safe."

My anger spikes. I whirl on him so we're chest to chest. He grips my chin to stop me from saying anything, and I slap his hand away, ignoring how his eyes harden.

"If you think I'm dangerous, then there's a whole room of people who will kill you without being asked twice."

My heart sinks. People—*organizations*—don't keep thousands of human bones in a catacomb if they're innocent.

Maddox tilts his head. "Who do you trust? The devil you know or the devil you don't?"

I have two options: run or double down. After how far I've come, there's only one right answer.

"I'm not leaving until you tell me what's going on." I curl my fists so he doesn't see them tremble. "You have information about someone I care about, and you're going to tell me."

He falters at my confession. This isn't the right place or the right time, but if I let Maddox go, who's to say he's ever going to tell me anything.

Shaking his head, he says adamantly, "No. You need to leave."

"Tell me first," I repeat.

His lips curl. "This isn't a game, Reyna. These people are dangerous. They're who I kill for. Leave. *Now.*"

For one horrific second, I wonder if Maddox might have something to do with Dad's death.

"Tell. Me." I demand.

He edges away. "I'll go out first so no one sees you."

I grab a fistful of his cloak so he knows that I'm serious, but I almost lose my train of thought when my hand brushes his chest. "Start talking, or I start screaming." I'm lying through my teeth. If he doesn't want me dead, then he needs to give me what I want.

Our eyes narrow simultaneously, and we stare at each other, neither of us willing to back down. He has answers I want. I'm not owed them, nor do I deserve them, but they're mine to learn, one way or another.

Maddox must see the determination written over my face, because he breaks the silence first, just as another round of applause sounds from the other room.

"We'll get you out of here. Then I'll answer *some* of your questions."

That's not good enough. "We go together, and you tell me everything I want to know, or I'm not going anywhere."

"Not happening," he says with an arrogance that no longer surprises me.

"If I try hard enough, I'm sure I can sneak back in here." That's the only thing that's going to happen if I can't find out what I want to know through him.

We still when the door opens. Someone stumbles out, sputtering a cough. Maddox wraps his arm around me, tucks me against him, and pivots to shield me from the person walking by. I grip the thick fabric of his robe with clammy hands as he rubs circles over my back that bring me very little assurance that we won't get found out.

But if I really think about it, that's not the reason I'm grasping on to him. I'm just not sure if the tears beading along my lash line are from fear, exhaustion, or the grief of losing him too.

Maddox curves his finger beneath my chin to tip my head up to face him. His heavy breaths mix with mine as I stare up at him, draped in shadows. Darkness dips beneath his jaw and curves around his mouth, highlighting his soft lips. This close, there's no mistaking the hollows around his eyes that tell a story of weeks of sleepless nights.

The pesky little butterflies in my stomach are under a misguided belief that he's tortured because he misses me, and that only makes me sadder.

We're in this limbo where he tells me he doesn't want me, yet looks at me like I'm the only thing that matters to him. I'll never mend my broken heart if he keeps coming back to break it, and looking up at him, I'm reminded of the fantasy I fooled myself into believing could be a reality.

"Fine," he breathes out reluctantly once the person enters one of the other rooms, breaking the spell.

My breath rushes out, and I nod, looking away so he doesn't see the tear fall.

Neither of us exchange another word as he grabs my hand and guides me back through the study and the catacombs, then out into the open.

I should snatch my hand away, but it stays right where it is. In his, where it's warm.

There's a whole other universe right beneath my feet—one that my dad was a part of. Holding Maddox's hand seems inconsequential in the grand scheme of things. So I let myself have this stolen moment.

A car pulls up in front of us, and he opens the door for me. I don't know where it came from or when Maddox might have ordered it. Whether out of blind faith or pure stupidity, I go in, missing his touch the instant he releases me.

"Where are we going?" My voice is hoarse. I can feel my body slowly giving out on me.

"To my safe house."

I frown. "Why?"

The way Maddox glances tensely out the windows sets me on edge. "If someone saw you, would you prefer to lead them to your place?"

A tremor works down my arms. Just because I made it out doesn't mean tomorrow is guaranteed.

I watch Maddox out of the corner of my eye. He's running his hand through his hair, and glaring out of the window. I haven't decided if I regret my decision to go down there since I've now dragged Maddox into my mess, and he of all people is concerned.

There's solace in knowing that despite everything that's unfolded between us, I know he's not going to let me get hurt. I truly believe he meant it when he said he'd give me answers.

My pulse races at the thought of getting closure after a year of feeling like a failure day after day because I still wasn't any closer to knowing the man my mother loved. I'd be a liar if I said I wasn't scared to learn about what my father was involved in. Nothing good, I'd imagine.

I'm functioning on autopilot, letting Maddox take me from a car, to the subway, to a cab, then back on a subway until we reach an unassuming apartment complex. I stop myself at the last second from taking Maddox's offered hand, and wrap my arms around myself to avoid the temptation to touch him.

My lungs stutter when he places his palm at the base of my spine like he needs the contact more than I do.

I step out of his reach. My anger spikes at his hurt expression. He doesn't get to be upset. I was the one who wanted to make this work, and he's the one who chose to blow up. *He* made the bed. He can lie in it.

If Maddox tells me what I want to know, then we can go back to being strangers. He doesn't have to make this any harder than it needs to be.

Padding behind him up to the apartment, I watch him enter the code for the front door: 26474. It feels important that he's letting me see it. Hope, the most treacherous emotion of them all, blossoms in my chest. Shaking my head, I focus on putting one foot in front of the other.

I couldn't have imagined Maddox owning a place in this building. The floorboards are uneven, there are cobwebs in every corner, and the occasional rung is missing from the banister. The most shocking part is that Maddox would buy property inside a building with a mix-match of warm- and cool-toned paint.

The tiny traitorous voice is still singing in my head, and my stomach swoops with misplaced glee. *He's showing me more of himself.*

I mutter my thanks when he stands back to let me inside his apartment first. When the light switches on, an odd feeling settles in my chest. It looks so . . . normal.

"I come here after a kill," Maddox explains as if sensing my thoughts. "Or to get away. It's my favorite one in this city."

I'm not sure what surprises me more. That he has more than one safe house or that he's divulging additional information without being prompted.

Saying nothing, I leave my shoes by the door to continue my perusal of his space as he busies himself in the kitchen.

It's a standard, open-plan studio, with a couch, desk, kitchen, and everything else I'd expect to find. Dishes are on the drying rack, a glass of water on the coffee table, a container of saltines in the middle of the counter, and even a plant next to the TV. The bed through the open French doors is unmade. There's a pile of clothes in the laundry basket and an unfolded pair of jeans on top of the duvet.

His safe house is more lived in than his actual house. It could be another one of his carefully calculated facades.

I deposit my coat and bag on the bench, hesitating before setting down the taser. I didn't realize I still had it gripped in my hand.

Maddox motions for me to sit on the couch as he finishes pouring two cups of tea. Seeing him behind the kitchen island hits harder than it should. It's a glimpse into the life we'll never have—one where he makes us tea before bed and we have breakfast together in the morning before rushing off to work.

A vision of what could've been.

Swallowing the lump in my throat, I do as he says. My back is ramrod straight on the edge of the seat. I'm here to get information about what my dad was involved with, then I'm leaving. There's no need to be comfortable and hurt my feelings more.

When he sets down the mug and a packet of biscuits in front of me, I'm too stunned to do more than sip the warm drink and stare at last week's newspaper on the coffee table. He relaxes into his seat on the opposite end of the couch.

"What were you doing there?" Maddox starts as if he knows I'm struggling to form words.

"I'm the one who will be asking the questions here."

He lifts a shoulder. "Tit for tat."

"That wasn't what we agreed."

"I'll answer your questions, but I want something in return."

"You're a real asshole, you know that?" I shake my head. I was stupid to think he'd be a man of his word.

"I believe you've shared your sentiments before." He's more at ease than I've seen him in a while. "Now, why were you there? How did you find it?"

I grit my teeth. He has no right to any information or to look as impressed as he does. But what choice do I have? It's not like there's a line of people wanting to divulge sensitive information. Giving him what he wants will shave down time and energy.

Gripping the mug, I glare at him. "Lawrence was wearing cuff links with the bee insignia on them." Maddox's brows jump up to his hairline. "So I followed him through the catacombs."

"Of course it was Lawrence. A brain-eating bacteria would starve in his skull," he mutters, shaking his head. "Maybe you are a decent stalker."

Lord, help me. "Tell me about the insignia," I demand.

His forehead wrinkles, although he appears unsurprised by my demand. "Why are you looking for information on it?"

I return my drink to the table and sit sideways on the couch to not miss any of his reactions. "It's my turn to ask the questions. What does the insignia represent?"

"A secret society."

Oxygen leaves my lungs. I read about it and saw it with my own eyes, but hearing him say it somehow makes it undeniably real.

"You better not be fucking with me right now."

"Did that look like a PTA meeting to you?"

As irritating as the sarcasm is, it does wonders at unwinding the threads in my brain and dispelling enough anxiety for me to think clearly. "What's it called?"

"The Order of the Hallowed Hive."

I frown. It's not what I expected, but it's better than being called the Order of the Beekeepers.

"And what's the purpose of the Order?" It feels foreign coming out of my mouth. "Is it like on TV where they're basically the underbelly of the city or whatever and call the shots? I heard someone talking about mergers and blocking a bill."

He nods. "My turn. How do you know about the insignia? Did someone show it to you?"

"I found it somewhere."

Green eyes narrow on me. "If you want to answer mysteriously, then so will I."

I grind my molars. *This is the path of least resistance,* I remind myself. "I was looking for information on someone and came across the emblem."

"Continue."

"That's it," I say stubbornly.

"A complete answer, Miss Sinaga."

I throw my hands up. "Fine. I saw a photo of that person in that room with the honeycomb ceiling, then an alumni book with the insignia, and in a shitload of other places. So I connected the dots and assumed they were linked." Telling him I'm looking for information about my dad is a level of honesty I'm not prepared for when he's kept so much from me. "Then I found a case where someone from Cresswell was institutionalized, and in his diary he was talking about a secret society. And tonight, Lawrence's fashion choice led me there. It's your . . . base, I assume."

He doesn't confirm, but the look in his eyes tells me all I need to know.

I give him an accusatory once-over. "Now, how and why are you involved with them?"

"My father is one of the leaders, and I frequently kill for them," he answers without hesitation.

If you were going to tell a girl you're an assassin, you'd think you'd spend at least a solid two seconds debating whether or not it's a good idea to answer.

"The kills I investigated—were they carried out for *them*?" I don't know what to call a secret society that dabbles in wide-scale political corruption and murder.

"I don't think you need me to respond to that one. You already know the answer."

The back of my neck prickles as I recall the photo of my dad in front of the beehive room, and the tears in Mom's eyes as Dad was lowered into the ground.

"Where were you on July 23, 2022?" It's the day my father died.

Maddox stiffens for a fraction of a second before composing himself. "Mind if I consult my phone?"

I nod, blood rushing through my ears as I keep my full attention on his screen. What if Maddox is the reason Dad took his last breath? What would I do then?

I swallow, silently willing him to move faster when he opens his calendar and scrolls back several years. "In Australia for an event." He shows me the entry where he left a week before my father's death, then flew to England for an exhibition.

My breath of relief is short-lived.

"I'm not the only killer they have on payroll," he adds. "Who is it that you're asking me about?"

I think I'm going to need a stronger drink.

Once I tell him, there's nothing about me that he won't know. Every secret I have will be out in the open while he keeps who knows how many. But if telling him is the only way for me to find out, then I'm willing to make that sacrifice.

"My . . . my father." I wait for a reaction that he doesn't give. "He studied at Cresswell University. He's the reason why I'm here. I think he was in the Order, or connected somehow."

"What's his name?" His curiosity isn't enough to mask the unmistakable hint of concern.

"Richard Talbot."

Maddox's eyes drop down to the floor, considering. It takes him a moment to answer. "What does he look like?"

"Light-brown hair, blue eyes, tall with broad shoulders."

"Very specific. That really narrows it down." His voice comes out monotone, but there's a tilt at the edges of his lips.

I fight back the instinct to roll my eyes. Is it wrong for me to miss his banter? To feel special that he's comfortable enough to take me here, let me in on a secret underworld while allowing his playful side to come out.

There's no point showing him the photo I found under Mom's bed. It's too blurry and overexposed to make out his face. My shoulders sag. I'm not sure where this leads me.

My forehead wrinkles as I mull over the information I have about the Order.

"Have you . . ." I start, unsure how to ask the question. "I'm guessing not all of your kills are creative, and some were executionary." I recall the victim with a bullet in his head and a honeycomb carved into his chest. Maddox might not have done it, but the society's pattern is clear. His hesitant nod confirms it. "Some were made to look like an accident?"

Again, he cautiously tips his head. "Sometimes I'm given specifics on how the scene should look—accident, execution, or someone who disappears from the face of the earth."

"Do you know how to make a car explode while it's in use?" The police told us there was a leak and a damaged fuse.

"Vehicles aren't my forte, so I couldn't say I'd know the first thing when it comes to that. I find simple poison and freak accidents easier to execute.

I'm aware there are a few mechanics and engineers within our ranks. But I'm unsure whether they're killing for the Order. We're kept apart for insurance purposes."

My lips flatten. "You wouldn't know what signs to look for?" If I knew, I could try to get my dad's crime-scene photos to check if there was something amiss and the police didn't notice.

He's forlorn when he says, "No."

Could it really just have been a simple car accident? Is there anything I'm not seeing? "How many assassins or killers—or whatever you call it—are there?"

Maddox runs his hand through his hair. "More than I'm aware of. People who aren't trained killers can be made to kill. People who aren't members of the Order can be coerced and blackmailed into doing things they'd never otherwise do."

Even if I did receive a set of names, what would I do with it? I'd be going up against a secret society that doles out murders like it's nobody's business.

I was following a serial killer around; I wasn't trying to hunt one down. I'm not the type to go on a quest for revenge. If my dad was murdered, I'd like to know the reason to understand his life. Beyond that? I can't bring him back, but maybe if I did know who killed him, I could bring him to justice. I'm not sure what Mom would have wanted. The truth feels more important to me.

A sickening thought hits me. "Could he have been one of your—*their* assassins?"

That could be why he was never around. He was too busy going off and doing what he loved—killing people—instead of spending time with his family.

Or maybe it wasn't safe to be around us, and he really did want to be closer but couldn't. Is that forgivable? Letting Mom die heartbroken because he would rather keep pulling triggers than do what needed to be done to make us a family.

Maddox almost looks guilty. "It's possible. The Order hides their weapons. I could walk past one of them on the street and not know who they are. You aren't meant to see the grim reaper coming."

Nausea churns in my stomach. I feel so hopeless.

"Who decides who lives or dies?" It's disturbing how corrupt this world is. I don't know what's real anymore.

"Any of the six high saints or the grand magistrate," Maddox answers.

"Is there a way to find out if someone from the Order killed my dad?" My voice comes out more vulnerable than I'd like, and the corners of his eyes soften.

"If there is, I'm not aware of it." The weight of his stare fixes on me like he's making sure that he has my full attention. "But I could check the Order's and the university's records for your father's name."

The offer takes me by surprise. "You'd do that?"

"Of course."

"I . . ." I clear my throat. "I would appreciate that."

I'm only agreeing because I want to leave no stone unturned. Not because it's an excuse to see him again, or because I'm hungry for his attention.

Maybe I'll never find out whether my dad was involved, but knowing what I stumbled upon is a start. Wiping any trace of emotion off my face, I look Maddox dead in the eyes. "Tell me everything else."

And he does—after some grumbling and glaring from both sides. He tells me about their monthly meetings, the hierarchical structure, all he does for the Order, and that he has many more victims not even I'd be able to link back to him. He tells me about how the world is a giant game of chess, and the Order is the one calling the moves. Why he was forced to agree to the engagement to Abi, and why their parents are pushing it for the sake of reelection.

But mainly, he explains that every bit of hurt he inflicted upon me was to keep Spencer from venturing down the dark path that's slowly killing Maddox, and because he's frightened of what the Order or his father might do to me.

It's like a cloud dissipates with every new piece of information, and light streams through. I should feel heavier from the weight of the truth, but it's oddly liberating. This is what I always wanted: to be let into the fold and trusted.

For a second, it's like I'm turning a page. Someone is seeing my value as a person.

I know he isn't telling me out of the goodness of his heart. Maddox probably thinks I'll keep pushing until I find something, and maybe he cares about me just enough that he doesn't want me to die in the process.

It's easier to tell myself we could never be together because of those chess pieces. It hurts less that way. That flicker of hope needs to be extinguished forever. No amount of praying and crossing my fingers will change that his brother's livelihood hangs in the balance between us.

I get it.

Maddox and I were never meant to be. It's not a question of fate; it's a fact. There are eight billion people in the world, and the one person who could fill the void is the one person I can't have. Not like he wants me anyway. He said so himself.

Maybe I'll get over this, grow old, and look back at the time I thought I could feel whole because of Maddox. Or maybe I'll be like Mom, a shadow of herself because her other half wasn't there to make her complete.

I feel like a kid begging for my parents' attention again, and I hate it.

I need to move on from Maddox and accept that some people weren't made to be loved. If he finds information about my dad, he can email me or something. Otherwise, I can't keep sitting here, tormenting myself by listening to him talk as if we're okay.

I need to figure out where to go from here with my dad, and if it's worth risking my life to know. And I need to get away from Maddox before he ruins me beyond repair.

Taking a deep breath, I keep my gaze fixed to the side and focus on keeping tears out of my eyes.

"Well . . . thank you for . . ." I wave my hand and rise to my feet. *Getting me out of there. Telling me everything when you didn't really have to give me that much. Even though you don't want me. Even though you think I'm not good enough for you.* "I'm going to head home. I'm sure no one is following me."

Maddox grabs my hand and pulls me back onto the couch closer to him. "Stay."

I'm exhausted and raw, and his games have gotten old. He just gave me a list of reasons why we can't be together, and now he wants to have a sleepover?

"Seriously?" I yank my arm away and jump to my feet. "I can't keep doing this. I can't stay under the same roof as someone who led me on for a bit of fun." My voice rises with every word.

"Stay." Why does he need to look at me like I couldn't be more wrong if I tried? Is he so self-absorbed that he doesn't realize how agonizing this is?

"I don't want to stay around someone who doesn't feel the same way I do."

"Reyna—"

"No." I whip my head side to side. My eyes heat with the urge to cry because everything he said about his feelings toward me was a lie. *"I'm me."* The girl whose own parents never chose her. *"And you're you."* The legend made flesh. Repeating the words he told me tastes like acid.

"Rey—"

"I'm no one," I choke. "Some wannabe with a camera up to no good. Who can't come up with her own ideas. A fucking *fraud.* A failure who will never be good enough for anything."

"Stop talking—"

Tears stream down my face, and I can't stop them.

"My father never wanted me. My mom didn't even stick around to see how pathetic her daughter became." I was a good girl. I got good grades in school. Ate my vegetables. Volunteered. Did my chores and homework without being asked. I just wanted my dad to come home and see me for me, not as an obligation. But I was always so *fucked in the head.* "I'm a nobody. A nothing. Someone who'll never amount to anything more than a decaying gravestone. I wouldn't dare soil your place with my pres—"

He clasps my face in his hands, stopping my rambling. "I'm obsessed with you, and I think it will kill me."

I suck in a sharp breath, searching his eyes for a lie. "Don't."

"I'm wholly, completely, and madly consumed by you, and it might kill me. Life and death lost meaning, and the only thing that made me feel human was art, and that was gone too. Until you came along. You haunt me while I'm awake. While I'm sleeping. I can't breathe because of you."

"Maddox, you can't." Can't keep lying. Leading me on. Making me fall for him, just to take it all away.

"I *can*, and I will."

I choke on a sob when he presses our foreheads together. It's all too much. I try to shove him away.

"No." I shake my head against his.

Lie, lie, lie, always fucking lying.

"Then why did you push me away like that?" I cry. "Why did you say the things you did and prove every awful thought in my head right?"

He claims he wants me, yet he threw me aside with no regard for the damage. I know now that he had to push me away, but he didn't need to do it the way he did.

"I know. I'm sorry. I'm so fucking sorry." Maddox's voice breaks and he tugs me closer. "I didn't want to, but I thought it was the only way I could keep you safe. Until the day someone puts me in the dirt, the only person I'll ever be is yours. My only regret in this life is that I made you think that you weren't everything to me, and I'll never forgive myself for that. You're all I've ever wanted and everything I shouldn't have."

I can't formulate the words to describe how I'm feeling right now; I just know it hurts a lot. My skin is burning. I want to remember what it's like to wake up and not wish that I hadn't.

"Please," I rasp.

Please don't lie to me.

Please don't break my heart again.

Please don't leave me.

"If I haven't made myself clear enough to you, the only person who isn't good enough is *me. I'm* unworthy of every crumb you have to offer, but I'm a selfish man who's unwilling to share you with anyone else. Because I'm me, and you're you, and I'll never be worthy. I never knew it would be possible for someone to see the real me, and still want me."

I squeeze my eyes shut. There's no realm of possibility where it isn't me who's lacking. I wish with everything I have that what he's saying is true, because in every lifetime that I'll live, no one will say that to me again.

"So stay, Reyna," Maddox pleads. "I need you to stay because nothing has felt right since you left."

The tears burn a path down my cheek and over his hands. I shouldn't be alone in this room with him, but it's the only place in the world that feels right. Here, with him, the universe could catch fire, and he'll hold me through it.

The sharp edges of my grief become dull when he's around. It's still there, waiting to cut me if I stray too close. But life isn't about getting rid of the feeling. It is about making the corners soft enough to live alongside. I've always known this, but it wasn't until Maddox that I thought it might be in the cards for me.

"You're *killing* me, Reyna. And I've killed for you. I'll be the dark, and I'll be the fucking shadows to your light, love. Our broken pieces fit together." His voice comes out in a gravelly rasp against my lips. "So don't leave. I promise you forever."

I shake my head. I want this to be real, more than just a blip in time.

"Please," he whispers, bringing me closer to him.

Moss-colored eyes collide with mine. They see through the cracks and the jagged shards of my psyche, penetrating the fibers that make up my being. *He sees me.*

Our lips brush together when I swallow. "But your brother."

Maddox tucks tearstained hair behind my ears. Frowning, he stares off to the side for a moment before refocusing on me. "He can make his own decisions. It's time I make mine."

"But . . . the video?" The Order is watching Spencer. We can't ignore all the risks. "They're going to break him. I can't let you do that for me." We're all victims of circumstance, and I'm not worth the repercussions.

"I'm not asking for your permission. I can't keep torturing myself if this is the life he wants. Spencer could never grow because I'm always there to stop it. He was never offered a choice in the matter, and I never had one. I'm going to end the engagement this week." He presses a kiss to my tearstained cheek. "If I'm living under someone's whim, I'd rather it be yours."

"And what happens once we walk out that door tomorrow?" I gesture to the entrance. I refuse to relive what he put me through again.

"We make it work." There's so much vindication in his tone.

Shaking my head, I release myself from his grip, anger rising. Those are the words I wanted to hear three weeks ago when I knocked on his door. He chose to tear me into pieces instead. "Why couldn't you have told me instead of making me think I'm the problem?"

A wounded look crosses his face. "I thought it would be easier for you to hate me and stay away than both of us fighting the pull. I'd take back what I said in a heartbeat if I could."

I can feel his guilt through the spaces where we aren't touching. But guilt isn't enough. I've been hurt by him and the people I care about too many times already. "I can't trust you won't pull the same thing on me again."

The vein in his forehead ticks, and his eyes harden as if he wants me to know what he says next is true. "Then I have a lifetime to prove it to you."

If I ask myself whether I'd regret walking out the door right now, my answer would be yes. I'm not sure whether he deserves another chance, but I want to have a chance at happiness. Or at least a semblance of it.

I shake my head, unsure what to do. He takes it as rejection.

"Is that what you want? To see me on my knees, *begging*?" Maddox slides onto the floor, dropping to his knees between my parted legs. "Because I'll crawl across glass if that's what you want me to do. I'll get on my knees every morning and every night if it means you'll look at me again."

He palms my thighs and rubs his hands over every curve of my body, anguished, like the only thing that can stop his torment is me and he won't survive if I let him go.

A sob builds in my throat. "I can't rely on your words, Maddox. They've lied to me before."

"I'll do anything. Name it, and it's yours. I'll gouge my heart right out of my chest if that's what you want. Kill my own father if it makes you sleep easier. Anything at all, and I'll do it." He drops lower onto his knees, gazing up at me in total despair. "Please, Reyna. Give me one more chance."

I avert my eyes and wipe away my tears with my sleeve. "I don't want to be made a fool of again."

"You won't. I promise."

I take a shuddering breath and twist my hands together. Is a chance with Maddox worth the risk of everything he's described? The very thought of the potential dangers sets me alight when it shouldn't. But his brother's life? Maddox's? We'll be playing with fire.

Saying yes to him isn't a declaration that we'll be bound to each other for an eternity. This can be a *we'll see what happens*. A trial period. If the risks become too grave, I can step away.

If he does anything—and I mean *anything*—that gives me pause, I'm out.

Looking back at him, I whisper, "No more secrets."

"None," he promises.

"No more lies."

"Never."

Taking a deep breath, I croak, "Please don't break my heart again."

"I'd rather die."

"Okay," I rasp. "I'll stay for now. But I can't . . . I can't blindly believe you again. This is temporary until I decide it's permanent—until I can trust that you really mean what you say and that I'm not just some pastime to you."

He nods. Grabbing the back of my neck, he pulls me down and meets my lips halfway. "I swear you won't regret it."

When he presses his lips to mine, I let him because I want this as badly as he does. I don't want to be alone anymore, and if kissing him is the only chance I'll get to feel like everything is all right, I'll take it.

Our lips move against each other, absorbing every ounce of desperation through the space where our bodies meet. I melt into him, silently urging him for more. To consume me so completely that I can forget my own name, and the pain that's lasted a lifetime. He grasps my legs, kneading my flesh through my clothes like it might keep him tethered to reality. But he doesn't get the hint.

My fingers wrap around his wrist to bring his hand up my skirt.

He pulls away, flicking his eyes between mine. "Are you sure?"

"Please." I push my hips forward to meet his hand.

A divot forms between his brows. I'm too raw to handle any rejection right now.

"Maddox." My voice wavers. "Make me feel good."

His frown dissolves. "Always," he promises.

He captures me in a kiss that steals my breath, and we move together like we were born to do it. I lift my hips so he can ease my woolen stockings down my legs. My skirt quickly follows suit. His lips don't leave mine until he pulls my sweater and blouse over my head.

I thread my fingers into his hair and deepen his kiss to savor the taste of him. No one has ever made me feel as good or as free as he has. It hurts to admit how much I missed him these past weeks. Even the act of simply talking to him makes the world seem a little less dull. But lately everything has turned back into various shades of gray. It's no way to live.

Maddox grasps my thighs to pull me to the edge of the couch. I shake my head when he begins to lower himself to the apex of my thighs. "No," I gasp, holding his head in place. "I just—" I choke. "I need to feel you."

He curses under his breath. In one swift move, I'm cradled in his arms, being carried over to the bed. Our gazes meet, and the intensity of his eyes threatens to bring tears to mine. They're filled with a hundred different oaths that would kill me if he broke.

The bed creaks as he slowly lowers me. The duvet engulfs me in its cool embrace. Holding my stare, he draws slow circles over my clit that leave me silently groaning and chasing his fingers. A bolt of pleasure flashes up my spine when he dips them into me, curling to make me see stars. His name falls from my lips, and I watch, mesmerized, when he shudders at the sound of the two syllables.

Moisture coats the inside of my thighs as he drives his fingers into me until I'm a moaning mess. Goose bumps cascade over my flesh from the visceral pleasure. My back arches off the bed, and I claw at his arms to keep him going.

Maddox barely leaves enough room between us for me to undress him, and like the other times we've done this dance, he leaves his top on. Questions form at the tip of my tongue, but I leave it in favor of keeping this moment free from more heartache. I wrap my legs around his waist, urging him to move faster.

"Reyna," he mumbles, attempting to loosen my legs from around him to keep working me with his fingers.

I shake my head, canting my hip to get closer to his cock. "I need you," I whisper.

With a strained grunt, he draws out of me and lowers himself onto an elbow beside me to cradle my head with one hand and wrap his arm around my waist with the other.

He pushes his cock up between my folds, and I let out a frustrated groan that he chuckles softly at, peppering kisses along my collarbone and up my neck as he continues teasing me.

A gasp rips out of me when he meets my lips and drives into me at the same time. My core clenches around him. It makes his muscles quiver beneath my touch. I curl my legs around him and raise my hip to take him deeper as his fingers find my middle to rub my sensitive flesh.

Maddox fucks me slowly. The kind of gentle that doesn't leave marks in the walls or shake the bed. Not once do his lips stop moving to press delicate kisses over my tender flesh. My heart feels full to the brim, and I'm worried it'll overflow and end in tears.

"I don't deserve you," he whispers, increasing the pressure with his fingers.

I squeeze my eyes shut and hold back a sob. He can't say things like that if he wants to keep me in one piece.

I pull his lips between my teeth to distract myself. I'm rewarded with a vicious thrust. His chest rumbles with pleasure when I moan his name again at the rising ecstasy. The pressure compounds in my core and makes me whine with need.

The rhythm turns more rapid, each thrust punctured to deliver every inch of him. A string of curses pulls from my lips, and my nails dig into the fabric of his shirt. My eyes roll to the back of my head, and everything after that comes out unintelligible. I'm a garbled mess of hiccuped moans and uncontained desire.

Pure, white-hot electricity zaps to every corner of my body, lighting me up until the pleasure becomes blinding. Maddox captures my cries and meets me with his own strangled groan. His cock twitches inside of me, spilling his come until it feels like I'm overflowing with him.

He rolls us over to have me lie on top of him. He carefully arranges the blankets without pulling out of me.

Maddox brushes his lips over the top of my head. "I'm never going to let you go."

My eyes drift shut, and I nestle against his chest.

I hope that's true.

32

REYNA

What an absolute shit show.

I splash cool water on my face and screw my eyes shut. It's absurd how I'm expected to attend class like everything is normal after what I learned last night.

This morning, Maddox and I left the safe house together. I went home to change, then spent the entire walk from the subway to the lecture hall looking around, wondering whether the room with the honeycomb ceiling was beneath my feet.

All I could think about was that they're watching. If I thought I was paranoid before, it's nothing compared to how I feel now.

Dropping my head into my hands, I groan.

It's going to be a long evening.

I exit the bathroom, then snatch my coffee off the kitchen bench and chug the lukewarm drink down before checking how far the Uber is. "Shit," I mutter, and grab my filming equipment and run downstairs, piling everything into the trunk before slumping onto the back seat.

I'm only running a couple of minutes late, but I'm getting a stress migraine just thinking about the work I have to do.

There's a text waiting for me from Maddox that I can't bring myself to read. Probably saying he couldn't find any information about Dad. He promised to meet me back at my place tonight, but after being told about the video taken in Spencer's bedroom, my apartment doesn't feel safe. I'm too scared to ask to go back to his house, because I know it serves multiple purposes, and managing my insecurities isn't one of them.

I've put myself into the Order's path. Maddox didn't confirm or deny it, but I heard his frantic calls when he thought I was asleep.

I was caught on video somewhere at some point, sneaking through their lair, and he was seen helping me. I don't know what that means for either of us. If they'd kill him for insubordination, or if I'd be made to sell my soul to them and perish later rather than sooner.

Until then, life goes on. Capitalism requires its sacrifice. I can't skip tonight's booking. They're paying me far more than I'm worth to film an ad for some big-shot finance guy. It's not the type of job I want in the long run, but it covers the bills.

When the car comes to a stop, I say a quick thanks to the driver and grab my stuff, then set it on the ground against the wall of the building.

Frowning, I survey the street. Unease trickles down my spine. This place is deserted.

I move out from beneath the lamppost and fumble for my phone to send the client a text saying I've arrived. I glance up and down the street, the prickle of unseen eyes crawls down the back of my neck.

The lump in my throat thickens. I check that the mini switchblade is in my skirt pocket, then my emails to confirm I have the right place.

I mean, it's the correct address.

I squint through the darkness at the sign above the door.

It's the right building too.

I shake my head. The events of last night are making me overly paranoid. Shaking off my nerves, I take a deep breath, put my business mask on, then try the handle. The door opens with ease. Silence greets me, but maybe everyone else is late as well? Sometimes people drive over in groups to avoid worrying about parking. Though someone is probably already here if the studio is unlocked.

With one last backward glance around the street, I slowly head up the stairs. My footsteps thump against the old wooden stairs, broadcasting my arrival to anyone in the building.

"Hello," I call out, only to be met with silence. "Anyone there?"

This feels like the start of a bad horror movie.

I call out again once I'm on the third floor, where the ad will be recorded. No response.

It's an open-space studio, not the largest I've been to, but by no means the smallest either. A blue backdrop stands against one wall, a wooden chair in front of it, and some plants and office props in the corner.

No windows, no moonlight, only the glare of the studio lights. If anyone asked for my input, I'd say it would be better to film in a real office building. Natural lighting would also make the guy seem more approachable, but I'm not getting paid to have an opinion.

The creative director decided that we're doing it in a studio, so I guess that's what we're going to do. But I won't be adding it to my portfolio any time soon.

I set my gear by the back wall and yell louder. Maybe whoever unlocked the door stepped out and forgot to close properly.

I slump down onto a nearby seat and send the organizer an email before begrudgingly setting up. The later they are, the later I'll have to stay. If rent wasn't due, I would have canceled and risked taking a reputation hit because I can't deal with any of this crap right now.

Twenty minutes later, I'm considering calling it quits. We were meant to start more than half an hour ago. I would bet my bottom dollar that the talent is a spoiled rich kid who gets away with holding everyone up. The director could have at least done me the courtesy of sending an email.

I throw my phone on top of my bag, then pull myself up and check out the other rooms. There are a couple of offices and studio spaces on the second floor and another on the third.

All empty.

And still no email.

This place is giving me the creeps.

Okay, I'm out of here.

I'll take the financial hit if they ask for their deposit back. I'm not going to wait around all night. I'd much rather be held by Maddox, in bed, hiding away from the world.

Wiping a hand down my face, I sigh and start to leave the studio. A hand clamps around my arm. The room spins before air punches from my lungs as my back collides with the floor.

The blood drains from my face as my eyes focus on the man looming above, dressed in black, wearing a balaclava, holding a hunting knife in his grip. A shrill cry escapes from my throat. I scramble back.

He's on me in the next second, straddling my hips. Raw terror tears through me. I try to scream again, but deadly fingers wrap around my throat, and fire instantly burns through my skull.

I put everything I have into trying to kick him off. It's useless. He's too strong, and dots are starting to blur my vision. I clamor for the switchblade in my pocket, struggling to get a good grip.

"Shut the fuck up," he snarls, bringing the knife up my cheek. "You—"

My mind blanks out. Panic drives my limbs, and instincts take over. The mini blade slices through skin and tendon until it's buried to the hilt in his armpit. A garbled cry tears from his throat. Or maybe it's mine.

Blood gushes from the wound at the very top of his inner arm. Warm liquid falls onto my chest and splatters a spray of scarlet onto my neck and face, seeping past the seam of my lips so I taste copper.

My eyes round in horror. A bloodcurdling scream tears from my lips. My hands fly out to shove him back. He barely sways, yanking the blade right out of his skin. Then he crashes, trapping me with his weight against the floor.

He's still struggling, holding me down with his hands on my shoulder and chest. Bleeding all over me. Something glints out of the corner of my eye, and I throw my hand out to grab the knife. He beats me to it.

I try to buck him off, slapping the floor around me in search of my switchblade. I can't feel anything but the paper backdrop beneath my slippery fingertips. My throat burns from screaming but I don't stop, hoping and praying I can grab anything to use as a makeshift weapon.

"No!" I beg, fighting him with my dwindling energy.

My foot catches on the nearby prop table and sends the items clattering onto the floor. He raises his arm, weapon gripped in his hand.

A muffled *bang* goes off. A spray of red splatters onto the blue backdrop as I watch the man collapse onto me.

Time slows. I stare at the dotted ceiling, crushed by his weight. The *drip, drip, drip* of thick blood trickles over my skin.

Someone just . . .

He just . . .

I blink up.

There's a dead man on me.

Nausea twists my stomach. Movement at the door kicks me out of my trance.

There's someone else in the room.

Fear clamps its claws into me in a solid vise. I scramble to throw my attacker's weight off me, then lunge for my bag to grab the can of mace. I hold it out in front of me, aimed, trembling and ready to let loose on the masked newcomer who snuck in without my notice.

A dead man was on me. His blood is still on me.

The intruder acts like I'm not even there, crouching down next to my attacker and lifting his mask off. I grab my phone, dial Maddox's number, and shove it into my pocket to focus on the man.

Pick up. Pick up. Pick—

My attention catches on the gaping hole in the side of my attacker's head. Red pools around him like a demonic halo. In the middle of the sea of crimson is the blade he was going to kill me with.

I was going to die. He was trying to murder me. He—He—I can't get enough air into my lungs. It's hard to hear anything beyond the roar of my pulse.

"He's one of your boyfriend's men."

My eyes snap up to the person who spoke. I gasp, and stumble back, aiming the can higher.

Alex. From class.

"You've been a giant pain in the ass."

The weapon rattles in my hand. *What the fuck does that mean?*

"Y-You're in the Order." A tremor threads through my voice.

Am I—Is he going to finish the job?

"We thought you might have worked it out, or had Maddox explain it to you." Alex eyes me. The hairs at the back of my neck stand on end when I spot the gun at his side. "I'm curious, what else do you know?"

He takes a step forward. Panic slices up my spine, and my back hits the wall. "Stay back!" I growl, waving the mace. "I'll use this on you."

Alex raises his brows in amusement. *I've brought mace to a gunfight.* "We're getting you out of here," he declares.

"Touch me, and I'll gut you," I threaten with enough conviction that I might even believe that I'd have the upper hand in a fight. I probably wouldn't last two seconds.

He slides his gun into the waistband of his pants, then raises both hands in the air. "You can either come with me willing—"

"The police are already on their way, Alex." I show him just enough of my phone so he can see that I'm on a call—at least, I hope I'm on a call. "Either shoot me and I empty this can on you, or leave. I'm not going anywhere with you."

I'm dead if he calls my bluff.

He works his jaw, eyes darting between my phone, the mace, and the corpse.

"Fuck," he groans, running his hand over his face and hair. My grip tightens as he paces, muttering words I can't make out. He takes a step toward me, then turns around only to turn back, racked with indecision. "Shit, shit, shit, *fuck.*"

I eye the switchblade on the ground between us. I might be able to make a run for it if he's distracted enough. Before I figure out my next move, Alex is running out of the door like there are hounds on his heels.

I stare at the spot he occupied seconds ago. White dots my vision. The sound of the door slamming shut stirs me into motion. He . . . It worked. He's actually . . .

I need to get out of here.

I snatch the switchblade off the floor, and run into the hall to the top of the steps. When I'm certain I'm the only one in the building, I check my phone to see if Maddox has picked up, and bring it up to my ear.

"M-Maddox," I stutter.

"Are you ok—"

"Th-There was a guy here. And he attacked me. And I-I stabbed him. But he took it out." I keep rambling despite his curse. I don't realize there are tears streaming from my eyes until the salty taste hits my tastebuds and mingles with copper. "And then—and then *Alex* came in. And blood splattered everywhere because he *shot* him. And he said he's your man and he thought I knew about everything. And then he left, and I-I don't know what to do. There's a body. He's still there. He's dead and—and I can't go to jail—and—and—and—"

"*Breathe*, Reyna." His voice is tense. "Stay on the phone. I'll be there in ten minutes."

No, no, no. That's too long. "I can't stay here. H-He might come back."

"Make it five."

I pocket my phone and run back into the studio.

They're going to send me to prison.

My career is over.

My fingerprints are everywhere. There's an Uber transaction and emails taking me straight to the crime scene. I'm covered in blood.

They're going to fucking kill me, because what did Alex mean by my attacker being one of Maddox's men? Did the Order send Alex to watch me? He could have called reinforcements already and it's just a matter of time before he realizes that the police aren't coming.

I can't wait for Maddox to arrive. Jumping toward my bags, I rush to pack everything up. I can't leave any evidence behind. But my fingerprints and—

The front door slams open. "*Reyna!*"

I stagger from the relief. "Third floor!"

Footsteps pound up the stairs as I finish putting all my gear away. Maddox's crazed eyes crash with mine and turn lethal in an instant. My muscles tense as I brace myself for the verbiage on safety when he storms up to me. His lips collide with mine, kissing me with frantic intensity.

"You're bleeding." Maddox's voice seeps with violence against my lips.

"It's not mine," I assure him, pointing at the corpse bleeding out on the floor.

Then it hits me. *I was set up.*

No one is here, yet the paper has been rolled out on top of a waterproof canvas, and there's a chair with duct tape on top of it. He laid out everything he needed to kill me, clean up, then dispose of my body like I was never there.

My chest heaves as I run through the facts. The booking was made a month ago. Has the Order been planning on killing me for that long, or did they sabotage my work after discovering me last night?

"He's one of my father's men." The predatory look from before turns downright murderous.

I suck in a sharp breath as another realization makes my heart stop beating. They want to kill me because of Maddox. They're going to keep trying to kill me because I'm the reason Maddox isn't falling in line.

He tugs on my arm. "We need to get you out of this building."

I nod. It's not safe for me in New York anymore. "I need to leave."

Tonight.

And I'm never going to see Maddox again.

33

MADDOX

I slam my phone on my kitchen counter hard enough for the screen to shatter.

I'm going to fucking kill my father.

I was worried this day would come. I simply didn't think Roland would be the one who signed Reyna's death certificate. I'll have a hit on my head if I take him out, but my options are limited.

"Fuck," I snarl, throwing a crystal tumbler across the room.

Shepherd will already know what's gone down since Alex is his favorite fresh blood. Why the fuck was he there?

It's been impossible trying to organize a clean-up crew to dispose of the body and wipe all traces of Reyna from the scene. Everyone I could send has ties to the Dornmonts or Roland.

I'm going to have to clean it up myself.

The sound of running water from the upstairs shower cuts off. We should have gone straight to the safe house, but she was shivering and scrubbing at his blood on her skin. I couldn't wait another minute watching her suffer like that when this is all my fault. None of this would have happened if I hadn't been selfish. Taking her to my townhouse was the only option.

My breaths come out heavy as I pinch the bridge of my nose.

I can't fucking lose her.

I fucking *can't*.

Any plan I devise now will result in sacrificing someone I care about. I haven't had the opportunity to talk to Spencer about my intentions or tell him the truth about everything I've shielded him from since he was born.

When I left Reyna with Lawrence a week ago, I realized that putting my brother first isn't enough for me anymore. I was lying to myself if I thought my dedication would ever satisfy them. They were always going to drag Spencer into their fold in some way. So what was the point of throwing away my one shot at happiness just to buy my brother a couple more years of freedom?

Freedom Spencer keeps fighting against because he's insistent on being involved with the Order.

Last night, I was convinced I would find a way to keep Reyna in my life against all odds. It's abundantly clear now that the only way it could happen would be if we disappeared. But hiding means ending her career. She will forever be running, keeping herself out of the limelight. Her talent would be wasted because Roland wouldn't rest until she's in a grave, and I'm back to being a leashed dog.

Unless I marry Abi.

Fuck that for a joke. I don't want Abi; I want Reyna. I have only ever wanted Reyna.

But if I married Abi, Roland would remove the target from Reyna's head. Spencer would be safe for a couple more years. My own career would dissolve into nothing because I'd never have a muse again. I'd be back where I started. A washed-up artist, fighting to hold on to something to call his own.

I may not be willing to ruin my life for Spencer anymore, but am I willing to spend an eternity being miserable if it means Reyna gets her dreams?

Yes.

I'd sacrifice my own happiness for her life even if it killed me. I told her I'm all in. I promised I would never do that again, but what the fuck am I meant to do? Try as I might, I don't have the power to protect her from the Order if we did go into hiding. The only way to keep her safe is to give myself over to them and do everything they say without question.

One thing I asked for. *One thing* I wanted. And I can't fucking have it. Gripping the edge of the kitchen counter, I hang my head beneath my shoulders, scowling at the marble countertop.

I could have washed my hands in holy water, bathed in crystal water, still, I should have been afraid of touching her, because one should never touch art. But for the first time in my life, I allowed myself to break that rule. To stain the art with my blood-soaked hands. Now, her name is painted and sealed in red.

It's all my fault.

Yet letting go of her is a road that will only lead to despair.

I can't do it.

I won't do it to her.

I'm not ready to say my goodbyes.

A click sounds beside me. I slowly turn my head to come face-to-face with the barrel of a gun.

"I told you to stay away, and look what happened." Shepherd's voice is a low cadence that doesn't betray his emotions. He watches me from the kitchen door, cataloging my downfall while wearing a designer suit.

I straighten to my full height and fail to hide my emotions because of my heaving chest. *I can't lose her.* I need more time.

"You had *one* simple task: focus on your engagement. And you couldn't do it."

My lips twitch. I can't bear the thought of being bound to Abigail Dornmont for the rest of my life. It should be Reyna who wears my ring. Not her.

"I'm going to," I lie.

"The damage is done. There's only one way forward." Shepherd sighs, the sound heavy with disappointment.

Fighting him will only guarantee my, Reyna's, and my brother's deaths. Either way, the distance between us means he'll shoot me before I can lay a finger on him.

If Shepherd orders a hit, it'll be carried out one way or another. No one is allowed to rest until that person's heart stops, because what the grand magistrate wants, the grand magistrate gets.

"Kill me, and you'll ruin House Shaw." Roland's, and potentially the Dornmonts', election campaign would take a substantial hit if I were to die—unless Shepherd makes it look like an accident, and he's very good at making it look like an accident.

A fake heart attack. Gas leak. Engine malfunction. Organ failure. An allergic reaction. Defying a direct command and keeping secrets are just two ways to meet the ferryman.

"You did that all on your own, son. As for Roland, he will bear the consequences of his decision." There's a hint of sorrow in his voice that I thought I'd never hear from the Order's supreme leader. "It's a shame it has to come to this. I saw you as one of my own."

"A couple more days." The years I spent dedicated to the Order *must* buy me this one last thing. "I need to clean up after Alex's kill, and make sure she's safe and taken care of for the rest of her life."

It makes me sick that I'm revealing my hand and showing him the full spectrum of my weakness, but I can't hide it. Reyna comes first. Always.

The slightest divot forms on his forehead. "You care about her?"

Inhaling sharply, I say, "I love her."

It's not a feeling I thought I was capable of, yet it's the only word to explain the lengths I'm willing to go to for her and the emotion that surges in my chest whenever I think about her. I need to tell her. *Fuck*, I wish I could have spent a lifetime showing her.

"And yet you brought her into this life? *Knowing* what could happen if she got too close." The edges of Shepherd's lips tip down. "You killed Reyna the second you decided to fall in love with her."

It's not something I can respond to. I knew the risk the moment I found myself gravitating toward her. Still, I took the plunge. I want to live so I can keep protecting her, but I'll never be able to escape the Order *and* keep her and Spencer safe.

My chest aches, like the dead weight between my ribs is struggling to beat. I wouldn't survive watching her fall in love with another person. Truthfully, I'm not certain I wouldn't kill them.

Why can't I fucking have this? I'll give up my art, my kills, all of it. Reyna is meant to be mine. I'm already hers.

"I need more time," I demand, slamming the counter. *More time to look at her. More time to hold her. More time to tell her that she means everything to me.* More time to decide whether we'll take our chances and run. I'll be fucking dead without her anyway.

"No."

Fuck.

I run my hands through my hair. Press my fist against my mouth to hold back the rage that's tearing my organs like poison. My throat closes. Everything fucking hurts.

I wish I could kill him.

I wish I could kill them all.

"Let me say goodbye first."

I can't leave without saying goodbye.

"Please."

I've never said that word to him before. I thought it was just something guilty men spat out. But when I heard Reyna say it, I knew I was wrong. That one syllable from her, and I'd destroy the world.

Looking at the man who sharpened me into who I am, I know he sees the same thing I used to see every time men would beg for their lives. To him the word is just a word.

"No. It'd be best for her if you disappeared for good." For a moment, I swear guilt flashes behind his eyes. "It's time, Maddox. Make your peace with the choices you've made. This is the only good thing you can do for—"

I whip my head toward the movement at the corner of my vision to find Reyna looking at Shepherd like she's seeing a ghost. His expression is of sheer, inexplicable panic.

I glance between them. The resemblance hits me for the first time: the rich shade of their eyes, the identical flick of their brows, the curve of their chins, even the little cleft in their noses.

"Dad?"

"Reyna," Shepherd gasps.

34

MADDOX

What the fuck?

35

REYNA

Dad holsters his gun under his suit jacket. "You shouldn't be here."

I blink, processing what he's saying. *He's real.*

"*I* shouldn't be here? You're meant to be *dead*."

"*He's* your sperm donor?" Maddox chimes, just as shocked.

The gun is back out of the holster and pointed straight at Maddox before he has the chance to step toward me. "Your father tried to kill my daughter. An eye for an eye," my dad tells him.

I can't bring myself to question why Dad's got a gun or why he's standing there.

He's alive.

He shouldn't *be* alive.

He died two years ago in a car accident.

Maddox holds his hands up. "I'm not sure if you've noticed, but your daughter isn't dead."

"*Why* aren't you dead?" I sound more disappointed than someone who just found out her father is alive should. "Mom died."

His eyes soften, and I can almost see the same pain Mom felt for him when he died. "I know. I'm sorry."

Sorry?

Fury hot and rapid rips through my veins. Mom's dead, and he's not. She's fucking *dead*, and she's not coming back. But him? He's standing right in front of me, suited up and clean-shaven like her passing meant nothing to him. Like the death of my only real parent meant fucking *nothing*.

She tried to blame her moods on the chemo, but I knew it was because the love of her life was dead, and there was nothing I could do to fill the hole he left in her heart.

Tremors shake my fist. I can't stand looking at him—breathing the same fucking air as him after everything he's done.

"My mother died with a broken heart, and you weren't fucking there," I spit.

I lost the wrong parent.

His throat bobs. "I couldn't—"

"I had to sit in the hospital room all alone and watch my mother die. And you weren't there," I repeat. "I had to *bury* her the same way I had to bury *you*. Except that time, I was alone. And you. Weren't. *There*." I choke back rage-filled tears. "I lost everything, and where were you? Huh? Where the *fuck* were you?" I scream.

The silence stretches as I wait for the answer. The room's temperature is rising, blanketing my body with a cloying feeling that makes it hard to breathe through.

"It was for your safety."

I gape at him, hardly believing my own ears. "Safety? You think I gave a shit about *safety* when I lost everything I cared about? Mom's last words to me were that I shouldn't cry for her because she'll finally be reunited with *you*." I sneer. "You without your work. Without secrets. Without anything getting in the way of your relationship. Mom died thinking that you'd be the first person she saw once she got to the other side, and *you aren't there*."

Salty tears trickle into my mouth no matter how hard I try to stop them from flowing. I'm mourning for the woman who raised me and never got her happy ending.

If there was one thing she cared about more than anything, it was him. She wanted that happily ever after with the family, the house, and the loving husband more than she wanted me. I know because I heard her begging too. I heard her on the phone telling him that I'd be going to college soon, and she could move closer to him so they could see each other more.

Mom spent every single day of her life wishing she could be with him.

He was everything to her. I was the one who had to help her through her depression when he inevitably left. I was the child who distracted Mom whenever she was missing him.

I saw how much it hurt her when I said that I hated him, so I kept it inside and seethed behind closed doors. I had to listen to all the lectures about why he's the most amazing person in the world, and I was the one who dealt with her disappointment when she couldn't convince me, and she'd say, *You just don't understand.*

And still, he wasn't there.

"Where. Were. You?" I scream.

I'm about to burst. Rounding on him, I shove him over and over, repeating the same three words until my throat is raw. I don't care that he has a gun pointed at Maddox. I'm so riled up that I wouldn't hesitate to stab my own father just to get rid of the tension winding around my heart so tight I fear it'll stop beating.

"What? No answer? Of course, you don't have an answer. You're a coward. A fucking *coward*!" I hit him in the chest again like I might be able to take away the pain Mom would have felt when she died and realized that he lied to her as well.

"I had to," he grunts when I shove him back hard enough to make him stumble.

"You didn't have to do anything! You didn't have to leave. You didn't have to have a kid. You didn't have to keep hurting us by coming back. You didn't have to pretend to die just to escape your responsibility." I can barely see him through the tears as he puts his gun away. "Say something!"

"He was here," Maddox answers when the man who helped create me doesn't.

I stare up at my father, waiting for him to confirm or deny it.

"Why?" I croak, stepping away from my father and closer to Maddox.

He answers again. "Because he's the grand magistrate. The supreme leader of the Order."

My stomach bottoms out. He's . . .

A maniacal laugh bubbles out of me. It keeps rolling out, becoming increasingly hysterical until I'm close to hyperventilating. My mother died alone because he chose power over us. My *father* would rather run a fucking secret society than show up for his family more than once a year.

"I may not have been present, but I have always been involved. If anyone knew about you or your mother, they would have killed you," Dad says calmly and evenly like it might stop me from losing it completely.

"Then why did you have a baby?" I yell.

I know the answer already. *Because Mom wanted one.* She wanted her perfect family. I've just never been able to figure out whether it was because she wanted to become a mother or because she wanted to keep a part of him.

She loved me. She did. But her love for me was never enough for her.

"So what?" I throw my arms up. "You asked Maddox's dad to kill me? Get rid of me so no one can hang me over your head?"

Dad's face contorts with measured fury. "Roland will pay for what he's done."

"Then what, Richard—is that even your name? Richard Talbot? Did you know that I was looking for you?"

His eyes flick away. That's all I need to know. "James Richard Shepherd."

My head turns to the side like I've just been slapped.

Find Shepherd.

That's what Mom said as she was dying.

It wasn't the ramblings of a dying woman. She was coming clean about my father's last name.

This whole time he knew I was searching for him, and he was never planning on making himself known. Seeing him right now is an accident. If he had his way, he'd be happy for me to live out the rest of my life as an orphan.

"Talbot was your grandmother's maiden name," *James* provides.

"Did Mom know?" My question comes out in a hoarse whisper. I'm not sure if I want to know the answer.

He nods. "Almost everything."

This is why he and Mom didn't want me to move to New York. They were worried I'd run into the man who I called Dad. I squeeze my eyes shut. My entire life was built on secrets, and everything is tumbling down like a house of cards.

"Two years ago, I buried a man named Richard Talbot." My voice shakes, and I force myself to look him in the eyes. "I was told he was my father. But I've never had one."

It's his turn to look like he's been struck. "None of this was ever my intention. Out of everything I've told you, believe this."

Another tear slips free. I've never felt so vulnerable. "I don't know you." How could a man who claims he loves me do this to his daughter?

"You do," he insists, holding a hand out to reach for me. "I'm your father."

I step back. "One day out of the year. Even then, you were only a father because of a piece of paper and Mom's devotion to you."

I wanted him to be around so badly when I was younger. As I grew older, I think I wanted the idea of a father more than I wanted him. It's why I thought searching for his memory would give me the father I thought was missing.

"I always looked out for you and your mother. I wish I could have done more, but everything I did, I did to keep you safe. Mora understood this," he continues on the same spiel.

"*Safe* isn't enough. It wasn't for me, and it *never* was for Mom." The house I grew up in always felt like something was missing. In truth, I think it was the part of Mom that my father took with him. "Keeping us safe is just an excuse you tell yourself to make you feel better at night when you're lying awake thinking about how you abandoned your family."

"Reyna—"

"No, I'm not finished." I quickly swipe the tears off my face. "Do you know how many times I begged Mom to ask you to come visit more often? How many times I cried, wondering if it was because you had another family or you were ashamed of me? Or that you were dead, and we didn't know it? Or because you hated me? I held my mother's hand, looked into her dying eyes, and *promised* her everything would be fine because you were waiting for her. I never wanted to be a liar but you made me one."

I inhale a shuddered breath when I notice my dad's eyes mist over. Maddox creeps closer to me, making his presence known by brushing his fingers on my forearm before dropping his hand.

"Let me make it up to you." There's the most subtle hint of desperation in his gaze that doesn't match his steady voice.

"You died. Two years ago."

"Reyna." His composure fractures into something raw.

I cross my arms, hugging myself. "There's nothing a dead man can do for me."

"Reyna, *please*."

"No."

"I was always there, Reyna. Even if you never saw me, I was there for you at every step." It's like his heart is shattering in front of me, and maybe it makes me a monster to feel happy that he's capable of hurting like I did. "I was sitting at the back of the lecture hall when you played a tree in second grade. You had a sneezing fit that made that boy you had a crush on, Justin, angry during his solo. I was there when you won the Chelsea Kennedy film grant and later came third at the Avery Film Festival."

"What?" I whisper.

"I paid for all of your film classes. Donated to your high school so they could expand the art department. I made sure Mrs. Norton retired early after she made you cry in class. I ensured a job position opened up for you at the museum near your old house. Did background checks on every one of your boyfriends before you went on your first dates. I fired two of your therapists so you could see someone better. Asked your mom to take you to art galleries because I couldn't do it."

He . . . The tears flow freely down my face. This whole time I thought I existed to him for a handful of days a year, and those hours were a chore for him. But he was there, loving me from afar.

"I agree, it wasn't nearly enough." He edges closer. "Allow me to make it up to you and your mother. It's what she would have wanted. We owe it to her. I promise that you are under my protection from here on out. Roland won't go anywhere near you."

My nails dig crescent moons into my palm as I try to get my emotions under control. I can't unpack years of neglect right now. Just because he did all those things doesn't change the fact that he could have texted or called to ask about my day once in a while.

Or not have faked his fucking death.

For a second I want to run up to my dad and cry into his arms like I never got to as a kid. All I wanted was for him to be around. Learning that he was always in the background? Finding out that maybe he loved me in his own way? It shatters everything I thought I knew.

"Why didn't you tell me? Why did you let me believe that you didn't care?" I ask through the tears.

His throat bobs. "We thought it was for the best. I realized too late how wrong we were."

We.

Mom didn't want me to know either? I cover my mouth with my hand to contain my sob.

Far too much has happened in the past two days—in the past few *years*. Maddox, James, and even Mom pulled wool over my eyes.

That changes tonight.

The road to forgiveness is a long one. If he really means it—if everything he says is true, then he can show me.

"If you, or any person in the Order, harms a hair on Maddox's or his brother's head, you *will* be dead to me. There will be no second chances." My safety means nothing if I'm the only one who survives. "And don't think I won't find out. I will, some way, somehow."

He tips his chin. "Understood."

"That means there will be no repercussions if Maddox calls off the engagement," I clarify.

It's hard to read his expression, but it's obvious he's going to disagree. "Roland and the Dorn—"

"*None.* No exceptions." I'm proud that my voice doesn't shake. "Mom might have turned a blind eye and forgiven you every time you hurt her, but I am not my mother."

"No, you're my daughter."

"In flesh alone."

"That will change in time." There's a challenge in his voice that I don't miss. "Anything else?"

I narrow my eyes as my mind churns to come up with something else. "The . . ." I swallow. "The man that I stabbed?"

"The place was cleaned out before Maddox made his first call." It's the most confident I've seen him tonight.

Oh, thank God. I'm not going to jail.

I tip my head up, meeting his challenge. "I want an apology."

"There are many things I regret. Leaving you and your mother behind is my greatest one of all. I apologize—"

"Not to me. I want you to apologize to Mom."

"I have every day since I left."

Out of everything he's said, it's the one thing I believe to be true without a shadow of a doubt, because somewhere deep down, I know he loved her too.

Maddox steps forward so that he's plastered to my side. "While we're on the topic of making demands, your daughter and I are together, and you won't be doing anything about it."

James becomes all hard edges, reaching for his gun again. "You aren't in the position to be making any—"

"Nothing," I emphasize. "No interference of any kind, or else your chance at redemption is over." It's up to me to decide whether our relationship is temporary or permanent. With both of them.

James doesn't hesitate to swing his stare at Maddox. His face is devoid of his emotion, but there's no mistaking the venom dripping from his voice. "You hurt her, and I have a bullet reserved for your skull."

Maddox leans back against the kitchen counter before I can snap, looking as relaxed as if we were having a friendly conversation. "At this rate, I believe she'll beat you to it if I so much as think about hurting her."

Their stare-off sets me on edge because I know how fake Maddox's casual demeanor is. I'm tempted to step between them to slice the tension in half. James must realize because he matches Maddox's laid-back stance, and takes a step away.

"Breakfast on Wednesday," James orders in the same voice he used on me when Mom told him I was slacking on the chores. "I'd like for us to catch up."

I shake my head. "I'm not ready for that."

Maddox's dad tried to kill me, and I just found out *my* father faked his own death. I'm going to need time to process. Maybe talk it out with a therapist, and potentially get blackout drunk with Kimi and Nicole.

"Being ready isn't a state of mind. It's a choice."

I nearly roll my eyes. He and Mom always loved his poster sayings. "Then you can wait until I've made that choice."

I'm unsure at what point in the conversation he thought he could start ordering me around, but he's sorely misjudged. If the strained look on his face is any indication, he isn't used to someone else calling out the shots.

He holds out his hand. "Truce?"

I hesitate before shaking it. "For now. *For Mom.*"

"I'll be at Harper's Diner at eight on Wednesday should you change your mind." Nodding my head, I take his business card. "Call me if you need anything—and I mean anything."

I won't. "Okay."

My knuckles turn white as I grip the card tighter, watching him walk out of the front door. The silence that follows the shutting door is maddening.

"You really are your father's daughter."

My attention snaps toward Maddox, who's still leaning against the counter and grinning, making me forget all about my rising anxiety.

"I am *nothing* like my father," I grit out.

"Whatever you say."

36

MADDOX

By the time I finish marking assignments, wash the paint from my hands, stop by one of my properties, and check in on Reyna, I'm well and truly on my way to being late to see Roland. A fact confirmed by a text from him at precisely 7:31, pointing out that I'm not there.

My natural reaction is to start driving below the speed limit.

The two individuals who created me chose to call an *emergency family meeting* after what I can only assume was a result of last night's revelations between Reyna and the man who trained me.

While I would much rather be in Reyna's presence this evening, a bandage needs ripping off, and I plan to do the removal while the wound hasn't closed.

Twenty-five minutes later, the valet takes my keys when I pull up to the apartment building I had the misfortune of calling home for several years. The filthy-rich citizens of New York occupy this street; from tech moguls to real estate tycoons, and now a businessman who may lose his seat in the Order.

The elevator climbs up until I'm on the top floor, where the family dining room is. Maria, the live-in maid and Spencer's old nanny, greets me as soon as the door opens.

It's 8:04 on the dot.

"Maddox," she beams. "I should warn you, he's mad you're late."

I shrug. "He'll get over it."

"Come, come," she urges, ushering me to the dining room as I slip a hundred-dollar bill into her hand. She shakes her head even though her eyes shine with gratitude.

The place looks as one might expect for the home of an old man in finance and politics who lacks any personality and keeps questionable tax records. A sculpture here, a war painting there, cream paneled wallpaper, crystal chandeliers, and antique mahogany furniture to match the wooden floors.

The scars on my back twinge with phantom pain as Maria walks into the dining room first. "Sir, Mr. Maddox is here."

A very upset-looking sperm donor sits at the head of the table, flanked by Spencer on one side and the woman who birthed us on the other. She scowls at me while Spencer shoots a nod my way before continuing to eat like the temperature didn't plummet to the negatives.

No matter, the doors to hell will open soon enough and heat this place right up.

"You're late," Roland says, slicing into his steak.

"That's because I didn't want to be here."

Maria shoots me a warning look while Roland says nothing. She pulls out my seat for me at the opposite end of the table—our usual show in front of the good and holy high saint.

"If I ask you to be here by seven thirty, then you are expected to be here by seven thirty." If I weren't so far away from him, I'd be concerned about his white-knuckle grip on the knife.

Maria fills my glass with sparkling water—which my sperm donor knows I despise as much as coffee. She offers to dish my plate, but I shake my head.

"No need. I don't plan on staying." I take the glass and look him dead in the eyes as I drink the disgusting liquid without flinching.

Maria must read the room because she makes herself scarce. I cut a glance to Mother, who says nothing, staring at her food. She hardly ever speaks in front of Roland at the dinner table, unless it's to take his side.

"I've summoned—"

He stops when a laugh rumbles out of me. I clear my throat, holding my hand up. "My apologies. Please continue about how *you* have summoned *me*."

Roland tightens his grip around his utensils, an arrogant gleam crossing his eyes. "We've decided to move up your wedding date to a month from now."

"Have you now?" I cock a brow.

"Yes. Annabel will arrange for the details to be sent to you," he says, spearing an asparagus without sparing a glance at Mother.

I swirl my glass, watching the disgusting clear liquid bubble. "Why the urgency?"

"Daniel is gaining more favor amongst the acolytes. The Dornmonts and I believe it is in the Order's best interest to do whatever possible to ensure he isn't elected." His eyes never meet mine.

"Right." I tap my glass against the table. "So this has nothing to do with your latest murder attempt?"

I see the exact moment the two words sound alarms in his head: *He knows.*

Oh yes, Father. I *know*.

His only tell is the briefest falter in his movements as he cuts into his steak.

Spencer's cutlery clatters onto his plate. "Murder? What murder?" He glances between us.

"Stop by my office tomorrow. We need to talk," I tell him. It's not a discussion we should have with either of our parents in the room.

Spencer narrows his eyes at me. We've never touched on such topics in front of him before.

"Murders happen all the time," Roland says noncommittally. "Am I expected to keep up with who dies?"

We stare at each other, waiting to see who will break first.

It was a gamble throwing the accusation out. It's not like Shepherd and I are texting buddies, but I figured that if he were half the man I think he is, he'd want to remedy last night's incident as quickly as possible—to keep his daughter safe and get his high saint back in line.

An acolyte had to kill another acolyte, after all. That doesn't happen every day.

"I suppose not." I shrug, taking another sip. "Alas, I thought it would be best that you heard it from me: I've spoken to Abi, and we're calling off the engagement."

In fact, I spoke to her just before coming here.

Mother gasps, and Roland slams his hand on the table. It's rather liberating to see the vein in his forehead pulse. It doesn't age him well.

"I don't know what paint you've been sniffing, son, but one month from now, you are marrying that girl. Should you change your mind, our *arrangement* will end." The tendons in his neck throb.

"Can someone explain what's going on?" Spencer insists, flicking his gaze between the three of us.

"Tomorrow," I promise before responding to Roland. "Then consider this a renegotiation of our arrangement. The wedding *is* off, and I will no longer be ordered around. Additionally, Spencer can choose what level of involvement he wishes to have with you and the Order."

Roland points the steak knife at me. "You're sorely mistaken if you think for one second that you have any authority over what goes on in my house."

"I never claimed to have authority. However, it would be most unfortunate if the acolytes discovered that the engagement was a farce coordinated by their high saint all along."

Fuck, it's hard not to grin.

"Are you threatening me?"

I smile because bloody hell this feels good. "You don't have to do anything you aren't comfortable with," I say to Spencer. "Roland will respect your decision."

"He's my son. He'll do as I say." Roland's voice is low and lethal.

I might be frightened if I weren't the killer in our family. "I have on good authority that *two* attempts were made on the life of the woman under the grand magistrate's protection." I murdered the first person to harm Reyna. From this day forward, I'll murder anyone else who tries again. "I believe Shepherd's only spoken to you about the one from yesterday. It would be a shame if he were to discover that one of Wilson Shaw's clients made another attempt on her life."

"There was no second hit." He glares.

I tip my head to the side. "Wasn't there? I saw it happen myself."

The man who attacked Reyna at Paddy's house was nothing more than a thug doing his boss's dirty work. It was just a fortunate turn of events that I discovered the aforesaid *boss* is a client of Wilson Shaw.

"If you ask me, that's not a transgression I'd imagine the grand magistrate would take lightly. Once is bad. Twice?" I shake my head, blowing out a whistle.

"He'll never believe your baseless claim." The vein in his forehead looks a second away from bursting. Fingers crossed that happens.

"Who is he going to believe? His favorite solider"—*and future son-in-law*—"or the man who was already caught once."

Roland's face falls.

Checkmate, cunt.

The wooden chair slides along the rug as I stand, gesturing for Spencer to do the same.

"Sit down," Roland orders.

Spencer glances between us, indecision ripe in his eyes. I'm not going to make choices for him anymore. If he wants to stay here, I won't hold it against him. In time, he'll learn the truth, and maybe then he'll decide he wants to distance himself from the Shaw name.

I lift my disgusting drink to my lips and down the remaining liquid. "Enjoy the rest of your meal, *Father*."

"Sit. Down," he grinds out.

I turn on my heel and waltz out the door, hearing him rise from his seat.

Spencer stays exactly where he is.

"I'm talking to you."

"Send the Dornmonts my regards. Oh, and let Daniel know that he has my vote," I throw over my shoulder.

My last name will still be Shaw, but I'm no longer part of its house.

37

MADDOX

"Act natural and pretend I'm not here," Reyna complains.

"I've never been able to ignore your presence before. That's not going to start now, love." I level her with a glare since she's been evading my questions all morning. "How was breakfast with the leader of a secret society? Life-altering? Mind-blowing? Inspiring?"

She blew Shepherd off on Wednesday and, to my surprise, agreed to meet him a couple of days later once he confirmed my engagement had been called off, with no repercussions.

Reyna and I have barely had time to see each other this week—which is utter bullshit, seeing as the only threat we now face is an HR complaint and the unlikely loss of the scholarship Shepherd set up solely for her a year ago.

With only a week until the exhibit's opening night, I've been going mad trying to complete everything and finish the painting for Theo's charity gala. It helps that I'm finally in the right headspace to clearly envision where I want to take each piece.

The extent of my interactions with Reyna lately have been in my studio, with her studying while I work. The only time we talk is during meal breaks, and that's wholly insufficient for me. Especially since our *conversations* have been turned into an opportunity for her to interrogate me on everything to do with Shepherd and the Order.

Which leads me to today.

I invited her to my house under the guise of filming behind-the-scenes footage for my exhibit. Little does she know that I have no intention of letting her leave until tomorrow morning.

"So?" I push.

She drops her hand, swinging the camera. "I chickened out. Okay? Can we not talk about it?"

I turn away from the half-painted canvas. "No. We're talking about it."

"I have nothing to say." Reyna brings the camera back up to focus on me, which is useless since the whole point of this is to have behind-the-scenes videos for the exhibit.

It's been rather tricky since half of the installations are a surprise.

Grumbling, she turns the camera off, then places it on the table before leaning against it, staring at me in distaste. My cock stirs when my focus goes straight to her thighs as she crosses her legs at the ankle.

Christ, I miss having them around me.

"Speak," I order.

She glowers at me. We both know I won't let this go. As much benefit as I might receive from being Shepherd's future son-in-law, and as selfish as I am for wanting them to rekindle so I can keep living the good life, Reyna should have a relationship with her dad. Even if he's a massive cunt.

"He lied," she says.

"Go on." I nod, adjusting myself to hide the hard-on I'm sporting while we're having a serious conversation.

"He faked his death."

She uncrosses her legs and folds her arms. Because I am but a simple man, my attention drops to the swell of her breasts. I clear my throat and force myself to think of dying kittens and accidentally breaking a brand-new graphite pencil. "Both very awful. Please continue."

"He was also *never* around. *And* he hurt Mom. Are we also forgetting that he tortured you?"

"We can both agree that he will never win any father-of-the-year awards. But he's also the reason your mother was able to have access to the best doctors in the country, why you were accepted into Cresswell midway through the year, and he got you into a nice flat with good security—"

"That you broke into several times."

"I don't count," I point out, pretending that I don't notice her chest rising with her heavy breath. "And he's probably the reason my father didn't try to kill you sooner, and why you're now one of the most protected people in this city."

She narrows her eyes at me. "How do you know all of this?"

"Because I met with him."

Her jaw drops. "*What?* When?"

"Eight a.m. this morning at the diner. I went in case you needed moral support—or if you needed help strangling him. Imagine my surprise when you weren't there."

"Was he . . ." Reyna averts her gaze to the floor. "Telling the truth?"

"I did my own digging after I left. He was."

The stool groans as I rise to my feet and pull her into my arms—which is a massive bloody mistake because now her body is right against me, and my dick is *very* aware that I could be buried inside her in five seconds flat.

"I'm not telling you to forgive him or give him a chance." I didn't deserve either of those two things from her. "A man in his position has a lot of enemies, and there might not be any second chances if something happens to him."

She leans her head against my shoulders, and my heart does a flip. "Mom always insisted I give him a chance."

I hum my acknowledgment as she groans and hits her head against my chest. "It's so stupid." She pulls back, and I cock a brow at her. "The whole reason I moved to New York was to learn about that prick."

"Believe it or not, you can now get your information straight from the source."

She rolls her eyes. "I know that, but I'm pissed off at him."

"Then stay angry. You don't have to push him away at the same time. Arm's length means that he's still reachable." I shrug. "And you could milk the situation for all it's worth."

She hits my arm playfully. "I don't want his money."

"I can afford to take us to Paris every month out of the year, but it would be much more satisfying to know it's on Shepherd's dime." I never received a cent for any of the shit I did for him. I am, however, pissed off at how little he left as Reyna's "inheritance." Admittedly, the bulk of the funds were used toward her mom's healthcare, but he could have covertly topped it up without putting a dent in his finances. "If Roland were a decent person, I might consider jeopardizing my precious brain cells to be in his company."

She purses her lips. "Would you want to get to know James if he were your dad?"

Fuck no.

I walked right into that one.

Shepherd recruited me when I was fourteen. The man clearly doesn't have much in the way of morals, and that's a lot coming from me.

A diplomatic response is the best course of action. "He's shown that he's committed to looking after you, even if you spend the rest of your life living as if he were dead. Now, tell me, Miss Sinaga, would you regret walking the other way if he died next week?"

"I'll text him tomorrow," she whispers reluctantly, innocently pressing her chest against me in such a mind-altering, cock-saluting way that I'm surprised she hasn't said that it feels like there's a loaded gun pointing at her.

Her fate is sealed when she levels me with the venomous glare that got me hooked on her from the very start. "Why did you have to make sense without being an asshole?"

Reyna yelps when I spin her around to bend her over the table, with my fingers threaded in her hair.

"What are you doing?" she gasps, supporting her weight with her hands.

"Being an asshole."

I yank the skirt up her waist and rip her stockings down her legs while her ass is up in the air.

"Maddox," she squeals, wiggling her hips.

Everything she does makes my cock fucking *ache*. "Apologize," I grunt.

"For what?" Her question comes out in that husky voice of hers that I've been obsessed with since day one.

I free my belt from my pants in a single motion and bind her wrists together. Her heady scent permeates the room as I pull the leather tight to keep her fingers from wandering places they shouldn't. "Calling me an asshole."

"No."

The one word earns her a sharp *whack*. She cries out at the impact, and a pink handprint blooms on her soft, tanned skin. The possessive beast inside of me preens with satisfaction when she squeezes her legs together, and a dark spot starts to form in the center of her panties.

She likes this.

My fingers trail over the scars along her hips and thighs as I massage the welt forming on her ass. It amazes me that she doesn't tense or cower away over having them touched. I want to ask if she's ever felt embarrassed by them, or if she's just learned to live with it.

"Beautiful," I mutter, because I'd fall for her in whatever shape or form she comes in.

I rub the red mark caused by my hand, appreciating the contrast of colors and the shape left beside her tattoo. "Say sorry, Miss Sinaga. Where are your manners?"

Looking up at me over her shoulder, Reyna raises her head in defiance, pupils blown out. "Make me."

Fuck, I bloody love her.

"I'd hate to have to punish you for your behavior."

My hand goes down on her pert ass, and she whimpers. One word that describes me is *sadistic*, and it perfectly describes how I spank her other cheek twice just to make the cherry-pink marks blooming on her pretty little backside even.

I wind her long hair around my fist. My other hand burns an achingly slow path from the back of her calves, curving into the dip between her thighs, up to her apex, where the cotton fabric darkens more with every second I leave her wanting.

A shuddered breath leaves her when I force her attention forward so she has to assume my movements by sound and touch alone. I brush her thighs before ghosting a touch over the back of her knees. The smallest whimper has me grinning, and I repeat the motion, sliding a finger against her pussy before running it down the back of her leg again.

When I have her squirming and shifting her hips, I bring my hand down on her supple skin, leaving another pink mark on her flesh. Reyna throws her head back as she cries out, pressing her legs together.

I do it three more times for good measure.

"Apologize," I demand.

"No."

It's her funeral.

My movements are languid, traveling back down the curve of her legs to her calves, imprinting every inch of her delectable body into memory as precome leaks from my cock.

Every exhale is breathy and strained, and I take that as the perfect time to change tactics, brushing over her weeping center each time I make it back to the top. I run my knuckles over her clit three times, then back down to her calves. When she—*I*—grow more desperate, I trace the line of her underwear, edging beneath the saturated fabric in a cruel tease.

If I don't sink inside of her soon, I'm going to lose my mind.

Her panties are completely soaked. She's hiccuping and pushing her hips against my fingers every time I come near her sex. Reyna could put us both out of our misery by saying one measly word. Yet here we are, both paying the price for her stubbornness.

The next slap comes out the hardest. She screams, breathing roughly through her nose.

I push her panties to the side to finally see what her pussy is doing for me.

I tsk, brushing the tip of my finger over her swollen flesh, and she bucks. Oh the poor thing is fucking dripping.

She whimpers as I knead her ass to undo all the hurt, only to bring it back, absolutely, utterly bloody mesmerized by the moisture seeping from her cunt and down her inner thighs.

My hand collides with her flesh four more times, alternating between each cheek before she finally says the two simple words I want to hear.

"I'm sorry," she cries, shaking like a leaf.

I lean over and pull her head back to see her delicate face. "Good girl," I praise, getting hit with another wave of desire when her lips part on a silent moan. "Now say, *I'm sorry, Mr. Shaw. I won't do it again.*"

Her eyes snap open as she tries to twist around to look at me. It's thrilling watching her anger dissipate the second I slip a finger inside her. Three strokes is all she gets before I withdraw, and her anger returns tenfold. Reyna gnashes her teeth and fruitlessly attempts to throw me off.

So I do it again.

Her anger washes away, then comes right back with a vengeance. Over and over, I bring her closer to the edge only to leave her vibrating with rage.

"Fuck you," she snarls when I pull my fingers out again.

"Say it."

"Maddox."

She begs so pretty.

"Say it." I rub her clit through her panties, and she thrashes against my grip in her hair.

"I'm sorry, Mr. Shaw. I won't call you an *asshole* again." She enunciates the word.

I smile down at her.

That's my girl.

I let go of Reyna and take several steps back. She frowns, pauses for a moment, hands still bound together in front of her, then whips her head toward me, otherwise staying exactly where I left her. "What the fuck?"

I grin, nodding at the object on the corner of the table. "Turn the camera on, love."

Her forehead wrinkles in confusion, remaining in place. "Excuse me?"

"Don't make me repeat myself."

I turn and grab one of my biggest canvases off the rack without waiting to see if she follows instructions. I can hear her hesitation seconds before she releases a dramatic huff and stomps to do as I said, muttering, *"Asshole,"* under her breath as she manages to undo the belt without my help.

Sexually frustrated Reyna is cute. Maybe I'll punish her again for her attitude.

I position the canvas on the wall across from the table. I prepped it weeks ago with today in mind. "Set the tripod up over there and make sure this is in frame."

She puts her hands on her hips. "You're seriously going to paint right now?"

"Miss Sinaga," I warn. "Do you need another lesson in manners so soon?"

Her eyes narrow at me, yet she does what she's told. She preps her medium, while I prep mine, using the palette knife to scrape onto the canvas the scarlet, sage green, chocolate brown, and cherry pink paints I made last night. Once all the colors are positioned in splotches on the canvas, I turn to find her waiting next to the camera.

"Take your clothes off."

Reyna wets her lips before wiggling her underwear down her legs in a slow tease. Just when I thought I couldn't possibly get any harder, her dress and bra drop to the floor, and she stands without a thread to hide her from me.

I smile to myself when I catch sight of all the bright-pink handprints covering her ass. I should start putting them there more often.

"Come here. Make sure the tape is running."

Panic crosses Reyna's eyes. "But I don't have any clothes on."

"Come. *Here.*"

She chews her lip in indecision before padding across the room. Softly placing a hand on her shoulder, I turn her so the camera captures every inch of her divine body.

If anyone comes across this video, I will gouge their eyes out of their skull and feed it to them. No one but me will ever get to see her like this.

A sharp inhale is the only reaction I get when I grab her hair off her shoulders to pile it up in a tight bun using the hair tie I stole from her room in the dead of night. I lower my lips to the smooth expanse of skin, kissing a trail from behind her ear down to the tip of her shoulder. She's bloody intoxicating.

A sound that's more beast than man rumbles from my chest when I curve my hand around her waist to coat my fingers in her wetness.

"Please, Maddox," she mewls, wiggling to fit my bulge against her ass.

My fingers curl around her throat to tip her head back, and I lower my lips against the shell of her ear. "I called you here to capture the process of creating art. Put your hands on the canvas so I can create."

I let go of her, stepping away so she can move on her own terms. Reyna glances at the canvas skeptically. "Do I have to touch oil paint?" She grimaces.

"It's *acrylic.*" The word tastes like dirt. "Just for you."

Taking a deep breath, she settles her hands on the canvas.

Her pussy quivers with anticipation as I stand back to unbutton my top and remove my pants, and underwear. My cock springs free, swollen and leaking from all the teasing. Edging closer, I run my cock up her slit. It's complete fucking torture. It takes every ounce of my fraying self-restraint to stop myself from burying inside her straightaway.

"Here's what's going to happen. I'm going to fuck you. You're going to scream. And you're going to be a good, *good* girl for me and say my name when you come." My voice is nothing more than a strained rasp. "Now say, *Yes, Mr. Shaw.*"

She jolts when I spank her once more, spreading the paint. "Yes, Mr. Shaw," she moans.

The thread holding me back snaps, and I sink into her, completely un-fucking-bidden. She takes me right to the very root, and I just about black out. Bloody heavenly.

She moves onto her forearm while the other hand slides across the paint, creating great big arcs and short, sharp strokes as she takes all of me.

I thrust into her gently, and so torturously slow, kissing each vertebra because she deserves tenderness. To be treated like she's a precious artifact. A treasure to be worshipped. She needs to know that I'm a demon in disguise, but I would never do anything to harm her. If she isn't here, I'll cease to exist. I would search for her in every life, because nothing holds meaning without her there.

No.

I can't do it like this.

I need to see her.

Reyna cries out when I withdraw from her and spin her around. My lips crash into hers, swallowing her gasp and plastering her back against the paint as I wrap her legs around my hips. I'm slamming into her before she gets a chance to recover, fucking her like she was handpicked by the divine to be my own undoing.

My hands roam over her body, from her waist to her tits, to the column of her throat, then to her paint-stained hair.

Reyna latches onto my opened shirt like she's incapable of letting go.

"Maddox, I—" She claws at me, slapping the canvas behind her before gripping me, smearing paint all over the both of us. Her teeth sink into my lips, drawing blood.

"Do you know how hard it's been not to drag you into my office every day and fuck you into the couch until you become nonverbal?"

Her answer is a jumbled compilation of incoherent words, choked by hiccuped moans against my lips. Her brown eyes glaze over, seeing me, yet completely unfocused. Lost, and like the only thing she knows is how it feels to be consumed by me.

I want every part of her. Even the parts she isn't ready to give or thinks I don't want. My life consists of her, and only her. Dying would mean nothing to me as long as I burn in hell with the taste of her still on my tongue.

My thrusts turn relentless. Her tightening pussy has spots clouding my vision. She's strangling my cock tight enough to feel like it might break. Nothing is as enrapturing as watching her let go. She quivers and shakes, chanting my name like I'm the only thing that exists in her mind. I can feel her climax in my bloody soul.

And I have it all on camera.

The canvas creaks as I continue, never giving her a second to come down from her high. She isn't just art; she is a goddess, perched on the altar for me to sacrifice myself in the name of worship.

"My devotion to you has turned me deadly," I whisper, even though she's too lost to hear me.

My lips meet hers so she can taste the damage she's done to me. I want to be an irrevocable part of her. I want her to always have a part of me, and know there isn't a second that goes by where she isn't at the forefront of my mind.

Love isn't strong enough for what I'm feeling. It's the maddest kind of obsession that turns a man insane.

Reyna's hand skates beneath my top, smearing wet paint across my waist as she reaches for my back. I capture her wrist and hold it above her head before I can ruin this moment. *I shouldn't have unbound her hands.*

"Take your top off," she moans, staring up at me with her deep-brown eyes that I picture before I fall asleep.

I shake my head. I'll do anything she wants, except that. I won't let anything ruin what's between us.

"Please." She tugs the collar.

I never would have thought someone could have so much control over me.

As soon as the clothes are gone, she'll see the truth of what the Order has done to me. Every foul, depraved wound caused by the people who were meant to take care of me. That I'm not a tortured artist; I'm a full tragedy.

I drop my head into the cradle of her neck and wrap my arms around her. I won't take my top off, but I can't stop her from finding out the truth. When she does, I don't want to see the pity on her face.

So when her hands move beneath the shirt to my back, I pull the soft skin of her neck into my mouth to pretend we're in a world where she doesn't know that I'm a patchwork of scars. Covered in burns and slashes from a time when being my own person was a fool's dream.

I hate those fucking marks with every fiber of my being. Every day, I wake up and go to sleep wearing the permanent reminder that I was bred to live beneath someone else's thumb.

I don't want Reyna to see me as weak.

Her body tenses against me, and I hold her tighter because if I lose a part of her to this, I at least want to know what it feels like to be wholly complete for a short while.

Reyna keeps running her fingers over my back regardless of how hard I'm thrusting into her, hoping I can make her forget that they're there. I'll never be as perfect as she is. One day she's going to realize I'll never fully escape the past. Then she'll stop looking at me like I was the one who hung the sun in the sky.

A crater forms in my chest when she pushes me back. I wish I hadn't asked her to put a camera up to capture the moment everything shatters.

She holds my face in the palms of her hands and stares into my eyes.

Then she kisses me.

She kisses me, and I almost break because she shouldn't be kissing me the way she is. Like they're just scars and she doesn't give a shit about the weight they carry.

I tangle my fingers in her hair to deepen the kiss, but she pulls back to rasp, "Please don't stop."

That does it for me.

I grip her hips and drive into her like a man who's lost all touch with humanity. She throws her head back with a cry, clawing at my back like she couldn't care less that I'll carry the evidence of my rotten childhood on my skin forever. I don't deserve her, yet it feels so good to be selfish.

Reyna's moans grow wilder as she thrashes around, choking my cock with her pussy. She trains her sights on me even though her eyelids are fluttering and she's shaking her head like the pressure is too much.

This time, when she comes, I fall over the edge with her. I watch her ride out her orgasm, eyes closed in utter bliss as she screams my name. White-hot ecstasy floods my veins when I spill myself into her, filling her to the brim until there's nothing left in me to give.

I'll never get over the sight of her. The paint all over her only makes her more beautiful.

I refuse to pull out, perfectly content with holding on to Reyna while I'm still buried inside her. It isn't until her bleary eyes find mine that I carefully peel her way from the canvas to carry her to the bathroom. My chest expands when she wraps her arms around the back of my neck and leans her cheek against my shoulder.

I turn the shower faucet on hot, take my top off, then step inside once steam rolls out into the room. The paint ripples off Reyna's back and flows down her hair, turning the water murky before it spirals into the drain. More washes away beneath my fingertips as I rub circles over her skin, tracing the dragon tattoo snaking up her spine as I do.

"Can you stand, my love?" I ask quietly when I've washed all that I can reach.

She nods, slowly unwrapping herself from me. It kills me to let her go, but it's not worth an accidental injury.

Carefully withdrawing from her, I lower her legs onto the floor and hold on to her just in case she loses her balance. A warm hand curls around my arm when I reach for the soap to continue washing her. Her lips are parted at the array of women's products I bought for her.

She doesn't ask any questions, reaching for the soap behind me. I watch with worry as she brings me under the hot spray of water and squeezes a dollop onto her hand before cleaning me the way I did her.

A dagger lodges in my throat beneath the tenderness of her touch, as if I might be as precious as she is. Anything I want to say dies on my tongue.

My muscles coil tight when she motions for me to turn around. Every cell in my body screams at me to deny her request because seeing the damage is different from feeling it.

Her soft gaze lands on my own, and with one look, she silences all the voices in my head. My nostrils flare, and I shift around, baring my back for her to see the wounds my father and the Order left. I try to notice any changes in her breathing pattern. But when her hand lands on my mutilated body, she cleans my back with the same delicate touch that she afforded the rest of me.

My muscles loosen, and my eyes drift shut.

To be understood is to know intimacy. That's what she told me the first time I met her. I get it now.

I turn around and drop my forehead to hers. I'm not sure how I ever lived a life without her.

"What happened?" she asks, tracing the lines of my face.

I press a kiss to the inside of her wrist. "I wasn't just made into a killer. I was beaten into one."

Reyna must see something that I've been desperately trying to hide from her, because her next words gut me. "You have nothing to be ashamed of."

A humorless laugh tears out of me, and I lean back against the shower wall. "I assure you, shame is not what I'm feeling. They are, however, fucking hideous."

"They're your story."

"Yes, and it's a fucking hideous story." I shake my head, putting some space between us. I bloody hate that she's seeing me like this. "It's like I'm a monster." *A leashed one.*

She wraps her arms around my waist to keep me in place. "You're a protector. Sometimes monsters and protectors are the same thing."

I stare at her, speechless all over again.

I know her just as she knows me.

Fuck it.

My lips crash against hers as I wrap her in my arms. Does she think she can say something like that and not disintegrate the mask I've had to wear? Only Reyna will ever see this side of me.

If I'm a demon, I'll make a hell just for us.

"What was that for?" Reyna gasps when I finally pry myself away for air.

"I've decided I'm going to be an asshole again. I want you on the bed on your hands and knees within the next ten seconds, Miss Sinaga. Or else your ass is going to be so red you won't be able to sit down for your exam."

A coy grin twists her lips. "Yes, Mr. Shaw."

38

REYNA

"Thank you." I force a smile as I hand over my coat to the attendant, shivering from the combination of cold and anxiety.

I run my clammy hands over my black dress, trying to pass the move off like I'm straightening it. I can't count how many times I've attended the opening night of an art exhibit, but this is the first time I've ever felt like throwing up from nerves.

Showcasing my work never gets any easier. It's worse since I didn't start recording Maddox in the creation process until all the pieces were relatively complete. Despite his assurances that I'm freaking out over nothing, I'm worried people are going to think I half-assed my job.

People walk around in suits and dresses that probably cost more than I make in a month. I recognize some as critics or artists who attended Mom's showcase. It's weird to think any number of people here could be part of the Order.

And anyone here could drunkenly tell me how bad the videos are.

I've been intentionally avoiding looking at the screens around the foyer since I arrived.

My eyes slip, just once, and I see something that spikes my panic to new heights.

People sidestep around me, grabbing drinks and canapés from the servers while they walk around the exhibit, but I can't move as he makes his way to me.

"Reyna, it's good to see you," Dad—*James*—greets. I can't decide which to call him yet. I've been interchanging them for the past week.

I took Maddox's advice and agreed to meet up with my dad. It went . . . surprisingly well. We exchanged stories about Mom the entire time, and even if it doesn't mend the bridge between us, it's nice to talk to someone who knows her as well as I do. Common ground is a safe place to start.

An awkward chill settles between us when he puts his hand on my shoulder in a show of what I can only assume is meant to be affection.

I clear my throat and shift my weight once he pulls away. "What are you doing here?"

An art exhibit is the last place I expected to see him. According to Maddox, neither of his parents will be attending tonight. If I thought he was an arrogant prick before, it's nothing compared to how cocky he is now that his dad is in the doghouse because of mine.

I mutter a quick thanks when a server offers me a glass of champagne. My dad looks at me with concern when I throw my head back and down the drink. Liquid courage is the only thing that will get me through tonight.

"I haven't missed a single one of Maddox's exhibits since he was a boy," he answers.

"Oh."

I shouldn't be upset that James was there for Maddox, sort of. Yet the thought of it makes my stomach sour.

"That's nice," I add, because I don't know what else to say.

"Miss Sinaga."

I turn toward the deep voice and almost dissolve into the floor. Maddox in a tux might be the death of me. The fabric fits perfectly, tailored around his frame in a way that has me wanting to wrap my legs around him. With one hand effortlessly tucked in his pocket, he oozes sex appeal.

His eyes darken when they land on me. The slow perusal of his gaze raises my temperature by ten degrees, getting hotter when his sights land on my cleavage that's peeking out above the sweetheart neckline of my dress.

Blush colors my skin pink. My professor is unashamedly checking me out in public.

I jolt when Dad clears his throat. "Maddox, we need to have a chat about the pieces you made of my dau—"

"I'll be stealing your daughter now, thank you," Maddox interrupts, placing a warm hand on the bare skin of my back to lead me away.

"Dinner tomorrow, right, Reyna?" Dad calls.

Glancing over my shoulder, I give him a hesitant nod. *Common ground is a good place to start.*

I'm slightly unstable walking next to him, both from the alcohol that's gone straight to my head and from Kimi's heels, which I thought would be a good idea to wear. The dress I have on isn't fancy by any means. Maddox had insisted on giving me his credit card to buy myself something to wear for tonight, but this dress has been sitting in my closet for the last three years, waiting for a special occasion.

Mom bought it for me before Dad faked his death, and after she died, I thought I'd never wear it because it didn't seem like anything good would ever happen to me.

So this afternoon, I put the dress on, did my hair, let Kimi do my makeup, and wore shoes that are outside of my comfort zone, because this is a new chapter. Growing was never meant to be comfortable or easy. If it were, everyone would be the best version of themselves.

The tips of Maddox's fingers dip ever so slightly beneath the fabric of my dress in a secretive show of intimacy. A hum of approval sounds from the back of his throat. "No tights?"

"No panties either."

Green eyes flash with excitement as he winks, grabbing a booklet from the reception desk to give to me. For months, Maddox has kept the collection's name private. Seeing it in bold lettering at the front of the book makes a funny feeling stir in my chest.

The Immortalization.

We come to a halt before reaching the threshold of the exhibit. "A private tour? You spoil me." I grin, feeling the champagne work its magic.

A soft smile tilts his lips. "Remember what I told you?"

My brows knit. "Which part?"

"All of it."

"Wow, yes. I know exactly what you're referring to. For sure." I roll my eyes, but unease settles in my stomach.

The nervous wrinkle on his forehead gives me pause. I can only imagine the pressure he must be under after being ridiculed by critics for years. In the time I've known him, he's always internalized any concern he might have over today's event.

"Are you all right?" I ask.

Sighing, he gives me a small nod, then holds his hand out, gesturing for me to go in first. His secrecy regarding aspects of the exhibit has my heart skip with trepidation.

I inhale deeply, grip the stem of the champagne glass tighter, then step through the open doors. The smooth strings of a violin and the piano in the corner of the room mix with the chatter of people congregating around each installation. Photographers and videographers move about the room to record the evening, capturing conversation and looks of what I hope will be awe.

Maddox's paintings and other mixed-media pieces are hung against the room's walls and dividers, and his sculptures have been placed strategically for people to flow between each piece.

My sights fall on the sculpture beneath the spotlight in the middle of the room. I recall seeing it in Maddox's studio the day we went to Halenbeek Museum. It was far from finished back then, but seeing it now, on display for the whole world to see . . . It's surreal.

The woman is sleeping in water, surrounded by a bed of . . . *peonies*. She rests on her side, using her hand and a lily pad as a pillow. Even without any color on the plaster sculpture, her face looks serene, as if she's miles away from all the world's dangers. My heart squeezes. I can feel her peace. It's unlike anything Maddox has created before. He's known for the dark themes he weaves into everything he makes. He's always tried to evoke sadness, disgust, or rage, but never contentment.

Slowly, I circle behind the sculpture to see what's attached to her back.

Wings. Big, sinewy wings lie against the water, as hornlike ridges trail from the top of her spine down to the tail curved around her leg.

My pulse races as I tentatively pad toward the plaque. Somehow, I know what the sculpture is going to be called without seeing it.

Tears prick my eyes when I read the engraved words: *The Little Dragon.*

I whip around, searching for Maddox, but he's nowhere in sight. My attention catches on a nearby sculpture instead; the one I saw in his studio when I woke up from my concussion.

A green two-headed serpent climbs up the scythe strapped to a woman's back as she cries pink tears. Poison ivy coils around her hand pointing heavenward. A cross between armor and silk covers her body and leaves a hole in her chest exposed.

Perseverance & Death.

Against the wall is the painting of an angel standing at the side of a cliff with seraphim-like wings. Her face was unpainted when I saw it, but now she . . . The painting is of me.

I'm the angel. *I'm* the one who was painted through the eyes of a lover.

Below the piece are two words: *My Muse.*

A tear breaks free. He painted me like a promise and signed it like a confession.

I move to the next painting and falter at the man plunging a spear into a beehive as he steps on the dead bees littering the ground. A small smile tugs at my lips as I read the title: *Liberation.*

Each piece in the exhibit pays homage to me: a woman bleeding into the same type of chrysanthemum that's tattooed on my thigh, another of a girl stabbing a dagger into a mountain of skulls, even one of a lady with the same hair as me. I move through the room, noticing the reference to things I didn't think he'd notice.

I'm his exhibit.

My hands are trembling by the time I make it back to the sculpture of *The Little Dragon*, and I open the booklet up. The cover page is the collection's name against a backdrop of dark scales. Turning the page, my lips part as I read the only other thing on both sides.

To my muse,

To be loved by an artist is to become immortal.
This is for you.

Yours always,
Maddox Shaw

"Penny for your thoughts."

I twist around to find Maddox behind me, appearing bashful like he's worried I might tell him that the collection is anything other than a masterpiece.

"I love you." I blurt the first thing that comes to mind.

I hate that I can't hug him. Hate that I can't kiss him so he knows how much this means to me. Hate that our relationship needs to be kept in the shadows until I receive an expensive piece of paper telling me I'm qualified enough to carry out my passion.

His eyes light up, and it's like the weight of the world has been lifted from my shoulders, and his cocky grin slides right back into place. "As you should."

I bark a laugh, feeling like a meteor could hit and it wouldn't matter.

"Not going to say it back?" I can't contain the smile spreading across my lips.

He shifts his weight to shorten the distance between us, still too far away for my liking.

"I believe I've shown it about fifteen times," he says, referencing the number of pieces in the exhibit.

I edge close too, practically begging for a scandal. "Tell me anyway. I'm not a very astute observer."

When his smile matches the intensity of mine, I swear the heavens open up.

"I've killed a great many men for you. Harassed a substantial amount of the teaching body for you. Created and dedicated an entire collection to you because you consume every one of my thoughts. You alone brought me to life. So let me say it simply: I love you too, Reyna." He pauses, then his smile turns wicked. "Now, if you'd be so kind as to follow me into the back, I need to see what your dress looks like on the floor."

"Maddox," I hiss. "This is your opening."

"I thought I'd made it clear that you take precedence," he murmurs. "As I said, after you, Miss Sinaga. There's no such thing as a bad time for private tutoring."

Epilogue

REYNA

Ten years later

"Take deep breaths and—"

"Stop telling me to calm down," I snap at Maddox. "I'm *calm*."

I'm going to throw up.

"Yes, you look like the very definition of calm."

He snatches my hand when I raise it to my lips to let loose on my poor fingernails. It's a habit I've picked up since I started this project three years ago.

Death Touched has consumed every second of my life recently. I feel ill thinking about everyone who's going to watch it, and the reviews they'll leave afterward.

Right after I graduated, Maddox slapped a ring on my finger, and we moved to California when I got a job as a runner for a TV show. Then many, many more assisting roles later, I managed to score a gig writing the screenplay for a box-office horror.

Fast forward to today, and my name is listed as *director* of *Death Touched* on IMDb. It may not be a box-office hit, but it's still my name there in shining lights.

I didn't expect that I'd direct anything that's even remotely romantic, and yet here I am, about to attend the premiere of a movie about a serial killer who falls in love with his victim. It's truly a wonder where I got my inspiration from.

Leaning against the headrest of the limo, I fidget with the bracelet Mom used to wear. I wanted her to be here for my official debut.

"Everyone's going to love it," Maddox repeats for what has to be the millionth time.

"I love you, and your opinion means the world to me. But you're biased. Nothing you're saying counts."

He chuckles, unbuckles my seatbelt, and pulls me onto his lap. I frantically swing my gaze to the front of the limo to make sure the divider is still up.

"If anyone says anything negative, I can always kill them," he offers.

I hit his chest. "You can't go around killing people for having an opinion."

Shrugging, he kisses my shoulder. "I'd do it for you."

I squeeze his hand because if I don't, I'll rip the skin from around my nails. I need a drink. ASAP. I settle for distracting myself by caressing the gray hairs that have started growing around Maddox's temples. I shouldn't be surprised that my old professor aged so well.

Minutes later, we pull up in front of the theater hosting the premiere. Photographers are already out front taking pictures of the cast and the various A- and B-list celebrities who wanted to attend for some reason.

Maddox steps out first, offering me his hand. The paparazzi go wild when they realize who's arrived. For a moment, I'm sure they'll start shouting for Maddox since he's been making headlines and has quickly risen through the art world, becoming as big of a name as Basquiat.

No one has ever particularly cared about my existence during premieres. It's fine by me because I prefer being behind a camera to let someone else have their moment of fame.

But no one is calling for Maddox this time. They're all saying my name. Even the cast and crew wave at me.

It's heady.

And downright nauseating.

Maddox gives my hand a comforting squeeze, and I plaster a smile on my face that hurts my cheeks. I'll never get used to posing in front of cameras or making small talk with strangers.

Beneath all the anxiety and panic, the elation whips the breath right out of my lungs. This is really happening. I know Mom is here with me in spirit, hanging around wherever Dad is, and telling all her ghost buddies that her daughter is a famous director.

I breathe a little easier once the cameras are away and there isn't so much commotion going on. Until the air is sucker punched out of me, and I'm bulldozed into Maddox. The high-pitched scream that follows pierces my eardrum and rattles my brain against my skull. I'm yanked right back to where I was only to be gut-punched by a baby bump.

People glance our way as Kimi starts yelling, "This is my best friend."

My cheeks burn from how much she's beaming. Owen pries her off me before she can do any more damage or rip my stupidly expensive dress.

"You fucking did it, bitch," she squeals. "If it weren't for this"—she points to her very pregnant stomach—"we'd be getting blackout drunk tonight."

"I'm excited for bed," I grumble through my grin.

Before Kimi can say any more, I'm crushed into a hug that realigns my vertebrae with a *click*. Dad lets go of me just as quickly, stepping back and fixing his mask into place.

He clears his throat. "Your mom would be very proud of you. *I'm* proud of you."

Oh God, I think I'm going to cry.

Kimi rushes forward to fan my eyes. "We can't ruin your makeup."

I laugh, taking in everyone who's supported me every step of the way and who became my family when Mom died.

Someone else calls my name, and Maddox follows close behind while I talk to them. He's forever playing bodyguard.

The room grows louder the more the drinks flow. My face hurts so much from smiling and laughing with the people I worked with to turn my dream into a reality. Most of the cast stays behind as we head into the theater to watch the movie Maddox and I have seen a hundred times. Kimi, Owen, and Dad sit at the back amongst people I don't know, while

Maddox stays by my side, occasionally giving my hand a gentle caress as a silent reminder that he always has my back.

As the movie starts, I genuinely think I might die. I'm not sure how I'll cope if someone walks out.

Maddox leans over right before the serial killer murders his first victim. "I forgot to ask if you credited me at the end."

I send a glare his way, biting my lip to contain the grin spreading across my face. Every person who's seen this scene has praised its delivery—it's the one I took the most control over. I wanted every minute detail to be perfected to the image I had in mind—and Maddox delivered.

Several people died in my creative pursuit. Whenever inspiration strikes, Maddox tracks down one of the subjects he'd been eyeing and carries the kill out in my vision. Then he brings me over to admire the aftermath of our art. What's a bit of love, lust, and light dismemberment?

We're a match made in a nightmare. Maddox and I work well together.

I'm his muse, and he's mine.

I've always been fascinated by death.

It's a good thing I've married a serial killer.

Acknowledgments

However long ago, I thought to myself, Pink Ink *would make a cool book title.* So I jotted it down in my notes app and promptly forgot all about it.

Fast forward to a year (?) later, I was tearing my hair out, drowning under the weight of a different deadline, when all of a sudden, I was hit with a bright idea: *Why don't I write a new book instead?* Off I went into my notes app, and lo and behold, the words *Pink Ink?* were staring right at me. My brain took those two words and *ran.*

Which brings us to today.

This book was a labor of love, hyperfixations, and a great many hours spent trying to think up creative murder scenes. And none of it would have been possible without you, my dear reader, for your endless support, and, in no particular Order (pun intended):

My incredible alpha and beta team, who quite literally saw this manuscript at its worst. Eve, you know you're always my number one. Jack, you truly did the most, and I love you for it. Amanda and Lisa, thank you for spending hours listening to me rant and work through things. Brooke, Nikki, and Kiza, you guys are a blessing.

Kylo and Stan, I could've done with less barking, but your slobbery kisses were always appreciated whenever I needed floor time. Orbit, the biting wasn't appreciated; however I'll let it slide because you're so cute.

To my fiancé, for always dealing with the evil version of me that comes out during deadlines.

Booksellers, indies, book boxes, librarians, and every book business that has supported me throughout my career.

My dear friend Leigh Rivers for your one-worded show of moral support and your borderline inaudible voice notes.

Kylie, you really are this book's number-one hype person. Whatever the opposite of humble is, you keep me feeling that way.

Jess and Lisa, you both keep me sane.

And finally, to the ones who made this dream a reality.

Thao, agent extraordinaire, thank you for believing in me and being an absolute champion for all of my book babies. Also, to the rest of the crew at SDLA, Nick, and Andrea, thank you for helping this book reach people all around the globe through various translations.

To my brilliant editor, Ghjulia, your love for this book and your unwavering enthusiasm for all things *Pink Ink* brought this novel to life in every sense of the word. Your ideas are always brilliant, and your comments of "Okay, but could we make this spicier?" bring me so much joy. Thank you for always answering my million emails (and often repeated questions) and for being a complete rockstar.

The incredible team at Gallery, you made this book happen. Thank you for all your support and guidance and for putting up with my endless tweaks. You took a chance on me. I'm forever grateful to be part of the team.

Stay smutty x

—ASG

About the Author

Avina St. Graves is a bestselling dark romance author known for *Death's Obsession*, *Skin of a Sinner*, and *The Saltwater Curse*. When she isn't reading and writing, doomscrolling, or figuring out how to make red flags look green, you can find her holed up in bed, combating the three *P*'s: back pain, neck pain, and knee pain. Born in Indonesia, she now lives in New Zealand. *Pink Ink* is her traditional publishing debut.